Seven of Druids

Sylvan Greenfield

Pixel Perfect
PUBLICATIONS

Seven of Druids

An archeology student makes a mystical voyage to save
his girl from the Voidshapers - or so he believes.

For hundreds of years, the druids of Eresa have been training in secret. The seven clans are battle-hungry. But nothing could have prepared them for what is coming.

Aaron Bishop, an archaeology student from Oxford, is on a holiday trip with his girlfriend Denise, when they are suddenly transported to a mystical realm. Gifted and cursed at the same time, Aaron has an ancient magic growing inside him. A Voidshaper, a merciless entity born of negativity, assaults Denise and turns her into one of them. Aaron's world shatters.

Burdened by his lover's fate, Aaron seeks counsel from the great Ouranis, a Phoenix of untold power, who claims she can give Denise her body back, but only in exchange for Aaron's help against the Voidshapers – a journey that will change his life forever.

Seven of Druids – Sylvan Greenfield

© 2015 Sylvan Greenfield & PixelPerfect Publications, The Hague, the Netherlands

ISBN book   9789491833243
ISBN ebook 9789491833236

PixelPerfect Publications
Bankastraat 107b
2585 EK The Hague
The Netherlands

info@pixelperfectpublications.com
www.pixelperfectpublications.com

Sylvan Greenfield

Sylvan Greenfield is a debuting fantasy writer from the Netherlands. For several years Sylvan has worked at a publishing house for children's books, which sparked his initial interest in writing. Both his BA in Mandarin Chinese and his MSc in Political Science have equipped him with a comprehensive knowledge of language systems, political ideologies and cultural diversity. These aspects, in conjunction with a life-long fascination with the fantastical, the exotic and the only-thought-possible-in-dreams, convinced him of his purpose in life: to invite  others along on his journeys of the mind. He has recently become a proud father of Lucas and, when he's not contemplating fictional evil, spends his days with his family in Uitgeest, a small village in the Netherlands.

Keep track
Do you want to keep track of Sylvan Greenfield, his new fantasy novels and our discounts? Send an email to info@pixelperfectpublications.com

Prologue

The sun beamed down at an almost vertical angle. Its golden rays bathed an olive branch in light. On the branch sat a squirrel. It had the see-through skin of a ghost and a bushy tail that shimmered silvery-blue in the sunlight. Every time it moved, the blueish shadow beneath its feet moved with it.

The spectral squirrel squinted against the dry Mediterranean breeze coming from the east. The breeze blew a single leaf up into the olive branches, where it was caught by the squirrel's fluffy tail; despite its ghostly appearance, the squirrel still had ways of interacting with its environment.

Down below, a procession of nine people trudged uphill over a half overgrown path. They were each garbed in white woollen robes, pulled up under sashes of various colours bound around their waists. The men, seven in total, had their robes cut short at the knees, while the women's went down to their ankles. Colourful shawls were draped over the women's shoulders to set them further apart from their male companions.

Sandwiched between his much younger companions, the man in the middle had only a small band of white hair left to protect his scalp from the sun. His features were serene and his gait resolute. Nothing about him betrayed a single doubt for what he was about to do. His companions shared his determination. But, in contrast to their spiritual leader, there did seem to be some internal struggle going on inside them. It was as though they wished there was another way, another path to take.

The moment the old man had disappeared out of sight, the spectral squirrel dashed down the tree and bounded through the vegetation after the group. More rustling noises followed and fleeting glimpses of blue could be spotted here and there on both sides of the path; a whole group of translucent creatures was speeding through the undergrowth like a miniature stampede.

Now the insects came. Dragonflies, horse flies, butterflies, mosquitoes, they all passed by the olive tree the squirrel had just abandoned for a better look. They all seemed to have suffered the same fate as the squirrel had; their bodies were but transparent versions of those of flesh-and-blood they once inhabited. Every single one of them was focused on the fellowship of nine and their solemn procession uphill.

The vegetation cleared and a great marble pillar entered the squirrel's view. It looked up towards the roof of a giant temple. Despite nature's best efforts to assimilate the building and turn its white to green, it still stood tall and strong. Following the row of pillars to the right, the squirrel was just in time to see the last woman venture inside.

Once inside the temple, the party of nine fanned out to form a circle. The eldest among them took position at the back of the room, in front of a stone basin filled with water. All seated themselves on the cold marble tiles in silence, and began to stare intently at an image of a solar disc cradled in cow's horns that was painted on the floor. An uncomfortable silence permeated the small chamber. None of them seemed eager to begin the ritual.

The rear woman looked up. 'The sun has passed its highest point,' she said, her voice soft. 'Shepherd, are you ready?'

In response, the elderly man in front of the basin closed his eyes and silence returned to the scene. Every head turned towards him.

The spectral squirrel was standing in the batch of sunlight that came in through the entrance. It was alone at first, but as the silence stretched on, more and more inhabitants of the forest trickled inside. There were mice, frogs, hares, and even a large porcupine invited itself in. Their shared transparent appearance made the band of animals look like a single many-headed, many-winged abomination.

The old Shepherd gave a slow nod of his head, the bald patch on his crown glinting in the light. Despite his stoic appearance, sweaty droplets dotted his skin. 'Andromeda, let us begin the ritual,' he said. When he opened his eyes again, some of the spirit animals at the entrance moved further in. Others simply stayed to watch.

'Druids, you know what to do,' said Andromeda, the rear woman who had taken the lead. 'Focus on the Shepherd and provide him with a steady supply of energy. Zeuxis,' she added to the old Shepherd in a heavy voice, 'may Ouranis carry you.'

At her final comment, all eight druids closed their eyes and pressed their palms together in prayer. The Shepherd did the same, but fixed his concentration on the painting of the solar disc on the floor.

One minute passed, then two. To the naked eye, nothing seemed to be happening. And yet, judging from the druids' faces, the ritual was well underway.

At one point, the Shepherd's eyes narrowed slightly and the spirit animals at the entrance startled. They began to jerk their tiny heads from one druid to the next, their faces curious. Some even began to retreat, caution muting their footsteps. Soon the tension was almost thick enough to taste.

The Shepherd's muscles now began to tremble as though something unseen was passing through them – a force that strained his muscles to an almost intolerable degree. Meanwhile, the pocket of air around the Shepherd was turning blue; such a tremendous amount of energy was being channelled into its body by his fellow druids that his aura was becoming visible.

Now a whisper licked the Shepherd's ears, one that only he could hear. The words slithered through the chamber like a viper, unnoticed by any of the other druids. The voice was silky and female. 'The Voidshapers are here.'

The sense of fear that coated the words sent a shiver through the old man and his gaze intensified immediately. The other druids stayed on task, unaware of the threat.

'More,' the Shepherd uttered through clenched teeth, while his muscles continued to complain against the energy that was passing through them.

'Shepherd...,' the woman in the back whispered in concern, her eyes remaining shut in concentration. She didn't understand the rush. The ritual was supposed to take at least half an hour.

'More, Andromeda! Do it,' the Shepherd said, barely able to move his lips. And because some of the druids had already complied with his first command, uncontrollable muscle spasms were making him labour to keep his hands together.

Andromeda's breathing had become heavy. 'As you wish,' she said obediently. 'Druids...'

Eight foreheads wrinkled up in concentration. Around the Shepherd's body, the band of blue light began to move like water being gently stirred. Sporadically and in slow motion, wisps of blue lashed out from the man's skin. Here and there a feather or a beak could be identified in the blue nimbus around his body, but they were gone before anyone would be able to point them out.

Standing on the solar disc before him, a figure was beginning to form. It was a woman in her early twenties, dressed in the same white garments as the two female druids present. Only her sash was orange, a colour unrepresented among the other druids.

Suddenly, every single animal that was observing the ritual either skittered or shot away; several tendrils of black fog came creeping in through the entrance. The shadows they cast on the marble floor were as black as their dark depths; not a single ray of light was allowed to pierce through the darkness.

The Shepherd's eyes flicked towards the invading fog. As a result, the figure of the woman standing on the painting, which had slowly become denser with every passing second, immediately started to fade.

'We're almost there,' said the Shepherd, his voice dry. When his eyes found the transparent woman again, the energy link between them was re-established and the transportation ritual resumed.

So intent was their focus, none of the druids beside the Shepherd had any idea of the danger posed by the advancing mist. The cloud of ash, for that was what it looked like, had its prey served on a marble platter. The entire entrance was now blocked by the darkness, and walls of fog were circling the group like a pack of wolves sensing imminent dinner.

9

The Shepherd's eyes bulged in fear. His mind was torn between the importance of the ritual and the danger the black mist posed. If he let go now, if he allowed the ritual to be interrupted, Ouranis' gift could be lost forever. He couldn't risk it. He mustn't.

'No... Andromeda...,' he muttered. His wrinkled eyelids filled up with tears.

The woman heard him. She opened her eyes. By now, the fog had reached both sides of the room and was slowly creeping closer to spring its trap. Andromeda, who was sitting with her back to the entrance, whipped her head to the side and stared the fog straight in the eyes. For there *were* eyes, two of them. They were like two blue, softly glowing sapphires being carried forth by the cascading waves of black ash.

The growl of a starving predator followed. With it came a snout, tufty ears and bared fangs; a hyena, black as shadow, jumped out from the cloud of ash. It sank its teeth in both sides of Andromeda's face, swung its body around the woman's shoulders, and snapped her neck with a loud, echoing crack.

Andromeda's limbs instantly lost all tension. Her arms fell down to her hips. Then she was dragged away by the hyena. Before the woman's legs had vanished into the mist, however, her body dissolved. Her flesh and clothes turned black and formed the lower half of a second hyena, including its bottlebrush tail. Before the Shepherd could see anything more of her transformation, she was gone.

Upon hearing the growl of the hyena, every single person present, with the exception of the Shepherd and one druid at his side, stood up. The remaining sitting druid was eyeing the scene with mixed shock and amazement, but was holding his ground regardless. He valiantly continued his efforts to supply the Shepherd with more energy.

'I am almost there!' the Shepherd called out to the druids, even though the image of the woman that they were trying to transport still looked far from solid.

'What *is* that?' one of the druids asked after coughing into his hand. With his other arm he was shielding his face as though he was afraid that another hyena would jump out and make him share Andromeda's fate.

The fog had filled up almost half the room. It was drawing closer and closer. With every square inch of space it swallowed, the druids took a step closer together.

'Aristion, I need two more to help me complete the ritual,' said the Shepherd, his hands still pressed palm to palm. 'The rest of you must protect the apprentice. It is the only way.'

During his short speech, as many as six hyena heads rose from the cloud of ash. Their beady eyes burned with blue fire. Their lower jaws were hanging loose in a silent cackle. Their tongues seemed to be already savouring the cornered lumps of meat.

'Now!' said the Shepherd. At once, two of the druids joined the one still sitting there.

Now the four druids on guard gave each other quick looks and nods. Something in their minds seemed to click in place and their expressions steeled. They knew they were in for a fight, a tough one, but in no case would they allow their Shepherd to die before he was able to transfer his power to his successor. Or else their duty to protect Ouranis' gift would fail and their connection to the animal kingdom, not to mention the great Ouranis herself, would be severed forever.

'For Eresa!' said the druid called Aristion.

'Ouranis, protect us!' said another, before he thrust his palms against each other and forced his entire body into a state of paralysis. A second later, a wolf, translucent like a ghost, sprang forth from his chest. It was as if the druid had been hiding the beast inside his body all along. The spectral wolf landed on all fours and in silence, charged its prey.

Aristion, who had just proclaimed his loyalty to Eresa, his beloved Sanctuary, had his hands pressed together too. With his mind focused on his animal of choice, three spectral eagles shot out from his chest, flooding the scene with silvery light.

As the spectral wolf threw itself into the black fog and between the hyenas, the eagles swooped in and aimed their hooked beaks for the eyes of the beasts. Gushes of wind battered down on the hyenas' heads, blowing most of the fog away in great swirls of darkness.

As the fog cleared away, the entire scene became suddenly clear. The wolf had sunk its fangs deep into the neck of one of the shadowy monsters. The remaining hyenas were gazing upwards, ready to rip feather from wing as the three ghostly eagles descended upon their heads. The druids watched how cascading waves of black fog continued to ooze from the hyenas' hides, painting the marble floor the colour of ash.

The success of the wolf and eagles instilled hope in the hearts of the druids. One saw a chance to use his spiritcraft as well and summoned a swarm of spectral locusts. The swarm spewed forth from his chest, zig-zagged upwards, then immediately began circling the group of druids like a tornado of twinkling lights. The advancing darkness retreated instantly, appearing to take a moment to adjust to the new situation. The druids used the time to regain their composure and regroup.

In unison, a threesome of hyenas broke through the cocoon of locusts. The attack came as such a surprise that two of the druids were lost before they had the time to retaliate. They were both dragged to the ground, one by the shoulders and one by the neck, and were forced to join the enemy.

The Shepherd was watching the battle unfold from his seated position. With every sacrifice his druids made to protect the ritual, he saw his chances dwindle. Panic was building inside him. If he should die today without passing on his power, life in Eresa would never be the same again. His people might even be forced to leave this world after calling it their home for centuries, and return to the homeland. Why had the Voidshapers chosen this time to attack? Had they sensed the energy generated by the ritual?

Aristion, with the eagles, and his only remaining companion, joined the Shepherd. They watched the cloud of darkness punch through the circular wall of twinkling locusts from all directions. The sparkles dowsed in quick succession as the locusts were swallowed by the fog, never to re-emerge. With them gone, the only light that still allowed the druids to see was coming from the three eagles and the wolf, all of which were being mind-controlled back by their druid masters.

'Shepherd, it's too powerful,' one of the seated druids said. Despite his best efforts to continue his duty, the man couldn't keep his eyes off the enemy.

The Shepherd had managed to steady his hands. He was biting his lip in an effort to think of a solution and keep control of his energy at the same time. Meanwhile the darkness was creeping ever closer. The hyenas had become submerged within the fog. Even the ceiling had now become completely obscured by the black mist.

'Shepherd…,' pressed the druid.

During the next few seconds, the Shepherd flicked his eyes from the three druids sitting beside him, to the two who were peering down with desperation enlarging their eyeballs. They didn't deserve this. They had no idea what they were up against. And he had sworn to the great Ouranis not to tell them. It didn't matter anymore. It was over. Or it was for him.

'Enough!' said the Shepherd, making the three sitting druids jump up in shock. 'You all need to get out of here. The ritual has failed.'

'We can't,' said one of the sitting druids. 'Shepherd, you'll die!'

A deep sigh made the old man regain his state of tranquillity. 'Do not concern yourselves with me,' said the Shepherd calmly. 'The Council must learn of what has befallen us. Eresa must be saved. One of you will have to become my successor and convince her to be content with it.' At the mentioning of "her", all ten eyes widened in disbelief. Sputterings of protest came from all directions.

'Go, now!' shouted the Shepherd and suddenly, the band of blue light around his body flared up like a bonfire.

The three sitting druids jumped to their feet. Then all five of them headed straight for the entrance, with the three ghostly eagles and the spectral wolf ploughing through the black fog before them.

The moment the druids were swallowed up by the enveloping darkness, all light went out.

The Shepherd's palms were still pressed together in a praying position, while the accumulated energy from the druids was continuing to race through his arms and torso. He could hear the growls of hyenas coming closer and closer through the pitch blackness. There was no road left to take but one. *Be kind to them, Ouranis. Be kind to... him.*

Meanwhile, the spectral squirrel that had followed the procession of nine to the temple had found another vantage point. It had taken up position high up in a carob tree. From behind one of the tree's succulent green legumes it was gazing down at the temple with its head tilted in curiosity.

Only the triangular-shaped roof was left of the temple, protruding from a sea of black, foggy darkness. Then the cry of a man, spine-shivering, rang out. It drowned all other sounds, including the other calls and shouts coming from the entrance, as well as the growls of hungry hyenas. A flock of translucent birds scattered, screeching in annoyance. Moments later, all was silent.

Chapter 1

A little over an hour before the attack on the druids, on the same island of Delos, Greece, my girlfriend and I were enjoying some time off in the archaeological museum. Neither of us had ever seen a druid, nor heard of a type of magic called "spiritcraft".

Denise and I were students of archaeology at Oxford University, and had recently moved in together. We've had a bit of a rough start, which convinced Denise's parents it was a good idea to send us here, to Greece. They wouldn't hear a word against it either. After last year's success – the four of us went on a tour around Egypt – they felt like another culture trip was exactly the thing Denise and I needed to iron out the kinks in our relationship. Naturally, we didn't try too hard to convince them otherwise; Greece was a place we had read and heard so much about during our studies and beyond, we felt like we had to see the sights for ourselves one day anyway.

After showing us around and highlighting the most significant artefacts the museum had to offer, our unfortunately named but enthusiastic tour guide, Adonis, had left us to marvel at the craftsmanship of the ancient Greek people by ourselves. Adonis had joined up with a colleague and went to see if he could "score a frappe", or so he informed me. By the way he looked at me you would think he expected me to want to go with him. Indeed, part of me was longing for an extra-large iced coffee, but I also didn't want to squander my time on Delos. Because chances were we would never be here again.

'You're still not feeling well, are you?' said Denise. I looked up from the ground, blinked, and there she was, standing with their arms folded.

'I told you, it's nothing,' I threw back at her. 'Just enjoy yourself, all right? We've only got half an hour left until we're out in that blazing heat again.'

'That's exactly the problem. I'm not so sure we should be.'

'Look, it's nothing. Remember Egypt? If I can survive that, I'll live through this one too.'

Denise shook her head. 'You're just as stubborn as your brother. I suppose it runs in the family.'

'No it doesn't. We may be twins, but we might as well not be. We couldn't be more different, Keith and I.'

'Really? You should've heard him talk to Patricia the other day. She doesn't know what she's getting herself into, poor girl.'

'You mean like you?'

'That's different. I've known you since high school.' A smile curved her lips. 'You're an acquired taste, Aaron Bishop.' With that she turned to a display case showing a variety of ancient clay figurines. I stared at her for a spell and used the time I wasn't being gauged to regain my composure. I did indeed feel a bit lightheaded.

When Denise spoke again, her voice was soft, but curious. 'Aaron, look at this.' She was pointing at a statuette of a woman with wings for arms and wearing a headdress consisting of a disk cradled between bull horns. 'It's a figurine of Isis, the Egyptian goddess. That's weird. What's a depiction of her doing here?'

So your curiosity won the battle over your concern for me, I thought. *Interesting*. Then I said, 'Didn't you know? There's a lot of overlap between Greece and Egypt here on Delos. Isis even has her own temple here. And I think…,' I produced the tour schedule from my back pocket with a flourish, '… yes, it's our first stop after the museum. No, sorry, the second. We're going to Hera's temple first.'

'I remember reading something about a religious trinity that was going on between Isis, Serapis and Anubis in the Graeco-Roman period,' I said, ploughing on before the subject changed back to my health. 'It was in that book you bought at the travel agency. The temples of Apollo and Artemis and the others are much older, though. But hers may still be worth a look.'

Denise acknowledged my words with a nod. 'It says here that Isis was known for her magical powers of protection and healing. And she was thought of as the ideal wife and mother.' A grin appeared on my face, which was spotted. 'What?'

'Nothing,' I said airily. 'I just thought it was funny that a figurine of Isis piqued your interest out of all these, being the ideal wife and all.'

'Yes, you would find that funny, wouldn't you? Well, let me tell you, there's nothing wrong with showing some concern for the man I'm planning to marry someday.'

'And… we're walking,' I said and stalked away briskly. I had barely taken two steps, however, when my mobile rang. I recognised the number. 'It's your mum. Why's she calling me?'

'Because my battery's dead, remember?' She took the phone and added, 'I forgot to charge it, again.'

I suppressed a sigh and turned to the life-size statue of a lion, which sat on a pedestal with its mouth gaping. By the look on the animal's face, it appeared to have been in the middle of an apology when the lion was forced to experience the calcifying results of one of the Medusa's tantrums.

'That was quick,' I said when Denise gave me back my mobile. Denise nodded. Something was obviously bothering her. 'Well?'

'My mum just came back from the hospital. Apparently grandpa managed to sprain his ankle.'

'You're kidding me. Now his ankle? He hasn't gone back on that roof again, has he? They only just removed the cast from his hip.'

'No, he slipped down the stairs, according to his own story. He's been lucky. It doesn't seem too serious.'

'Not yet, you mean. I'm telling you, you should tell your mother to call the roofing company before he tries to get up there again. He's almost ninety for heaven's sake!'

'She promised to keep an eye on him,' said Denise dismissively. 'Let's focus on something else.' There was a moment's pause, during which I put my phone back into my pocket, then, 'Do keep it on, though. You never know.'

After about an hour's worth of sweat, and with our minds flooded with more impressions of the ancient Greeks, we were shielding our eyes against the mid afternoon sun. We had just finished our visit to the temple of Hera and were making our way uphill to the one that had been built in honour of Isis.

As was the case with most temples and statues on the island – since not much was left of the ancient culture – the power of our imagination was put to the test once more. It had been one ruin, broken pillar and eroded statue after another, but our guide was fantastic. Adonis' exuberant personality and colourful descriptions made it easy for our creativity to fill in the blanks and almost see the white-robed worshippers bring their offerings for the Gods they so deeply venerated.

'If you come a bit closer, you will be able to see what the image on the disc represents,' the guide said when Denise and I joined the group in front of the temple. 'Who can tell me what it is?'

Denise wasn't paying attention to the tour. She had noticed me screwing up my eyes in discomfort, which was quite remarkable since she was walking behind me. 'You do know you can't hide it from me, don't you, Aaron?'

I quickly straightened up and ironed my face. The effort forced me to take a deep breath, something not even Denise's x-ray vision could prevent. 'Just don't, Denise. We've been over this. It's probably just the sun.'

The fact was, ever since that morning a strange sensation of dizziness had been bugging me. It felt like a host of insects had taken up residence in my skull and had used my brain for a game of toss. I thought I managed to hide the worst of it from Denise, but after exiting the museum it had only gotten worse. And just a couple of minutes ago, the insects appeared to have gotten bored and deemed it more entertaining to grab my thought-container in their tiny legs and take it for a spin.

Denise screwed up her lips in disappointment. 'I told you what, ten times already? You should drink more. Here, you can have some of mine. And don't bother giving it back before it is empty.'

'I'm fine, really. I don't want to run out. We've got the entire afternoon ahead of us.'

She had already taken one of her bottles out of her backpack and handed it to me. 'Drink,' she said, using a voice that told me I could try to bribe her with the world's most amazing back massage and she would still insist.

'All right, all right, I'll have some. What about you?'

A second bottle was already out. While draining over half of its contents, Denise tuned both eyes and ears back to Adonis. He was ushering the band of tourists inside the temple, which was a funny sight as the entrance was basically all that remained standing of the once great structure. Before I knew it I was watching Denise's black ponytail bouncing against her backpack as she followed the group inside.

'I guess I'll carry this for a while,' I said to no one in particular, as I thrust her empty bottle between the ones inside my own pack.

Even though I fully intended to refer to the bottle, I was seconds away from discovering this sentence could have referred to something else entirely.

The cry of a bird unlike any I had ever heard suddenly battered down on my eardrums. The sound embraced me like a mother reunited with her long lost child. The cry was that of a fearsome predator of the skies, and something in its voice reminded me of desperation – and the will to protect. The noise sent painful spasms past my eardrums. I let out a cry of my own. I didn't even realise I was already down on my knees, and that my hands were pressed against my ears as though they were afraid my skull could crack in two at any moment.

I heard Denise call my name somewhere far away. I couldn't look up. The pain was too severe. My backpack was kicked aside and I felt a hand on my back. It was a woman's touch, gentle, but unfortunately it couldn't soothe my agony. It was obvious Denise couldn't have heard what I had. She might have been tough, but running towards me and lending a hand would have been the last thing on her mind if she had.

My mind was racing. *Am I suffering from some kind of heat stroke? What was that cry? Where did it come from?* Slowly I opened my eyes. An annoying and persistent bottle of water was obstructing my view of the ground.

'Drink, Aaron,' I heard Denise say. 'Don't be so hard on yourself. Here.' The bottle disappeared, then returned without the cap.

Traces of the cry still echoed around my skull like a flock of ducks. I pushed the bottle away.

'It's not that,' I said, somehow knowing it was the truth. Not to mention the fact that my stomach barely seemed able to keep down the contents of the first bottle I drained. More people had joined us by now, which was obvious due to the crunching of sand and stone under their feet, and the many murmurs coming from all around. I looked into Denise's concerned eyes. 'Just let me breathe for a second, Denise.' Her hand was still on my back. It felt hot.

Before me stood the entrance to the ruin that had once been the temple of Isis. Slowly the half collapsed structure acquired more detail. But, even as I thought I was coming back to my senses, they seemed to betray me once more. Out of the entrance, from behind the four stone pillars that were all that was left of the temple, a duo of azure globes made their appearance. The light they emitted painted the pillars blue. I was now convinced it was the heat stroke throwing me another curve ball and causing me to hallucinate: this couldn't be really happening.

The globes were mesmerisingly beautiful. My eyes felt enchanted and they had no choice but to follow them. Everyone else was looking at me and my rolling eyeballs, probably drawing their own conclusions. I paid no heed to their muttering.

The pair of translucent orbs was barely visible against the clear sky. Twisting and turning they danced through the air like two hummingbirds performing a mating ritual. Then, after another double corkscrew, they changed trajectory and started heading straight for me.

I gave a loud curse and threw myself backwards, thrusting my hands into the sand behind me. Fear was clutching my chest. I could barely breathe. Now Denise saw the globes too. She grabbed my shoulder so forcefully that my T-shirt objected with a loud ripping sound. Others joined in and were able to either jump aside or utter screams of surprise of their own. I wasn't.

Two forceful impacts followed when the azure orbs slammed into my chest, forced the breath from my lungs, and pressed my back into the gravel. The scene dissolved into darkness, black as pitch, and I lost all sense of self. I figured this was what it must feel like to fall unconscious.

Seconds, or perhaps hours, later I blinked my eyes. Nothing changed. Whether I closed my eyes or used them to gaze at my surroundings, they couldn't pick up anything but blackness. And, at least for the first few seconds, there was no sound either. There was just me, the earth, and the intense darkness around me. The air tasted like ash, which stuck to my tongue and palate with every breath I took.

A girly scream came from my left. It was followed by a blue squirrel, or perhaps a ghost, running across my chest. Whichever it was, however, I could still feel its claws digging into my shirt and skin as it used my body for a race-track.

'Denise?' I asked as I recognised the voice. The scream she had uttered acted like a talisman against fear.

'Aaron?' she asked in return. She sounded very close and I could hear her hand searching the ground. So I reached out and grabbed it into my own.

'I'm here. Are you all right?'

'I... I think so,' she said, sounding unsure. 'What happened?'

'I think we died,' I said bluntly, as it was the only thing that made sense to me. *It may sound stupid*, I thought, *but what else could have happened?* 'Did you see that squirrel?'

The sudden growl of a canine predator made Denise grab every part of my body she could find and hug it. 'I did,' she said in a voice that could have belonged to a petrified ten-year-old.

'Whatever you do, don't let go,' I told her, squinting blankly into the darkness. I had to blink every other second, as my eyeballs were drying out at an alarming rate. Denise made a whimpering sound to acknowledge my words and intensified her grip. I figured she must be pressing her lips together to prevent the ash from entering her throat.

Voices came, shouts, then more growling. They seemed to have come from higher up the hill. 'Go, quickly,' I whispered through tight lips, pushing Denise away from the din. 'And stay close.'

We had to be careful not to trip, for the path we followed downhill was half overgrown with vines and different types of vegetation. I tightened my grip around Denise's wrist; we could easily lose each other in this pitch blackness. The notion that we had died already and this place was either heaven or hell, or anything in between, had no place in my mind anymore. The ingrained habit of moving away from danger was powerful enough to overrule any curiosity for what was happening.

'Who are you?' I heard a male voice say. It had come from back up the hill. Denise and I halted instantly, listening. Had they heard us?

'Your Shepherd,' said another, a woman this time. 'What has happened here?' But instead an answer, the first half of a cry of pain came from the man's mouth, before a cough and a great deal of sputtering followed.

Then a blinding flash bathed our part of the hill and the forest around us in light. Both Denise and I squinted against its dazzling power, as well as the gusts of wind and ash that were being blown into our direction by two massive wings. There, hovering in front of the entrance of a Greek temple, was a giant bird, sharing its size with that of the average automobile. At first I thought it was composed of silvery dust, but as my eyes adjusted to the amount of light, I realised it had the same ethereal appearance that the squirrel had when the tiny beasty jumped on my chest earlier.

Positioned directly under the bird I saw a buxom young woman with an attractive, heart-shaped face. She was dressed in white garments with an orange sash around her waist and a similarly coloured shawl draped over her shoulders. Her palms were pressed together tightly, as though she was praying for something. Beside her, lying on the ground, was a figure wreathed in black smoke. The woman was studying it with an expression of mixed horror and incomprehension; she evidently had no idea what she was looking at.

I couldn't see what the black figure represented until it got to its feet and cocked its head at the bird above it. The figure resembled a black hyena, but one so filthy, it seemed like it was actually sweating the ashy grime I could taste on my lips from every square inch of its body. It was perspiring so profusely in fact, that the grime was flowing copiously down its pitch black hide, staining the grass around its paws.

Evidently taken by surprise, the woman whipped her head from left to right. 'Druid, where are you?' she said while backing away from the hyena. Her hands still seemed glued to one another for some reason. 'Adrastus, was that you?' Then her eyes fell on Denise and me. 'You there, watch out!'

What happened next went by so quickly, neither Denise nor I had time to react. A second hyena had used the undergrowth and the confusion to mask his escape. And Denise couldn't have chosen a worse time to brush away a translucent wasp that was annoying her. By doing so, one of her hands was just close enough for the hyena to snap off a fingernail while continuing its rapid retreat though the vegetation.

'Denise!' I called.

She clamped her other fist around the injured finger and hissed in pain. Tears were gushing from her eyes, mirroring the slow trickle of blood that immediately began seeping through her fingers.

'Oh, no... Denise...'

I had just put a consoling hand on her back when a great flapping of wings made me look up at the temple. With this, the giant bird shot away into the darkness, probably chasing the first hyena, and took all light with it. Slowly the dark fog withdrew and the rays of the sun were finally able to break through. The long, blonde hair of the woman in white came into view again. She was running towards us.

'Is she all right?' asked the woman when she had come close enough for me to judge her age. I figured she had to be in her early twenties, although the confidence with which she carried herself could easily add ten more. Her face looked bewildered. She seemed just as confused about what was happening as I was.

I looked down at Denise's finger, then into her eyes. They were hard, though they weren't squinting in pain anymore. 'I think she's going to be...' My breath faltered. 'Denise?'

Denise had slipped out from under my arm. She fell down on her knees and hands, and began staring at the ground with her eyes bulging in shock.

'Denise, what's wrong?' I asked in desperation. I looked up at the blonde woman. 'What's wrong with her? Do something!'

'I… I can't,' she said, looking shocked. She glanced back over her shoulder at the temple and added, 'I don't understand. None of this should have happened. Where is everyone?'

'None of what? Where's who?' I didn't wait for an answer. Quickly I kneeled down beside Denise. Judging by the way she was trembling all over, however, I wasn't even sure she remembered my name.

'Aaron…,' Denise said beseechingly, 'forgive me…' Tears shattered onto the tangle of leaves and vines between her hands. They were dark, as if fallen from an ink bottle.

'Wha…' A hand was laid on my shoulder. I felt it tighten around my shirt and pull me up. 'What are you doing?' I asked the blonde woman, who had her gaze locked on Denise, her expression hard as granite. 'Let me go!' I slapped the woman's arm away.

And then, as I stooped over Denise to satisfy my urge to help, something taken straight from the mother of all nightmares began to unfold. First Denise began to cough and wheeze horribly as though someone had emptied an ashtray into her mouth. Then her clothes bulged as black smoke accumulated between skin and fabric. Tendrils of dark fog began to rise up from the ends of her sleeves, the legs of her trousers, and the bottom end of her shirt.

'Denise, no!' I said. 'W–What's happening?'

'Stand back,' said the woman, as though from very far away.

Soon Denise's entire body was cloaked in darkness. There was nothing I could do. On top of this, the blonde woman, whoever she was, was doing her best to prevent me from getting close. And in my current, desperate state of mind I was doing a poor job of fighting her. A few seconds into Denise's transformation, a sense of estrangement from my own girlfriend washed over me. It was like my own mind was trying to save itself by telling me to get away; it recognised the danger.

I felt tears roll down my cheeks. My entire world was shattering to pieces as the woman I had come to love so deeply was now being taken by the monster of all transformations. A single word rang from my throat, carrying every drop of my affection as it echoed through the woods around me. 'DENISE!'

At the mention of her name, the shadowy face of a black hyena with beady, blue eyes emerged from the gloomy fog. The transformation was complete, or it seemed that way. And, as Denise moved forwards, her slender, doglike body left most of the dark grime behind, while more of the greasy substance kept exuding from her skin like a fountain of black chocolate. I gasped.

A voice came shooting up the hill. 'Selena!' A young man, sharing our age and also dressed in white, now came running up the path and two more people followed. Seeing them together reminded me of the recreations of ancient Greece I had seen back in the museum we had visited that same afternoon.

Denise halted in her step, one grimy paw hanging motionless in the air. She began whipping her head between Selena and me and the advancing threesome, apparently figuring out what to do. A low growling sound came from her throat. Then she crouched into a retreat, but the tree behind her and the thick vegetation surrounding it made it difficult to choose an escape route.

The young man in the lead had short black hair offset by a single strand of white. He gave the dark hyena a quick frown and said, pointing to one of his companions, 'Peleus saw the smoke coming out of the water. We came as quickly as we could.' His entourage passed him and more eyes fell on Denise.

'By Ouranis' hind feathers!' the man named Peleus exclaimed. The young woman behind him gasped in an almost exact imitation of me a moment ago.

'Briseis, Peleus, circle it so it can't escape,' said the young man, trying to drown the fearful murmurs with his command.

'Please, don't hurt her!' I said, and turned to Selena. 'Tell them, please. She's my girlfriend!' All heads remained fixed on Denise, who was bowing her head submissively and lowering her back in an attempt to look as unthreatening as her monstrous demeanour allowed. Selena was evidently still trying to make sense of the situation.

'Leander, no,' Selena said suddenly. She was clearly not used to issuing commands, but she tried it regardless. 'Stay back. I don't believe it is here to hurt us.'

It? I thought while my mind was desperately trying to make sense of the situation. My whole world had been thrown into turmoil. *Her name is Denise! She saw her transform, didn't she? What's going on here?*

Leander, who seemed to enjoy a certain level of respect from the other two, looked back at his companions' shocked faces. 'Are you sure about this?' he asked. Selena said nothing. 'What about you? Has the ritual been completed?'

'I... think so,' Selena said thoughtfully.

'And the others? Where are Andromeda and Aristion?'

'They...,' Selena began, then breathed out through her nostrils. Her eyes travelled to Denise, to me, then to the vegetation that the second hyena had used to escape and back to Leander. 'I can't say for certain.'

'Hmm.' Leander looked doubtful. 'But you are sure there are no more of these things? Never mind,' he added quickly, 'we can't take the risk. Let's have a look around. Whatever happened here, it must've had something to do with that dark fog.' As he finished his sentence, he gave the grime beneath Denise's paws a scrutinising look.

'I already have, Leander,' said Selena, which seemed unlikely considering the tiny amount that the dark mist had allowed us to see. 'Andromeda and the others can take care of themselves. They probably headed down to the coast to see where the fog came from. We should get back to the Sanctuary instead and report to the Council. Aaron here came from the homeland.'

Leander, whose eyes didn't seem able to see me before, finally noticed me standing there. His eyes grew slightly as he linked his homeland, wherever that was, with my face and he swallowed Selena's lie without a second thought. 'The homeland. That explains a lot,' he said, indicating my clothes with a nod of his head. I didn't think my leather sandals, cotton trousers and shirt were all that different from the white garments and *straw* sandals these people were wearing, but it still impressed him. 'Peleus, have you ever seen anyone dress like that?'

With difficulty, Peleus removed his eyes from Denise and looked at me. 'Never. He must be telling the truth then.' He gave me the impression he wasn't the brightest, quite in contrast to Leander and especially Selena; behind Selena's eyes I imagined a brain that was continuously processing past events, in preparation of sketching all the possible scenarios in her head. The only thing on Briseis' mind seemed to be Denise. She looked appalled by her appearance and didn't seem to care much for anything else at the moment.

'Do you know how he crossed over?' asked Leander. 'And why?'

'That is for the Council to work out,' said Selena with finality, as though hoping Leander wouldn't press the matter any further.

Leander chewed on the words for a moment or two, then said, 'Fine. So you're absolutely sure we can't do anything here?'

'I am sure.'

'Well, you're the Shepherd now,' said Leander, as though that settled the matter. 'What about this one?' he added, turning to Denise. 'Do you want to take them both with us? The Council is not going to like it, I can tell you that.'

I was quite surprised, and pleased at the same time, for the light-hearted attitude Leander took towards Denise's appearance. For someone who had evidently never witnessed anyone or anything like her, he seemed remarkably fearless. In fact, the same held true for Peleus as well, although his eyes never left Denise for more than two seconds.

Selena and I looked into each other's faces. Mine had to be burning with the desire for her to agree. 'It will be fine, Leander,' said Selena. 'I will help them see reason.'

I turned back to Denise. Despite her feral appearance, her posture showed a level of anxiety only matched by my own frantically beating heart. She was obviously as confused as I was, probably more. In the presence of this many strangers, she seemed to melt in place until there was nothing left but a shapeless hump of foggy darkness with two beady eyes shining from its depths. *Is this really my Denise?* I questioned in silence. I thought back at the other two black hyenas I had seen. *She's definitely different compared to the other creatures, but… is this still her? My Denise wouldn't cower away like this.*

'Are you coming?' said a voice. 'We can talk on the way if you like.' I looked up and saw Selena standing there with an inviting look on her face. The others had already begun moving downhill, but stopped and turned when they caught Selena's words.

'How about "no"?' I said, my voice gathering strength with each word. 'Not before you tell me what is going on. Who are you people?'

Selena's pupils moved to the corners of her eyes, then took a step towards me. I mirrored her by taking a step backwards, teeth clenched. She stopped, held up a hand in a soothing gesture and said softly, so that the others couldn't hear, 'Please, come with me. I have answers, if you let me. But you need to trust me.'

'And why should I do that? First tell me what happened to Denise and how to get her back, then we can talk.'

Selena bit her lip. 'I'm afraid I don't know. But that doesn't mean I can't help you. Please.'

My fury continued to build. 'How can you help me if you can't do anything for Denise? What else do I need, new sandals?'

'Selena, is there a problem?' asked Leander.

'Everything is fine,' said Selena. She gave me a meaningful look, saying, 'We'll be right there.' I folded my arms. And before I knew it, Selena had closed the gap between us and bent towards me, whispering, 'You're on a small island. There is no one here but us. Your girlfriend is in mortal danger and I am the only chance you have. These four truths are absolute. The choice is yours.' And with that she wheeled around and walked briskly towards the others, who were all staring at us as though unsure what to make of Selena's funny behaviour.

'So…,' said Leander, pointing at me. Selena joined them, saying nothing. Leander withdrew his finger and used it to scratch his head, looking befuddled.

What on Earth is going on here? I asked myself. *This is so messed up. These people are the only ones around? Do I even have a choice? I have to find help for Denise. And that Selena knows something she's not telling, I'm sure of it. But can I trust them?* I sighed and steeled my resolve. *Fine, but they better have the answers we're looking for.*

'I am very sorry for this,' said Selena, as she and Denise and I started following the others down the hill. Denise was walking in front of us, with her snout almost scraping the overgrown path and her bottlebrush tail dangling between her legs.

'Me too,' I said curtly, frustration colouring my voice. 'Now can you please tell me where we are?'

It took a while for Selena to respond, and even when she did, her mind didn't seem fully present; during the time I took to make my decision, she seemed to have been contemplating recent events as well. 'I was right about you coming from the homeland, wasn't I? Incredible,' she added in answer to her own question. I searched her face. She was looking at Denise, but no expression related to the word "incredible" could be found in them. Behind those blue pearls, I knew her brain was still working tirelessly. 'Did you see anything of the ritual?' she asked at length, without averting her eyes.

'A ritual? No, I didn't see anything. But you said you had answers for me.'

'I have some, yes. My name is Selena Zaro,' she said, sounding like she wished we could start over the conversation. 'I am a druid. And you have just entered the realm of Ouranis.'

'Realm of Ouranis? I've never heard of such a place. My name is Aaron Bishop. Hers is Denise.' Despite my need for information, my attention was attracted by the cloud of ash that was continuously being emitted by Denise's skin. The trail extended about a yard or two behind her, where it evaporated into thin air before our boots and sandals could step into the inky substance.

'I'm pleased to meet you, Aaron,' said Selena.

'So, this realm of Ouranis, it's somewhere in Greece?'

'Greece?' Selena shook her head. 'I don't know what you mean.'

'You don't? Then what are you saying, we've travelled to another dimension?' Despite the severity of the situation, I gave a chuckle. A memory now replaced my current thoughts. 'You said I was from your homeland. So that must mean you do originally come from where I'm from.'

Instead of answering, she began murmuring to herself, of which I repeatedly picked up the words "council", "captains" and "shepherd". Instead of asking any more questions, which Selena was obviously reluctant to supply anyway, I chose to observe and listen for a while. I was rather annoyed by her reserved attitude towards me at first, though from the way Selena was shooting her fellow druids occasional, haunted looks, it seemed she was almost as upset by what had happened to Denise as I was. As a result, I felt the emotional walls erected by my irritation crack slightly.

The silence between us lasted until Leander's voice carried up the path. 'Selena, this is your chance.' We found the young man standing just beyond the forest's edge, where the path led us out of the woods and continued to snake through a colourful flowerbed. Leander had his finger aimed at a cluster of flowers for a reason that was not immediately clear to either of us.

Selena's eyes kept searching until her head stopped and a wry, unsure smile appeared on her face. I could see it too. The large ears of a hare, blue and translucent like the squirrel had been earlier, were sticking out of the vegetation. They were difficult to spot because the hare was so far away. Yet we managed it because the hare's silvery outline contrasted starkly with the green and yellow of the flowers behind it.

'Please be silent for a moment,' Selena said softly without diverting her eyes from the hare. The rest of the group kept watching her intently, as though hoping for Selena to turn the hare into something with a lot more translucent meat on it with her druid magic. For a long spell nothing happened. Then Selena shook her head. 'Nothing yet.'

Disappointed, the group wordlessly turned back to the path. I was glad to see Denise had the presence of mind to comply and continue with them. For a second there I thought she wouldn't, for she seemed entranced by the hare's translucent appearance. The blue light in her eyes matched the blue skin of the hair perfectly.

After topping another hill, a smaller one this time, the panorama opened up and I found myself overlooking a semi-circular shoreline with a pair of wooden docks sprouting from the shore like fingers jabbing into the sea. Up ahead was a tiny island with one end almost nudging the shore. The small landmass was covered with thick forest and fenced by a low wall that seemed to encircle the entire isle, reminding me of the balustrade of a mediaeval castle.

'Eresa,' Selena said to my raised eyebrows.

'Sorry?'

She pointed ahead. 'It is the name of our sanctuary.'

I nodded. As I glanced back at her, there was a certain preoccupied look in her eyes. 'And that's where you're bringing us,' I said, deliberately pointing out Denise and my lack of freedom.

26

Selena's troubled look changed to one of compassion. 'Your friend's… accident gave us no choice, Aaron,' she said, lowering her voice again to prevent anyone from eavesdropping. 'You will understand why soon enough. It is clear that the Shepherd ritual, which apparently chose me, has gone wrong somehow. There were supposed to be eight druids waiting for us. We need to understand why they weren't there. Or why most of them weren't,' she added in a smaller voice.

'Chosen for what?'

'To become the next Shepherd and receive Ouranis' gift.' A jolt of confidence straightened her back. 'And because none of the druids were there to meet me,' her face dropped a little, 'it is of the utmost importance that we find out whether Ouranis' gift is still with us.'

'Does it have something to do with what happened to Denise?'

'I've been thinking about that same question, and I think it is possible. I cannot be sure, however. We have never encountered anything like these black creatures before.'

'You're talking about my girlfriend,' I said in a harsh, almost menacing voice. After everything that had happened, it was impossible for me to keep my voice from sharpening the edges of my words.

'I apologise. Your friend, Denise, does seem different compared to Adrastus. He was transformed into one of these creatures as well.' She looked uncomfortable. 'I suppose you may have seen him near the entrance of the temple.'

'You mean the one who was scared away by that giant bird?'

A weak smile curved Selena's lips. 'I suppose you may call her that,' she said enigmatically. 'As for Adrastus, I didn't know him very well, regrettably. Though of the little that I knew of him, not much seemed to be left after his transformation. Denise on the other hand, appears to be more in control of her actions.'

'She's strong,' I said, a sense of pride in igniting in my stomach. 'But I can't detect much of her personality either, unfortunately. You do seem to know a thing or two about these transformations, though,' I added quickly, now that our conversation was finally getting somewhere. 'I'm sorry, but it's just odd to see you being so calm if you've never seen them before. The same goes for all of you.'

'I understand your confusion, Aaron, You must also understand, however, that all of us,' she pointed out the group with her eyes, 'have spent our lives training for the possibility that one of us would become the next Shepherd. So changing one's shape may not seem as unnatural to us as it does to you.'

'And you know this how, exactly? Or are you saying you were waiting for me as well?' Once again I failed to leave the frustration out of my voice. Everything about this whole situation seemed so otherworldly and unfair, part of me was thinking it didn't really matter what I did or said, because I would wake up from this nightmare any time now anyway.

In response, Selena seemed content to just give me another cordial smile and look at me for a spell. Then she gave me the most unsatisfactory answer she could possibly give me. 'I have to ask for your patience, Aaron. All will become clear once we are back in Eresa.' I shook my head, silently conveying this was a giant mistake. 'I understand how you must be feeling, Aaron. I promised you answers, and you will get them.' In a whisper, she added, 'But I'd rather discuss this somewhere more private.'

'Have it your way,' I muttered. *But if she can't help me, I'm going straight to that Council of theirs.*

We reached the shore. Absently, I gazed at a blue speck which I figured had to be a bird of some kind. It had seated its feathery behind on a branch half way up a Juniper tree, a tree that sprouted from the edge of the island called Eresa, located a little off the coast. Directly ahead there was an opening in the low wall that circled the island. It gave access to a path leading to the island's centre. There was only one problem.

'Where's Trionyx?' Briseis asked the group. She was shielding her eyes from the sun with her hand and was searching the body of water between us and the island.

'What is she looking for?' I asked in a whisper. I didn't even know why I was whispering.

'Trionyx, our transport,' said Selena. 'He should be here.' She fell silent again and joined Briseis in her search. Leander and Peleus were giving each other confused looks and they too joined in the search.

'Right,' I said to no one in particular. I turned away to see how Denise was doing. She was gazing up at me with her beady eyes glowing from their black sockets. 'Are you all right?' I mouthed soundlessly. The monstrous hyena continued to look at me with an unblinking stare. I thought I could see her jaw moving up and down, but was unsure whether she was trying to talk back or wondering which limb to tear off first. *Don't worry, Denise, I'll find help. These druids apparently know a thing or two about changing one's shape, so one of them must be able to help us.*

'Selena, you're the Shepherd,' said Leander. 'Try to call for him. He can't be far. He just ferried us.'

I wasn't paying attention. 'I'm going to help you,' I mouthed to Denise, supplementing my words with hand signals as best as I could. 'Help… you…' Even a wag of her bottlebrush tail would have given me at least some idea of what was going on inside her head.

Unfortunately, nothing of the sort happened. And this new monstrosity of a face of hers was so shockingly different from anything I knew, any facial expression she was able to pull would be too hard for me to read. Not to mention that over the next half a minute or so, her body cloaked itself in such intense darkness, it was hard to discern one facial feature from the other. By now, pointing out a fang or even one of her tufty ears was nigh impossible.

'I'm not sure if I'm doing it right, Leander,' said Selena. 'I'm supposed to hear the animals' thoughts, but I can't. I believe we have no choice but to swim across this time.' Several disappointed groans followed.

'Great,' muttered Leander after a sigh. 'Everyone, you heard the Shepherd. It's time to get wet.'

'What about this... *thing*?' asked Peleus contemptuously. It took me a moment to realise who or what he was talking about. Then I saw the druid jabbing his finger at Denise like a thrusting spear.

'You leave her alone,' I told him, my voice low and threatening. Pure bravado was carrying my words, which instantly drowned all conversation. The group's spirit changed with a snap of a finger.

'Excuse me?' Peleus said into the silence, rounding on me. For some reason he began moving his hands towards each other until his fingertips met. Judging from the look he gave me I half expected him to draw a dagger or some similar small weapon from under his robes. I knew it couldn't be anything larger, as I had already ensured myself none of them carried any such weaponry, evidenced by the shape of their garments.

'You heard me.' I stepped closer to Denise to convey my resolve, though not close enough to offer a few fingers as lunch. Peleus appeared frozen, as if unsure whether to hit me, yell at me, or back off.

'Peleus, don't,' said Selena with quiet authority. The tone of her voice took him by surprise. 'Aaron is our guest. And so is Denise. Don't let her appearance guide your actions.'

'Guide my actions?' Peleus repeated as his hands parted. Finally he lowered his arms, slowly, his fists tightly clenched as though they were indeed holding daggers. He appeared to suffer another moment of internal struggle before he turned his back to us. 'It's not its looks I'm concerned about..., *Shepherd.*' His last word had a sour taste to it. Selena uttered a heavy sigh.

'Thank you,' I said to her. Selena gave me a cool look that told me she wished she could get rid of the itch named Aaron Bishop on her back with a simple scratch.

'Selena, are you going to tell us your plan before or after we show our new friends to the captains?' Leander dropped at us. I could see in Selena's eyes he had hit the right chord with her, yet she managed to keep her composure. 'Look, I'm only asking because I don't think that whatever you're planning is going to work,' said Leander, his face slightly apologetic. 'You know the Council. They never agree to this.' Whatever "this" was, he indicated with a swift glance at Denise. 'And since when are we not on talking terms anymore? You know you can trust us.'

Selena spent a moment considering his words. 'And you can trust me, Leander. I'm not doing anything behind the Council's back. I am going to speak to them directly, in fact, in a meeting.' By the tone and hesitancy in her voice I had the impression she had just made up her mind about this. 'That is all I can say, I apologise.'

'A meeting,' Leander repeated questionably. His eyes leapt from one face to the next. Nobody said anything. He took a deep breath. 'You know I hate it when you do this,' he then told Selena. 'But I guess you have to have done something right to earn your Shepherd sash.' Selena produced a small smile. 'Peleus does have a point, though. We don't even know if… she… can even swim. Without Trionyx, I fear we can't risk it. Neither do I think we can fly her across. Or can you?'

'I've never tried letting her carry anything,' said Selena after a short pause. 'It might be possible, but I'm not sure. Also, I have no idea how Denise's body will react to my phoenix, or how tightly I need to grip.'

We all watched the weird grime flow from Denise's body. It did indeed seem you needed much bigger claws than those of Selena's bird to grab hold of her.

'Then we'd better not try,' said Leander. 'If your energy doesn't last or something unexpected happens, she'll drown for sure.'

'There is another option, though,' I said. 'Hyenas can swim, can't they? Dogs can.'

Peleus whipped his head towards me, his eyes granite, but it was Leander who responded in words. After shooting Denise another look he drew closer and whispered, 'Look, I don't know what is going on between the three of you, and frankly, I'm not sure I even want to know. But if you are indeed from the homeland, you have a long way to go to earn the Council's trust. And Selena has bigger responsibilities now.' Peleus turned away, his jaws clenched, to which Leander added, 'And let me tell you, you cannot afford any accidents right now.'

By almost kissing the grass with her snout, Denise was attempting to show her obedience to the group. Or that was what I thought she was doing, since the front part of the cloud of ash shrunk suddenly. None of the druids acknowledged her efforts, however, not even Selena.

I've heard the word "trust" a little too often for my taste, I thought. *How can they expect me to trust them if they don't give me any reason to? By giving me answers, for example. Still, Leander seems like a good guy. It's obvious he wants to avoid conflict and I clearly don't need any more problems.* 'Okay, I see your point,' I said, feeling a sense of appreciation for Leander growing inside me. 'Then what do you propose?'

'Unless Selena wants to risk it,' he looked at Selena, who shook her head in reply, 'some of us need to stay here to wait for either Trionyx or a druid to show up who can help us across. Or you two can swim ahead, but I'm still worried about that dark smoke. It must have gone somewhere.' He turned to Selena again. 'You could ask Lycomedes to come back for us. You can tell him about the ritual on your way back. I suppose I'd better stay here with Aaron.'

'I agree,' said Selena. 'I'll be back as soon as I can.'

'Peleus?' Leander asked. Peleus gave a curt nod and joined us.

'I'll wait for master too,' said Briseis, which somewhat surprised me. Of everyone, she was definitely the least comfortable being in Denise's presence. Selena, who realised she was going to have to make the trip by herself, shot Briseis a discomfited look. Then she seemed to make up her mind and nodded her approval.

'Oh, and Selena,' Leander added as Selena prepared the orange shawl around her neck for a cold dive, 'Congratulations.'

Chapter 2

With Selena gone, the five of us, Leander, Peleus and Briseis, Denise and I, began our wait for this surreal world's version of a ferryboat to come and pick us up. Peleus still didn't seem to have much love for either Denise or me, but fortunately, Leander and Briseis were more than talkative. Our conversation reminded me more of a boxing match than a normal heart-to-heart, however, as both my side and theirs tried to direct as many questions towards the other's ears as we could in the time we had until Selena got back.

Despite my many burning questions about this strange place, it was difficult to keep my mind from Denise. So I decided to use her bizarre fate as a catalyst to find out as much as I could from the druids, so as to put myself in the best position to give Denise her old body back and get her home.

I was surprised to learn that my earlier guess of this place being located in another dimension wasn't that far from the truth; the island which Denise and I found ourselves stranded on was actually the one our trip to Greece had led us to, the island of Delos, albeit a different version. But they too knew the island only by the name of Delos, even though they had never heard of Greece or Europe. In fact, Leander told me the temple I had seen on the hill was none other than an intact version of the Greek temple we had departed from, oddly enough. So I figured that the two azure globes, which I thought had knocked me unconscious, must have either teleported us back in time, or indeed to some strange, unknown copy of the world I knew. Always supposing this wasn't some feverish lucid dream, that is. Or the afterlife.

The druids also told me that their home, Eresa, was known by another name: The Phoenix Sanctuary. It was a name which I guessed may have something to do with the fact that, aside from those born and raised inside Eresa, every druid that lived here had abandoned their previous lives for the opportunity to start afresh. After all, I knew that the Phoenix, as a mythological creature from ancient times, was generally associated with rebirth and regeneration. Both of my companions were uncharacteristically evasive when I tried to explore the subject, however, and they quickly changed tactics.

When it was their turn to begin the assault, Briseis grabbed her chance and liberally sucked me dry of any knowledge I had of the ritual that had been performed at the temple, the manner in which I had found my way here, and more even about the world I came from. With Selena gone, the thread that had stitched her lips together had apparently snapped and she showed no restraint anymore. Unfortunately, neither she nor Leander, who mostly listened, could tell me how I was able to understand their language, or they mine.

More remarkable even than what they told me about their world was the fact that they were perfectly all right with me coming from a place they couldn't reach by boat or on horseback. And despite the fact that they had no idea how to get there, and that they didn't have any knowledge of anyone else coming here recently, their kind apparently knew of the existence of my own world all along.

Apparently, a previous Shepherd by the name of Zeuxis had told them about the world their forefathers came from long ago. He had learned it from the great Ouranis, a being with whom Selena was soon to have a private conversation with, and in doing so, receive the blessing of the Shepherd. I had heard the title of "Shepherd" mentioned several times now, and I imagined it to be some kind of mediaeval bard, whose jobs included both storytelling and giving directions. How the druid Council fitted into the political picture, I wasn't quite sure yet.

'There they are,' said Peleus suddenly. He was on his feet in no time. I could almost taste the impatience coating his words.

'Leander, I don't understand,' I asked softly so Peleus couldn't hear us gossiping. 'Have I done something to offend him?' It was obvious Peleus was rather uneasy with me being here, not just Denise, and I wondered if the few words I shared with him were the cause.

Leander eyed me for a moment, obviously considering his answer carefully. Then he nodded his head to the opposite shore. 'Aaron, take a look and tell me what you see.'

A small, elderly man and a blonde woman had emerged from the depths of the forest on the opposite bank. The man had his hands pressed together. I saw something blue and silvery appear in the water before him. It created a sloshing sound that was audible even from this far off. They both stepped onto the raft, which then began moving towards us with an elegance no average tree trunk could imitate and without any visible means of propulsion. Only when they had sailed about half the distance did the tell-tale movements of the raft betray what it actually was.

'Is that a crocodile?' I asked in disbelief.

Leander smiled at the wonder in my eyes. 'Not exactly. It is the manifestation of Lycomedes' energy. As is the case with every druid in Eresa, our empathy with a specific type of animal enables us to link with their essence and mould our energy into the shape of their image.'

'Well that makes a lot of sense,' I said sarcastically, already confused.

Leander let out a chuckle. 'I suppose it doesn't until you see how we live. I still needed to tell you this in response to your question. You see, Peleus over there has spent almost his entire life connecting with the spirits of jackals. I didn't want to stir something up, but when you compared... hyenas,' he added with a glance at Denise, 'to dogs, you did indeed offend him. Every druid takes great pride in the animals they have chosen, Aaron. You would do well to remember that. And once in Eresa, I advise you not to make the same mistake again.'

'I was just trying to help,' I said earnestly. 'We wouldn't have had to wait if we had just swum across as a group. But I know that would have been a gamble with Denise looking the way she does,' I added in a lower voice. Though I hadn't discussed it with them, I still found it odd that neither of them had asked me a single thing about Denise, about who she was, and why she was with me. I figured it was simply Selena's seemingly magical influence over them that made them refrain from asking about her. Or they might have thought they would alienate me if they did so, and thus making me reluctant to answer any more questions.

'You shouldn't worry about it, Aaron,' said Briseis. 'At least it gave us the time to learn something about each other.' I returned a thankful smile.

'Very odd indeed,' said the old man named Lycomedes a few minutes later, when he had drawn close enough to take in Denise's black-as-pitch features. He was dressed in white like everyone else, and had the same orange sash bound around his waist. His hair was a dark shade of grey, his eyes auburn and sharp. His crocodile had disappeared into thin air the moment he and Selena jumped off. 'You said it has been a girl once?' he asked Selena. 'Human?'

Selena looked at Leander first, who didn't look as surprised as I expected him to, then to me. 'She was. And this is the man who came with her.'

'Hmm,' the old man said thoughtfully, undressing me with his eyes. 'What's your name, boy?'

'Aaron Bishop.'

'Aaron,' Lycomedes repeated, moving his jaw in a way that told me his facial muscles didn't quite agree with the motion. 'Bishop it is, I think.'

I thought I could see a blush appear on Selena's cheeks, but paid it no heed. There was something much more pressing gnawing at my brain. And judging by the feat the old man had just displayed with the translucent crocodile, I figured he might be the right one to ask. 'Can you do anything for Denise?'

In a dual motion, a frown appeared on Lycomedes' forehead and he pointed at Denise. I nodded encouragingly. 'No,' he said, as if his answer was as obvious as the existence of butterflies. 'I am but a ferryman. And a poor replacement, it seems,' he added, counting the seven heads, himself included. We were indeed quite many. 'We'll need Trionyx, or it will never fit.'

'Master, please,' Selena threw at him, appearing flustered. 'This is serious.'

'Yes, about that,' he said curiously. 'Where's Andromeda, and the other ritualists?'

'I told you, something went wrong with the Shepherd ritual,' said Selena. 'We don't know where they are.'

'I'm not talking about the ritual,' he said dismissively. 'That ended a while ago. Why haven't they come back?'

'I told you we should have looked for them,' Leander snapped at Selena. 'You barely could've had the time to search properly.'

'Don't be so dramatic, Leander,' said Briseis. 'It makes your feathers fall out.' Selena suppressed a snort. 'This is Andromeda we're talking about. Aristion, Adrastus, they were all there too. I don't believe there's anything to worry about.'

'Selena, we do need to take a final look before we head back,' said Lycomedes, evidently making up his mind on the spot. 'If something did go wrong with the ritual like you told me, some of their energy canals may have overloaded. It could be the reason why they haven't come back to the Sanctuary.'

'If you deem it necessary,' said Selena. 'You should go. I wish to remain here with Aaron and Denise.'

'No, I'd rather have you come with us and show us where you've looked. It may narrow our search area. And you know how much I hate circles, especially if I have to hike them.' This last comment didn't make much sense to me, yet it seemed like I was the only one.

Selena shook her head. 'I have something important to discuss with Aaron, Master, and I don't believe he wants to part himself from Denise.' Selena gave me a look that told me I had better say nothing or I'd end up being chased all the way back up to the temple by a summoned beastie of her making.

You treat me like some GPS ankle bracelet, and yet I should continue to trust you? I commented in silence, while my insides started boiling again. *If only I had another option… Well, there is, but not one that can help Denise.*

'As you wish,' said Lycomedes, throwing both hands in the air. 'You're the Shepherd now.'

It surprised me how easy it was for Selena to persuade the others to leave her alone with Denise and me, especially since the last time, when as many as three druids were needed to make the group feel safe enough to split up. Currently, Selena and I were watching Leander, Briseis, Peleus and Lycomedes cutting a straight line through the flowery meadow and heading back up the hill.

Denise had put her tailed behind into a cluster of flowers and was eyeing Selena with a stare that could scare away any pride of lions, ghostly or corporeal, with ease. Waves of foggy blackness were continuously billowing from her hide, causing her to become enveloped in dark smoke a few seconds after she had sat down. By now even her head had become barely distinguishable, while her blue, piercing eyes continued to burn brightly. It was like she was carrying her own cloak of concealment everywhere she went.

'I don't know how much time we have, so we will need to act quickly,' said Selena without preamble. 'Listen, Aaron, the reason why I decided to leave the others in the dark, as it were, is because I have a theory about what transpired during the ritual. As I said, I believe something went wrong, disastrously perhaps, and need you to help me discover if I'm right.'

'Finally,' I sighed. 'All right, let's hear it. What is this ritual thing about, exactly?'

'Yes, well,' said Selena, slightly flustered, 'the ritual, the one that has been performed at the temple this afternoon, is designed to help the Shepherd choose his or her successor. With the help of a small group of druids, they channel their energy and in doing so they summon the most worthy candidate to his location. How he does it is not important right now,' she added in response to my questioning look. 'Just know that as it happened, I was the one who was chosen.'

'Okay, so you're the new Shepherd. What does that have to do with me, or Denise?'

'That is my point. I don't believe I am the new Shepherd. I was chosen, yes. Yet for some reason, Ouranis' gift, the Shepherd's power, was not bestowed upon me. At least I don't believe it did.'

'Are you saying…,' I began, pointing at Denise. I couldn't even voice my thoughts about this so-called "Shepherd" being able to transform into something that no one would want to encounter in a dark alleyway. After all, it was Selena who had hinted that the Shepherd was able to change their shape.

'I already told you I have no idea what happened to Denise,' said Selena a little impatiently. 'No, the most prominent among the Shepherd's abilities is the one that allows him to communicate with animals. But I have yet to hear any of their voices.'

'So that's what you were trying to do with that hare we saw earlier, you were trying to read its thoughts,' I said. Selena nodded pensively as though she was reliving the event in her head and was contemplating the disappointing silence. 'That still doesn't explain what all this has to do with us.'

'Well, I believe that, because of what happened at the temple at the time of the ritual, the Shepherd's powers went into you instead of me.'

My jaw dropped and kept hanging there for a spell. Then I let out a snort. 'Oh, come on… Are you serious?'

'Why shouldn't I be?'

'Me? A real-life Dr Doolittle? Well, I'm sorry to disappoint. But even given the circumstances I haven't heard a thing out of the ordinary. And I daresay I would have heard my own girlfriend, if she counts as an animal now. I've been focused on her the entire time.'

'Perhaps you were not listening properly. Senses can be easily manipulated by emotions.'

'Look, Selena, I don't know what is going on here, but I just want my girlfriend back and to go home, all right? That's all.' I paused for a moment. My better judgement, fed by the look on Selena's face, told me I needed to switch tactics immediately. 'It's not that I don't appreciate everything you've done so far, defending us against the others and all that, but…' I took a moment to think about my next words. 'All right, fine. I'll continue to play along if you promise me right now that you will do everything you can for Denise.' Selena gave me a blank stare, as though she could see something she couldn't see before. 'I mean it. I need your promise.'

'You wouldn't have to ask me that if you knew what is at stake,' said Selena. 'But since you don't, I promise.'

'Thank you. Now, if there's anything I can do for you, I will. Just… don't give me this rubbish about special powers and everything. I'm afraid I have enough on my plate already.'

'That is fair,' said Selena, then looked out across the water and drank in the shoreline of Eresa. 'Aaron, on our way here, I've been thinking about how to handle the situation, and I believe I can be reasonably sure that Andromeda and the other druids are not coming back; or at least some of them aren't. If my suspicions are correct, Adrastus, who I saw change with my own eyes, might even have been the last of the ritualists to be turned into one of these hyenas.' She held up a hand to keep me from interrupting. 'What this means is that if Lycomedes, Leander, or anyone else learns about what has befallen them, it would be disastrous for you and Denise.'

'Because of how she looks,' I filled in.

Selena nodded. 'At the very least, they will want to use her to find out what happened to the ritualists and how to get them back. We cannot allow this to happen, not before we know for sure that the Shepherd's power has not been transferred to you. All faith in you, in the Shepherd, would be lost.'

'Why? I don't understand. Why is this power so important? I mean, talking to animals?'

'I cannot go into too much detail now, because I cannot be certain how much time we have left. Just know that the Shepherd is very important to us because it is he or she who can claim audience with Ouranis. She means everything to us. And to lose our connection with her would be... unimaginable.' It was evident by the wet glint in her eyes that even the word "unimaginable" fell short of what she truly meant.

'And you think I am that connection?'

'Again, I do not know. This is why I was hoping for an opportunity to put my theory to the test before we enter Eresa. Either way, it is imperative no one is given any reason to doubt the fact that I am the new Shepherd, because it is our belief that only the one who is chosen by the ritual can become the Shepherd. It has always been that way. Therefore, at least until we can find some kind of remedy for Denise's condition, we will need to keep today's events a secret. My peoples' faith in Ouranis, and our connection to her thoughts are not to be questioned, Aaron, especially not by an outsider. I hope you understand.'

'Oh, I do understand,' I replied sincerely. 'I just think you're making a fuss over nothing. I mean, you probably just need some practice or guidance, or something. I'm still willing to give it a try, though, if you want to be sure.'

'Good, then prove it,' said Selena, standing up. It was evident she didn't want to give me time to have second thoughts. I quickly went after her with Denise loping behind. She seemed just as interested in watching this play out as I was.

Upon reaching the shoreline, Selena halted and began peering into the distance. I emulated her but could see nothing but blue stretching in all directions – and the floating forest called Eresa. Distant mountains and coastlines were blocking our view of the horizon behind it. I had noticed them before, but had been too preoccupied to pay them any attention.

Now that I had a few moments of peace, a thin line of sparkling silver attracted my eye. It was positioned at about the same height of the water line between the sea and the island of Eresa. Every time the water receded to prepare for another wave to batter against the few feet high wall that closed off the island, the twinkling line came into view once more.

I pointed them out to Selena. 'Those are periwinkles,' she explained absently. 'They are a kind of snail that has a symbiotic relationship with the island, and us I suppose. We supply a safe living environment for them, while they keep the Sanctuary afloat.'

We fell silent again until after a minute or two, Selena said, 'This is what we will do. Aaron, I'd like you to close your eyes and focus your mind on contacting Trionyx. He should be around here somewhere, but for some reason I can't see or hear him. And because he is already used to interacting with humans, it should be an easy task for the Shepherd to call him. Remember that we also need him to bring Denise to the island, so it is important that you succeed.'

'Okay, I'll try.' I gave Denise a glance, then asked, 'Just his name, Trionyx? You're not giving me anything else?' Selena shook her head and with a sigh, I closed my eyes.

The first thing I noticed was that my eyes seemed more than content with the action. I felt tired, despite the fact that the sun was still blazing down on us. My thoughts were swimming this way and that like a single-sailed fisherman's boat caught in an autumn storm. Blue lights popped up in my mind one after the other: the twin globes that had sent me to this odd place, the beady eyes of Denise, the tapered ears of the hare we had passed. They made it difficult to focus on any one thing at a time.

Tri-onyx, Trio-nyx. I repeatedly called out the name in silence and envisioned projecting the thoughts outwards like homing pigeons, all sounding slightly different, and each in a different direction. None of the pigeons returned. Again and again I tried, until not even the peace-inducing sound of the waves fist-bumping the shore was able to keep my mind arrested any longer.

'I told you it wouldn't work,' I said dismissively, opening my eyes. 'It was my great grandfather who herded sheep, not me. I'm no Shepherd.'

My bad attempt at a joke did not crease any of Selena's features. She merely kept staring into the distance. 'Try again.'

Again I took a deep breath. But, just as my lids fell over my eyes and I was about to start resuming my efforts, a great disturbance in the water wrenched them open again. The surface of the water bulged, causing a miniature tidal wave to soak our sandals and grime-covered paws. Denise gave a yelp that could have belonged to a dog whose tail had just been squashed by a bull hippo.

To my astonishment an enormous, grey, overturned bowl rose up from the watery depths. The sight brought images of giant jellyfish to my mind, though it would have had to be one that had mated with a sea turtle; a turtle's head the size of a mature grizzly bear came next. Every single one of the beast's features was silvery blue and translucent, allowing me to see his pointy tail moving up and down through the long length of his body. Even more remarkable was that, because of his transparency, Trionyx's body acted like diving goggles, enabling us to peer several feet into the body of murky water underneath him.

'There you are,' Selena greeted the giant beast with a warm voice. 'You had us worried.'

In response, the turtle lowered his massive head and started to approach us like a horse longing for a bit of affection. Every foot the turtle came closer, Denise and I met with a step backwards. I didn't realise I was still moving until Selena stuck out her hand and placed it between the turtle's nostrils. The turtle halted immediately – and Denise and I did as well.

'Aaron, Denise, meet Trionyx,' said Selena. With each caressing movement of her hand, a trail of silvery light remained behind until it faded a few seconds later. It was like seeing the moon play with an ice sculpture on a starlit night, except, of course, the scene was being played out in full daylight. The sight was simply awe-inspiring. 'Thank you, Aaron,' Selena added without looking away from Trionyx.

'Not me,' was the only part of my thoughts that made it to my mouth. I swallowed, then said, 'It wasn't me.'

'Sure it was. I didn't call for him.'

'Then he must have seen you standing here. You did say he was already used to you.'

'Why don't you come closer?' asked Selena, ignoring my discomfort and staring pointedly at my feet standing a few yards behind her. They felt as though glued to the ground. 'You might as well become used to him now, don't you think?'

'I'm not him,' I said exasperatedly, still holding ground. 'I'm not the Shepherd. Don't you get it?' The name "Shepherd" felt like a ball and chain every time it passed my lips or eardrums.

'Why is it so hard for you to believe?'

'Why is it so hard for you not to?' I returned. 'I'm just an ordinary guy. It almost sounds like you're glad you haven't been given these powers. You've been training for this opportunity for a long time, haven't you?'

Selena's cordial features changed within the span of a snapping finger. A mixture of emotions I couldn't immediately place fell over her face like a blanket. Upon seeing them, I recalled what Leander and Briseis had said about Eresa being a sanctuary for people who either chose, or were forced to, abandon their lives and desired a new start. Orphaned children, or men and women traumatised by what they had done or seen in the past, everyone was offered the chance to find new purpose, to become someone else. It made me want to take back my words as I wondered in which category Selena could be placed.

'I'm… sorry. I shouldn't have said that.'

'It's quite all right,' said Selena calmly, breathing away whatever emotional trauma had bubbled up. She turned back to Trionyx and resumed her long strokes along the turtle's snout. His large eyelids began to droop in delight. If the oversized reptile had belonged to the feline family, I was certain his purring would have sent an earthquake through the island, one that would have been palpable even to the search party over at the temple on the hill.

Slowly I moved over to Selena's position. Denise stayed behind. 'Why do all the animals here look like this?' I asked Selena in a quiet voice. 'Or don't they?'

In response, Selena nodded to her own hand resting on Trionyx's nose to indicate I was to do the same. When I did, she appeared content, and for a long spell we didn't speak again. The skin of Trionyx felt smooth, like water having turned solid, though not cold like ice. It reminded me of the curdled skin formed on top of a bowl of pudding after having cooled down without a cover. It was the weirdest experience I had ever gone through, and one of the most unforgettable. I had heard of people touching elephants and being awed by the animals' sheer size and the feel of their enormous lungs filling up with air. I now knew exactly what they meant.

'They have always been this way,' Selena said at length, answering my question about the animals' wraithlike appearance. 'Did you expect something different?'

'Well, I didn't expect anything that has happened to us thus far, to be honest,' I said. 'It's not like we are here by choice. But this… Where I, where we, come from, animals don't look like this. Our turtles have scales and pupils, and they can't squash you if they're not careful.'

Selena smiled. 'I see. Then I believe you will enjoy your meeting with Ouranis, Aaron. She is magnificent.'

I let out a heavy sigh. 'You're not giving up on this Shepherd business anytime soon, are you?'

'Neither should you.'

'Yeah. So, that hare we saw earlier, and Trionyx as well, they are different from the animals you druids are able to summon? Leander has told me a little about you druids being able to manifest your energy in the shape of animals. I'm still trying to understand what he meant by this and it is kind of confusing when I see no difference between, for example, Trionyx and that crocodile Lycomedes created. Aside from Trionyx's size, of course.'

'What Leander told you is correct. As druids, we have learned to connect with the spirits of animals and use their image to shape our energy.' Selena eyed me with recognition. 'I can see the same kind of confusion in your eyes that I see in those of all the people that come here. Briseis only joined us a few years ago. You remind me of her, in some ways. As for your question, it is indeed true that even though they look similar, the animals we are able to summon are quite different from living entities like Trionyx. In short, Trionyx has a spirit, while our summoned animals do not. They are merely manifestations of our energy, temporary shapes, you might say, which we use to express our skill in spiritcraft.'

Selena turned once more to Trionyx. The sunlight reflected by the giant turtle's shimmering forehead cast a blueish sheen over her face. 'I wouldn't put too much thought to Trionyx's existence, however,' she went on. 'We have vainly wasted much thought on that already. In the end, we have accepted that he might be the result of druid experimentation performed in the past, which might explain his fondness for druids. We suspect he can not only see us, but feel our energy as well. He is always there when we need him. Well, almost,' she corrected herself.

Lycomedes and the other three druids soon returned from their search. Or perhaps the time only appeared brief, since being in the presence of such an impressive creature as Trionyx probably made the time seem to go more quickly. As Selena had predicted, the party returned empty-handed.

The moment the great turtle realised he hadn't been called here for a pat on the nose, of which I still wasn't sure was actually my doing, his ghostly eyes switched to Denise. The, from his perspective, tiny monster cowered in fear as soon as Trionyx laid his solemn eyes on her, and began to retreat backwards. As she did, she was forced to leave the sanctuary of her cloud of black smoke behind, making her appear even smaller.

Because of Trionyx's reluctance to carry Denise, a battle of words followed. It was one that meandered between Peleus defending Trionyx's position, Selena arguing there was no other safe way of getting Denise to the island, and Leander offering to stay behind with us until the Council made a decision as to what to do with my girlfriend. In the end, Lycomedes came up with a solution. He proposed a three-split with him taking Denise and me on two of his summoned crocodiles, while the rest of the group followed on Trionyx.

Whether Denise was afraid this new body of hers wasn't able to swim, or if she feared she would be left behind if she fell off the crocodile, I couldn't tell. But her shaking paws and her tail, which was trying to disappear between her hind legs, told me she wasn't going to forget this trip anytime soon. When she stepped onto one of Lycomedes' summoned crocodiles she gave me one last fleeting glance, before she returned her stare to the surface of the water, probably to anticipate the incoming waves. A few seconds into watching her standing there on top of the glass-like crocodile, with her legs wide and back rigid, her motionless body became devoured once more by black fog.

It was smooth sailing over the relatively calm waters. Lycomedes and I took the lead and it didn't take long for me to become accustomed to the crocodile's movements as it moved up and down with the rolling of the waves. How Denise was doing I couldn't really tell; by now her smoky secretions had enveloped both her and almost the entire length of the crocodile. Only the translucent nostrils of the beast were left visible as its snout stuck out from the cloud of black fog. Behind the two of them, the giant figure of Trionyx was ploughing through the water with Selena, Leander, Briseis and Peleus on his back.

'Selena told me you were from the homeland,' Lycomedes said suddenly. His voice came as a surprise, and my resulting start almost made me tread on the crocodile's head. 'Interesting tale I have to say, and I am looking forward to the sequel.'

'Yes, I am,' I replied, feeling unsure how to respond. I had been so transfixed on Denise, the thought hadn't even crossed my mind that, by acquiescing to Lycomedes' travel plan, I would have to spend some time alone with yet another person I didn't know. Another barrage of questions was soon to follow, I was sure.

'My name is Lycomedes Papadopoulos. Selena is, was, an apprentice of mine.' I could only see the corner of one of his eyes when the old man looked over at the druids on Trionyx's back, but the pride in them was as clear as the sun glinting from our crocodile's spectral hide. 'She's always been a promising student.'

'I can imagine,' I said, thinking of the way she had managed to keep her composure after learning that some of her colleagues, perhaps even friends, had gone missing. 'So, uhm, I'm sorry to make this about me, but I was hoping to ask you if there is anything you can do for Denise. I know you said "no" before, but perhaps you know someone else who can help us.'

'I might,' said Lycomedes mysteriously, 'but not before someone decides to tell me who did this to her. Selena may think she can keep her secrets hidden from me, Bishop, but she is disappointingly bad at it. I thought I taught her better than that.' He chuckled, and then said in reminiscence, 'I would know, I've known her since she was only half her size. And I am talking about her length, not her weight. She could lose some of that too, along with her habit of plotting behind my back. Which I've cautioned her about more than once, mind you.'

I pressed my lips together to prevent a laugh from forcing itself through. It resulted in a snort which made Lycomedes look over his shoulder in disgust. 'Sorry,' I said, mopping myself up with the sleeve of my shirt.

The old man's look of revulsion changed into one of mirth. 'Now that you are amused, Bishop, you can go ahead and tell me who did this to your girl.'

At that exact moment, before I could even open my mouth to speak, the sound of great, snapping jaws came from behind. It was accompanied by a torrent of splashing water, which raked against the insides of my knees, legs and back. My heart skipped a beat and my muscles cramped from the shock and fear of what was happening behind me.

I spun my head around and came eye to eye with a small, sapphire-like orb, set in the face of a massive shark. Like Denise and the other hyena, the shark's body was black as pitch. Moreover, again like Denise, dark grime was oozing from its rubbery skin. The glowing sapphire turned out to be its eye.

I had only a second to look. With a single bite, the shark had bitten off the crocodile's head, after which the black assassin had continued to propel itself upwards and out of the water.

The shark was at least twice my size. There was a seemingly infinite moment during which both Lycomedes and I gaped at the giant creature towering over us. Then Lycomedes dispelled it with a cry of fear. After its unexpected decapitation, the summoned crocodile was apparently not able to keep it together, its body lost cohesion, and we plunged straight through the shimmering outlines of Lycomedes' formerly helpful avatar, and into the dark water.

I was fully submerged when my eyes shot open in shock. The second rush of cold was even more overwhelming than the first. I couldn't see anything but blurs of blue and grey – and something much darker to my right. With an almighty kick I broke surface and gasped for air, but my aching muscles denied my ribs the opportunity to fully expand. They shot daggers of pain into my chest.

With my eyes squinting blearily and one hand wiping the sheen of water from my face, I saw a dark shadow moving past me. It had to be the shark, hungry for more. The growl of a canine predator came next, then a yelp as Denise hit the water's surface; the shock had caused Lycomedes to lose his focus and her crocodile had vanished as well.

'Denise!' I yelled, but she was quick to resurface. Her paws were aiding her surprisingly well and she was already closing in fast. With her mouth hanging open and treading through the water in a fast, if frenzied, doggy-paddle, she seemed to be doing a better job against the cold than I was.

Fear was enveloping me, a death grip that was trying to throttle me into submission. The shark had to be close. I couldn't see it anymore. Neither was there any sign of the old man. 'Lycomedes!' I called to no avail.

Only now did I register the calls and shouts from Selena and the others. Thus far, Trionyx had apparently made sure he kept his distance from Denise. But now that Denise's crocodile was gone and therefore my girlfriend no longer had a foothold to make a jump for his eyes, all caution of the black hyena seemed to be wiped from the giant turtle's mind; he was coming for us at ramming speed.

The wallowing sound of something haphazardly breaking the surface came from my left. I wheeled around just in time to see a hand submerge again. With a few forceful kicks I was already on top of it, but Lycomedes had no need for my help. His head appeared and he took a great lungful of air. To make sure he wouldn't go down again, I quickly positioned myself behind him and grabbed his robe by the shoulders.

'Are you all right?' I asked as my lungs continued to fight the shivers.

Lycomedes didn't respond in words. Instead he had his palms pressed together, his teeth clenched, and began to utter a long, continuous grunt of concentration. Despite the numbing effect of the cold, I could feel my fingers starting to tingle as if I had sat on them for too long and blood was beginning to flow back. It was the old man's energy, it had to be.

'Mr. Papado…,' I began, but the cocktail of fear and cold made me forget his last name. 'Lycomedes?!'

Then I saw it. Directly in front of us, the black fin of a shark, at least two to three feet high, was racing towards us. A contrail of dark smoke wafting behind it made it appear like a missile. Lycomedes was ready. He had already gathered the energy for a counter attack.

The water in front of the fin surged and the broad, flat nose of the shark thrust its way towards us. The sheer size of its head sucked every ounce of my attention towards it. My breath high in my chest, I watched how a wave rolled by the shark's flank, flicking one of the glowing eyes of the shark on and off like a light bulb.

'Lycomedes!' I heard Leander's voice call out. 'Selena, hurry! I'm almost ready!' But whatever he and Selena were about to do, they were too late.

The shark was almost upon us. Several rows of black, jagged teeth entered my view. The gaping mouth of the shark, hungry to produce more of its kind, was all my eyes were aware of. Pure dread paralysed my remaining functioning muscles.

My body was about to give up when a cry of defiance from the old man regenerated my courage and fuelled my will to survive. His robes were still in my fists and I tightened my grip.

In the splintered second before the shark's jaws were able to snap close on us, something large and blue shot out from Lycomedes' chest. It was the head of one of his crocodiles. Twisted sideways at a ninety degree angle, the crocodile's jaws collided with that of the shark at only an arm-length's distance from the two of us. The impact travelled all the way through the half of the crocodile's body that was protruding from the old man's chest, through Lycomedes himself, and into my arms.

The giant shark was a formidable force. Even after colliding with the crocodile's head, it still ploughed on like a battering ram breaking down a castle wall. I was forced to let go as Lycomedes' robe was ripped from my fists and he was propelled backwards through the water. Due to their speed, continuous waves of water were rolling over Lycomedes' shoulders and head while he and the shark sped away from me. I received a slap to the shoulder by the monster's tail fin as it shot past me. I could do nothing but watch how the battling beast and Lycomedes left me in favour of the open sea, the ghostly crocodile's head being the only shield between flesh and black fangs.

With the shark and Lycomedes now absent from view, Denise came into sight again. She was still trying to reach me. The dark secretions coming from her body had formed an oil-like stain on the water that seemed to travel with her as she swam closer. Though my body remained buoyant this time, my heart dropped like an anvil; her repulsive features were even worse from up-close.

'Denise, go back. That way,' I said as I tried to hold her off. Her kicking paws barely missed scratching me a couple of times, and I knew that with monstrous sharks patrolling the area, this was a bad time to become injured; sharks could smell blood from miles away.

A flapping of wings made me look up. A pair of giant claws, blue and iridescent, came into view. The next thing I knew I was being dragged backwards through the water with bird claws digging into my shoulders. I saw Denise's head becoming smaller and smaller while she uttered a series of howling barks.

'No, let me go!' I tried to wriggle myself loose. 'Denise!' The claws only sank in deeper.

'Don't fight her, Aaron!' Briseis said from behind. 'We're trying to help you.'

'Selena, talk to Trionyx,' said Leander. 'We need to go that way. Lycomedes has just gone under. I was too late to do anything for him.'

As my back slid across Trionyx's smooth shell, I realised it was actually Selena's bird who was dragging me onto the giant turtle. 'Please, we need to help Denise,' I said to the group while scrambling to my feet. 'She's over there.'

'Lycomedes first,' said Leander, aiming for everyone at the same time. 'Selena, get Trionyx to move closer, quickly.'

Selena had her palms pressed together to focus on her energy. Her giant bird was already flying off to search for Lycomedes. Without saying a word to Leander she gave me a meaningful glance over her shoulder. I caught it and sent a nod back to her, indicating I was going to have another attempt at the Shepherd abilities.

Wasting no time, I closed my eyes and focused on what Leander was asking for. I used every ounce of willpower I could muster to send a message to the great turtle, as I not only wished to save Lycomedes, but I also knew that Denise's time was running out.

Turn right, turn right. Over and over again I tried to implant this simple message into Trionyx's translucent skull. It didn't work. No reply came in words or pictures, nor did any of the druids call out in triumph to announce I had succeeded.

'There he is!' said Peleus suddenly. 'Over there!'

I opened my eyes. A spectral crocodile was lying in wait for a command from his master about thirty yards to Trionyx's right. Two hands were resting on its back. And now Lycomedes, with his white robes glued to his skin, was heaving himself onto the back of the creature. A large, growing red stain was colouring his neck and shoulder.

'Trionyx, come!' Briseis was trying to attract the attention of the giant turtle's eye by standing on the outer edge of his shell and waving frantically. 'This way!'

The great beast paid her no heed. He was continuing to plough forwards with great haste, apparently dreading the moment the shark would leave Lycomedes for a bite of something much larger. The only things on his mind seemed to be to shed the load off his back as soon as possible and then retreat into deeper waters.

'Selena…,' Leander urged, noticing the lack of success of Briseis' efforts.

I was just about to try it again when help arrived from an unexpected source. Denise, who was still labouring to keep her head above water, was approaching the left side of Trionyx. Like an elephant suddenly spotting a mouse, the giant turtle pulled back his head – either in fear or distaste, I couldn't really tell which – and veered off-course to the right.

'You're doing it!' Peleus told Selena. Evidently he hadn't noticed the black hyena in the water. It was also the first time I saw any positive emotion in the man's dark eyes.

Selena had only eyes for her giant bird, which seemed to be guarding Lycomedes while the old man was tacking towards us on the back of his crocodile. With his hand he was trying to suppress the bleeding from his shoulder wound. His wet robes were turning scarlet at an alarming rate.

'Selena, the shark!' I called when I saw the black fin break the surface of the water once more. It was heading straight for the tail of Lycomedes' crocodile. I heard Briseis hiss through clenched teeth as she too watched the scene unfold with unblinking eyes.

Selena breathed in forcefully through her nostrils. In response, her giant bird pulled in its feathered wings and suddenly dropped like a stone towards its prey. Its beak and talons were pointed downwards and aimed directly at the shark's fin. There was a chaos of dark smoke, splashing water and twisting, silvery trails, and the shark and the bird vanished. My jaw dropped at the sight of their short-lived fight, while Lycomedes' crocodile continued to paddle frantically, battling the waves that emanated from the point of impact.

When Lycomedes was finally back among us, the invisible blanket of pent-up anxiety was suddenly lifted from the group. Our greetings and concerns for the old man's shoulder had to be kept short, however, since Denise was still treading through the water – and without any hope of being allowed to climb onto Trionyx's back. And there was still some distance left to the opposite bank.

Brushing away Selena's hand as she tried to assess the damage, Lycomedes immediately called on his druidic abilities once more and summoned another pair of crocodiles, one of which he then guided to Denise. He mounted the other himself, probably to make sure the first one would stay on course.

'You see? There's nothing wrong with you,' Leander told Selena as we watched Lycomedes and Denise sail off. 'And if you can talk to Trionyx, it's only a matter of time before you can do the same with other animals.'

Selena gave me an appraising glance. 'I suppose so, Leander. Did you find any sign of the ritualists at the temple?'

'I told you, nothing,' said Leander, suddenly looking like he had just chewed on the skin of a citrus fruit. 'There was no sign of a struggle or anything similar. It appeared like they just, well, vanished.'

'It must have had something to do with that smoke we saw,' said Peleus. 'What could it have been? I've never seen anything behave so strangely. And that shark…, it looked exactly the same as that foul hyena.'

'Her name is Denise,' I said, feeling another wave of frustration rushing to the surface. Nobody paid me any attention.

'I wonder what the connection is between the two,' Peleus continued, squinting his eyes at Denise. Currently none of her features were distinguishable. She looked like a black cloud floating across the water's surface, although one with a blue, translucent tail of a crocodile propelling it forwards.

'It *is* odd,' said Leander.

'I don't know what you're all thinking, but Denise had nothing to do with this,' I told the group, more forcefully this time. 'I can promise you that.'

'So can I,' said Selena, joining me at the shoulder. 'Denise has yet to show a single sign of aggression.'

Leander shrugged apologetically and looked at Selena, then at me. 'We are simply considering all possibilities, Aaron. Nothing more. I only hope for your sake that the Council will do the same.' When I looked away, Peleus' narrowed eyes made me clench my teeth in anger. If anything would happen to Denise, anything at all, I felt ready to wreak havoc unlike anything these people had ever experienced. I could promise them that too.

Lycomedes and Denise were waiting for us when we approached the island. Due to the small opening in the low wall and the thickness of the forest, there was only a narrow strip of grass for us to moor on. So we had to jump from Trionyx's back in single file and continue heading up the path that cut through the forest to make room for the next person. As soon as the last of us had departed, Trionyx gave an annoyed grunt and returned to the watery depths.

As we proceeded on through the dense forest, light became increasingly scarce. The canopy above our heads was like a sea of green with small chinks here and there to let the occasional shaft of sunlight lick our faces. It seemed as though Denise and I had entered an entirely different world, again.

Selena, Denise and I brought up the rear of the procession. I soon noticed that, for whatever reason, Selena was purposely trying to distance us from the rest of the group.

'Do you know what's going to happen?' I asked her quietly.

Selena shook her head almost imperceptibly. Her eyes were fixed on the backs of the druids in front. 'I have tried to guess the Council's reaction to today's events, but we have never encountered anything like these creatures, or that fog. It is difficult to say.'

'Then how come you don't seem as freaked out as I am? I mean, we almost died out there.'

Selena looked at me, and then turned her head in thought. 'Because I'd rather stay focused on the present, Aaron. There are much more dangerous things here than sharks.'

'That's comforting. So you're still not going to tell your Council about the connection between those druids at the temple and the other hyenas?'

'Not at first. It would generate too much bias against you and Denise. We can't risk it. I want to see how they will react to the two of you first.' She met my eyes. 'It does mean that, if I do this, we are in this together, Aaron. I hope you keep that in mind.'

'I will, thank you. So, what *are* you going to tell them?'

'The truth, or at least the things I know for certain. I cannot deny that the Council does need to know about the fog, for whatever it is and might be capable of, we need to find a way to guard against it. Peleus was right about the shark, Aaron. It did appear similar to whatever Denise has been turned into. And if these creatures can get this close to Eresa, there is no telling what kind of danger we are in.'

'What about Denise, then? Is it even safe to bring her to the Sanctuary?'

'I have thought about that too. The way I see it, you have two options. Either you leave Denise here in the woods and you make sure no one will see her, or you bring her with us. Keep in mind, however, that keeping secrets from each other is not a habit of ours. We generally have no need for them.'

'Say that to Lycomedes,' I said with a chuckle.

'He spoke to you about me?' Selena asked, managing a smile. 'I imagined he would. It does prove my point, however. Eresans pride themselves in being candid.'

'That makes perfect sense,' I said dryly.

'We've spoken about this, Aaron. This is an exception. Now that I think about it, perhaps it is best to explain the situation to Lycomedes as soon as we can. It would do us no favours if he finds out on his own that something has gone wrong with the gift, and he may be able to help us with our situation. But he won't be happy about it,' she added in a lower voice.

I turned my attention to the hyena walking behind us again. 'So what do you suggest I should do with Denise? Take her with me?'

'I do think it would be a mistake to conceal her presence from the Council. Druids often train in this wood, which means you won't be able to find a place that is entirely safe for Denise. What's more, concealing her could become even more problematic for you if my suspicions about you being the new Shepherd turn out to be true.'

I sighed. 'Not that again. You do know it wasn't me who turned Trionyx around, don't you? It was Denise, not me.'

'I do,' said Selena in a voice that betrayed that part of her had hoped otherwise. 'But I also know that if I was indeed the one who received the gift, at least some sign of the Shepherd's abilities should have been apparent by now. There have been none, however,' she added wistfully.

'Same here,' I replied with a shrug.

'That may be true, although due to my training, I know, in theory, how I am supposed to use them. Lycomedes has prepared me well. And with that in mind, I see only one road left to take. We will just have to train you as well.'

'Until we find a way to give these powers to you.'

'Correct,' said Selena, a little too hesitantly for my taste.

'Hey, Aaron,' Briseis said as she turned around, walking backwards to keep up with Leander and the others. 'Welcome to Eresa.'

I received a soft hand around my upper arm before Selena's whisper tickled my ear. 'Stay close, Aaron.'

Chapter 3

The trees began to thin out along the path. Increasingly, one to two storey buildings began to push them aside. Nature did not seem to be completely comfortable with this arrangement, however, for the homes we passed were slowly being devoured by moss and vine, one square inch at a time. Not many people were out in the streets, at least not on this part of the island. I welcomed it. It meant that Denise and I could get used to the staring eyes before they became too numerous.

A man emerged from one of the homes. His robes were white, cut short at the knees like those of Lycomedes and the other men, and a yellow sash was bound around his waist. A certain amount of unease washed over me as I looked at the man walking up the street. His presence made my skin prickle as though it was attacked by tiny insects.

Now my eyes fell upon the barely visible ribbon of blue energy that connected the palms of his hands, which were hanging loosely by his sides and swaying back and forth with his gait. The ribbon was constantly moving, and pulsated as if it was having difficulty staying alive. It reminded me of seeing a fish out of water, gasping for breath.

A blue and translucent wasp was buzzing in front of him, apparently guiding the man to the centre of the path. The man's emergence seemed deliberate somehow, though he didn't show any sign of noticing us until he halted. Slowly his head turned and an expression of mild interest fell over his face.

'Captain Helios,' I heard Briseis whisper. I detected a hint of fear.

'He is the Vespine captain,' said Selena in response to my questioning look. Then to herself, she murmured, 'I didn't know he was on guard duty. Not good.' She began chewing her lip like a piece of gum.

Captain? I thought. *Wasn't this supposed to be a druid sanctuary?* 'Do you want to turn back, or?' I then asked Selena.

'It's too late now anyway,' she said. 'We have no choice but to let it play out. Say nothing, Aaron. I mean it.'

Stay close, say nothing, do nothing, got it, I summarised, feeling annoyed again. *Don't mind me. I'm just some alien visitor from another world.* The four in front came to a halt, and so did we. No one spoke. The only sound that disrupted the silence came from a translucent lemur high up in a tree as it skittered away from the scene.

'Lycomedes,' Helios said, the ribbon of blue energy connecting his palms intensifying slightly. His profile barely hinted at any emotion.

'Helios,' Lycomedes returned curtly, with a slight inclination of his head.

Slowly, Helios eyed each of us in turn. His eyes lingered on me a little longer and when they fell on Denise, his entire body, with the exception of his blinking eyelids, seemed to freeze. Devoid of any detectable fear, and with his gaze remaining locked on Denise, he asked, 'Where is Adrastus?'

'He's missing, as are the other ritualists,' said Lycomedes. 'We are on our way to send word to the Council. And do not concern yourself with her,' he added, indicating Denise with a glance. 'She poses no threat.'

At these words, Helios turned to the old man. Again he paused for a short spell, then said, 'That… is obvious. Although the fact that you are escorting her into the Sanctuary is no proof of that.' Lycomedes didn't respond. Visible signs of unrest were making their way through the party. 'You know the rules, old man.' Lycomedes still held his ground, which made Helios spend a moment considering his options. At length, he said, 'On your head?'

'On mine.'

'Very well.' And with that the druid captain went back into the house. Selena let out a sigh in relief.

'Nice guy,' I commented, my eyes lingering on the open doorway for a moment.

'And very powerful,' said Selena. 'Of all the druids in Eresa, he is one of the last you will want to upset, Aaron. Trust me.'

That word again? 'We've done nothing but trust people since we got here.'

Soon the midsummer sun managed to get a good grip on us once more as the trees parted and we found ourselves overlooking a large square full of people. The square was sandwiched between two enormous Greek temples, both made entirely of white marble with great pillars propping up the outer walls. The larger of the two, the one on the right, featured an image of a spread-winged Phoenix. It was carved in the pearly marble above the double doors by a skilful hand, so it gazed upon anyone who ascended the steps to the entrance.

At the centre of the square there was a raised platform with marble columns sprouting from each corner. It was difficult to gauge its function, but no one seemed to dare tread upon its white tiles.

Astonishment washed over me. Not at the sight of the temples, the platform, or even the people crowding the plaza. What was truly jaw-dropping was the fact that we seemed to be crashing a party where humans and ghosts were intermingling without restraint. None of the ghosts were human, either. Animals of all shapes and sizes were represented in one way or the other, each of them as transparent as the next. It was as though this whole area had once been a zoo, one in which the residents had been killed by some disastrous catastrophe and hadn't yet moved on to whatever afterlife may await animals.

'A sanctuary for druids,' I stated, repeating Leander's words. Selena offered me a smile, which seemed to contain more than just the simple pleasure of seeing someone being impressed with her home.

Then, bit by bit, as I stood there watching, the realisation for the truth behind Leander's words began to sink in. For none of the wild beasts that were running, flying and chasing each other across the square were actually real. They couldn't possibly be, because after they had been called to life by their druid masters for a single charge, a bite or a swipe at their spectral opponents, or to stay for a longer battle, they simply vanished into thin air. On top of that, their throats were silenced. The sight rivalled anything I had seen thus far, including Trionyx.

'Are you seeing this, Denise?' I asked the black hyena behind me. Now that I looked at her properly again after seeing so many beautiful, almost fluorescent, creatures, Denise looked more out of place now than ever. Denise, however, had no eyes for me. Her sapphire-like eyes were moving this way and that as if she was watching an absurd and chaotic version of a tennis match.

'Master, you're back!' a young woman said as she came running towards us. 'We wondered where you were. We've been asking around, but nobody knew anything.'

'I'm glad to be back, Lanike,' Lycomedes said, holding up a hand in greeting.

'Your robes!' said Lanike, as her jubilation shattered and she ground to a halt. 'What happened? Are you all right?'

In the meantime, while everyone in our group was focused on Lanike, a black shadow slunk away from us. Denise, who had been hiding behind me until now, had just entered the corner of my eye.

'Denise, where are you going?' I asked in a hoarse whisper. I was too startled to keep my voice down properly, but it wasn't enough anyway; she did not seem to have heard me. Throwing all caution to the wind, I attempted to grab her by the neck to prevent her from heading further up the square. But to my astonishment, everywhere I placed my hands the dark, grimy cloud that continuously oozed from her skin just repealed them like an opposing magnet. I couldn't touch her.

An almost girly scream suddenly filled the air. It was so high and shrill, that it instantly drowned all sounds coming from the square. I looked up at Lanike, who had clapped a hand over her mouth and was staggering backwards with shock etched on what little I could see of her face.

Murmuring followed, low and menacing, and everywhere I looked druids were closing in; the combination of Lanike's scream, Lycomedes' blood-soaked robes and Denise's monstrous appearance made everyone form their own opinions about what had befallen us. And judging by the dominance of anger and suspicion in the many faces, neither Denise nor I were seen as an asset to the community.

I glanced back at Selena, who appeared to be frantically trying to think her way out of the situation. I could see doubt form in her face. Had it been a mistake to bring us here? Lycomedes, Leander, Briseis and Peleus seemed just as unsure about what to do, but not nearly as concerned about it. After the encounter with the black shark, the relief they felt for being home again was evidently too strong to share in Selena's distress.

The entire scene had changed. Except for the occasional live, but still translucent, butterfly or wood mouse dotting the crowd, every single sign of ghostly presence had vanished. Like a single entity, the square full of people was slowly forming a semi-circular wall of bodies to barricade our access to the Sanctuary beyond. The druids' eyes were hard and mirthless, like those of firefighters having been called off a poker game because someone had set fire to a neighbour's house. The only way out was to go back.

'Everyone, calm down!' Lycomedes said imperially. 'Aaron and Denise are our guests. They pose no threat, I promise you.' His commanding voice easily carried over the murmurs, but received no response. Even Lanike, who was evidently an apprentice of his, walked away embarrassedly and joined the crowd.

Finally Denise seemed to realise what she was up against and fell back. I took up position in front of her to shield her from the piercing eyes. It didn't seem half as effective as I was hoping for. 'She's done nothing wrong!' I said. 'She's harmless!'

'Aaron,' Selena said warningly. When I looked at her she was shaking her head. I gave her a look as if asking, "Why not?", and she actually attempted to shush me into silence.

'I won't let them touch her,' I said a little louder than I needed to, hoping that more would hear. 'I'm serious.'

Selena was looking angry now. She bent towards me and whispered, 'You know what is at stake, Aaron. Please.'

'Yes, my girlfriend's life,' I snarled at her. 'There's nothing more important than that. Nothing. You hear me?'

A tall, imperious-looking woman shouldered herself through the crowd. Her robes were white as everyone else's, yet her shawl and sash matched her black hair perfectly. Her black was one of the least represented colours among the crowd. 'What is going on here?' she demanded.

Selena ignored the newcomer. 'And what do you think you're doing, exactly?' she asked me. 'Protecting her? You will only make it worse if you resist.'

'Resist?' I said in exasperation. 'I can't believe I actually let you drag me over here. First that shark and now this? What's next, a prison cell?'

Before Selena could answer, our attention was drawn to Lycomedes. He was staring up at the tall woman. Behind her, the druids who had been thrust aside to allow her entrance were quick to close the gap behind her. By the look on many of the druids' faces, it was obvious the woman enjoyed a great amount of respect.

'This is it,' Selena whispered into my ear. 'No more games, Aaron, or it's all over.' I gave her a sharp look, but she didn't catch it. She seemed entranced by the scene that was playing out before her.

'Megare,' said Lycomedes, greeting the woman with a small bow of his head.

Instead of returning the greeting, Megare looked from Lycomedes' robes to me and then to my feet, behind which Denise was still hiding. Finally she gave a slight incline of her head in return and said, 'Please explain, Lycomedes. What has befallen you? Who is this man?'

'My tale deserves a little more time than is prudent to take here, as well as a more private setting, Megare,' Lycomedes answered. 'But I assure you, they pose no threat.' Megare's expression did not change. 'If it suits you I would like to call a meeting. It concerns a matter of great importance.'

Megare narrowed her eyes in thought and realisation seemed to strike her. 'Which one is it?' she asked a little more enthusiastically, her eyes travelling between Leander and his peers.

'Selena is the new Shepherd,' said Lycomedes, loud enough to carry over the many heads. His answer shushed the crowd as suddenly as if a switch had been pulled.

Like marching soldiers receiving the command to look right, all heads turned to Selena. The many frowns and loose jaws baffled me; even though I knew the role of Shepherd was important to them, I had never expected to see this much reverence in their eyes. It almost made me wish Selena was right in her assumption that I had been given the Shepherd's powers. Countering this was my gnawing desire to get out of this place as soon as possible: to possess these powers would no doubt complicate things if the response by our audience was any indication.

'I see,' said Megare. 'Then I suggest she joins us at the meeting. Selena, will you follow us?'

'Of course,' said Selena with a small bow of her own. Then turning to me, she asked, 'Are you going to be all right?' I could almost taste the doubt in her voice.

'Don't worry about me, I'll be good,' I said grudgingly, though reassuringly. The sincerity in my voice finally seemed to calm her. And, with a nod in my direction, she followed Megare and Lycomedes to the taller of the two temples.

With Selena and Lycomedes gone, it felt like they had taken my symbolic breastplate and shield with them; I couldn't help but feel uncomfortably naked with Leander, Briseis and Peleus being only people by my side who could validate that Denise and I were indeed harmless.

Luckily, however, we weren't just left to the mercy and perhaps malicious entertainment of the crowd. When Selena and her two escorts left through another gap in the wall of druids, two men traded places with them and beckoned Denise and me to follow them. They brought us to the same temple Selena had entered. There we were taken to a small, Spartan room, furnished with a table surrounded by high backed chairs and a locked wardrobe. After closing the door the two men stayed to guard the door – easily noticeable because they didn't bother to keep their voices down.

'Did you see that thing?' one of them asked. 'It was all black and… something must have gone wrong with it. Could the rumours be true?'

'Oh, come on, Anthaeus,' said the other, 'you don't honestly believe those, do you? Experimenting with spiritcraft is one thing, but this? I don't know.' In a lower voice, he added, 'I must say, Captain Ione *was* acting rather strangely last time I saw her. Perhaps she and the other Canines did find a way to infuse spirits. But then, what was that thing doing with Lycomedes' apprentices? None of them are Canines, are they?'

'Peleus might be one of them, I believe,' said the first one. 'He should be getting his Canine sash any day now if he manages to pass his test.'

'There's no way Peleus has been able to learn to infuse spirits, even if the Canines have succeeded,' said the other. 'Nah, it must be something else. Then there's the Zaro girl as the new Shepherd.' He gave a derisory snort. 'No surprise there, right? First being saved by Ouranis and then being allowed to share the link with her. Lucky girl. And so young, too. It's unprecedented. From the moment she was brought to Eresa, I knew Selena was destined for great things.'

'Yeah, imagine what she'll be able to do once she finishes her training,' said the first. 'I wager she'll be able to turn into the great Phoenix herself.'

'Don't be ridiculous. Shapeshifting into Ouranis?' The man let out a hearty laugh.

'You can laugh all you want,' said the first. 'I've heard some extraordinary tales about the Shepherd's abilities, and if even half of them are true, we are looking at truly historic times.'

The laughter stopped and now a snort came through the door. 'What are you even doing in druid robes, Anthaeus?' the second guard asked. 'You should become a writer, a poet. You would become rich beyond your wildest dreams.' The last two words were thick with mockery. Another burst of laughter followed.

I gave a sigh and turned to Denise. I had heard enough. My head was swimming with memories and impressions, the likes which had never even occurred in any of those wild dreams the guard was talking about. Denise was sitting on her haunches in a typically canine fashion and was staring at me like one of the marble statues of dogs so common in Egyptian architecture.

'So this is it,' I said, repeating Selena's words to her. 'We're alone, locked up, and I haven't got the slightest idea what is going on in that head of yours. Oh, Denise, this is so messed up. If I just had you. If I could just talk to you, I would have at least someone who understood me. And you can do that better than anyone. That's why I love…'

A realisation struck me. 'Wait a minute,' I said. 'Maybe I can. If Selena is right, and I do have these powers, I should be able to do this… this telepathy thing. Let's try it. It sure beats waiting for Selena to burst through the door. That meeting of hers could take hours for all we know.' *Or our executioners*, I added as an afterthought.

I closed my eyes. The second I did, a picture bubbled up that caught me completely by surprise. With my mind's eye I beheld my own immovable back. Denise's hyena snout was resting on my shoulder, with the ashy substance dripping down my shirt. I was hugging her.   I felt my muscles ease. I knew it was my subconscious yearning for a connection. I longed to know she was doing all right, that she was even still in there. The thought consumed me. Nothing else, not my memory of the black shark, nor that of Trionyx or the druids, was able to interfere. I wouldn't allow anything to come between us.

My mind reached out. I imagined my thoughts trying to pierce that black skull of hers and penetrate her mind. I wanted to grab her spirit, to hold on, and if possible, to pull my girlfriend out of that alien body. Deeper and deeper I sank into the well of concentration. Flashes appeared. Some seemed to be mere shapeless blots of light, while others were fragmented memories. But all seemed to be my own. None gave me the impression they had come from Denise.

I opened my eyes again. Denise was still staring at me with unblinking, blowtorch eyes. The flow of grime that radiated from her skin was reduced to a slow and steady rippling, which followed the length of her legs down to the marble floor. It had formed a pool of darkness around her black behind. Despite the continuous downpour the pool remained the same size, for the outer edges seemed to vanish into nothingness.

'I'm so sorry,' I whispered breathlessly. It was the only thing I was able to produce. Denise gave a sigh through her nostrils, bent her front legs and lay down on the ground. For a long spell I kept watching her. I felt a single tear roll down my cheek. It hit the marble tile next to my hand and shattered. 'I *will* fix this, Denise. I promise. Just… just give me some time.'

The door swung open and a column of light split the dusty atmosphere in two. But it wasn't Selena or Lycomedes who came to pick us up. It was Leander. 'They gave me permission to show you the Sanctuary,' he said with an inviting smile. 'What do you say?'

'Sure, that'd be great. But what about Denise? Will the other druids be okay with her?'

'It's supposed to be just you and me, Aaron. Sorry.'

I looked at Denise, then back at Leander. 'In that case I'm sorry too, Leander. I'm staying with her.'

'Aaron, I really think you should go with me,' he said, a little more insistent now.

'Why? What's wrong?'

'I'll explain later. For now just come with me.'

'As much as I want to, I really can't, Leander,' I said apologetically. 'I won't leave Denise here alone.'

Leander sighed and he stepped aside, his indisposition slowing his movement. 'Sorry for this, my friend.'

Replacing him in the doorway were the two guards, who entered in silence. They walked straight to Denise as though I wasn't even there. She, in turn, bent low to the ground and bared her pitch black fangs. A long, continuous growl escaped through them. With every two steps the men took, she took one backwards until her behind hit the back wall.

'Leander, what is this?!' I called at the door as the guards passed me. 'Where's Selena? Selena!' Leander appeared again in the doorway. He was looking downcast, but didn't say or do anything to help me. 'Get your hands off her!' I told the guards, who were continuing to back Denise into the corner. 'I mean it!'

As Denise had already retreated as far as she could, she resorted to shrinking in fear instead. Meanwhile her head was whipping left and right, searching for an escape route.

'Orders are orders,' said one of the guards. 'It's for your own good. If you can tell it to come with us, no harm will come to either one of you. You have our word.'

'Come with you where?'

'Just help them, Aaron,' said Leander. 'She'll be all right. We can't take any risks. You understand, don't you? It's for your own safety as well as hers.'

My heart and mind battled for dominance. I knew Leander was right. I couldn't walk around the Sanctuary with Denise looking the way she did. Of course I couldn't. And yet my heart didn't care about right or wrong. It was time to make a decision. 'All right, I'll help,' I told them, 'but I'm going with her. I'm not leaving her alone.'

'Whatever you wish,' one of the guards said. 'Our orders concern the creature only. You are free to do as you please. However, you should know that it isn't necessary. Every life is sacred to us.'

'We're not the enemy here, Aaron,' Leander added.

'Well, the same goes for Denise.' I paused and looked at her. She had apparently given up on finding a peaceful solution to her predicament, and was preparing for a bloody one instead. 'No, I can't leave her,' I said resolutely. 'She needs to know I'm here for her.'

'Understandable,' said Leander.

Instead of being brought to either a prison block or an underground dungeon, which I had expected, we were led deeper into the temple. For all I knew, Selena was probably sitting somewhere in its labyrinthine depths without the slightest idea of the treatment we were subjected to.

This part of the temple seemed quieter and less populous. At length Denise and I found ourselves looking into a room like the one we had just left, albeit one with a heavy lock glinting in the light of the torches. This one contained a simple bed with a grated back and a thin mattress on one side, and a small table with two chairs on the other. In both corners in the back there were pedestals, each featuring a pair of unlit candles and a small, wooden statue of a prancing deer.

I felt something bump against the inside of my knee. Next I saw Denise rubbing the side of her head and most of her flank against my leg in an attempt to make me turn around. 'It's going to be all right, Denise. I'm going to take care of this. Don't worry. I'll be back soon.' Denise looked up. Her eyes were shining a lot less brightly now. I felt my heart crack as though it were hit by a sledgehammer. 'Just go, please,' I said, my voice breaking. 'It's only for a little while.'

With the constant murky flow trailing behind her, Denise looked as though she was crying from every pore in her body. But into her cell she went, with her nose almost scraping the marble floor, and the eyes of the guards and Leander following her with a mixture of disgust and sorrow. It seemed that, even to the guards, locking up Denise went against everything they stood for.

'Let's not talk about it anymore, shall we?' I asked as Leander proffered another apology. We had made it back to the entrance of the temple and the square opened up before us. Only about half of the druids from before were still showing off their skills to each other. The other half had probably left to tell their friends and families about the events of the afternoon. 'What's done is done. We'll just have to make sure we'll get her out of there soon.'

'Fine with me,' said Leander. 'I only want to say this: during the time I have spent in Eresa, we've never had to detain anyone before. You may find we are not as adept at it as you might expect.'

Realising that Leander couldn't be much older than I was and knowing that he had lived in the Sanctuary for the majority of his life, this was rather hard to believe. 'Never?' I asked him. 'Then what do you do if someone does something wrong? I mean, I don't want to offend you, but it doesn't look all that peaceful around here from where I'm standing. At least, not as much as I had expected when you told me this was supposed to be a sanctuary.'

'You must be thinking about Captain Helios,' said Leander.

'Among other things. Those thuggish guards, for example.'

Leander produced a small smile. 'Do you remember what I said about Eresa, and about what kind of sanctuary it is?'

'Of course.'

'Then you should realise that many of us have pasts they are not proud of, and most do not think lightly of people who make them relive it. So yes, problems do sometimes arise. But our method of dealing with them is usually convincing enough to prevent most people from acting against our laws. In fact, it is executed right over there.' He pointed at the structure on the other side of the square.

Without preamble Leander exited the temple and began to make a beeline for the smaller building. I hesitated; I wasn't as keen as he seemed to be to be out in the open again.

'If you don't mind me asking, I keep hearing about this Ouranis,' I said, catching up with Leander. 'Does she have anything to do with a Phoenix?'

'She *is* the Phoenix. She is our guide, our mentor. She is the one who taught the first of us, the first druids of Eresa, how to use spiritcraft.'

'Your magic,' I said to clarify. Leander shrugged in confirmation. 'I see. So that's what Selena meant.'

'She talked to you about Ouranis already?' he asked in mild surprise.

'A little,' I said, choosing my words carefully. 'She said something about your people's connection with her and that it is important to you.'

Leander nodded in agreement. 'She must be really looking forward to meeting her. It is a great honour.'

'I can imagine. And this ritual that chose her as the new Shepherd, I assume it has something to do with the connection between Selena and Ouranis? Besides the obvious, I mean.'

'I'm not quite sure. Today was the first time that the ritual has been performed since I arrived here. Why do you ask?'

'Just out of curiosity,' I said with a shrug to add a nonchalant air to my words. 'I just thought there must be some way for this Ouranis to know who the new Shepherd is, right?'

'Ouranis is connected to all beings in our world in one way or another. But the Shepherd is the only one who can actually communicate with her. Selena may have some problems still with her abilities, but she'll be all right,' he added with confidence. 'It's only her first day. I'm not too worried.'

'Is everything all right, Leander?' a slender, red-haired woman in her late twenties asked from further up the square. She had an impressive air about her and was eyeing the two of us with a feline interest. Joined to her hip was a teenage girl and more people were on their way for a closer look.

'Keep walking,' Leander whispered from the corner of his mouth, trying his best to ignore the gathering crowd. It took me a second or two to realise he meant me.

'Flying off so soon?' said the woman, more to the crowd than to us. 'I'd say he's a true Avian already.' People started sniggering, which seemed to add fuel to the woman's fire. 'You should go to your captain and ask for your sash, Leander, instead of...' A realisation seemed to strike her. 'Ah, you're gathering supporters,' she added, undressing me with her eyes. 'And not just from Eresa either, I see.'

'The duel is off, Phoebe,' Leander snapped back at her. 'If you don't like it, I suggest you take it up with your Captain, Niobe. She's the one who cancelled it.' I received a hand in the back as Leander continued to propel me in the direction of the temple. It was evident he didn't want to linger for longer than was necessary.

'That's not what she said,' said Phoebe, a little louder now. 'I heard it was postponed because of the Shepherd ritual. It will still happen, you know?'

'Then you heard wrong,' said Leander over his shoulder. To me, he added, 'Up here.' And together we scaled the stairs of the temple. Behind us, the babble of dozens of urgent conversations became a throbbing hum through which individual voices could no longer be discerned.

'What was that all about?' I asked, as we made our way inside.

'Phoebe,' he said, a bitter taste on his tongue. 'The name alone should have been enough if you were one of us. It's only a bit of rivalry between her captain, Niobe, and our master.'

'You mean Lycomedes?'

Leander nodded. 'It's not his fault. And I'm not only saying that because he's my master. Trust me, no matter how powerful a druid becomes, nothing changes inside their heads.' He breathed out forcefully through his nostrils. 'Even Lycomedes is prone to respond to their silly games, which he shouldn't. His level of spiritcraft doesn't come close to that of a captain.'

'So what happened? They called him out or something?'

'Not exactly,' said Leander, looking thoughtful. 'You see, whenever a new druid joins us, no matter at what age, he is obliged to reveal his past. When he does, whatever he has done before his initiation is forgiven, though not always forgotten. He is allowed to join our order no matter what has transpired, if and when he pledges fealty to Ouranis.'

Leander fell silent and turned to the temple interior. The structure had only one floor, but made up for its lack of height with the other features. Inside, there was large rectangular pit of sand. Marble columns, like those adorning the outer walls but smaller, circled the pit. They served as support beams for the roof to rest on. The courtyard itself was roofless.

'The Arena of Repentance,' Leander said proudly. 'Or "the Pit", as some of us prefer to call it.'

I acknowledged his words with a series of nods and gave the arena a good sweep. 'So you settle your disputes here? How?'

'Isn't that obvious? Both sides send a representative and they battle it out,' he said simply.

'You've got to be joking. How does fighting each other say anything about who is right?'

'It doesn't,' Leander answered. 'If a dispute arises where it actually matters who is right or wrong, it is brought before the Council. In most cases it is simply a matter of butting heads, which is easily remedied by allowing both sides to… butt heads. Albeit in a safe environment, of course,' he added. 'Fighting each other with the intent to hurt is forbidden beyond these doors, the exception being if we are ordered to do so, of course.'

As I looked behind me and through the entrance at the square, I fell silent for a spell. *This place looks more and more like some Buddhist martial arts monastery than an actual sanctuary*, I thought. *It can be both a training ground and a safe haven at the same time, I suppose. Only when they told me it was a home for druids I did expect something more… peaceful.*

'You still haven't told me what happened to Lycomedes,' I said at length.

'True.' Leander breathed in the scent of earth that suffused the air. 'Well, normally when an aspiring druid pledges his fealty to Ouranis, he needs to confess his misdeeds and whatever else he needs to get off his chest. In short, he is required to tell the tale of his past. It is still possible for him to lie or omit things, of course, but a druid can only connect with the spirits of animals and learn spiritcraft if he is washed clean of the negative energy that surrounds him, if there is any. That's just the way it is.'

'Now this cleansing can only be performed by fellow druids, preferably by druids with the same kind of affinity for animal spirits,' he went on explaining. 'It is the main reason why we have clans in the first place. Or, at least, it was probably the initial reason. Things have changed. Nowadays it's all about training. Anyway, if too much negativity is found when weighed against the probable emotional impact of the druid's confessed misdeeds, he will be banished from Eresa forever. We don't like secrets, or the people who keep them.'

'I know. Selena told me.'

'Then you should be able to understand the problems people had, and still have, with our master. Because Lycomedes either never had to undergo the ritual, or he's done it in secret. For no one I know has attended it.'

'Yet you still became his apprentice. Or didn't you have a choice?'

'Oh, no, we can choose whoever we like, if they take us. And I chose Lycomedes, even though I knew full well there were things about him that were not mine to know. Lycomedes may act a little... eccentrically sometimes, but I still believe he is one of the best. He's a great mentor.'

'I'm still confused, though. If you people value honesty so much, why is Lycomedes allowed to keep his secrets?'

Leander gave me a look that told me I had hit the truth square in the face. 'Luckily for him, what is allowed, and what is not, is not for us to decide. It was the Council's decision. Remember that if it was something really horrible, he wouldn't have been able to use spiritcraft and wouldn't really pose a threat to the Sanctuary. I believe that if and when Lycomedes wants to tell us about it, he will do so himself. Until then...'

'There you are,' a familiar voice said. 'Leander, did you have an exchange with Phoebe again?' Selena was standing in the entrance, frowning. Leander gave an uncomfortable grunt in response and looked away. 'She has gathered quite an audience,' she said accusingly. 'I told you, you should stay out of her way for a while. This could rapidly escalate. Phoebe is young, Leander. She has much to learn. She hasn't been a druid for as long as most of us.'

'Neither have I,' said Leander defensively.

'You can't compare yourself with her. You have Lycomedes.' There was no disputing this fact, and acknowledgement showed in Leander's face.

'She came up to us,' muttered Leander in response. He seemed to regret his comment the second it had left his mouth.

Selena shook her head. 'You should know better. Lycomedes doesn't need another outburst from Captain Niobe and you know how good Phoebe is in extracting those.'

Before Leander was able to respond again, I was quick to jump in. 'Have you asked your Council about Denise?'

Selena didn't seem at all taken aback by my reaction. It was as if she had actually been waiting for me to butt in. 'We have discussed the situation, yes. It is one of the many things I would like to discuss with you as well, in private.'

'That's fine,' I said quickly. 'Sorry, Leander.'

'Don't worry about it,' Leander said airily, yawning. 'I'll get you your...' His sentence was cut short when his eyes fell on the extra white toga Selena was unfolding. I hadn't even noticed her carrying it. She performed a quick check for any stains its previous wearer might have left before she handed it over. There was a pair of the druids' knitted sandals too. 'Never mind,' Leander finished.

'It's a Phoenix, isn't it? The bird you're able to call,' I asked Selena as I busied myself trying to get the knot in my sash to look the same as hers. It was coloured the same too, bright orange. By now we had managed to sneak away from the square and were about to make our way back to the jetty where we had last seen Trionyx. Currently we were hiding in the bushes, while Selena took a moment to make sure we weren't followed.

She let out a soft chuckle. 'I told you, druids do not call upon animals, Aaron. We simply conjure their image. Here, let me.' She grabbed both ends of my sash and pulled them tight. The knot that appeared a few seconds later seemed to be mirrored by my intestines.

'Let's go through here.' She pointed deeper into the forest. 'Captain Helios was called back for the Council meeting, but knowing him, he didn't leave without finding a replacement first. And I'd rather not find out who it is. You were right about the Phoenix, however,' she said at length, her eyes keeping a tag on our environment. We had a clear view of the path and whoever may be treading it. So far, we had been lucky. No one had gone this way. 'I was saved by Ouranis after both my parents had been killed. I was the only survivor.'

'Oh, I'm sorry,' I said, feeling uncomfortable.

'Don't be. It is nothing to be embarrassed about. I was only six years old at the time. I can't remember much more than the thundering of feet and the many shouts coming from the upper deck, and the many vases I was hiding behind. I think my parents were merchants, since we were on a small ship at the time. I must have crawled into the hull. When I finally braved the climb up to the deck, I was alone. That was when Ouranis appeared. She took me away and dropped me off near Eresa.' She paused briefly, then said, 'We can go there if you like. We will be able to talk and practice there without the fear of eavesdroppers.'

'I'd like that, but what about those creatures? What if those hyenas come back, or that shark?'

'We will be relatively safe if Trionyx is still willing to help us across, I believe. I will keep my energy down just in case. If that is how these creatures found us, it will hopefully prevent them from doing the same again.'

'You will keep your energy down?'

'My spirit energy, yes. We use it for spiritcraft. There is no need to worry. I can accumulate more if the need arises.'

'I don't understand what you just said, but that's fine,' I said. *This is hardly the time to ask for a lecture about their magic*, I added silently.

'Look, Aaron,' said Selena, 'I realise there is a risk in leaving Eresa, but we need to find out which one of us has the gift and we can't do that here. I am not a very good liar and if the wrong person sees us practising together… No, it's too risky. I am not even allowed to show you how to use spiritcraft before you are ready. You are not a druid yet.'

'Yet?'

'Shh, Aaron.' She held up a hand and I fell silent. A fellowship of druids passed us. We tucked in our heads so we were hid from view and watched the druids stride by the building where, in all probability, Helios' replacement sat out his duty shift. The druids were evidently going the same way we were, to Delos.

'Another search party?' Selena whispered. 'The Council must have sent two. Aaron, stay close. We have to be careful they don't see us.'

Only when we had made it to the shoreline and the search party had been taken across by Trionyx did I dare speak up again. There were still a lot of questions I needed answering. 'So what else did you talk about at the meeting, if it's okay to ask?'

'The missing ritualists, for one thing,' said Selena absentmindedly as she peered across the broad band of water to the opposite shore. 'Look.'

I followed her outstretched arm and saw Trionyx lying on the bank of the main island like a washed up sea monster. His diagonal fins were lying lazily at his sides as he watched a host of people sprinting across the flowery meadow.

'Do you think they will find anything?' I asked.

'As I said before, I believe Andromeda and the other ritualists either, like Denise, have been turned into whatever these hyenas are, or some of them might have found a place to hide. Either way, should either of the search parties find out, it would not bode well for us – especially when considering Denise's current location. It would be virtually impossible to get her out of the Phoenix Hall in time.' She shook her head. 'Even if Denise survives the experiments, she will not be the same again. I can assure you.'

I couldn't believe my ears. 'Experiments? What? We have to go back! I have to get her out of there!'

Selena's hand was even faster than her objection. 'Aaron, no. We can't.'

'Sure we can! I'm not going to let them experiment on Denise. What kind of people are you? You never said anything about…'

'Please, keep your voice down,' said Selena, her hands pushing the words back into my mouth. I stepped back from her, my mind racing. 'As long as the search parties don't find anything, Denise will be safe.'

'As if I am going to wait for that! Screw this!'

'It is too late, Aaron. You will be detained as well if you try to free her.'

'It's better than doing nothing. Can't you do anything?'

'Even as the acting Shepherd, I can't,' said Selena, almost pleading for me to hear her out. My body felt numb and my brain empty. I had already taken a few steps back towards the Sanctuary, but halted because of the desperation in her voice. 'The search parties, as well as Denise's guards, act on the Council's orders, and I have no say against it. The only thing that could possibly sway the Council is proof that you are the real Shepherd. It is the only thing that might convince them that something has gone wrong with the ritual and that Denise is a mere victim of the event. Now do you understand why I wished to keep this quiet? If they had started experimenting on Denise and you had tried to come to her aid, which obviously you would have, you would have been detained immediately. If that happened, it would have become impossible for me to find out the truth about what happened to the gift.'

'This is crazy. We should never have come here.'

'To Eresa?' said Selena hesitantly. I gave her a nod. 'It was a gamble, though I still believe you made the right choice, Aaron. If you had stayed on Delos, alone, you would eventually have been spotted. At that point it would have become very difficult to earn the trust of the Council. No, I do believe you did the right thing.'

'Time will tell, I suppose,' I said, unconvinced.

'If you want my advice, you should focus on what you can do to change the situation, not dwell on things that are beyond your control. In fact, I believe that if you do turn out to be our new Shepherd, things will become very interesting, as my master would say.'

I sighed and felt the majority of my anger seep away. Then I asked, if only to provide a little distraction, 'How is Lycomedes, by the way? He was injured pretty badly during his fight with the shark.'

'I believe he will be all right,' said Selena. 'The cut isn't too deep. His soaked robes made it look worse than it is.'

Attracting Trionyx's attention was easier than I thought it would be. After the search party had disappeared from vision, he turned around and spotted our waving hands. It took me a second or two to get used to his size again, a time which Selena used to express her relief for the fact that none of the black shark's companions, if there were any, had come to see if there was anything left to feast on. After all, Lycomedes had lost a lot of blood and sharks, at least in my world, were known as the scavengers of the seas.

Once back on the main island, Selena walked me past the docks until the trading vessel moored there was no longer within sight. We continued west along the shore until we had circled part of the woods in which, somewhere up the hill, the complete version of the temple of Isis stood. During this time, Selena kept her thoughts to herself, but occasionally glanced over at a tiny island in the distance. From this far away the island looked like the jagged peak of a mountain, one whose bulk was too large to hide below the surface completely.

Suddenly I realised Selena was no longer beside me. The silence had lulled me into sailing a lake filled, not with water, but with my own thoughts; my imagination had been toying with me all the way here, juggling with my memories in a spiteful fashion. Everywhere I looked, Denise's pretty human face was staring back at me with a longing in her eyes I knew I wasn't able to satisfy anymore, physically or mentally.

'Is this the place?' I asked Selena. The blonde woman was standing with both hands on her stomach and was gazing into the distance. 'Selena?'

Without looking at me, she whispered, 'Ouranis…' She closed her eyes and, for a short while, she fell silent again. Finally she turned to me. 'Sorry? Yes, this is the place where Ouranis left me for the druids to find.'

'Okay, so what's the plan? I assume you want to practice first, right? To see which one of us is the Shepherd?' Selena gave a slow nod and began to look around. 'And what if neither of us possesses these powers? What if whatever happened during that ritual completely messed up the transference?'

'Let us hope we will not have to find an answer to that,' said Selena curtly. 'Come with me, please.' She brought me to a small patch of green grass shielded from sight by two trees standing on either side, indicated for me to sit down and once again looked back to the tiny island.

'In case I do end up having these powers,' I said when her attention returned to me, 'I want you to know I never wanted this to happen, Selena. You know that, don't you?'

Selena turned serious. 'Don't think like that. You should give it your all, Aaron, especially since we don't know what news the search party will bring back to the Council. If they find so much as a twig that can connect Denise to the disappearance of the ritualists, you will need the gift.'

'Yes, you already made that clear. What do I do?'

'Close your eyes. Ease your mind and control your breathing. Let the sea calm you down.' I followed her guidance. 'When you are ready, try to listen to the forest, the rusting of the leaves, the animals, anything you can hear behind you.' She paused for a spell to give me time to adjust to the rhythm of nature. 'Now wait for the first animal that enters your mind and focus on its image. Try to see nothing but this single animal and examine it in detail. Focus on its characteristics one at a time. Take them in as if you had to draw a picture of the animal into the soil once you open your eyes.'

Selena fell silent once more. For a long while I did nothing but focus on my hearing, my smell and my mind's eye. The aroma of the forest, of fresh grass and resin, was soothing, while the salty scent of the sea invigorated me, preventing me from being lulled into slumber. The soft breeze playing with the trees as well as the rhythmic frothing of the waves were slightly distracting and didn't help me much. I wasn't used to them, born and raised in busy Oxford. The sounds conjured images that had nothing to do with Selena's exercise.

I did manage to choose a creature, however. In fact, despite the flipping of the pages of my mind, the creature remained stubbornly in sight. It was as though the squirrel was actively fighting off any thought that was trying to come between us and jumped back into view every time it was pushed away by another memory. I didn't dare speak up out of fear of losing my focus. I was quite amazed by the proficiency with which the tiny critter was keeping my mind fixed on its face, yet nothing else worthy of note appeared to be happening. It was just there.

'Once you have succeeded, try to listen to the creature's voice,' Selena said at length. 'Try to understand what it wants. Ask it something.'

Ask it something? I repeated in my mind, bewildered. *Ask it about what?* I dismissed the thought as being unhelpful. I decided to start listening to the squirrel first, to see if I could hear it at all. But the harder I listened, the more intrusive the rustling of leaves and the noise generated by the waves became. The sounds might be soothing in any other situation, but at a time during which I was supposed to listen without utilising my ears, they didn't do me any favours.

Doubts began to permeate my thoughts. Because even if the squirrel was able to produce anything with its tiny throat, I couldn't imagine that I would be able to understand it. *At least I would have something to ask it*, I thought as I felt a faint smile play on my lips. *"Can you say that again?"*

'Did you hear anything?' Selena asked. I figured she had seen my smile.

'I can hear a lot, just nothing coming from it,' I said while trying to keep my focus. 'I don't think this is working.'

I felt a hand coming to rest on my forearm. 'Are you certain about that?' Selena asked in a peculiar fashion. A soft squeeze made me open my eyes.

My mouth fell open. Before me, sitting on the grass, were a host of about a dozen squirrels. They were hard to count, since judging from their appearance, they all seemed to have died long ago, only to return in spirit form to haunt the forest they called home. Their pointy faces, beady eyes, bushy tails and tiny claws, every one of their features was as silvery blue and transparent as most other creatures I had seen in this strange world.

'Did I do that?' My eyes refused to leave twelve of the cutest faces I had ever laid eyes on.

'The hare did not come to me when I called her,' Selena replied in an almost "I-told-you-so" sort of way. '*They* did come for you.'

'But I didn't call for them. I did think of a squirrel, and I could see it clearly in my mind, but I couldn't hear anything except for the noise around here.'

'It will come in time, Aaron,' said Selena. 'You are right about the ambience, though. I didn't realise how inexperienced you were. And you are clearly unaccustomed to nature's presence. Perhaps next time we'd better choose a quieter environment to practice. But this is a promising start.'

'Yeah, I guess. But these are real squirrels, aren't they? I mean, there are alive, not like those energy manifestations you druids can summon with your magic.'

Selena produced a smile, though not one that reached her eyes. My success was a bit of a double-edged sword for her after all. 'No, these ones came from the forest. It takes years of training until you would be ready to summon an animal body with your energy. And like I said, you need to establish a link with an animal first, before you are able to manifest your energy.'

'I understand. So, what's next?'

Focus returned to Selena's face. She looked over to the tiny island contemplatively. 'We need to make sure,' she answered in a soft voice. 'If we are anything less than fully confident about you being the Shepherd, Aaron, the Council will surely sense it. The proposition that Ouranis' gift has been transferred to an outsider is difficult enough to believe as it is, especially since I am the one who was chosen by the ritual. They might not want to believe it unless we can prove we have her blessing.'

'So I take it you want to go there?' I said, indicating the island with my head.

Selena nodded. 'If she is in her den, that is where she will be.' Her mind seemed to be somewhere else now. 'I do not want to use Trionyx. His absence may attract too much attention.'

'How so? Doesn't everyone think you are the Shepherd? I thought the new Shepherd was supposed to meet this Ouranis.'

'That is true, but normally there is an inauguration ceremony to welcome the era of the new Shepherd. It is at this ceremony that the new Shepherd meets Ouranis and receives her blessing – as well as her guidance.'

'Another ritual?' I asked. 'Do you druids get a day off sometimes too?'

'It is a very important event,' said Selena severely. 'In this case, however, I don't believe we have much of a choice. We cannot afford to wait.' She stood up and brushed the forest debris from her white garments.

'When is this ceremony supposed to be held?' I asked her.

'Tomorrow.'

We headed to the docks. Moored, on the closest pier opposite the much larger trading vessel, was a wooden boat, but one that was still large enough to offer half a dozen men a place to sit. Selena and I didn't share a word until we arrived at the pier, a silence that was mostly due to our haste. Selena didn't appear to have much interest in talking anyway. She was like a lightning rod charged to full, which would burn my hands, shock my hair and blast me off my feet if I were to prod her with my finger.

'This way.' And with that Selena walked briskly up the pier. The place looked like it was used only rarely, made obvious by the creaking of the planks as we sped to the boat.

'Uhm, Selena, is that old fishing boat even seaworthy?' I asked reluctantly, pointing at our transport. It did indeed look like it had been a time since anyone used it. 'It doesn't even have a sail.'

'Fishing? I am not quite sure what you mean by that, but yes, it can take us there.'

'It's for catching... fish...' My voice ground to a dumbfounded halt half way through my sentence; I suddenly realised something. 'You don't eat meat, do you?' I asked. 'You can't. Not if all the animals here look the same as those squirrels.'

Or could they? I added in silence. *If those squirrels are truly alive, I suppose it is also possible they could be hunted and eaten.* The surreal thought of a blue and translucent barbecue steak lying on a dinner plate pushed most other thoughts away. *But if so, would the druids even consider eating them? Animals are their lives, their everything.*

Selena seemed to have a hard time understanding me. She quickly lost interest, and then turned back to the boat. I could see doubt showing in her face. 'I have to try,' she muttered under her breath. 'I have to know. I hope I have the energy to do this.' Her voice found strength again and she said, 'Help me with the ropes, Aaron. We need to move quickly.'

'All right, all right. I'm on it.'

Chapter 4

Selena was sitting on the front bench. I was watching her from my seat as the incoming waves continuously rocked the boat this way and that. Naturally, since the absence of a sail or oars meant that there was no way to use either wind or muscle to propel us forwards, we had barely moved an inch since we took our seats. So unless I jumped out and propelled the vessel to the island, we were victims of the current – which, fortunately for us, was directed at the docks, not Ouranis' den.

Selena would never have chosen the boat if she didn't have a way to move it, I was sure. And yet, a few minutes in, I was still waiting for Selena to give me a command, or give any sign of life at all. I looked back at the flowery meadow stretching behind me. As far as I knew, the search party hadn't returned to Eresa yet.

I thought of Denise and how different everything would be if she were with me. We hadn't been together for that long, and we were still in the process of figuring things out together, but it had felt right almost from the moment I met her. *If her parents only knew about where they had sent us… Hopefully this Ouranis can help us.*

Then, just as the memory of Denise's transformation began to intrude once more, the hairs on the back of my neck twitched. My fingertips began to prickle uncomfortably. Like a tribe of ants marching across my hands and arms, the prickling spread to other parts of my body. I turned back to Selena. Shock impacted my chest as a pair of brilliant, blue, silvery wings suddenly sprouted from Selena's back. Larger and larger they grew until the giant phoenix that emerged exceeded even the size of our boat. My eyes felt like they had grown just as large. After being summoned into being, the bird began to hover obediently above the stern.

'Aaron, grab the rope,' Selena said in a strained voice. I jumped up and saw she had her hands pressed together in a praying position. Blue slithers I could only describe as *energy* were licking her fingers like flames. Talking was evidently taking her great effort. 'Throw it.'

The rope soared through the air like a leaping python. Selena's phoenix snatched it out of the air with deadly precision. I felt a hard tug on the boat. Selena had anticipated it, but I had not. And when my back met the bench behind me, I could actually hear my own teeth grating in pain.

'Don't fall out,' Selena whispered hoarsely. 'We need to keep heading forward. I definitely don't have the energy to do this more than twice.'

'Good to know,' I muttered irritably, rubbing my back.

The phoenix was as powerful as it was enchanting. With its great wings it flapped powerful gusts of wind, one after another, against the rolling waves below. With each consecutive wave of its wings, foaming tops were whipped into the air as though the phoenix was actually trying to push the water away to decrease our drag.

I looked back over my shoulder to watch the shore receding with every passing second. It was already becoming difficult to discern one flower from another. Turning back, the island belonging to the real Phoenix was, in contrast, increasing in detail. I beheld a narrow path, one that served both as a landing and a means to scale the jagged peak.

If her phoenix is this strong, I thought, *why didn't she try to carry Denise across the water earlier? I know she said it was because of the inky substance, but she could have at least tried. Maybe she didn't want to do it because she wanted to talk to me first, before taking me into Eresa. It's probably good that she did; I never would have allowed them to throw Denise behind bars if I hadn't heard her out first. It won't be for long, though, not now I know about those experiments.*

Soon I came to realise the island wasn't as tiny as I first thought, and the jagged peak was one that any amateur climber would think twice of braving. Also, the wind was starting to pick up, turning from a soft breeze into a hefty, and slightly worrisome, gale; by the way Selena's phoenix bowed its head against the building wind, I realised even this one trip might be beyond Selena's capabilities.

I gripped the sides of the boat with my hands and braced for impact. But a second before it appeared it would crash into the desolate mountain, Selena's phoenix made a swift turn and moored us, with a loud scraping of the bow, onto the strip of pebbled beach. The moment we hit the shore, the phoenix vanished into thin air and Selena's arms fell down at her sides. She looked exhausted.

I placed a hand between her shoulder blades. 'Selena, are you all right?'

Selena swallowed and took a deep breath. The front of her robes was saturated and showed quite a bit more of her figure than Denise would probably have liked me to see. It surprised me how much I was affected by the sight, but I shook it off and focused on her eyes again.

'We're here,' she said with relief, her eyes squinted against the wind. 'I could do it after all. Now it's time for answers.'

The interior of the mountain was breath-taking. We had just entered via a cave on the south side of the island and found ourselves gaping at a display of crystals far beyond my imagination. The walls, the ceiling, the floor, every surface of the tunnel looked as if covered with blue ice; though the slightly dry warmth belied this.

My straw sandals had a tough time with the slippery floor. Inching onwards, we passed a cluster of man-sized, crystal daggers sprouting from the rocks. I could actually see my own face and chest reflected multiple times. Up ahead the tunnel opened up to a cavern of whose parameters, in the dim light radiating from the crystals, was impossible for me to ascertain. About half way there, Selena stopped.

'Ouranis?' she asked into the silence. Her voice was echoed back several times before it dissipated. There was no response. She tried again.

'I don't think she's here,' I said, stating the obvious. My nerves were affecting my legs and my mind began fantasising about the size of the giant bird, her claws and beak in particular.

Selena took a moment to consider. 'We need to be certain. I need to know.' I was sure she meant to say, "*We* need to know", but for some reason it didn't come out that way.

After a lengthy and careful walk, the tunnel indeed opened up to a cavern, one that I could now see was wide enough to hide a herd of dinosaurs – and high enough to do the same with a cathedral. There also turned out to be another entrance, for the mountain turned out to be a dormant volcano with the main vent opening to the sky above. If the volcano had once been active, it must've been a long time ago, since there was no dried lava to show for it.

When I found her again, Selena was squinting at the light that came down the shaft, which ricocheted from one crystal to the other until it lit up the wet surface of her eyes.

'You were right,' she said, her voice a cocktail of relief and disappointment. 'She's not here.'

'Do you think she'll be long?'

'I know her only through our previous Shepherd, Aaron. I have never been here before. So I can't say.'

'Great. Now what do we do?'

'We have no choice but to wait,' said Selena. 'I have to rest for a moment before we can go back anyway, if we choose to do so.'

'Well, I'm not going to wait too long. I want to be back in Eresa before those search parties return.'

'We will be,' said Selena, failing to sound very reassuring.

'Right.' I sat down on the ground next to one of the crystal fingers. Out of curiosity I tapped it with my fingernail and a resonant, glassy sound swam across the chamber.

'We can't stay here, Aaron,' said Selena. 'We'd better retreat to the mouth of the cave.'

'Why?'

'Because, in normal circumstances, no one but the real Shepherd can get close to Ouranis. It isn't simply a matter of being allowed,' she elaborated to my furrowed eyebrows. 'No one but the Shepherd is capable of withstanding the high energy pressure that continuously emanates from her body.'

'Seriously? Then what am I even doing here?' I sprang up and hurriedly joined her inside the tunnel; speed seemed to help my straw sandals maintain traction. 'You're not suggesting I can get close to her and you can't? You're way more used to this energy business than I am.'

'Used to, yes,' said Selena, stopping halfway through the tunnel. 'But this is not about skill. Even our captains cannot approach Ouranis. So to think that I would be able to without her gift is foolish, despite how much I wished it. I merely wanted to take a look,' she added in an awkward voice.

'Are these captains that powerful?' I asked. Selena nodded in acknowledgement. 'Hang on, I thought you said it was Ouranis who saved you from that ship and brought you to Eresa. How is that possible if you can't get close to her?'

'Aaron, part of becoming a druid, in my experience the most important part, is establishing a spiritual link with the animal of your choosing. You said you have already spoken with Leander about this.' I nodded. 'Then he may also have told you that this connection can be achieved either via direct contact with a living specimen, or through the guidance of fellow druids. For me, when Ouranis grabbed me the night our crew was attacked, I became linked with her without me even realising it. And when I started my training as a druid some years later, I wasn't able to bond with any of the animals represented by the clans, or beyond. That was when I found out that something was wrong.'

'That must have been weird, considering the way you people live.'

'I was scared,' confessed Selena. 'Scared that I wouldn't fit in and of what would happen to me if I wouldn't be able to establish a link. No one is allowed to leave Eresa once they become a druid.' She took a deep breath. 'I tried and tried. I was determined not to show weakness and to prove to them I was capable. Lycomedes was the only one among the grandmasters who saw me for who I really was. It took me many years before I was finally able to summon my first phoenix.'

'So how did you find out you were linked with Ouranis?'

'I didn't, at least not by myself. It should never have happened according to our knowledge of spiritcraft. Ouranis is not a regular animal and, as far as we know, cannot be chosen by a druid to link with. The same holds true for Trionyx.' A small smile appeared on her lips. 'Some have tried. Instead it was Zeuxis, the previous Shepherd, who sensed Ouranis' energy inside me. He told Lycomedes about what he had learned and the two of us started experimenting with my energy.' The mentioning of experimentation again side-tracked me back to Denise, and I had to force my mind to remain fixed on the present.

'The problem was,' Selena went on, 'I had only a vague idea of what Ouranis looked like, as I only had my memories of when I was a little girl to guide me, and the one time I had seen Ouranis leave her den with my own eyes. Zeuxis tried to help me by asking Ouranis to show herself to me. We thought she might be willing to do so, since she was the one who saved me. We thought I might even have become immune to her energy pressure. She never gave us the chance to test this theory, though. And Zeuxis' efforts didn't do him any favours; Ouranis isn't one to be commanded. So I returned many times to the place at the beach where she had left me for the druids to find, and stared at the sky for hours at a time, hoping that the great Phoenix would show herself. As I said, I only saw her leave her den once, which is why my own version is still incomplete.'

'Incomplete?' I repeated exasperatedly. 'It looks amazing.'

My enthusiasm took her by surprise. 'Thank you.'

'So, about those druid clans, how many of them are there? Leander told me a bit about them too.'

'There are seven in total, but not every druid in Eresa belongs to a specific clan. Our master is one of them.'

'I see. Yes, Leander told me that Lycomedes had a little trouble of being accepted.'

'The Felines, Niobe's clan, have a hard time accepting anyone but their own,' said Selena sourly. 'Other clans have that same problem, but most choose to ignore rather than confront. Unfortunately, some druids allow certain characteristics of the type of animal they linked with to carry over and change their personalities. Then there are others, like Phoebe – you met her on the square – who have been venomous from birth.'

'Now just a few days ago a duel was scheduled between Captain Niobe and Lycomedes,' Selena went on. 'However, the Council talked to Lycomedes and decided to cancel the duel, probably partly because of the upcoming ritual. It is very rare for the Council to interfere with duels, but they can and they did. I haven't seen Captain Niobe since, but knowing her, I imagine steam still boils from her ears.'

'But Captain Niobe's a captain… obviously. There is no way Lycomedes could beat her.'

'That is not necessarily true. You have seen the arena. It is a relatively small place. And neither contestant is allowed to damage the building or they lose the match. The outcome of a duel consequently depends for the most part on the contestants' wit and quick thinking. Of course it doesn't hurt to be physically fit as well.'

'So does that mean druids always choose an animal that's good at fighting? I mean, you can't expect to win against another druid using grasshoppers or, I don't know, peacocks.'

'It is not a rule or a requisite to join our community, but yes, most druids do tend to go for an animal that can prevail in physical combat. That said, the animal kingdom is one where the fittest survive, and it might surprise you how much damage a peacock can do when it is forced into a corner. Again, do keep in mind that the animals we summon are not actually alive. They have no conscience and can use any weapon at their disposal without restrain.'

I nodded, but I still wasn't entirely convinced. 'So about Lycomedes and this duel. Did it have something to do with…?' The rest of my sentence became stuck in my mouth, as though pushed back into my throat by Selena's outstretched hand. 'Is it Ouranis?' I added in a whisper.

Selena shook her head, but remained quiet. Her hand was still in the air. Her eyes were glassy, as though every one of her brain cells was currently assigned to her hearing. Now I heard it too. There was an occasional flapping sound, not of wings, but of fabric. It was mixed with the sound of something large cutting through the water. Then a sound of hundreds of pebbles being crushed to fragments, and a grinding of wood against stone, entered the tunnel. This din was followed by an almighty crash of yielding rock and splintering planks. The collision sent a vibrating earthquake through the side of the mountain.

Without a word Selena and I scrambled out of the cave and into the late afternoon sun. The potent gale was still present, yet it seemed to have stabilised after we entered the cave. Shielding us from the wind was a large two-master, at least twice the size of the trading vessel moored at the docks near Eresa. The ship reminded me of the warships the ancient Greeks went to war with around the Hellenistic period; a trireme. It had apparently tried to bore itself a third entrance into Ouranis' den.

The sight stunned us into silence. There was rock and wood debris scattered everywhere. The collision had bored a hole in the hull, one that was large enough to enter without the need to bend double.

'Incredible,' Selena whispered, drinking in the ship with her eyes. There was not a single sign of life anywhere.

'Yeah, but… where is everybody? Hello?!' I called with both hands aiding my voice. 'Is anyone up there?!'

Selena followed my example, but no reply came. Not a single word, no cry for help, nothing. 'Let's take a look inside,' I suggested. 'There has to be people on board.'

I was just short of touching the torn hull when a calloused hand grabbed the edge. Next came a head, as a man in his late forties came into view. He stepped out through the hole, a ragged and soaked brown chiton covering one shoulder, his belly and his upper legs. Pressed against him was a young girl, ten, perhaps eleven years of age, with unusually long, black hair obscuring her shoulders and front. The girl was wearing a plain green dress.

The man eyed each of us in turn before his knees gave way and dug into the pebbled beach. The pain barely faced him; all of his attention remained focused on the girl. He only just managed to keep her upright.

Selena and I shot forwards and helped both victims further up the beach. The man breathed out a sentence, the only audible words being "... any help", then sunk tiredly against the rock face. After catching his breath, he asked, 'How's Sophia?'

'Unconscious,' I mouthed to Selena, checking on the girl.

'She's unconscious,' Selena answered, somewhat bluntly. I shot her an angry look. 'But she appears to be well,' Selena added hastily. 'Can you tell me what happened to you and your crew?'

At the mention of his crew, the man's eyes narrowed slightly. 'Who are you people?' he asked in return. His voice bordered upon rudeness.

Selena's eyebrows went up in mild surprise. 'We are from Eresa, the Druid Sanctuary,' she said, displaying the slightest hint of concern for the man's boorish behaviour. Perhaps it was because she had already assessed he was no threat to her.

'Druids…,' muttered the man. He took a deep breath and tried to sit up properly, but couldn't. Settling for the next best thing, he let his head fall to the side and took a long, hard look at the girl. 'That means we've made it.'

'You were on your way to Eresa?' Selena asked incredulously. Even I had a hard time believing it. From what I had been told so far I knew that most people seeking sanctuary in Eresa were orphans and loners, those who were looking for a new start. It was no place to raise a family, although I remembered Leander mention that some of the druids had had children.

The man now looked at Selena with regret. When he turned back to the girl, his face softened and he seemed to come to a decision. 'The ship… was part of a prison transport,' he said, dropping the words like a lump of meat for piranhas to feast on.

'What?' My eyes immediately searched for the girl's face again. Again, she couldn't be more than eleven years old and to think she had committed a crime worthy of incarceration was ludicrous.

Selena had stood up and backed away. Her hands were level with her chest, presumably in preparation of being able to summon another phoenix the moment either tried to pull a knife. As I looked at her stern countenance I wondered where her jumpy reaction came from; neither the man nor the girl seemed even remotely threatening, and I had thought she felt the same way.

'It's the truth,' said the man, closing his eyes and turning his face to the sky. 'You need not be alarmed though. You have no reason to fear us. We have done nothing wrong.'

'Then how did you end up on the ship?' I asked him, trying to infuse my words with the unstated advice to choose his words carefully. 'Or weren't you one of the prisoners?'

The man looked up. 'I was. We both were. But not anymore, it seems. As far as I know, we are the only ones still alive. My name is Pelegon Linard, Sophia's my daughter. I was a guard at Arcturus' keep, but that was some time ago.' Pelegon began shaking his head and then scowled. Something seemed to be adding to his strength. 'When I learned about his plans for battling the Darkness, we fought him with everything we had.'

I looked back at Selena to see if she understood Pelegon's story. She appeared as puzzled as I felt. 'You have to take a step back here, Pelegon,' I said. 'Who is this Arcturus? And what do you mean by "the Darkness"?' The moment the words passed my lips, however, a suspicion was aroused. After all, how many different kinds of dark entities could this world hold?

'I believe I can answer that,' Selena replied in Pelegon's stead. 'Arcturus is one of the ruling lords, and is said to be a benevolent leader. I don't know much about him, however, since we don't concern ourselves too much with the world outside Eresa.'

'Lucky you,' Pelegon muttered. 'Trust me when I say that "benevolent" only concerns the *old* Arcturus, the one whose guard I joined. Or, you might call him "selectively benevolent" these days, because apparently it only applies to those who follow him like earthworms seeking fresh dirt. Without eyes to see his fall from grace, a mouth to speak about his disgusting lack of ethics, or ears to hear his victims scream, he might appear to foreigners as a benevolent leader. Not to us he doesn't.'

Hear his victims scream? I repeated inside my head. Pelegon read my thoughts from my face.

'You heard me, boy,' Pelegon said, giving me a nod, his memories reducing his eyes to slits. 'Arcturus is beyond reason, as are the other lords, none of whom have attempted to stop him.'

Again I looked back at Selena to see her reaction. She seemed to have lost all interest, though, and had returned to watching the sky for any sign of Ouranis. 'You were talking about the Darkness,' I told Pelegon. 'What do you know of it?' It was difficult to keep the eagerness for more information out of my voice, which Pelegon evidently didn't appreciate. He eyed me reluctantly.

'The same thing everybody does. What do you think ate the crew and the other prisoners?' He gave a nod towards the ship. 'A giant sea monster?' He let out a cynical laugh which ended in a rasping cough. His throat sounded so raw, I half expected his hand to hold more than just saliva when he withdrew it to stroke his neck.

A groan came from the girl. 'Father?'

'Sophia!' The man was suddenly on his knees again, adrenaline visibly putting his eyes back into focus.

A gasp from Selena made me look up. She was staring at the sky with both hands touching her belly. Her eyes were as large as rubies and her lips appeared to be moving on their own accord, though no sound came out.

There, diving under a mass of white cloud, was a ghostly figure with the silhouette of a predatory bird. It was still tiny, but, knowing it was so far away, my brain became confused by its impossible size. It was like seeing something that couldn't really exist according to nature's rules, yet was there nonetheless. Breaking free of the shadow of the cloud, the great Phoenix initiated her dive and, mere seconds later, disappeared out of sight behind the mountain peak.

'Selena, do you want to take a closer look?' I asked, pointing to the shoreline behind us.

'We will never be quick enough, Aaron,' she said with reverence in her eyes. She acted like she had just seen her personal deity, which, of course, she had in a way. 'Ouranis is already here.'

'How can you say that without even trying? Come on.'

I had barely taken a few steps when a great flapping of wings came rapidly closer. At its peak I could see two vast, feathery wings, silvery and translucent, appear on both sides of the tip of the volcano. Shortly after they had disappeared, the sound of daggers digging into a glass surface echoed towards us through the tunnel; Ouranis had arrived.

A muttered curse was forced from my mouth, generated by the rush of nerves that came stampeding up my legs and which grabbed my insides in a stranglehold. The imprint of the enormous wings I had just witnessed kept dancing before my eyes. *Is this really happening?*

When my eyes found Selena, she was staring straight back. At the periphery of my sight I saw Pelegon crawling closer to his daughter. He put his arm around her, a pained expression on his face. Sophia was looking at us instead. Her profile was strangely dispassionate; it was as though she had experienced so much pain, becoming a Phoenix's meal would only be a merciful end to a life of strife – perhaps even a blessing.

'What do you want to do?' I asked Selena in a whisper. My nerves were preventing my throat from speaking normally.

'We proceed as planned. Pelegon and Sophia's lives are not in danger, and they don't appear to be bleeding. We will wait for you here until you get back. What happens then will depend on Ouranis' reaction.'

'So you're not going with me after all? The ritual chose you, didn't it?'

'Don't tempt me, Aaron,' said Selena grimly. 'It is difficult enough as it is. I made a mistake earlier when I followed you inside. It is supposed to be you.'

I gave Selena hard, sceptical look, and said, 'This better be worth it.'

One foot at a time, and while keeping my shoulder pressed against one side of the cave, I made my way deeper into the Phoenix's den. The feeling of the rocky surface gave me a sense of security, so that I didn't feel so naked. My heart pounded. I kept swallowing, as though trying to prevent my heart from climbing up my throat and turning tail on its own. All the way I kept thinking of Denise and the need for us to learn the truth about what happened to the Shepherd's gift.

Every now and then I could hear sharp objects scraping against crystal. Something large and elongated moved in and out of sight in the distance. It was too indistinct to make out what it was, as the white and blue of the crystals behind it provided the perfect camouflage. Judging by its size and because the lines reminded me of feathers, I guessed it might be one of the Phoenix's wings.

I inched closer to the inner mouth of the tunnel. My heart suddenly sank and became as quiet as a skewered knight fallen in battle; the bundle of feathers I had spotted turned out to be only a part of her tail. She had to be enormous.

I finally made it to the inner mouth. Ouranis' feathered eyelids were half closed. Her entire demeanour reminded me of an old lady having returned from a long holiday. She was tilting her head this way and that and stretched her beak wide, a beak that seemed large enough to snatch up a mature grizzly bear with ease and gulp it down.

With a loud, echoing noise, her beak snapped closed. Then she shut her eyes completely, rubbed her wings against her enormous bulk, and sat down on the crystal floor in a typical, birdlike fashion. A few seconds passed in which I couldn't do anything but stare at her transparent body. Then a voice, female and gentle, entered my brain. It seemed to circumvent my ears entirely.

'Why have you come, druid?'

The voice took me completely by surprise. I had been watching Ouranis the entire time, and I was sure I hadn't seen her beak moving. Nor was there anyone else in the vicinity who could have voiced the words.

Not knowing whether to speak or to think my answer, I decided to send out my thoughts and hope for the best. *Sorry to disturb you, Great Ouranis,* I thought back. *My name is Aaron Bishop. Can you hear me?*

'Why have you come?' Ouranis repeated, the same patience coating her voice.

I apologise for this intrusion. I was sent here by Selena... I forgot her last name. I can't believe how hard it is to talk like this, I added to myself. *I mean, she is the real Shepherd of Eresa. The new one. We think something went wrong with their ritual and I may have received the Shepherd's abilities. So I have come to see if this is true.*

The Phoenix opened one languid eye. Then, with remarkable speed for such a huge creature, her head flicked towards me. My heart shrivelled and everything became numb. We locked eyes. For a spell that seemed to last for minutes we did nothing but stare at each other. Then without warning she lurched to her feet and shot forwards like a swan protecting her young.

My legs refused to comply with the screaming insistence of my brain to flee. On their own accord they *were* shifting backwards, but that was about all they could respond with. I felt paralysed, cold in every part of my body except my face, which felt like the only thing still working.

There was no word of reply from the charging Phoenix, nothing.

I'm sorry! I yelled without speaking. The words seemed to serve as a catalyst for my legs and they jerked into action. Seconds later I was already half way back through the tunnel, slipping as I went. As the light at the end of the tunnel came into view, a powerful gust of wind swept me off my feet, carried me the final stretch to the beach, and launched me belly-flat onto the water's surface like a skimming stone. During my flight I could just see the heads of Selena, Pelegon and Sophia, who followed my trajectory all the way until I hit the hard surface of the waves.

'You people are mad!' I heard Pelegon say as Selena dragged my soaked body across the pebbled beach.

'What happened, Aaron?' Selena asked, bending over and checking my head.

'Isn't it obvious?' I said contemptuously. 'I don't think she likes me too much.'

'I meant, what did she say? You didn't offend her in any way, did you?'

'What? No! I didn't do anything. I just told her the truth, that something had gone wrong and that I may have received those abilities. She probably didn't believe me, or...' A curse escaped through my lips. 'I knew this whole thing was a bad idea. I'm not the Shepherd and we're going back, now.'

Selena bit her lip thoughtfully. 'Yes, you are. If you were able to hear Ouranis' thoughts, you undoubtedly possess the Shepherd's gift. Perhaps we should try it again, together this time.'

'You've got to be kidding me. *Now* you want to come with me? Denise is running out of time. We have to go back.'

'Ouranis needs to know you are telling the truth,' Selena told me, clearly content that this served as an explanation. In a less assured voice, and with her gaze anxiously searching the cave entrance, she added, 'Perhaps I can convince her.'

I rolled back my eyes and stood up so quickly, I almost knocked Selena off her feet. 'If you think I'm going back in there with that thing, think again, Selena. There's no way. You didn't see her face as she came charging at me and chased me out of her den. If you had, you wouldn't be suggesting this, believe me.'

'Aaron...,' Selena said, almost pleading.

'No, I have enough. If you want to give it a shot, I wish you the best of luck. But I'm going back and get Denise out of that temple. When those druids come back from the forest, which is probably any minute now, they'll start their experiments!' My voice broke and I sniffed. My throat was stuck, my eyelids watered. I blinked and a tear rolled down my cheek. But my resolve was as steel. 'It's not her fault they turned her into a monster! And there's no way I'm going to let them do that to Denise. Not when I still have a breath left in me!'

Adrenaline was pumping through my veins. My heaving chest was refusing to calm down. Selena's profile showed both a mixture of respect for my resolve and a desire to indeed try her luck with Ouranis herself. After a moment of juggling with her options, she decided on neither, and instead walked over to the former prisoners.

'Pelegon, you said you knew something about the Darkness,' she said. 'How would you describe it?'

Pelegon looked at his daughter for a moment, as though asking for her permission. She gave him a quick glance, then closed her eyes and curved her lips downwards. 'It is evil at its purest,' Pelegon answered in a low voice. 'Nobody I know can tell you where it came from or how it came to be, but it seems to be able to change its shape according to its needs. As I told you, it's what attacked us on our way here.'

'In the form of hyenas?' I muttered, wiping my tears and silently cursing at the fact that I had allowed Selena to take the reins again. I continued to feel like a leaf caught in an autumn storm. My back was killing me too. It had taken quite the punishment.

'Why were you on the ship in the first place? Why did you rebel?' Selena immediately followed up, more logically.

Aided by a stern glance from Selena, Pelegon chose her question over mine. 'The resistance I later became part of staged an attack to convince Arcturus that there were other ways to fight the Darkness. But his mind was set. He had this whole speech about sacrificing one thing to gain another, to stop the violence in a *civilised* manner.' Pelegon chewed on the word "civilised" as though it was a bad date.

'As his guard, we were standing right next to him on the balcony, watching the people's faces turn,' he went on. 'I had never seen this much fear in anyone's eyes, let alone hundreds at the same time. We were all terrified. Something had to be done, we all knew that. But the more we fought, the stronger the Darkness seemed to become. And Arcturus was becoming more desperate by the day. I could see it in his eyes. They were like cornered rabbits every time he spoke about this evil.'

'Sophia's mother was chosen,' Pelegon pressed on now he still had a steady voice to speak. 'One of the guards who came to take her from our home was a friend of mine. I was prepared to fight him to the death. The anger...' He breathed out forcefully through his nostrils. 'I was spared because of my position as one of Arcturus' guards, but after the beating I took I was forced to watch helplessly how they carried her off. She was so brave, my Raisa. I haven't seen her since. That was when I joined the resistance. Arcturus thought he could keep off the Darkness and stop the onslaught by sacrificing some of us to save the rest, the fool,' he said, as though cursing his former Lord with every word he spoke. 'Of course it wouldn't work. Something as diabolical as the Darkness cannot be controlled, ever.'

I winced at these words and had to force myself not to launch into a retort, for Denise was one of *them* now, or something in between. And hearing a stranger like Pelegon talk about her in such a way was downright painful.

'If what you are saying is true,' said Selena severely, ignoring my discomfort as always, 'I wonder what this Darkness is doing all the way out here. It can hardly be attracted by the food supply.'

'Selena!' I snapped harshly. 'You're talking about the girl's mother.'

'It is quite all right, druid,' said Pelegon calmly. 'Sophia can handle it. She's tough like her mother.'

'If you say so,' I said, watching Sophia turn away her head. The girl hadn't shed a single tear since she arrived at the beach, which I guessed was either because she was still in shock, or simply that she had no tears left to give. 'And by the way, I'm no druid,' I added. 'In fact, my girlfriend is a prisoner as well.' Pelegon's eyebrows were almost touching his hairline. Even Sophia looked interested, despite her earlier lack of attentiveness. Selena shot me a look as though she was ready to send out her Phoenix to exact punishment. I returned it with one that spelled "try it you'll never see your precious gift again". 'It's the truth, isn't it?' I then said to her.

For a moment I was sure Selena was going to shout. Instead, she said in a surprisingly propitiatory tone, 'Then let us go back to Eresa and change it, Aaron. Your reconciliation with Ouranis will have to wait for another time.'

'You mean that?'

'Your only other option is to go back inside and try to receive your blessing from Ouranis. There is no other way to save Denise from the Council if the search party returns with damning evidence about the fate of the ritualists. Although I have to say, it will be difficult to prove you have her blessing without the Council actually seeing you enter her den. We might still have some time before the search party finds anything, however, if we are lucky. But these creatures, this Darkness, are probably still around here somewhere, because I doubt they have already found what they are looking for. This means it will only be a matter of time before the Council finds itself forced to take more drastic measures to gain information.'

'At the expense of Denise,' I said scornfully. Selena nodded. 'But you're sure you still want to help us? I can understand if you don't.'

'Like I said, we are in this together now, Aaron. The fact that you could get as close to Ouranis as you did and, again, were able to communicate, proves you do indeed possess the Shepherd's abilities.' She paused, then added in an emotional voice, 'Or it does to me. Anyway, since we don't have a way of convincing the Council that you have Ouranis' blessing, at least not yet, you need to take Denise away from Eresa and stay out of sight for a while until we know more about this 'Darkness', as well as the full extent of your abilities.'

'What about them?' I said with a nod to Pelegon and Sophia, who had been listening to the last part of our conversation in silence.

'That is for them to decide.'

'We cannot go home, even if we wanted to,' said Pelegon, looking at the ruined transport. 'Even if you gave us a ship, there is no place for us in the world anymore. After we escaped from Arcturus' dungeons, we managed to stow ourselves away on this transport. Then the black things attacked, and I hid the two of us in the shadows of one of the cells. They must have missed us. I think the screaming of the other prisoners and the crew drew the Darkness's attention away. And yet Sophia still kept her cool during this time.' He turned to his daughter with pride gleaming in his eyes. She didn't smile back. 'I managed to grab a few apples and a water jug one of the prison guards left behind when he was eaten, but that was the last bit of food or fresh water we have seen in over two days.'

'Do you know the original destination of this prison transport?' Selena asked.

'That's the thing,' said Pelegon ominously. 'They were being sent here.'

I looked at Selena, then asked, 'To Eresa?'

Pelegon nodded. 'The Sanctuary is not widely known among my people. Its existence is almost like a legend, a myth. The same goes for druids. Nor do I recall Arcturus ever sending people here. I'm sorry I can't tell you why he did it this time. He keeps his own counsel nowadays. And, like I said, my days of serving him are gone and wasted.'

'People that come here usually do so out of own volition,' said Selena. 'I am very surprised to hear this, Pelegon. Especially since Lord Arcturus does not have any authority over us. We are an autonomous society. It is therefore difficult to imagine any benefit to him if we would turn these prisoners, as you say, into druids.'

'Well, it's all a big mystery, then,' said Pelegon, giving Sophia a glance. 'And frankly, I don't really care. My only wish is for my daughter to be safe. Can you arrange that?'

'You shouldn't take the choice to enter the Sanctuary lightly, Pelegon,' Selena cautioned him. 'And neither should you, Sophia. My experience tells me that seeing how we live can be enticing. And once you choose to become a druid, which you will be asked to, there is no going back. Nobody leaves Eresa. In addition, since you have no transport of your own anymore – and we are not in a position to supply any – you cannot leave on your own.'

'We understand,' said Pelegon, his voice belonging to a man whose other options had been eliminated by fate.

'Uhm, Selena,' I said, 'I don't want to make this about me, but I worry about how this would impact my own problem. You know, Denise?'

Selena fell silent. Her eyes lingered on each of us in turn. 'I see what you mean, Aaron. If Pelegon and Sophia tell their life's story it would indeed incriminate Denise. Or so it would seem to the Council. However, I do not believe it would alter her fate too much if the search party has found any evidence against her anyway.' She took a long, hard look at Pelegon, then asked, 'Pelegon, can you keep a secret?'

The boat we used to cross over to the island of Ouranis seemed only just capable of carrying all four of us – three and a half if counted by size. But the thing that concerned me most during our journey back was the increasing amount of sweat that was drenching Selena's forehead. It told me she hadn't yet recuperated from our last trip through the waves. Add to that the extra weight of Pelegon and Sophia – as well as the current, which seemed to be carrying us south instead of east – and I found myself contemplating my options for a backup plan. But aside from a cold dip, the only option was using the planks we were sitting on as paddles.

Pelegon and Sophia had no eyes for Selena's sweaty brow or, indeed, for makeshift paddles they could potentially kick loose if needed. Both pairs of eyes glinted with lines of blue and silvery light and their mouths were transfixed in expressions of awe; this was obviously the first time they had the privilege of seeing a phoenix from up this close. For me it was definitely a treat as well. Although after seeing the original version of Ouranis, I could see why Selena said that her phoenix wasn't entirely perfect.

'We made it,' I heard Selena breathe when we were a few yards from the shore. The moment the words had left her mouth her entire demeanour changed and her body crumpled as though hit by a tranquiliser gun. She rested her elbows on her knees to prevent her chest from hitting the floor of the boat, while her phoenix evaporated into silvery wisps. Seconds later, to my back's dismay, the boat ploughed into the bank of the main island.

We hadn't headed straight for the docks, as that would probably have been too taxing for Selena in her current state. Instead, aided by the current, she had brought us to a place further down the island to the south. I was first to jump out of the boat, then Selena. Next was Sophia, supported by her father in the back and my outstretched hand.

One of her tiny sandals was at the edge of the boat, and I could see Sophia's muscles contract in preparation of the jump. At that moment, a great splash and a forceful hissing sound made her grip my hand so tightly, the tendons in my fingers popped painfully. Into view came the massive head and body of a great, pitch black anaconda. It had reared up out of the water at the other end of the boat and was shaving the vessel's starboard side, aiming for my throat. As it did so, the now familiar black filth from its skin flowed into the boat.

My brain froze. At the same time, an adolescent scream pounded my eardrums and my knees collided painfully with the wooden hull; Pelegon had pulled his daughter back into the boat and, in doing so, me along with her. A giant muzzle snapped shut mere inches from my face, yet remained there like a grim statue. The whole scene froze.

The head of the snake, mouth wide and fangs bared, was hanging motionless inches from mine. Waves of the dark grease were continuing to ooze from each of its features, including its dagger-like fangs and its blue eyeballs. The snake's neck was being held in place by the beak of Selena's phoenix, which had sprouted from its master's chest. Selena was standing wide-eyed, panting heavily, with both her hands in a praying position.

My own eyes and the blazing ones of the snake locked. When they did, the snake's mouth opened again and a hiss escaped that carried such force, its forked tongue vibrated uncontrollably. There was a groan of effort from Selena, then both the anaconda and her phoenix disappeared in slithers of black and silver. Selena slumped sideways and landed on the wispy grass, looking exhausted.

'Sophia,' said a worried Pelegon. 'She fainted.'

I reached down to help hoist Sophia out of the boat, but she was already stirring. Pelegon gave a sigh of relief and whispered, 'The Darkness, it must have followed us.'

'No, Pelegon, it was already here,' I told him. 'In fact, we shouldn't be out here at all,' I added accusingly to Selena.

'There is time to point fingers later, Aaron,' said Selena, still recumbent and trying to catch her breath. I offered her a hand, but she refused. Then with another deep intake of air, she rose to her feet again. 'We need to move, now.'

'Father,' said Sophia promptly, 'look.' She was pointing in the direction of Ouranis' den.

We watched as half way between us and the island, black fins rose up from the water's surface. Instead of swimming towards us, however, the fins began to dissolve into smaller creatures which, after forming, congregated into an elephantine swarm of bats. The combination of their tiny bodies and their wildly flapping wings made the bats as indistinguishable from one another as raindrops in a storm. The alarming rate at which the cloud grew told me that the anaconda was but the scout of a much bigger army.

'Run, everyone!' said Selena. 'Quickly!'

In a mad dash we began racing up the shore as fast as our feet could carry us. Even the exhausted Selena seemed to have been injected fresh energy: after seeing the cloud of death amassing above the stretch of water, her second-wind was quite astounding.

'It's coming for us!' Pelegon called from the back. 'Grab my hand, Sophia!' Next thing I knew both he and Sophia were passing me with bounding strides, purpose etched in Pelegon's profile. His daughter Sophia appeared to have only half her mind focused on the present, though. The other half was evidently somewhere I couldn't follow.

The swarm of bats rapidly closed the gap. By the time they reached the shore behind us and spun in uncanny unison towards us, I could already sense our speed faltering; the adrenaline fuelling my companions' legs was beginning to dissipate, replaced by lactic acid. With one hand pushing against Selena's back I watched how black, dog-sized blobs dropped down from the dark cloud that was pursuing us. It was like watching a storm cloud raining giant, inky hailstones onto the grassy beach.

One by one the shapeless masses met the grass. As though hitting the ground running, black panthers shot out of the grimy blobs the moment their claws met solid ground, their blue eyes burning with hunger and a thick ribbon of dark smoke trailing from each of their tails. With a jolt I realised that the creatures must have some strange, hive-like connection with the bats' minds; they knew exactly in which direction to continue their pursuit.

I turned my head back and closed my eyes, if only for a moment. The fear was overwhelming. With every passing second, the rapid sounds of light paws hitting the grassy bank behind us became more and more distinct. I pressed my hand a little harder into the small of Selena's back, so as to prevent her from flagging. The closer I got to the blonde woman, the louder and more laboured her panting was becoming.

'Selena, it's no use,' I told her between breaths. 'We can't outrun them.'

'Into the woods,' she said in a ragged response, followed up by a huge gulp of air.

'Good idea,' I said. 'Pelegon, the woods! Go!'

Pelegon glanced back over his shoulder. At the sight of the panthers pursuing us his eyes shot open and he jumped into the first opening he could find, half dragging Sophia through a caper bush. As he did so, the bush exploded into a fountain of white petals. I had no choice but to follow them and push Selena right into the gloom beyond.

A few seconds of confusion followed, there were leaves and branches everywhere. Once we were free of the dense band of vegetation and the forest opened up, the light thudding of footsteps behind us changed to claws raking through grassy roots; the panthers had seen us change tactics.

I couldn't see Pelegon or Sophia anymore. Now my entire shoulder was boring into Selena's back and I literally had to push her up the hill. Fatigue was getting the best of her. Behind me I could hear the pack of panthers crashing through the underbrush with unearthly growls. I knew our only chance of getting out of the woods alive was to distract them, but asking Selena to summon one was no use.

'Sophia!' Pelegon's voice sounded from up ahead. Then a shattering of bark and a splintering of tree trunks came thundering down the hill.

Selena yelled and launched herself sideways. I felt a hand on my robe. She pulled me down with her, but I was just in time to see a spectral water buffalo stampeding down the trail the four of us were following. As it passed us to scatter the panthers like bowling pins, thick, red liquid I recognised as blood coated one of its translucent horns.

'Captain Kriton,' Selena sighed into my ear. Her voice carried both vexation and a hint of relief.

Now the danger had subsided I realised I was lying on top of her, and quickly dug my hands into the earth to relieve her of my weight.

'Who?'

'The search parties,' she explained in a whisper, closing her eyelids and swallowing hard. 'They're still here. Bless the Goddess.'

Someone was running down the hill with reckless abandon. As his large bulk flashed by, I saw that the man was keeping his hands steady, while a silvery blue thread of energy connected his palms like a chain. The man's wide grin was dripping with delight, teeth showing. More people followed, but they were less reckless, and dug their heels into the ground to control their speed.

'We need to let him know we're here,' said Selena, pushing herself up with her elbows. As an entire search party had just ran by, I reckoned that the "him" was she was talking about was this Kriton fellow. 'Aaron, please.'

Confused, I helped Selena to her feet. She looked as if she had just survived a date with a vampire. 'Pelegon, Sophia!' she called as loud as her breath allowed. 'This way!'

When father and daughter appeared, it was like experiencing an unusual kind of déjà vu. This time it was Sophia carrying her father's arm around her shoulders, and it was Pelegon who looked as if he had one leg already in the afterlife. A blood stain, one as large as a grapefruit and still growing, was colouring Pelegon's chest. I immediately connected the stain to the blood on the stampeding buffalo's horn.

'Oh, no. How bad is it?' I asked Sophia, as it seemed that asking Pelegon would be pointless in his current state.

'I don't know,' she said tearfully, her eyelids refusing to open completely. 'He... he pushed me aside when he saw that creature coming. It's my fault.'

'No, don't say that,' I said consolingly.

'His wound will have to wait,' said Selena. 'We have to hurry. Sophia, if you want to stay here until we get back, it's okay. But I need you to be very quiet, all right?'

'What's up with you?' I snapped at Selena. 'We can't leave them here. He's bleeding. We need to get him some help.'

'I know that, Aaron. I will explain later. But first, come with me.'

'We'll be back, I promise,' I told Sophia. After uttering a grunt of disapproval, I reluctantly complied.

Once we broke free of the forest, I found myself stunned by yet another confrontation. The black panthers, about a dozen in total, were locked in a stalemate between them on one side and Kriton and his water buffalo on the other. Backs bent and ears flat, the group of panthers was slowly circling the man, their muscles stiff from anticipation. While doing so, the dark secretion that oozed from their hides began to fuse together. It formed a ring of black fog around Kriton that, seconds later, was already threatening to shield him from view. The rest of the search party was standing a little to my right, doing nothing but watch.

Selena was shaking her head, a curious look on her face.

'Hey, why aren't they helping him?' I asked her.

She shot me a glance, then said in a defeated voice, 'Aaron, meet Captain Kriton. He is the captain of the Bovine clan. He must've told the others to keep their distance.'

'What? That's insane! There are like six of them.'

'Do yourself a favour and don't tell him that, Aaron,' Selena said earnestly. 'Captain Kriton is not the most forgiving among us, nor accommodating, even amongst his own. To call him insane could be a fatal mistake. Captain Kriton lives for one thing and for one thing only: fighting. And if anyone, including druids from his own clan, poses a hindrance to him, he would go through them like one of the bulls they venerate. It has happened before.'

As I looked into Captain Kriton's face, which was the only part left of him I could still see in detail, there was a thirst for blood and a hunger for competition you would only expect from a psychopath. His eyes were almost burning with pleasure as he sized up the competition, while his single water buffalo was doing its best to keep two of the panthers from closing the circle completely.

'Can't you give him a hand from here?' I asked. 'You can use that phoenix of yours.' In a smaller voice, I added, 'What if he loses?'

Selena didn't return my glance. Her face was hard and focused on the battle. 'He'd be satisfied.'

None of the spawn of darkness had eyes for us. With a snarling growl, one of the panthers leapt, aiming for Kriton's back. I watched its dark figure and blazing eyes arc through the air through the semi-transparent fog. Its companions responded a splintered second later.

There was a moment in which the thread of blue energy flowing between Kriton's palms intensified. The light emanating from the thread lit up the ring of black mist that surrounded him. And from his body, four more massive water buffaloes came charging out in different directions, their blocky heads lowered, and their glowing horns pointed forwards, ready to impale flesh.

As the buffaloes smashed through the encircling fog, the neatly skewered bodies of panthers jerked spasmodically on their horns. The panthers then lost cohesion and dissolved, with the buffaloes, their task completed, disappearing soon after. Lacking enough of the strange oily darkness to remain intact, the ring of fog shrank like a magician's curtain. There stood Captain Kriton, his teeth clenched and a wide, malicious grin on his face.

More of the mist vanished. My jaw dropped. Kriton, panting with fatigue, yet still appearing to have the time of his life, had two of the panthers hanging down from his corded shoulders. The errant felines had apparently made it through the counterattack of stampeding buffaloes and had seemingly buried their fangs into the ample flesh on Kriton's bones. Even as I watched, my brain was screaming at the druids to help their friend. But Selena's earlier warnings made me hold my tongue, and also, I was too concerned with any more panthers that could be lurking behind the treeline.

With a groan of defiance, Kriton thrust his muscular arms behind his back, somehow grabbed them by their spines, ripped them loose from his shoulders and sent them airborne. He then slammed his hands together with a resounding clap and a sixth buffalo came charging out of his chest. The buffalo dispatched the panthers with a single swing of its head, the duo uttering piercing snarls that I could feel running down the entire length of my body. The remaining slivers of darkness retreated back to the sea and all fell silent.

'I received a soft hand on my arm and I looked sideways into Selena's eyes. 'Look at his shoulders,' she said.

I did and, incredibly, witnessed a pair of buffalo horns, each sprouting from one of Kriton's shoulders; despite not knowing what he was up against, or perhaps because of it, Kriton had taken no chances. By using his spiritcraft, the Bovine captain had summoned a pair of buffalo horns to act as shields against the panthers' poisonous fangs. In unison, they evaporated.

At that moment, a pair of blue dots appeared in the corner of my eye. After what happened with Denise, it seemed that my eyes had become attuned to them, for I was the first to notice. 'Selena, look out!' With that I thrust my shoulder into her ribs, trying to force her out of the monster's way. In mid-flight, I heard a feline growl, a rustling of leaves, and saw a black shadow leap from the undergrowth. Selena and I hit the ground, my heart pumping in my throat.

Yells erupted and all around us, hands were clapped together in preparation for the druids' magic. I felt the beast's paws press down on my back and the next moment, there was an explosion of black ash behind me. Even as I lay on top of the startled Selena, I felt the grime from the defeated panther flow across my back and into my robes. To my left, a blue and translucent figure in the shape of a goat continued its charge for a few yards, then vanished; one of the other druids had saved us. As I watched the goat disappear into thin air, my ears slowly tuned in to Selena's breathing.

'That was close. Are you all right?' I asked.

'I am, thank you,' said Selena, studying me. It was as though, briefly, I had allowed her access to my emotions, which were previously stowed away in a metaphorical jar and sealed with my devotion towards Denise. I quickly shut them away again. *I have to stay focused.* Over at the shoreline, Kriton was looking at the lapping waves. A small smile curved my lips, cutting through the rush of adrenaline, then I whispered, 'And I always thought buffaloes were herd animals.'

Chapter 5

I was lying on my back, staring vacantly at the ceiling. I had tried to close my eyes a few times, but every time I did, my drowsiness induced flashbacks of events I didn't want to relive. Denise's transformation, my attempt at invoking the Shepherd's abilities, my disastrous meeting with Ouranis, being chased up the beach by monstrous spawn of darkness, it all appeared like a nightmare I was unable to wake up from.

The stretch of white marble I was looking at was rapidly turning a darker shade as twilight crept its way into Denise's cell – or quarters as Selena so comfortingly called them. Beside the bed lay an empty plate. Bits of fruit and cooked vegetables dotted its surface; I had no stomach for carrots or grapefruit. I never had.

I let my head fall down to the side. Denise was lying curled up at the other end of the room, her body completely obscured by the nimbus of dark secretion around her. I had willingly locked myself up in here, not only as a comfort to her, but also to give me another chance at connecting with her mind. Unfortunately, I had yet to see any sign of whether this was even possible.

After hours of trying I was forced to conclude that either her thoughts were too alien for me to penetrate, or whatever happened with the spectral squirrels back on the island of Delos had merely been a fluke. Once we made it back to Eresa we had split up in different directions. I had sped to the temple for a chance to try what I had learnt about my abilities on Denise. Once I entered her cell, however, something had changed inside her. I could feel it.

She wasn't aggressive or anything of that nature, but there was a distance in the way she behaved and looked at me that wasn't noticeable before. The first thing that entered my mind was that she blamed me for what happened to her, or perhaps she was just angry at me for leaving her behind to go with Leander and enjoy a tour around the Sanctuary. But if that were true, it wasn't like her. The real Denise, whose personality I had to believe still resided somewhere inside that hyena body, wasn't one to bear a grudge like that. Quite the opposite in fact. If she had somehow retained her vocal chords, I reckoned she would have urged me to find out as much as possible about this strange world we found ourselves stranded in. She wouldn't want me to stay with her and start crying over spilt milk, she would want me to fight, to search, and to never stop trying. That's the kind of girl she was. That's the girl I loved.

Currently, while part of my brain was busy interpreting the many shapes it could discern in the cloud of black smoke surrounding Denise, another part of me was pondering on a different, much more worrying explanation. I thought back to the moment just before Denise's transformation and tried to focus on the cause of her fate, not on what happened to her body afterwards. Then I thought back at what Selena had said about the difference between Denise's behaviour and that of Adrastus, the druid we had seen turn into a dark hyena in front of the temple.

Even she had acknowledged that Denise seemed to be more in control of herself than the druid had been. This, combined with the fact that Denise had received only a minor injury on her finger by the hyena that bit her, made me think that perhaps Denise's transformation had not been complete when I last saw her. In fact, for all I knew it could still be going on inside her. Perhaps her mind took longer to convert than her body.

As I watched her lying there, for a fleeting moment I thought I could see blue dots lighting up within the grimy secretion. I felt my stomach twist once, then a second time as a lock turned and the cell door swung open. Selena, her long, blonde hair cascading over her shoulders and her face frozen half way through a frenzy, was standing in the light as it came flooding in. Her forehead was wet and her eyes troubled.

'Aaron, Aristion's back,' she whispered. Even though her voice was soft, the message pulled me back to the here and now with the force of a steam engine. 'He was among the team of ritualists that was attacked. Aaron, he knows about the Darkness. You two need to get her out of here, now!'

Looking completely unconcerned and moving in slow motion, Denise's head emerged from the nimbus of black smoke. Judging by the way she was eyeing the scene I half expected her to stick out her tongue at Selena, cover the floor in a lot of drool, and go back to sleep. Instead she slowly turned her glowing eyes to me as though interested in my reaction.

I jumped to my feet. 'One of the ritualists is here? How? Why now?'

'Never mind that. You need to hurry. Before the Council connects his story to their prisoner.' With her hand Selena indicated Denise, who had, seemingly reluctantly, stood up and was now making her way towards me. Her rumbling growl told me she sensed that something was wrong, though she could also be disapproving of Selena's presence. 'And Captain Kriton should already have informed the rest of the Council of his encounter as well,' she added.

'But where will we go?'

'I have arranged transport,' said Selena. 'Please, we don't have much time.'

'All right, lead the way. I'll take Denise.'

'I have sent the guards to the main entrance,' said Selena as we entered the empty corridor. 'Being the Shepherd does have its advantages. My lie won't keep them there for long, I'm afraid. This way.'

We took a right and sped on. 'I'm glad to see you're enjoying *my* new position,' I said meaningfully.

Selena glanced back over her shoulder with a smirk on her face; she had no trouble decrypting my comment. 'I suppose we will have to share our Shepherd responsibilities for the time being, Aaron. That is, if you are inclined to consent to this proposal,' she added pompously.

I snorted. The acoustics of the marble temple made it appear so loud that I slapped a hand to my mouth to prevent another from escaping.

Selena started and grabbed my wrist so my hand stayed where it was, and I remained silent. 'Quiet! There is someone here,' she whispered. Our corridor-eating strides were instantly reduced to a delicate, almost tiptoeing walk. I felt Denise hit the inside of my knee with her head and heard her retreat at once, scraping her nails across the floor and again growling her disapproval.

Selena offered us a fleeting, angry look before turning back to the hallway before us. My heart was pounding in my ears, making it hard to hear anything but a rhythmic thumping. For a short spell nothing happened and Selena slowly began to speed up again. She had released my wrist, but she kept her hand dangling in front of me to stop me if needed. It also served as a silent command to keep quiet.

Then a voice came echoing down the hallway, young and female. 'I didn't ask you to come. I only wanted to see him once. He should be around here somewhere. Mother said he was staying in one of the guest quarters near the library.'

All three of us, even Denise, kissed the wall with our shoulders, frozen. *Guest quarters with a lock, you mean,* I corrected the unknown woman in silence.

Selena pursed her lips and indicated with her finger that mine should remain shut. 'It's Aerope. An Avian.' As I had no idea what an "Avian" was, my eyebrows fused together into a frown. 'Bird clan,' Selena added in minor annoyance for my ignorance. 'It means trouble.'

Of course it does, I added in annoyance. *Why would anything go our way?*

'Did Captain Cyrene say they were going to offer him a cleansing?' a deeper, masculine voice followed up. 'I know it's standard procedure, but he is from the homeland. I mean to say…'

'Not for at least a couple of days,' said Aerope. 'I don't think the Council will perform a cleansing so soon after the Shepherd's ceremony, and that is supposed to be tomorrow. I hope Selena is ready for it. Zeuxis always had our best interests at heart, but I think we could use a new wind blowing through Eresa. Don't you think?'

I could only just see two bodies appear around the corner when another, more familiar voice halted them in their tracks. It was Peleus, one of Lycomedes' students and, being a future member of the Canine clan, the very person I had unwittingly offended by comparing Denise with a dog.

'Aerope, what a coincidence,' said Peleus, his voice easily carrying through the corridor. 'I was hoping for a word.'

'Peleus?' said Aerope, evidently surprised.

Peleus came into view as he stepped out from the opposite end of the T-junction. When he spoke next, he sounded quite a bit less confident than his strides made him appear to be. 'Yes. I was on my way to see your captain, because I was hoping she could clear something up for me about the Shepherd ceremony. Perhaps you can help me instead.'

For some reason Peleus kept speed to his strides, passed between Aerope and her male companion, and chose the fork Aerope and the other man had just ventured from. As he disappeared out of sight, Aerope and the other man both had to turn their backs to us if they wanted to continue the conversation, which Peleus was insisting on.

'What is he doing here?' I heard Selena whisper to herself. 'He was supposed to be waiting for us at the exit.' Turning to us, she added quietly, 'This is our chance. Come with me.'

I glanced back at the clearly still disgruntled Denise, who only had eyes for Selena, after which we followed the blonde all the way to the end of the T-junction and the talking trio. Peleus, Aerope and her companion didn't seem to notice us due to the intensity of their conversation. By the sound of it Peleus was only a few seconds away of receiving a kick in the family jewels when we took a right and proceeded down the short hallway to the open door at the end. Greyish moonlight came flooding in through the doorway, which meant that this would be the last stretch before we tasted the late night air.

I indicated for Denise not to fall too far behind. She seemed to be struggling between a choice of either coming with us, or doing something I didn't even want to consider.

A curse suddenly bounced our way across the hallway, carried by Peleus' voice. 'Selena, watch it! They've spotted you! I'm…!'

'What is this?!' Aerope's male companion roared, drowning Peleus' voice. 'Is that the Shepherd, and the prisoner? I knew something wasn't right the second I saw you, Peleus!' The sound of flesh hitting flesh pierced the air and Peleus let out a cry of pain. 'Aerope, assist me. We can't let them escape.'

As I looked over my shoulder, Peleus was on the ground with both hands covering his face. The man standing over him had his hands pressed together in a praying position. Aerope stood perplexed, her wide eyes locked onto me, her expression confused. Her arms, which she had raised out of instinct, fell down to her sides.

'Aaron, against the wall!' said Selena. Her command jerked me right back to reality. The next second I was sharing my space with a man-sized phoenix, which launched itself at Aerope and her companion like an ostrich gone wild. The sight was remarkably similar to seeing Ouranis' charging at me, but in miniature and reverse.

When Selena's phoenix arrived at the intersection behind us, it flapped its wings forwards, pushed itself up from the marble floor with its claws, and enveloped Aerope and the man with its wings in an imprisoning hug. The lumpy package of the druids wrapped in the unyielding, see-through body of the phoenix fell to the ground. Peleus, still recuperating from the punch in the face, was just in time to roll away to avoid getting crushed.

I received a hit to the shoulder. 'Run, Aaron!' said Selena. 'Master is waiting for us at the shoreline.' We immediately continued our dash.

With the sun having tucked in for the night, the waxing moon had taken over. The backdoor of the temple lead us to a path that cut straight through the forest and branched out at odd intervals to other parts of the island. Here, the landscape was a lot different from the simple green and brown of the parts of Eresa I had seen thus far. It was neat and abundant with flowers, as though we were running through a king's well-tended garden as opposed to anything formed wholly by nature. I imagined that, if not for the scarcity of light and our haste, it would have been quite a sight.

We arrived at a blossoming tree sprouting from a mound of rocks in the middle of the road when a voice turned my stomach upside down once more. Its nerves-inducing power was astounding. 'Even the Shepherd is not above our laws, Selena!'

I looked back and saw the same man closing in on us with Aerope at his side. Also bounding after us was a pair of spectral jackals, controlled by the bruised and bloodied Peleus, who was lagging behind, his hands pressed together and his expression fixed in concentration. Selena came to a slipping halt and I followed suit. It was still a long way to go to the island's edge, which I couldn't even see from our position.

'Leave us be, Lydus!' said Selena. 'What we're doing is important. It doesn't concern you.'

Lydus' eyes flashed. 'Important enough for the new Shepherd to act against our laws on her first day? Think about what you're doing, *Shepherd*. Do you even know these outsiders?'

Aerope, slightly behind him, seemed to want to say something, but held her peace. She couldn't keep her eyes off me. Peleus' jackals arrived and took position, like bookends, on opposite sides of Lydus and Aerope. Lydus paid them the same amount of attention he did to the star-filled night sky. My gaze alternated between him and Aerope. My desire to shift attention from Denise, and perhaps offer a distraction for Selena, was fuelling my courage.

'What laws do you speak of?' I asked Lydus. 'I thought you people weren't in the habit of taking prisoners.'

'Aaron, don't,' said Selena, her voice brittle, but angry. 'Just because we don't often use them doesn't mean we do not have laws for situations like this. Now please, let me handle this.' In a barely audible voice, she added, 'When I say run, you take her and run. Understood?'

Lydus' eyes narrowed. 'You're not only cutting them loose, but now you are conspiring with them as well, Shepherd? Where's your pride, Selena?'

'I told you, this does not concern you, Lydus,' said Selena. 'Go back and I will explain everything once I have dropped them off.'

'You can explain it to me now or directly to the Council when you return. Those are your options. The decision is yours.'

Even from this distance I could hear Selena swallow. Aerope, clearly torn, still seemed to be stuck somewhere between action and inaction. The night was silent, feeding my fear that this breakout was a very bad idea.

Like old light bulbs blinking their last, the two spectral jackals winked out of existence, causing a thin blanket of darkness to cover the scene; when they disappeared, the light that had been beaming from their hides went with them. Behind Aerope and Lydus, the thin sheet of energy between Peleus' palms had now disappeared as well. His attention had clearly shifted from the drama in front of him to the blood pouring from his nose, which had changed from a trickle to a gushing flow.

The decrease in light didn't do Lydus' haughty, slightly equine face any favours. It could have been carved out of an oaken branch for amount of humanity it displayed. He lifted his head, causing him to look literally, as well as metaphorically, down his aquiline nose at us. 'Is this what Zeuxis gave his life for?' he barked. The words tasted foul. 'You're not even really one of us, are you, Shepherd? Just like your master.'

'Lydus…,' said Aerope in a weak, yet reproachful voice. Her eyes had finally turned away from my face.

'You leave my master out of this, Vespine!' Selena snapped back at Lydus, silencing Aerope. 'You know nothing of Lycomedes' reasons for not joining the Viperines. His intentions are just as pure as that of any druid in Eresa. And, for your information, there is more to joining a clan than teaming up with people that happen to have chosen the same type of animal.'

'Happen to have chosen?' Lydus repeated derisively, chewing on every word. 'My, my, Shepherd. Aren't you the perfect person to bring the true spirit of our druid ancestors to the surface?' Slowly he began to raise his hands and brought them level with his chest. While doing so, and without displaying even the tiniest amount of emotion, he said, 'You may not have chosen a clan just yet, but I think you know what a vice captain is capable of. Or don't you?' The moment his last word left his lips, a thick thread of blue, pulsing energy exploded into being between his hands. His entire face lit up and his lips locked to form an impassive, horizontal line.

Aerope, Selena and I all took a step backwards. The girls' eyes met, Selena's requesting aid and Aerope's, for reasons of her own, powerlessly denying it. Half a dozen yards behind Lydus, Peleus returned his attention to us once more as he slowly withdrew his hands from his face. His face was livid.

Selena's whisper tickled my ear. 'Run.'

The word sent a jolt into my legs that stirred every single one of my muscles into action. Then Denise and I bolted, shouting, 'We're not leaving without you, Selena! You better come after us!'

'No one leaves without the Council's consent, outlander!' Lydus' voice thundered after Denise and me as we sprinted under the blossoming tree and resumed our dash along the garden path.

Selena let out a scream that swam through the trees in all directions. 'NOOOO! AARON!'

A buzzing sound of hundreds upon hundreds of bees swarming up behind me arose. Looking over my shoulder, a blue and silvery cloud of insects, every single one of their tiny wings twinkling in the moonlight, was congregating for a feeding frenzy. Denise saw them too. She let out a yelp as though she could already feel the ghostly stingers pumping poison, or whatever else they were hiding inside their translucent venom glands, into her behind. She instantly doubled her speed, leaving me labouring to keep up.

The static noise generated by the bees became louder and louder. By now it was loud enough to drown any shouts from Selena and the other druids. It also made it impossible for me to surrender, as no one would be able to hear it. Soon I could see a small opening in the distant trees behind which, hopefully, safety stretched towards the horizon in the form of the open sea. But even if the edge of the island was really as close as it seemed and Lycomedes was indeed waiting to pick us up, I knew I had marshmallow's chance on a barbecue to make it that far.

There was only ten feet left between me and a thousand glowing stingers. My mind could do nothing but focus on the potential pain of the incoming machine gun drilling into my back, as I imagined this was what it would feel like to have each of those tiny needles boring into my flesh. There was six feet left and my legs started to become numb with dread. There was two feet left and I could feel my chest inching forwards to try to postpone the moment of impact. My entire body was prickling in fear.

In the final moments, my eyes closed. Cold sweat mixed with tears seeped down my cheeks. Then the din of a thousand insect wings exploded: the swarm had split up moments before hitting me. Fear stricken and with limbs flailing, I opened my eyes again and watched how the two swarms passed me, then merged together in front of me. I came to a scraping halt and immediately started backing away from the menacing mass of glittering creatures.

Not knowing where to go or what to do, I braved a look behind me and saw Selena sprinting towards me. What was happening behind her was hidden behind her body.

Suddenly the buzzing sound intensified and the swarm split up again like a pair of guards jumping aside to avoid the slash of a sword. It wasn't any mediaeval weaponry that was threatening them, however. It was something much older, or at least one part of it. Emitting the unearthly, high-pitched howl only a hyena can produce, Denise came charging in through the separating halves of twinkling lights, snapping left and right as she went. As the summoned insects fell prey to Denise's jaws, the victims vanished into slivers of blue and silver, which snaked through Denise's fangs and were lost to the night air.

'Denise! Thank God!' Everything inside me was itching to throw open my arms and catch her in a well-deserved hug. But even if I had done so, Denise probably would not have noticed it; she appeared to have gone into a blinding rage.

'Go, Aaron, go!' said Selena. Looking back, I saw that Selena was almost upon me, her hands pressed together, preparing to summon another phoenix. 'I'm right behind you!'

With no time for second thought I sped to Denise, who was still snapping wildly to keep the swarm away from her back. I passed her, back bent and my head tucked between my shoulders, yelling, 'Denise, let's go!'

The flapping of wings, and a scattering of leaves yielding to the might of Selena's phoenix, drowned out all noise. It reduced the thrumming of the bees to nothing but a minor annoyance. As soon as it emerged, the phoenix obediently began its assault on the swarm. My heart lifted. With each well-aimed lunge of the phoenix, Selena drove the bees higher into the air. It was like seeing a sheepherder commanding his dog to drive his flock up the slope of a hill.

Lydus' voice reached us from far in the distance. 'The Council will never approve of you, Shepherd! My captain will make sure of that! Zeuxis must have made a mistake! It's over, you hear me?'

A sudden flash bathed the surrounding forest in blue light. The buzzing coming from above became magnified to a tinnitus-inducing extent. I looked up at the phoenix surrounded by bees and over the next few seconds, the number of insects increased exponentially. My eyelids climbed up as if trying to retreat into my skull. The muscles in my face contracted, squeezing all blood down into my body. My skin was tingling all over again.

A growl and a toothy snap came from below; Denise was trying to attract my attention. I glanced down at her, shook my head to get rid of the fuzziness, looked back at Selena and said, 'You can't win against that, Selena! Hurry!'

Selena looked on the verge of collapse. She was labouring for oxygen, chest heaving like a bellows. Her blonde hair was flapping behind her in the wind, while some inner strands were glued to her neck. As I was watching her, now dashing madly from the multiplying swarm, she released her hands, severing the connection between them to focus on running. Instantly, her phoenix vanished.

As though joined at the hips, the three of us ran, Denise's tongue dangling from the side of her mouth. Lydus must have realised his words had no power over us anymore. Now swollen to over four times its previous size, he finally deemed his swarm ready to continue the attack and sent it into pursuit once more.

I cursed angrily; having recently only barely escaped from the bats, we were now being pursued by yet more magical flying entities. *I can't believe this. Why is he doing this? And against his own people?*

The swarm was closing the gap at an alarming rate. It would be only seconds before they would floor us, the druids would detain us, and cage us like criminals. And with the ritualist Aristion now back in Eresa, and his story about to become public, it would only be a matter of time before my Denise would be subjected to the druids' experimentation. My brain was beginning to feel light and drowsy. It was as though my mind was trying to lull me to sleep as though in an attempt to shut itself down as an escape method, or perhaps it was simply recognising the hopelessness of the situation and was giving up.

'We will never make it, not like this,' I heard Selena mutter to herself between laboured breaths. 'I need to… connect…'

Connect... connect... connect... Selena's words kept dancing around in my head like a siren's song. They bounced and pivoted; as though trying to lure me away from the scene, and I was glad to follow. I longed for anything to take my mind away from here. Then a flash of blue, bright and blinding, ignited in my mind. Selena's words had triggered something, something ancient and unfamiliar. And, without the need for a conscious thought, the path before us became clear again, perfectly clear in fact. I was here, I was alive, and I wanted nothing more than it to stay like that.

My body felt as light as a feather. My eyes were fixated on the road before me. Then curiously enough, I felt my hands or feet, I didn't know which, grab hold on something. Wind was rushing against my face more forcefully than ever. The sensation of moving at an impossible speed washed over me. At the same time, the vegetation to my left and right lost all detail and became reduced to nothing but ribbons of colour.

The opening in the forest ahead sped towards me with near inhuman speed. There was a gap in the low wall that circled the island. Lycomedes, dressed in white and an expression of shock etched in his lined face, was waiting for us. He had a lit oil lamp in his hand and was standing on the back of one of his spectral crocodiles. His mouth was hanging open, gaping at... me.

It was as though the entire scene, the gap in the wall, Lycomedes on his crocodile, and the moonlit sea beyond, was rammed into my face like a boxer's glove. At least that was how it felt before all lights went out and my world was turned into one of darkness, silence and sleep.

Chapter 6

Through the gloom, Lycomedes' low, raspy voice touched my eardrums. 'Yes, curious indeed. If I hadn't been fortunate enough to see it with my own eyes, I wouldn't have believed it either, Selena. Although I have to say, stranger things have happened.'

'They have?' asked Selena. 'Like what?'

'Like the fact that we managed to get here in one piece, as one of them. This Darkness must still be around here somewhere. I have no doubt about that. Not after the encounter you had with that snake this afternoon, and the rest of them.'

A short silence followed, then, 'How is your chest feeling, Master?'

'Cracked a few ribs,' said Lycomedes, audibly shrugging the thought away. 'The shoulder is worse. Old age, you know? Weak skin.'

The scraping of Denise's claws and the crunching of pebbles reminded me of the narrow shore of Ouranis' island. I tried to open my eyes. A sharp pain in my forehead made me wince and close them again. I tried once more, slower this time, and Denise came into view. She was standing on a short strip of pebbled beach next to a large, half-buried boulder; we had indeed been shipped back to Ouranis' den. *Thank goodness, she's all right*, I thought. She looked straight back at me, and I thought I could see relief in her eyes as well.

Lycomedes and Selena were there too, obviously. Both had fallen silent again and were eyeing our reunion with expressionless faces. Lycomedes was evidently having difficulty breathing, though he seemed otherwise fine. Both he and Selena looked at me expectantly, as if whatever they were going to say or do next was dependent on the first word that would pass my lips.

'You're all okay,' I sighed.

'Can the same thing be said about you?' Selena asked, a twinge of fear in her voice.

'I think so. What happened?'

A sigh of relief escaped Selena. 'You proved me right a second time, that's what happened. You are the Shepherd. There is no denying that anymore.'

'What?'

'You shapeshifted to escape Lydus' efforts to uphold the law, it seems,' said Lycomedes in Selena's stead. 'I believe I am the only one who actually saw you do it. Lydus' vision was obscured by his bees, Selena only had eyes for the road as she dangled from you like an unfortunate rodent, and your girl was focused on keeping up with you. Yet it is the truth all the same. You don't remember any of it?'

I tried to produce a frown, but even that small movement hurt. I thought back at how oddly *feathery* I had felt moments before I passed out and how the entire world – and Lycomedes' face in particular – seemed to come at me with a dazzling velocity. 'I shapeshifted? I… It's all kind of a blur.'

'That is to be expected,' said Lycomedes. 'I don't believe I have ever seen anything fly that fast, let alone *anyone*. Then again, I've never had the fortune of seeing Ouranis in person,' he added to himself. 'I have to ask, have you been in any physical contact with Leander since you arrived here by any chance, Bishop?'

This time my frown did appear, regardless of the pain. 'Physical contact? Not that I know of. Why?'

'That *is* curious,' said Selena, nodding thoughtfully. 'Are you sure it was a *horned* owl, Master?'

'Positive. Bishop, I can't say I understand how you did it, but in order to expedite your escape you managed to change your shape into that of a horned owl,' explained Lycomedes. 'And one that was large enough to take both Selena and Denise with you to my location. Not that this, in itself, is so remarkable; not even the Shepherd can alter his body mass. What is interesting, however, is that horned owls are Leander's, my apprentice's, favourite. I find it quite peculiar you chose that shape in particular.'

Despite the utter sincerity in his voice, or perhaps because of it, I found myself grinning. 'Peculiar, well, that's one way of putting it. Though anyone I know would say the shapeshifting itself is more peculiar than the animal I chose. In fact, I didn't consciously choose anything. I just wanted to get away, and quickly. That's all, really.' Selena let out a nervous laugh, and even the grave Lycomedes produced a smile. Selena's face soon turned stern again, however, presumably contemplating the dark path the breakout had set us upon.

An idea occurred to me. 'Did I appear as translucent as the other animals here?'

'Certainly not,' said Lycomedes. 'A Shepherd needs his skin to feel and his lungs to breathe, would he not? It is only his shape that changes, be it feral or furry. By no means does he *become* the animal whose shape he borrows. That would be impossible.'

While doing its best to make sense of this, it felt like my mind had stopped halfway through Lycomedes' explanation. It probably feared it would throw the rest of what I thought I knew into turmoil as well. In some weird way, what Lycomedes told me made sense, considering how the druids lived and what the fauna in this world looked like. But then again, what kind of creatures did the druids categorise as animals, if they had no use for lungs? Were the animals here even alive?

My eyes fell on Selena again. Her expression was glazed, absent. 'I guess it didn't really go as planned,' I said in an obvious understatement.

Selena's eyes flicked, then began to stare dejectedly at the coastline of Delos. She breathed in deeply. 'No, it didn't.' By the moist look of her eyes I expected a tear to roll down her cheek any second now.

'Lydus has no authority over us or the Council, my dear,' Lycomedes assured her. 'I wouldn't be too concerned.'

'Perhaps not, but his captain does,' said Selena. 'Lydus threatened to go straight to him, and Captain Helios knows how to play the other captains, especially the commander.'

Lycomedes shook his head. 'I doubt Helios will disrupt things based solely on Lydus' word. It takes more than one malcontent to persuade him to disturb his precious peace. No, we will just have to see what happens. There is no point in guesswork. The best we can do is tutor Bishop towards convincing the Council that he is the new Shepherd. It is the only thing that can make them see the validity of your actions.'

'That's exactly what I was hoping to accomplish by bringing Aaron to Eresa,' said Selena, her face brightening a little with the knowledge that there was someone else who agreed with her plan. 'It's also the reason why I kept the fate of the ritualists a secret. Because Denise's fate would have changed for the worse if the Council learned about it.' She gave Denise a concerned glance, and received an indefinable one in return.

Denise now wheeled around and stalked off to the water's edge. She had apparently heard enough, or sensed maybe. While she obviously had greater understanding of events than you would expect a real hyena to have, how much she comprehended, and more importantly, what remained of her original personality, was still a mystery.

'Denise, don't stand too close to the water,' I warned her. 'We still don't know if the Darkness is…' My voice trailed off when Denise looked from me to Selena, then sniffed loudly and began gazing at her own distorted reflection in the now placid water. I sighed and turned back to Selena, who gave me an apologetic smile. 'I think we can all use some sleep,' I said. 'So why don't you say what you have to say and be done with it, all right?'

Selena nodded. 'As Master said, we need to get you ready, Aaron. This means you need to learn to use your Shepherd abilities at will. Only then will we be able to return to Eresa. If we returned before that, we would certainly be split up and there would be no way for Master and me to help you, nor would we get a fair chance of explaining ourselves. Attacking a fellow druid outside the arena is a serious offence.'

'You were just trying not to get us stung by that swarm,' I reasoned. 'They can't fault you for that. It's self-defence.'

'It was me who attacked first, remember? I summoned my phoenix as a decoy when we were making our way out of the temple. When we got out of Denise's quarters and approached the corridor leading outside, Peleus must have seen Aerope and Lydus coming from the other end and decided to try to distract them. I asked him to guard the door before I went to get you. But unfortunately, because Aristion, the surviving ritualist, was already on his way, I didn't have time to go over the plan in more detail. I needed to break you out immediately, or else the Council would have strengthened your guard and I would have had no chance in getting you out. I also did not expect anyone to take the route Aerope and Lydus did.' She shook her head. 'Peleus' heart is in the right place, but I cannot expect him to lie for me to the Council. He's a Canine, or he is about to become one, and he has to think about his standings with his clan. His future captain, Ione, is a very loyal member of the Council. And with those three asserting my guilt, it would be pointless for me to claim otherwise.'

'The same holds true for facilitating Selena's escape,' said Lycomedes. 'As a grand master, I should be upholding the law, not breaking it.' Once more his slightly stolid personality shone through; his face displayed far less concern than I would have expected in light of what had transpired. 'The only thing I might have going for me is the fact that, as far as I could see, Lydus was the one attacking the three of you, not the other way around. And because Selena is my apprentice, saving her could possibly count as a justifiable reaction by a sentimental old man. And, I must say, it is not far from the truth.' Selena, touched by her master's words, smiled fondly back at him.

'I really don't get this whole clan business of yours,' I said. 'It seems to me there is a lot of tension between your clans. Yet Peleus did come with Leander and the other druids to the temple when they saw the dark smoke. And they seemed rather friendly with each other too.'

Lycomedes nodded in agreement with my observation, but it was Selena who answered. 'What you are referring to is a lengthy topic, Aaron,' she said. 'There is a lot of history involved, for the clans have existed since the founding of Eresa. Leander, Briseis and I know each other because, as you know, we have all chosen Lycomedes as our master. Peleus was also one of his apprentices, he still is actually, but he is about to graduate and join the Canines. It was simply a matter of coincidence that they were all together when they saw the Darkness creeping into the forest. Now, you need to remember that there might indeed be a little bit of barking, growling, and, indeed, screeching and bellowing between the clans, but we have always managed to work out our differences without too many casualties.'

'Using the Arena of Repentance,' I said. Selena nodded. 'I'm still confused, though. How can you simply pit people against each other in what's basically a gladiatorial free-for-all? Doesn't that mean the strongest person always gets his way?'

For a moment, Selena looked at me as though she didn't understand what I was trying to say. Finally she said, 'Aaron, you must understand that for us druids, the most important thing is our connection with our animal. It is what we carry with us every hour of the day and what we strive for to deepen and explore. Many of us even experience changes in their personalities as the bond deepens. We spend our days meditating on the animal we admire and compete with other druids to hone our skills.'

'And I get that, I do,' I said earnestly. 'I just don't understand what fighting each other has to do with improving this bond you speak of. I think if I was you and I venerated a certain animal, summoning it to fight my friends would be the last thing that would occur. I understand the whole meditation thing, or I think I do. And believe me; I would be the last person who tries to judge someone else's lifestyle. I just don't see what loving an animal and seeing it get destroyed in ritual combat have to do with each other.'

Selena had to think about her answer, so Lycomedes stepped in. 'I believe the proper way of explaining it is to say that duelling is a way of testing our bonds and comparing them with those of other druids. Many centuries ago, when Isis brought our ancestors to this world, Ouranis received us and taught us how to live as one with nature. Only a small proportion of our ancestors desired the life we live, and the many who didn't left to seek their fortune elsewhere. Ouranis herself will be able to tell you more when you meet with her, I believe. I know your predecessor, Zeuxis, knew more about this than he let out. Yet it is my view that Ouranis' teachings are what inspired the thirst for competition in the druids' hearts, which, on a personal note, I do not agree with.'

'You don't?'

'I have said it many times, and I will say it here once more. The life of a druid completes something in me, as it has in so many others. But the focus on progress in battle is the very thing that caused the division between them all those years ago. It wasn't Ouranis who created the clans, but the druids themselves. Someday, be it in my lifetime, my apprentice's or their students', it will lead to outright conflict. I am convinced of that. And when it does, it may very well mean the end of the Sanctuary and the way of life we hold dear.'

None of us spoke for a good while until Denise, seemingly tired of contemplating her reflection, re-joined us. Her approach caused an idea to float to the surface of my mind. 'You spoke about Isis bringing your ancestors here, to this world,' I told Lycomedes. 'So, am I right in saying that this Isis came from my world? Is that why you call it "the homeland"?' I had heard the name "Isis" mentioned several times now and I was beginning to wonder if these people actually thought that the Egyptian goddess of nature and magic once walked among them and conveyed her teachings to the human population. Then again, the druids did have a giant transparent Phoenix living in their backyard.

'You have a sharp mind, Aaron,' said Lycomedes, nodding thoughtfully. 'And I daresay you are going to need that as our new Shepherd.'

I felt my cheeks redden; now there was no denying any more that I possessed the druids' gift, the only things left were awkwardness and an even more complicated future. 'I wish you could go in there and tell that to Ouranis then,' I muttered, jabbing my thumb at the small mountain we were standing next to.

As I looked into Lycomedes' solemn face I suddenly understood why Selena and his other apprentices chose him as their teacher in life. 'A man's resolve is his greatest weapon, Aaron,' he said wisely. 'Find it and you can achieve anything.'

'Aaron, aren't you missing something?' Selena asked. I was continuing to gaze vacantly at Lycomedes. At hearing Selena's voice I turned away, scanning the pebbled beach.

'It's Pelegon's ship! It's gone.' Sure enough, the depression of where the prison transport had dug into the beach was still there, as was a portion of the debris. But the vessel itself had vanished.

'Indeed it is,' said Selena. She had obviously noticed this fact long before now.

'Do you think Ouranis…?'

'She must have,' Selena answered before I could finish the question.

'Maybe she sank it or took it somewhere to prevent the whole of Eresa to come over and see what happened,' I said. Grimly, I added, 'It makes sense, considering her aversion to visitors.'

Engrossed by the very idea of Ouranis emerging from her den to tow away the ship, Selena muttered, 'She must have.'

Chapter 7

The following day, morning arrived mercilessly early. My back hurt from sleeping on the smooth crystal around the cave's mouth, and my forehead still throbbed from hitting Lycomedes' chest. On a more positive note, the soft frothing of the waves, although apparently not working for me when I needed my mind focused for meditation, did help to fall asleep. This combined with half of the golden circle at the horizon warming my cheeks with its sunny rays – and gently pulling me back to the waking world – did me a lot of good.

As I opened my eyes a fraction to prepare them for the light, Selena and Lycomedes' raised voices bounced back and forth like a heated tennis match. I couldn't see them due to the sunlight on my face, but I didn't care either. Not with a body that felt like that of a decrepit old man, one that ached with every movement I made.

I slowly let my eyes adjust to the morning sun. The sight stunned me. I had never been fortunate enough to see a sunrise at sea, and was therefore mesmerised by the golden orb rising up from the island-dotted horizon like a gilded snail climbing a blue window. In that blissful moment I forgot all about the bad things in life, including my back.

I got up with a groan and joined my two companions, who I found glaring at each other a little deeper into the cave leading to Ouranis' den. Denise was there too. She was standing even further in, staring into the distance with her back rigid, her round, soft pointed ears aimed at the ceiling like satellite discs, and her tail lifeless like a blackened branch. It was evident she hadn't moved from her spot for a while; the dark mist that continuously oozed from her hide was confined to a small, circular pool of blackness around her paws.

'What are you two arguing about?' I asked Selena. I found it difficult to keep my eyes off Denise and wondered what she was doing. It wasn't like she could actually be aware of Ouranis from her position, unless her senses, if not her looks, had been improved during her transformation. I also doubted something as ethereal as the Phoenix carried a scent.

'Apparently,' Selena said with a reproachful glance at Lycomedes, 'I'm not allowed to go with you.'

'Go where?'

She gesticulated angrily. 'Inside.'

'I merely *advised* her to stay here,' said Lycomedes, clearly addressing his remarks to Selena instead of me. The old man looked exhausted, which was no surprise after yesterday's events and his insistence on keeping watch during the night. 'If she still wants to go, I won't stop her,' he added loftily.

'You won't need to,' Selena retorted. 'And you know it.'

'That's what you two are arguing about? I probably could have heard you from the other end of the mountain.' Selena said nothing, but continued to glare at the old man. As neither of them seemed to be willing to let it go, I said with a shrug, 'Well, there's no point in arguing about it, since I'm not going.'

'Of course you are,' said Selena.

'Of course I'm not.'

'You're the Shepherd.'

'And she's a terrifying, forty foot tall mythological monster come to life.' The words were out of my mouth before I had time to think about them.

Selena paused. I clearly took her by surprise. Then again, she had never seen Ouranis from up close. 'But it's your destiny,' she said, slightly bewildered by this turn of events. 'You have to go.'

'No, it's not. It's yours.'

'We've talked about this, Aaron. We were going to find out who possesses the gift, and that person will be the new Shepherd. That person's you.'

'Yes, we *have* talked about it. And we've decided that you do the talking part and I use the abilities.'

'We've decided no such thing.'

'Then it's time that we do. And to make this clear: Ouranis falls into the talking category, and the same goes for that Council of yours.' The anger in my voice could be attributed to the dream I just woke up from. It concerned Denise sitting in a small room, snapping at a group of Eresa's faceless physicians carrying an assortment of needles and feet-long probes.

'Is that so?' Selena narrowed her eyes. 'And how am I supposed to get close to Ouranis without the Shepherd's abilities?'

'You just said you wanted to go with me, didn't you? So you'll just have to pretend that I'm there, because I'm not going to risk my neck again just to have a little chat. Who's going to prevent Denise from being experimented on if that bird, or whatever it is, snaps my head off?'

At the mention of her name, Denise finally deemed it safe enough to come closer. The way she staled towards me, eyes blazing, made me again wonder how much she had already been changed on the inside by the Darkness, because by the looks of it she was slowly changing from my girlfriend into my personal guard dog. Although, given Denise's personality, this, in itself, wasn't a huge leap in character. But it still made me feel that the animal characteristics were gaining precedence. I could only hope that the process was still reversible.

Neither Selena nor Lycomedes had an answer and fell silent. 'Figures,' I mumbled.

I couldn't even tell where all this negativity that I felt inside was coming from, as both Selena and Lycomedes had done nothing but help me since I arrived here yesterday. I figured it was probably caused by the fact that no matter how hard I tried, I couldn't help but feel like a feather caught in a storm. And if there was one thing I couldn't stand, it was being told what to do, especially when I knew I had to do it.

Flawed logic or not, I was fully aware where my feelings against authority came from. My father had died when I was very young and I was raised by my mother. She was a very loving and free-spirited woman, my mother, and I always enjoyed great freedom under her wing. This meant that I was used to doing my own thing and make decisions for myself. I wouldn't have it any other way, either. Now almost a year had passed since I moved in with Denise, ten months that had taught me a great deal about compromise. And yet, despite my aversion to bossy people, the woman I loved so dearly knew exactly what she wanted, said exactly what she desired, and managed to get exactly what she asked for. Most of the time.

'Ready for this?' Selena asked quietly a few minutes later, a time during which our heads had come back together as a team. Despite our disparate priorities, we still needed each other.

I looked over my shoulder and saw Lycomedes standing on the beach near the mouth of the cave with Denise sitting next to him. By now the dark secretion had once again formed a nimbus of inky blackness around her. It had swallowed her body, leaving only two shiny, blue sapphires where her eyes were supposed to be. *Nothing has changed, Denise. I still love you.*

'Aaron?' Selena tried again.

'I'm fine,' I lied, winking back a tear. 'And you? Ready to meet your childhood hero?'

'I thought I would be,' said Selena in a small voice. 'I cannot believe how wrong I was. I can't even feel my toes.'

'It gets worse once you see her, trust me,' I said, mentally squeezing more nerves into her bloodstream. 'I just hope I still have toes when the running and the screaming ends.'

'No more games, Aaron, please,' she said, tension causing her voice to catch.

As we inched our way closer to the central chamber, the crystal layer lining the walls of the cave became noticeably thicker. For some reason the floor seemed even more slippery now than it had the day before. I was once again confronted with the fact that the druid sandals Selena had given me yesterday were an inconvenient down-trade to my leather, hiking ones. Their rubber soles were specifically designed to offer the wearer increased traction, something these straw ones evidently lacked.

'What do you think?' I whispered from the corner of my mouth. 'Shall we go together, or…?'

'I'm not sure,' Selena whispered in reply. 'Honestly, I expected to feel something by now. The energy pressure from Ouranis is said to be too great for anyone but the Shepherd to approach her. But it has been a while since anyone tried it. Let us go in a little further, slowly.'

I nodded and took a few quick steps to take the lead. Selena didn't object. Upon reaching the inner mouth of the cave, our backs scraping the crystallised surface of the wall, I placed one hand on the edge and braved a look inside the chamber. A few seconds passed, during which my eyes drank in the size and emptiness of the den. It was so quiet that I thought I could hear the sound of my breath echoing back at me. Then without warning, a giant bird's head, silvery and translucent, appeared around the corner. My heart did a full somersault and seemed to grab the inside of my throat.

I jumped back in shock and collided with a something behind me. An intake of breath followed, wheezing and labouring, and Selena fell to her knees and hands. Instinctively I reached down to help her up, but found her staring blankly at the ground, her eyes bulging and her senses turned inwards. In an instant I was back on Delos again, but in thought only. It was like I was staring down at Denise when she was about to transform into the black hyena. 'No, Selena!'

Horrified, I wondered if my errant elbow could have caused this damage, but then remembered what Selena had said about the high energy pressure coming from Ouranis. As I stood there, helpless, I could hear the splintering of tears on the crystallised floor. Her face was covered with them.

Selena couldn't form a reply. She was labouring to supply her body with oxygen, for her throat seemed to struggle with her wishes. The great Phoenix, well over twice the size of an African elephant, had come fully into view. Fortunately the mouth of the cave was too small to fully accommodate her vast bulk. Our eyes locked. Meanwhile, my mind juggled between the options of retreat and trying to shift Ouranis' attention away from Selena.

Ouranis continued to stare at me in silence. I knew that the blonde woman at my feet, currently fighting against total collapse, was my only solid link with the druids. She had been with me from the start and was my best chance of finding help for Denise and returning home. There was only one choice to take. 'Take my hand,' I said, as Ouranis raised her head like an Egyptian queen inspecting her offerings. 'I promise I'll do whatever you want once you're safe. Just grab it.'

Selena had her teeth clenched. I had no idea what she was going through, but each time she inhaled, I felt like I was suffering with her. With effort she raised her head and shot a pained glance at me. Her eyes were squinted to slits, her lips contorted; her proximity to Ouranis was quickly becoming unbearable. I was so fixated on her suffering, that when she suddenly grabbed the wrist of my outstretched arm she almost pulled me to the ground in the process. On top of this, an immense flare of silvery light dazzled my eyes the moment we touched.

The light came from everywhere. It was similar to the explosion of light I had seen in my head moments before I shapeshifted the night before, only much stronger. It was like a lightning bolt entered my arm and spread to my entire body. Once it reached my brain, it overloaded all of my senses at the same time, rendering me stupefied.

Next, the energy thundered all the way down into my legs and rapidly began to dissipate through the soles of my feet. The moment it was gone, a resounding crack echoed through the tunnel. I could feel my feet sink an inch or so into the floor as though standing on quicksand. A split second later, a great shattering of glass followed; all around us, the crystallised coating on the walls and ceiling of the cave broke apart, showering our heads with glittering shards of crystal. Only when the priceless waterfall had stopped did I realise what I had done.

Selena's hand and my wrist were glued together. And in my efforts to shield Selena from the glassy shower I had rolled her to her back. I was on my knees, seemingly unharmed, and Selena, blinking up at me with a nonplussed expression on her face, appeared to be perfectly all right as well.

Behind me, the toes in my sandals were digging into a sizeable pair of joint craters filled with crystal shards and silver dust. My head was spinning like a carousel. It was like the energy had turned my brain into a rat that was now searching the inside of my skull for a way out, gnawing frantically every time it found a weak spot. At the same time, my nostrils, my throat, as well as the rest of my body felt like they had been burned clean by a group of tiny blow-torch wielding imps.

I swallowed what little saliva I had left in my mouth. My throat felt raw. 'Are you okay?' I asked almost inaudibly. I coughed and repeated my question. Selena nodded, but didn't say anything. She merely blinked a few times, still looking utterly perplexed. Then she turned her head to Ouranis, who was still standing at the mouth of the cave, staring appraisingly at us.

Lycomedes' voice came stampeding towards us. 'SELENA?!' Though no hurrying footsteps followed.

'Do not let go of her hand if the druid's well-being is of interest to you,' said a female voice inside my head. It was sharp and gentle at the same time, careful not to touch anything that didn't belong to her.

Strengthening my grip, I looked up at the giant Phoenix. The voice could belong to none other than her. *Will you let her leave?*

'That is not up to me,' Ouranis answered simply.

I took a moment to consider, then thought, *If I come back, will you agree to talk to me?*

'Why are you here, young Shepherd?' she asked in return.

At least she's willing to talk to me this time, I thought. *Crap, did she just hear that? I mean*, I thought quickly, turning my attention back to Ouranis, *I was brought here by accident. I didn't choose to come to your world.*

'Your mouth speaks as though you believe that anything happens by accident,' said Ouranis. 'Every effect has a preceding cause, as well as its own nest of necessary conditions. You must know that.'

I wasn't trying to say I was brought here by chance. Meanwhile I was helping Selena to her feet. *Like I said before, something went wrong with the druids' ritual. If I understand it correctly, it chose to transport Selena to their temple, but it transferred the Shepherd's abilities to me. I didn't ask for any of this.*

'Fate does not supply on demand, young Shepherd. Come back after you have sent the druid on her way.' Her voice was patient, though commanding. 'And bring the one who has been taken. We have much to discuss.'

Did she mean Denise? I asked myself as Selena and I made our way towards the morning sun. *She must have. But then, what is she planning to do with her? Should I risk it?* There was only little time left to think, as I wanted to get back into the den as quickly as possible. I was quite surprised by this, though I figured that if I had to talk to Ouranis anyway, I might as well do it on the best of terms. And keeping her waiting was probably not the way to show her my best intentions.

We stepped out of the cave and into the morning light. The sun blinded me for a second or two, and I found myself staring into Lycomedes' distressed face.

'What happened in there?' he asked. 'I thought it would only make the situation worse if I came after you.'

'I think it was a wise thing to do, Lycomedes, thank you,' I said, handing Selena over. She still looked groggy. Denise, on the other hand, was again staring into the cave and was impatiently scraping the crystal coating with her paw. 'If I have to guess, I think Ouranis was testing us.'

'And that explosion? Did she attack you?' Lycomedes sat Selena down on a boulder and eyed me inquisitively. It was almost as though he was expecting a "yes".

I shook my head and caressed my throat. 'It wasn't like that, not really. I'm not sure what did happen, though. Denise, it's all right,' I added to the hyena. 'I'm okay.' She didn't seem to understand me.

'It was her aura,' said Selena. She was still having difficulty breathing, though she seemed to be all right otherwise. 'I expected something like this to happen, but I wished to see her anyway.'

'Was it worth it, coming with me?' I asked.

'Every second.' A small smile curved the corner of her mouth.

'It still doesn't explain that explosion,' said Lycomedes, alternating his gaze between Selena and me.

'It happened when I touched Selena,' I said, showing him my hand. It was still rather white on top, while my palm and the inside of my fingers looked red and dry, almost burned. There was a similar tender patch on my wrist. 'I wanted to take her back, but when she grabbed my wrist I saw this silvery light and everything around us exploded.'

'You must have created an energy bridge,' Lycomedes observed, nodding at my near injuries.

'Excuse me?'

'It is a method we druids use if we want to teach someone how to connect with the spirits of animals. If an aspiring druid has difficulty creating the link himself, we can offer him the chance to experience what the energy feels like by transferring some of our own. This method is particularly effective if the apprentice wishes to connect with the same type of animal the experienced druid uses. It is the foundation on which the divide between the seven clans is built. And the same method is used to perform a cleansing. There has been talk about performing one already.' The look he gave me left no doubt about whom he meant. In fact, I remembered Lydus and Aerope talking about a cleansing to be performed on me as well.

'Okay, this is all very interesting, and I do mean that, but I really need to get back in there. I'm supposed to bring Denise too. What do you think I should do, Lycomedes? Will she be safe?'

'Hmm.' The old man looked at Denise. She had gone further into the cave and was looking at the ceiling as though inspecting the coating. 'She seems to think so.' After this, and Lycomedes' not so helpful advice to remain as unassuming as possible, Denise and I began shuffling our way to Ouranis' echoing chamber.

'The legendary Shepherd, able to copy the strength, speed and agility of any creature he comes in contact with,' said the Phoenix, as we came upon the inner cavern. 'The nexus between realms, the link between worlds. It is an honour to meet you.'

This is different, I thought. *She has to be pulling my leg.*

'Your words are mine, young Shepherd. This is different indeed. Bring her forward.'

Just a moment, please, I thought, gesturing Denise to wait back in the tunnel. *I want to know what you're planning to do with her first, if you don't mind.*

'As you wish,' said Ouranis playfully. She seemed to be rather enjoying herself, though it was hard to tell, as her feathered head and her beak of translucent bone made it difficult to actually make out different expressions. The only thing I had to go on was the tone of her voice in my head, as well as her body language. 'I merely wanted to see if I had something to bargain with,' she added.

The word "bargain" triggered an entire host of negative emotions. *What do you mean by that?* I took a step back towards Denise. *She's not for trade, or anything like that. She means everything to me.*

'It was not her spirit I was referring to, young Shepherd,' said Ouranis patiently. 'See it as an antidote to the poison she has, I suspect, unwillingly been infected with.'

You mean you have a cure for her? I felt my heart lift and my guard drop at the same time.

'Most definitely,' said Ouranis. 'There is, however, one minor problem.'

I give you anything, do anything for you. The mention of the trade was still on the forefront of my mind.

Ouranis raised her head in thought. 'Again, you misunderstand me. The problem is that I am uncertain what will be left of her body after I have removed the... poison.'

Left of her...? I couldn't even finish the sentence. I swallowed as hope seemed to pour to the bottom part of my body, away from my brain which so desperately needed it. *You mean she may... die?*

Ouranis turned and walked off, her giant claws digging into the crystal coating with every step. When she appeared to have found a suitable spot she sat down like an overgrown chicken, wriggled her body to readjust her wings and feathers, then turned her head to me again. 'Perhaps,' she said in an unsettlingly blasé manner, her beak remaining shut. 'Although I do expect her spirit to survive. It is merely her body I am not too certain about.'

And what will happen if we leave her like this? I was surprised I was even considering the option.

'She will stay the way she is,' Ouranis said matter-of-factly.

Right, never mind. I don't see any other way out of this, so just do it. I'm sure it is what Denise would say if we had any way of asking her.

'I am afraid it is not that simple, young Shepherd,' said Ouranis.

Oh, right, I thought, realising my mistake. *Well, I've already told you I'd give or do anything, so just name it.*

'No matter how tempting, I cannot accept your offer.' Her voice was suddenly wistful. In fact, her whole demeanour seemed to change after this simple sentence. In addition, as she spoke, the light in the crystal-coated cavern appeared to dim slightly and an ominous feeling crept over me. It felt chillier too. 'For there is indeed one thing a Shepherd could possibly do for me.'

What is it? I interrupted her eagerly, my hands touching my belly like Selena's did every time her eyes fell on Ouranis' island. I didn't even know why I did it. Since no answer was immediately forthcoming, I added, *Tell me, please. Anything.*

Ouranis' eyes narrowed. 'I can see your heart is in the right place, and your resolve might even triumph over that of your predecessor. The strength of your abilities as well as your experience, however, are like a yet beardless boy, conjuring wisps with his spiritcraft, when compared to the seasoned veteran thus is the one who came before you. I am afraid you cannot help me.'

Then teach me. How can you know I can't do what you ask of me before you've even asked it?

Ouranis bowed her head. I could see her chest expanding like a giant bellows. Then a rush of wind escaped through her bony nostrils, blowing back my hair. 'Come join me, Shepherd,' she said, her voice solemn. 'I realise I have put you on a disadvantage the first time we met and I can see you have suffered as a result.' She made it sound like the relationship between us was more of a duel than a growing bond. 'You couldn't have come at a worse time, and I apologise. Now, allow me to begin afresh and tell you the story I have told most of the Shepherds before you. Perhaps at the end of my tale you will have a fair understanding of what I, in a regrettably weak moment, was thinking to ask of you.'

I indicated for Denise to follow me, because I figured that the more empathy I would be able to create for Denise's situation, the easier it would be to convince Ouranis to help her. For a moment or two, Denise seemed to struggle to decide which one was stronger, her desire to be beside me should I need her, or the fear of being snapped in two like a brittle twig in a storm. Deciding to set an example, I threw my fear into the back seat and walked over to the Phoenix. There I sat down on a small boulder, coated, like everything else in the cave, with crystal.

Denise's small paws weren't exactly suited to negotiating the ice-like surface with any sort of speed. Despite the occasional slip, her eyes remained transfixed on Ouranis as she followed me all the way there and sat, bolt upright, mere inches away from me. I could feel the ashy blackness from her skin flow down the side of my body like a never-ending waterfall, which quickly threatened to swallow her whole. Ouranis' slanted eyes were surveying the scene with curiosity. Her eyes seemed to welcome the distraction from her thoughts.

'The crystallisation process is a result of the energy my body is continuously emitting,' Ouranis explained, telepathically. 'The dark cloud your friend produces is similar, although not quite. You will understand more about this deeper into my tale. For now, I would like to start at the beginning. Can I count on your patience, young Shepherd?'

Of course.

While listening I tried my best to keep my thoughts as objective as possible out of concern of interrupting too frequently. To keep my mind calm I decided to treat Ouranis' tale as a story my history lecturer from back at the university was unfolding, and repeated parts of it in my mind as soon as I felt an intrusive comment bubbling up.

'Some three millennia ago, when animals still ruled these lands and mankind had no presence here, a human male arrived at the same temple you did yesterday,' Ouranis began.

She wasn't kidding about starting at the beginning, I thought before I could help myself. *I mean, three thousand years ago at the temple of Isis. Got it.*

Ouranis paid no heed to my thoughts and ploughed on. 'This human called himself Pharaoh Akhenaten, a leader who, during his reign, had difficulty convincing his people of the changes he was trying to bring about in their traditions. It was a name which, I suspect, he had chosen for himself. For to this day, the descendants of his followers refer to him as Amenhotep, or the snake lover.'

The name "snake lover" caused a memory to unfold of a giant black anaconda rearing up out of the water before being caught in mid-air by a translucent phoenix's head protruding from Selena's chest. It was the one where Sophia, Pelegon Linard's daughter, narrowly escaped a bite to the head, were it not for her father pulling her away in time.

'Interesting,' said Ouranis.

It baffled me that the snake hadn't even crossed my mind once after we brought Pelegon and Sophia back with us to Eresa. In hindsight I figured my disappointment of failing to connect with Denise in the hours that followed had probably thrown the memory in chains and suppressed it. Or perhaps everything else that had happened seemed just as compelling and my mind simply didn't know what to focus on anymore but the present.

It was that Darkness again, I thought to myself. The moving pictures of ash-black panthers, bats, a snake, a shark, and then Denise shot across my vision.

'Darkness,' repeated Ouranis. 'A rather simplistic name, yet elegant. The precise term of reference is Voidshapers, however, as they are not a single entity. They are bound to an intellect I have designated as the Void Hive. Strictly speaking, it is not even appropriate to refer to the Voidshapers as living beings. They are merely manifestations of the Hive's mind, spiritless and essentially bodiless. I can see you have become quite familiar with them.'

How could I not? I commented with a sideways glance at Denise.

'I understand. Unfortunately, the Hive is spreading its wings and is becoming more powerful every day. Your... mate,' she said after a pause during which my brain felt a little more crowded than I was comfortable with, 'is evidence of that. And a victim. Yet I will leave the Voidshapers for last, for it will be some time before they make presence in my tale.'

'Now, the human Akhenaten wished for nothing more than to create a place for his followers, a paradise, to live and worship this new deity he desired to bring to his people,' Ouranis went on. 'He called this deity Aten, or the Sun. To him, Aten was the prime deity and should be worshipped above all others, which, as I told you, was not received well by many of his people. However, with the help of the goddess Isis, he entered this world and continued to make use of Isis' mastery of spiritcraft to create a living entity his people and their descendants could worship for all eternity. He called this creature a Sphinx, with the body of a lion and...'

The head of a human, I finished for her.

'You know of it?' Ouranis asked in surprise. 'Very peculiar.'

Of course I know of it, I thought, not realising what I was saying. *Everybody does, in my world at least. They've built a giant one in Egypt near the pyramids.*

'Egypt?' Even though the protagonist of her story sounded much like an Egyptian pharaoh, the word "Egypt" seemed to sound alien to her. 'Who are these people you are referring to, young Shepherd?'

Egyptians, I guess. No one is really sure who actually built our Sphinx, I think. But I could be wrong. I don't know that much about Egyptian lore. Why? What's so special about a Sphinx?

Ouranis drew her head back in astonishment. 'The Sphinx, if completed, would have possessed powers akin to the goddess herself. The Sphinx's golden breath of life, which was supposed to shine as brightly as the sun, would have been able to heal any ailment. It was even supposed to bring eternal youth to those of full health. The Sphinx would also have been able to offer passage to this world to anyone who was willing to convert and worship the one deity, Aten. And these were only some of the abilities the Sphinx would possess.'

I see. Well, our Sphinx is just a statue, so you don't have to worry about any powers, I thought dismissively. *But let me get this straight, if I may. Akhenaten wanted his people to worship one deity, this Aten, and to do that he used the help of another deity? That doesn't make a lot of sense.*

To be honest with myself, not much about the story made sense so far, not least the fact that a human could contact a goddess and ask for her aid. But even before Ouranis had started her tale I had decided to try to keep an open mind, no matter how far-fetched the tale would become, and I was determined to continue to do so. I knew the upcoming story would probably throw my understanding of the world into chaos, but what choice did I have? Anyway, if this all happened three thousand years ago like Ouranis said, perhaps her story was simply an allegory, a mythologised reinterpretation of events that were actually quite explicable.

'Akhenaten did not blaspheme against the known deities, nor did he deny their existence,' said Ouranis. 'This does not mean his followers did the same, unfortunately.' Ouranis looked away. The blue line that painted her lower eyelid seemed to thicken. She blinked and it returned to normal, though it took her a while to carry on.

'The goddess Isis was deceived,' she said at length. 'It was her wish, like Akhenaten's, to found a paradise where Akhenaten's people could live in peace and would not have to worry about the oppression of opposing religions. However, as I mentioned, Akhenaten wanted more. After he and his followers were brought to this world by Isis, Akhenaten somehow found a way to keep the link to Isis' abilities open and funnel her energy into a single being.'

The Sphinx, I filled in.

'The Sphinx. Now before completion, Isis realised what her abilities were being used for and wanted to put a stop to it. This was no easy task, and not without great risk to this world's inhabitants. At the time of the ritual, when Akhenaten was channelling Isis' energy, Akhenaten's followers – as well as many of this world's original denizens, animals in your eyes – were attending the event. And it so happened that before Isis realised that Akhenaten was about to drain her of her energy and pour it into the Sphinx, too much of her energy had already been released from her body.'

This may sound stupid, I interrupted her, *but too much of her energy was released from her body? What do you mean that?*

'You may visualise the energy as coloured threads that linked Isis' incorporeal body with that of the Sphinx. They were needed to feed the Sphinx Isis' life force.'

Threads of energy? Could it… No, that's stupid. The image of two azure globes dancing through the air above a temple ruin bubbled up. The picture was almost as clear as the real thing, moments before I was brought to this world.

'Curious might be a better word to describe what your mind beholds, young Shepherd,' said Ouranis. Her beak moved a little closer. 'I can see what is troubling you. Curious indeed. Never have I seen energy behave that way, for it is indeed energy that made up the orbs that currently clog your mind. Perhaps in time we will find the answer, together.' I felt a soothing wave of warmth wash over me, unrelated to her breath on my face. I swallowed.

'To continue my tale, Isis became aware of the deception,' Ouranis went on. It was obvious she wanted to get this story off her chest as fast as my human mind could interpret it. 'But if she would sever the link with the Sphinx rather ritual was still underway, the sudden release of energy would have meant the death of all those present, humans and animals alike. To Isis, who to the present day is revered for her ability to love and nurture, this was to be prevented at any cost. And it cost her dearly indeed.'

'It is said that a single tear rolled down her cheek when she pulled the threads of energy from the Sphinx's incomplete body, which disappeared instantly. The threads ran amok as they began twisting and coiling on their own accord. Finally, in her attempt to seal the energy away, Isis guided all seven threads to form separate creatures, each imbued with a part of Isis' magic.'

She's your mother, I thought, realising this. *The goddess Isis. It's true, isn't it?* The thought of a giant Phoenix was, even for this world, too crazy for Ouranis' story and her existence not to be linked. But there was more. The emotion in Ouranis' voice indicated she was more strongly connected to her tale than the average storyteller.

Ouranis bowed her head in acquiescence. 'The seven Celestial Beasts were born, the Gryphon, the Cockatrice, the Hippocampus, the Chimera, the Pegasus, the Manticore, and, finally, me. Or you could say we are all part of Isis herself, as the seven of us have her energy sealed within us.'

There are still some things I don't understand, though. A lot of things, actually. For example, why did Isis help Akhenaten in the first place? She's a goddess. Didn't she know that her magic would be transferred to the Sphinx? And why did she even care about this Akhenaten?

'I know these facts only from witnesses of the event and what my siblings and I have been able to put together. Now humans have a colourful imagination. And when tales pass from mouth to ear, they have a funny way of adding or omitting things they shouldn't. In addition, you may not have noticed it yet since your abilities are still developing, but animals have rather unique ways of interpreting events, and all interpret them differently. Like the notion that the tear which rolled down my mother's cheek during the Sphinx's creation was caught by one of Akhenaten's followers and was placed in a stone basin at the temple. I have never seen it for myself.'

Never? Needless to say I was quite surprised by this. *Why not? It can't be more than five or ten seconds away if you give it a little effort. It sounds like a pretty big deal, a tear from your mother.*

'I rarely leave my abode, young Shepherd, and only for the direst of circumstances. Neither do I allow myself to be seen by the Eresans more often than is necessary.'

Well, if you don't want to go there, I can bring back some of it for you if you'd like. It's no trouble, really.

'Are you suggesting to scoop up a portion of my mother's tear?' Ouranis asked, her voice riddled with reproach. A rustling of feathers swam through the cavern.

No, no, of course not, I thought hastily. *Forget it, I was being stupid.*

'I will most certainly try,' Ouranis said in a small voice. Despite knowing that my suggestion was forged out of the best intentions, I could slap myself for being so witless. Not to mention that I didn't have the slightest idea how Selena and the other druids would react to their new Shepherd sticking his hand in their hallowed water.

So about these other Celestial Beasts, I thought quickly to kick our conversation back on track. *Do they live in dens like this one as well?*

As was the case with my suggestion about the tear, I was trying to keep my thoughts light and unassuming. Upon seeing Ouranis' reaction, however, my knack for throwing salt in a wound while I thought I was adding sugar, hit me in the face for a second time.

Ouranis' massive head drooped, her eyelids closed, and her wings, previously neatly folded against her flanks, slid to the ground.

Not again…, I thought miserably. *I'm so sorry, Ouranis. I did it again, didn't I? I'm such an idiot.*

Ouranis' beak was so close to my face, I could actually feel the sucking force as she inhaled deeply through her nostrils. 'The fault is not yours, young Shepherd. You could not have known. Being reminded of my brothers and sisters' fate by another is simply… unpleasant.'

Still, I shouldn't have said it so casually, I thought apologetically. *And you certainly don't have to answer me if you don't want to.*

'It is not a matter of desire,' she said darkly, raising herself up. 'It is a matter of trust.'

Well, I don't want to state the obvious, but I have come here to ask you for help, not the other way around. You can definitely trust that I want to do what is best for Denise, and you said you could help her. So if it's a question of motivation…

Ouranis fell silent for a spell. 'You are not like the others, young Shepherd. Most druids that come here have an agenda of their own, but not you, aside from the obvious.'

My only agenda concerns Denise. I moved my hand subconsciously to pat Denise on the back. About halfway there I changed my mind. In the corner of my eye I saw Denise's hyena head turn towards me. It was the only part still visible because of the nimbus of blackness that surrounded her. *And getting out of this place in one piece*, I added. *Particularly after of our prison break yesterday. I don't even want to think about what is happening over there.*

'I apologise. That is not what I meant,' said Ouranis. 'I am not used to conversing with humans. Zeuxis wasn't the most talkative among the Shepherds, although it might have been my fault that we didn't talk much. I have had a lot on my mind lately. You saw the results of that during your first attempt to meet me. Instead, I was referring to your lack of prejudice and assumption. You seem to take life on its own terms. I admire that. It is not an easy thing to do if you have existed as long as I have.' The weight of her voice told me she meant more than she said.

I shrugged and thought, *I suppose it's because I don't like people who judge others. It's how I've been raised. You'll have to thank my mother for that.*

'My place is here,' Ouranis stated primly.

Yeah, uhm, never mind that. I paused for a moment to refocus my mind on Ouranis' tale. *There was something else I didn't understand in your story, though. We're still in Greece, aren't we?* Now something else bubbled up, something I had asked Leander and Briseis yesterday, but had yet to find an answer for. *And yet you all speak English, my language. In fact, this Amenhotep or Akhenaten, or whatever his name was, was obviously an Egyptian pharaoh. So his followers, the people who came here, were Egyptians. But then, how come we all speak the same tongue?*

'Greece, Egyptians, the names mean nothing to me,' said Ouranis. 'I know this world as the Land of Aten, for it is this how Akhenaten named it, as did our mother. The language you speak is the language we all speak. I do not know what else to tell you.'

So it's possible I'm speaking another language without even knowing it? Could the Shepherd abilities have something to do with it? I mean, if they enable me to talk to animals... But then, what about Denise? Maybe she can't understand me because I'm not speaking English anymore.

'Like I said, I do not know what else to tell you, young Shepherd. I am merely glad we can understand each other.'

Me too, Ouranis. But I had another question, if you allow me. Because before Denise and I arrived here, we were taken from our version of Delos. That's in a part of my world we call Greece. And you just said that Akhenaten arrived at the temple of Isis too. But he was an Egyptian pharaoh, meaning he's from Egypt. So why did he come to Greece? Or was the island of Delos the only place that had a gateway?

'I cannot tell you what I don't know,' said Ouranis. 'What I can say is that ever since I took my first breath, I have never heard of another place beside my mother's temple where living beings are able to travel between this world and yours.'

I guess it doesn't really matter, I thought with a glance at Denise. *But, uhm…*

'You wish to know if I still have the intention to help you,' said Ouranis, interrupting me. 'I can sense your desire.'

Actually, I believe the question is not whether you want to, but whether you trust me enough to tell the rest of the story, I thought, choosing my words carefully.

'A very sharp mind.'

That's what Lycomedes said, I thought to myself, chuckling softly as the old man's face swam by.

'The wandering druid,' Ouranis stated with a queer edge to her words. 'One who is without allegiance. Do you know him well, young Shepherd?'

As well as anyone can get to know someone in less than a day, I thought. *I know he won't be winning any popularity contests anytime soon, that's for sure. He is not very popular with the druids*, I added quickly to Ouranis' quizzically tilted head. *But Selena likes him, and I think I do too. He's already helped me a great deal.*

'I understand.' Her voice had a lack of emotion which instantly pulled my eyebrows together in consternation.

Is that a problem? I thought tentatively, hoping against hope that my fraternising with Selena's master had not damaged my chances with the giant bird.

'Not in a way you would expect,' Ouranis answered vaguely.

What's that supposed to mean?

Ouranis looked sideways. 'It means this conversation is over, young Shepherd. For now. I need time to think.'

Uhm, okay. I rose to my feet.

'Young Shepherd,' said Ouranis, 'I must ask you not to discuss the Voidshapers with anyone.'

My mind felt like a bowl of mousse after being ravaged by an excited three-year-old. All the memories, experiences, and information I had received in the shockingly short span of only twenty-four hours, were jumbled together like a tangled thicket of brambles. And Ouranis' abrupt end in our conversation certainly didn't help. There were just so many questions.

'I wonder why she wanted Denise to remain if she didn't say she was going to cure her,' Selena thought out loud. 'It must not have been easy for you to let her go.' We were standing on the pebbled beach before the mouth of the cave, and I had just finished telling Lycomedes and Selena about my visit. At Ouranis' requests, I left the Voidshapers out of the story.

Apparently, the tale of Akhenaten was nothing new to them, which meant that they must have heard it from the other Shepherds before me. They could also add that the other Celestial Beasts, Ouranis' brothers and sisters, had passed away long ago. Ouranis was the only one left. This, of course, explained a lot about her emotional reaction when her siblings entered the tale.

'I had to do something,' I said, as a numbing wave of helplessness washed over me. 'Now that everyone knows about the Darkness, it's become too dangerous for Denise to be out in the open. You said so yourself. And Ouranis said I was welcome to come and see her any time *my heart desires it*,' I added with emphasis. Neither of my two companions showed any sign of understanding my emphasis, which reaffirmed their claims that neither of them had ever heard Ouranis in their own minds. 'At least this way the other druids can't get to her anymore, since they can't enter Ouranis' den,' I added. 'And I must say, I do feel a bit better now that I don't have to worry about her so much.'

'I'm glad,' said Selena. A small smile brightened her face, but it was only there for a second or two. 'What about our situation? Ouranis was supposed to offer you guidance on the journey ahead.'

I scratched my head, perusing the pages of my memory in silence. 'I don't think she said anything about that, no. I had the feeling we were getting to that when she suddenly decided to end the conversation. I don't really know why, to be honest.' I saw Lycomedes turning to the cave with a thoughtful, slightly dubious, expression on his face.

'She decided to end it?' Selena asked, appearing taken aback. 'What was the last thing you talked about? You haven't said something to offend her again, have you?'

'Nice, thanks.' My voice dropped slightly. 'You are right, though. I think I did say some things I shouldn't have. I didn't know it at the time,' I added quickly in response to Selena's scowl. 'And she forgave me, so that can't be it. No, actually…,' I paused to make sure this was the route I wanted to take and turned to Lycomedes, 'we were talking about you.'

The old man was still staring blankly at the cave, his mind absent. When he suddenly realised he had become the centre of attention, a jolt of shock shot through his body. His face quickly began to hop between Selena and me like a frog having a hard time deciding which lily leaf served best to attract a lonely princess.

'What's that? Me?'

'Is there something you want to tell us, Master?' Selena asked in return.

'Lots of things, though nothing that would be of interest to the great Ouranis,' he said. 'What did she say about me, Aaron? Anything positive?'

'Not really. She just wanted to know what I knew about you. So I told her the truth, that I've only known you people for less than a day.'

It was quite funny to see the two expressions change – Lycomedes' turning downcast, but Selena's glowing with relief. If I were in Lycomedes position, I would certainly go for relief as well; by size alone I would rather stay out of Ouranis' spotlight, be it positive or negative.

'So, to cut the tale short, you have no idea where to go from here,' Selena paraphrased neatly, crossing her arms and sounding like she was blaming me for the abrupt dead end.

'Well, she did mention something about a certain… thing I could do for her,' I said, realising I had left that part out of my tale.

'What kind of thing?' Selena asked enthusiastically.

'She didn't tell me.' Selena gave me a look that was instantly familiar. It was the one Denise used when I had forgotten to pay the electricity bill, again. 'I mean it. She didn't want to tell me because she didn't know whether she could trust me.'

'You did say she could, didn't you?'

'Of course I did,' I snapped at her. 'What do you think I was doing in there anyway? Of course I want her to trust me. But it's only natural that she doesn't. I'm not even a druid. And even if she did tell me, what can I do that she can't do herself? Or she could have asked the previous Shepherd to do. What was his name, Zeuxis?'

'You might think so,' said Selena, rolling her eyes. 'At least it gives us somewhere to start.'

'It does?'

Selena opened her mouth to answer, but Lycomedes waved his hand in a hushing gesture, silencing her instantly. 'You disappoint me, Selena,' he said. 'Almost your entire life you have aspired to become the next Shepherd, to meet the one being you bonded with when you were but an callow girl. And now you are chosen, you are so close to achieving your life's ambition, and you don't ask the one question I would assume would be your first.' Selena seemed at a loss for words, so Lycomedes answered for her. 'Did you receive the blessing?' he asked me, throwing up his arms to highlight the simplicity of his question.

'Ah, yes,' said Selena, smiling despite her master's rebuke. 'Did you, Aaron?'

'Uhm, she did call me Shepherd,' I said guardedly. 'Young Shepherd, but Shepherd nonetheless.'

Selena and Lycomedes looked at each other, seemingly thinking the same thing. 'I've never actually seen a Shepherd receive the blessing,' said Lycomedes. Selena nodded. 'Normally it happens at the inauguration when the Shepherd enters Ouranis' den for the first time. The ritual is quite the spectacle. The Piscines supply the whales for transport, everyone's there, and wherever you look, people can't resist showing off their prowess just for entertainment's sake. But, sadly, the receiving of the blessing is only for the Shepherd to see.'

'Well, sorry to disappoint, but I think I've seen enough spectacle for the time being, if you don't mind,' I said. 'Especially those in which I'm the living target.'

Selena let out a snort, while Lycomedes threw his fist into the air in triumph. 'Ha! You've seen nothing yet, Bishop. A true artist saves the best for last. And you're becoming a fine one indeed.'

Chapter 8

After hearing Lycomedes and Selena's comments I had the impression that this whole idea of Ouranis' blessing had the same veracity as a fairy tale; a few truths glued together by a healthy dose of fantasy. It was probably just another ritual, something that was important to them but had no real meaning outside the druid community. I could be wrong, of course, but after hearing Ouranis talk about the Shepherds in general, and seeing how I had been treated by her thus far, there was no doubt that she didn't see the position in the same awestruck light as the druids themselves.

I continued to feel like a knight on a chessboard, useful, but dependent on my master's whims. Except that my master wasn't one person, but several. And, with Ouranis added to the mix, the number still seemed to be climbing. But as long as she had the antidote for Denise in her claws I was hers to command, for my pledge was sincere; I would do anything to get her back.

Fortunately, despite my earlier fiascos, something was going my way at last. Ouranis and I had had a real, honest conversation and, for the moment, she seemed satisfied with me carrying the Shepherd's torch. She had even agreed to watch over Denise for the time being, which induced a sense of relief much more powerful than I was comfortable with of showing Selena or Lycomedes. It was something private, a sense of elation that, perhaps a bit selfishly, I did not want to share. Perhaps it was because I felt that if I shared it with someone, if I let someone have a taste, the cream of happiness would be soured. It felt too fragile for anyone to come near. Denise was everything to me, especially now. It was the only real, tangible thing I had left of home.

With Denise safe from any druid experimentation, the three of us agreed that the most promising way out of the mess we had created was to find a way to Ouranis' heart. She was the key, not only for my goals, but for Selena and Lycomedes' as well. For Ouranis was the only one who could convince the druid community of me being the rightful person to be Zeuxis' heir. However, not only did we think it a bad idea to badger the Phoenix any further, we also felt it was too dangerous to press our luck with the Voidshapers much longer. We may have been lucky so far, but with the jaws or claws of the Voidshapers potentially hiding behind any wave or tree, there was only one option, one road for us to take; we had to get off Ouranis' island and head back to Eresa. It was the only guaranteed Voidshaper-free place beside Ouranis' den, which was obviously off-limits for my two companions.

But to go back now meant that we still had no way to prove that I was the Shepherd, neither by skill or with this mysterious "Blessing of Ouranis". On the positive side, with Denise out of the picture, there was no real need for the druids to know, either. In fact, between the two of us, Selena was obviously the better choice for the druids to turn to for guidance. Selena had been chosen, she was well trained and was definitely capable, if Lycomedes' judgement was any guide. She may not have the requisite abilities to validate it, but, to use Lycomedes' own words, no one in his right mind would expect Selena to be capable of displaying any as yet.

'Niobe probably will ask, but she's just a cat,' Lycomedes said dryly as we made our way to the central square of the Sanctuary and his two spectral crocodiles melted into nothingness behind us. Judging by the grimace he pulled, and the way his hands balled into fists, the old man clearly had a radically different relationship with cats than most.

As we approached the square, the increasing silence between us was unsettling. I couldn't speak for the others, but to me it felt like yesterday's breakout was floating above our heads like a thundercloud. I couldn't believe that anything, not even an evil sentient cloud of ash with the ability to swipe, bite and sting all at the same time, could persuade me to come back here. At least Denise was protected this time.

'Where is everybody?' Selena asked, her voice ebbing away over the deserted plaza. We listened to her voice going the way of the dinosaurs. There was only the rustling of the leaves around us. It was like a spell of silence had been cast over the area and everyone had ran off somewhere to regain their ability to speak. The two temples now looked like forgotten ruins, waiting for time and weather to consume them.

'Now this is more like it,' said Lycomedes, nodding at the square as if it had finally lived up to his expectations. 'This is the kind of peace I was hoping to find when I first heard about this place. Young men and their dreams…' He produced a smile that dripped with happy memories.

'Master?' Selena asked tentatively. One look at her face told me she was hoping to be treated to a tale she had been longing for years to hear; the tale about Lycomedes' past.

Lycomedes looked back over his shoulder and the twinkling in his eyes disappeared. The memories were gone in an instant. 'It isn't natural,' he said sincerely. 'What are you staring at?'

'You, Master,' said Selena. 'You've never told me why you wanted to become a druid. You don't even like crocodiles. You were talking about young men and their dreams just now. Why *did* you want to join the druids?'

'Dragons, my dear,' he said, his voice worthy of that of a mediaeval bard. 'Big, scaly, toothy dragons. But no one has ever seen a dragon, has he? So it's out with the quibbles and in with the experiments.'

'But if you liked dragons, how did you end up with crocodiles?' I asked him. 'I thought the Greeks…' I swallowed to rephrase my sentence, '… I thought dragons were more serpent-like.' Indeed, from what I knew of Greek mythology, the ancient Greeks pictured dragons to resemble snakes more than crocodiles.

'And how would you know about that, Bishop?' said Lycomedes. 'Have you ever seen a dragon?'

'No.'

'Then there's your answer,' he said. 'Speaking of snakes, was there a meeting scheduled that I wasn't informed of?'

'Hey, hold on,' I said, reminiscing. 'Wasn't that ritual for the new Shepherd supposed to be today? Maybe that's where they've gone off to.'

'Nah,' said Lycomedes throatily.

'They can't be, Aaron,' said Selena. 'They need the Shepherd for that. Also, the Council has to know the full extent of everything that has been going on by now, including the existence of the Darkness. Aristion is bound to have told them, even if Pelegon and Sophia have kept their word. Fortune may have been on our side during our trips across the water, but it could have been just that, luck. You saw how that dark smoke retreated into the water after Captain Kriton defeated those panthers. And we know the Darkness is able to change its shape, because we saw those bats do so.' She shook her head. 'I daresay we haven't seen the last or the worst of this Darkness. What I can tell you is that if the Council has been informed of the Darkness, and, again, we must assume they have been by now, they will never approve of sending a whole procession of people to Ouranis' island before they know it is safe. And I think we can be reasonably sure that, after what happened during your escape yesterday, my inauguration won't be the first thing on the Council's mind anymore.'

'Don't fret, my dear,' said Lycomedes, unconcerned. 'This isn't the first time Lydus has tried to pull the Council's tail.'

'Like I said before, Master, it is not just Lydus,' Selena replied, her words dripping with anxiety. 'If Captain Helios supports him and Aerope backs him up, we will have a hard time convincing the Council otherwise.'

'It's quibbling, nothing more. You shouldn't let it wind you up.'

'So what do you want to do?' I asked Selena, to break the moment of silence that followed. 'You said you wanted to explain yourself to the Council?'

'I still do,' said Selena, visibly running the scenario through her head. 'We should go to the Phoenix Hall and hope they are there. It wouldn't be helpful to our cause if we are found first, especially not by certain people.'

Two hollow knocks echoed through the hallway. Lycomedes, Selena and I were standing inside the Phoenix Hall, in front of a door behind which the central chamber was supposed to be. It was here where the Council held its meetings. It took another two knocks before the door finally squeaked open. In the doorway stood a woman in her early thirties with a neat, auburn braid hanging down her shoulder, bound together by a brown strip of cloth. Its colour matched the sash around her waist perfectly.

'Shepherd,' she said. I looked up into her eyes, fully expecting a return glance. They were fixed on Selena instead. She looked away and added, 'And Lycomedes.'

'Ione,' Lycomedes greeted her with a small nod.

'It's *Captain* Ione, Lycomedes,' said Ione. 'We are in the middle of a meeting. What brings you here?'

Now an aged, squeaky voice came from inside the chamber. 'We have what we need. You may go.'

Ione stepped aside for a young man with black hair offset by a single strand of white.

'Leander,' Selena said in surprise.

Leander looked troubled, or he did until he saw who were waiting for him. 'Selena. I mean, Shepherd,' he said, quickly correcting himself. 'You're back.'

'Very good,' said the same squeaky voice. 'Bring her in, Captain Ione.'

'Shepherd, you heard Commander Xenokrates,' said Ione. 'You're being summoned.'

Selena looked first at Lycomedes, then to me. I shrugged as if conveying, "This is what you wanted", and said, 'Good luck.'

'You too, Lycomedes,' said Ione in a fanged voice as Selena shouldered herself between her and Leander, and then vanished.

'Me?' Lycomedes asked, looking around with a hand on his chest, as though he was expecting to find a couple more people named Lycomedes behind him.

'She is your apprentice and you are responsible for her escape, both by your position and your deeds.' Despite the feathery softness of her voice, there was something oddly savage in Captain Ione's eyes. 'Lydus claims he saw you leaving with her and the prisoners. It is high time you explained your actions, old man.'

'Easy, easy. There's no need to bare your fangs, Canine, thank you.' Without further ado he passed Ione, who followed every move the old man made with narrowed eyes. Her feral gaze reminded me of a stray dog watching a butcher carry a tray of juicy sausages.

With a nod in my direction, the captain said to Leander. 'You watch over him. He will be the next one to be questioned.' And with that, the door slammed shut.

'Talk about walking into a lion's den,' I said, feeling queasy. 'What about you, are you all right?' Leander sighed, seemingly overcome by the effect of the wringer that had just been used on his brain. 'That bad, huh?'

'It's not good, no. And that's partly because I don't understand half of it.' He rounded on me. 'You should never have allowed Selena to take you away from the Sanctuary, Aaron. She's not in her right mind. I see that now.' He breathed out forcefully through his nostrils. 'We should have looked around for Aristion before we headed back to Eresa. Selena must not have searched properly, she can't have. And now the Council is considering a purification.' He looked as though he was expecting to hear a gasp and see my hand slap against my mouth. It conjured an image of a dozen druids in hazmat suits ripping off my clothes and starting to scrub my back.

'It means they are going to strip Selena of her spiritcraft,' said Leander, as anger seemed to rise up inside him with every word he uttered. 'The purification will take away everything, including the abilities she acquired when she became the Shepherd. It's the only way to forcibly remove Ouranis' gift.'

'What?! They can't do that!'

'Oh, really.' He nodded mockingly, though his voice dropped immediately. 'Well, unfortunately for her, the Council is perfectly capable.'

'But I didn't…' I choked on the lump of bile that had formed in my throat. Leander eyed me with a glance that was entirely devoid of empathy. As I stood there, once more the sensation of powerlessness embraced me. It was an intense feeling of looking helplessly at the world without having a clue how to put things right. I saw a world that was both pitiless and relentless, a world that was continuously toying with me and the people around me, sacrificing one piece to win the game. Hatred bubbled up. My mind started racing.

Why can't Denise and I just leave this place and be done with all this? Wouldn't that solve everything, and save Selena at the same time? She can be the Shepherd. I never wanted these abilities, she did. If we could only leave these so-called druids to their own games, their stupid little laws, and in particular, their idiotic rituals. It felt like the entire world was closing in on me, pressing me down.

I was still fuming as Leander slid down the back wall and sank to the ground. 'This is going to take a while,' he sighed. He pulled in his legs and crossed them. 'You might as well sit down too, Aaron. They've got a whole list of questions for them, I can tell you that much.'

I didn't respond. Instead I turned to stare in the direction of the door, behind which, in my mind, Selena and Lycomedes were suffering some extreme form of mental torture. The heavy entrance door appeared to be carved from a single slab of wood, with the natural lines of the original tree's heartwood serving as the only imperfections. I barely noticed any of it. The image of Selena's determined expression, born out of her need to lie, was the only thing I could think about.

'If you want to talk about it, I am available,' Leander said, hope cutting through his ill feelings. 'I tried my best to defend you in there, you know? Peleus did too, surprisingly. Or at least that's what he told me. You never know with Canines. They are loyal, but rarely do they care about people outside their clan.' Again, I remained silent.

'All right, then,' he said. 'If you don't want to tell me what's on your mind, then tell me this: Where have you been hiding out since yesterday? They've been searching both islands all night. You can't have gone to Ouranis' den, that's for sure. Neither was there a boat missing from the docks, so you must have used Lycomedes' crocs. So, where did you go?'

I forced my lips into a smile, intimating that none of his ideas were even close. Chuckling animatedly, I asked, 'Why couldn't we have gone to Ouranis?'

Leander produced a smile of his own. 'You may not know this, but no druid is allowed to set foot on the island except for the Shepherd.' At hearing his words, the recollection of Selena wheezing and heaving on her hands and knees came floating across my vision. Its colours and detail were as pronounced as they had been inside the cave. 'Ouranis' gift mitigates the effects of her aura. So be advised and don't go there.'

There is that gift again, I thought. *But no druid is allowed to set foot on the island except for the Shepherd? Is he just flat out lying to me, or is he really this badly misinformed? We had no trouble approaching the island whatsoever, twice no less. And Selena only collapsed when she was really close to Ouranis. Lycomedes didn't feel a thing either, and he was right outside. No, forget that. If Leander knows, Selena certainly must have as well. Yet she brought me to the island anyway without knowing which one of us was the Shepherd. Or did she think only druids could be affected and I would be safe, Shepherd or not?*

It seemed the ordeal fate had put me through had messed with my mind. Only now did I remember the conversation Selena and I had when we first found Ouranis' den deserted. *No, wait a minute, she did know. She told me she knew she couldn't get close to Ouranis without the gift, but did it anyway because she couldn't resist trying to catch a glimpse of her.*

'I ask again. Where have you been?' Leander pressed me.

I looked down into his questioning face. He raised his eyebrows even further, indicating he was still waiting for an answer. 'It's better if you don't know, Leander. The less you know...'

'The more boring it is for me,' Leander finished in my stead, pursing his lips. He scoffed and said, 'Yeah, never mind. I don't know why I even care. I only hope for your sake that hyena friend of yours is far away from here, Aaron. And that she knows how to keep her head down. Because once the Council is done questioning you, I'm sure they will continue looking for her. And you'll be hard pressed to keep anything from them. That is to say, you better tell the truth.'

I had my reply ready and opened my mouth to speak, but no sound came out. For some reason the words became stuck somewhere half way from my brain to my mouth.

'Oh, but I have no intention of being questioned,' I then heard my own voice speak. It carried such a confident air, it was almost as if a third person was behind me, moving my jaw as would a ventriloquist.

Leander appeared to be at a loss for words. As he looked up at me, flabbergasted, he blinked a few times. He seemed not to notice his mouth was still hanging open. There was definitely confusion in those wet eyeballs of his. There was even a smattering of fear. As his mouth closed, his lips twisted into a small, insincere smile. 'Now don't be stupid, Aaron,' he said, his voice quivering slightly. 'It's only questions.'

Because I could see and hear the scene play out, I didn't immediately realise that there was something unnatural about my behaviour. After all, experiencing nerves getting the better of you is something any college student is familiar with, especially one who had as many class presentations under his belt as I had. Now, however, as I vainly tried to scratch my neck, I realised something was wrong. I simply couldn't do it. I tried again, and again my muscles didn't respond. I felt my mind trying to produce a frown, but my eyebrows wouldn't move. A surge of dread raced through my unresponsive body. A helpless passenger in my own skin, I could only wait passively to find the source of this new nightmare.

'You're not looking too good, my friend,' said Leander, shaking his head worryingly. He was on his feet again. The threat of me leaving, and he having to explain my second escape to the Council, had evidently evaporated. 'Come, sit down for a minute.' As he took my arm, I could feel his fingers touch my robes and press down on my skin. Yet it didn't feel like my skin at all, or not the way I was used to.

'Don't,' I whispered, forcing the word from my throat. I knew it was wrong to touch me. It felt invasive, as though Leander was trespassing the already transgressed boundaries of my body.

'What are you...?' Leander began, before he gave a cry of surprise and started violently. Were it not for his grip on my arm, he would have toppled like a domino. Because as his feet jumped backwards, his hand remained tightly clenched around my arm; he couldn't let go.

A thunderbolt suddenly raked through my body, originating from Leander's palm. As it dissipated, it left a tingling sensation on my skin, and yet my body was still beyond my control. Then, slowly and unbidden, my free hand was being raised and placed on Leander's. Upon touch, the tingling sensation quadrupled in intensity.

'No!' he said in a hoarse voice, one that was more breath than sound. He doubled over as though about to puke. With his back bent and his face gazing at the floor, he began taking one wheezing breath after another; just as Selena had done at Ouranis' den. 'Stop! Please!' he beseeched me. 'Don't take away my owls!'

Tears hit the marble floor, shattering. Finally I somehow seized control of the invading mind and pulled my arms back. The moment I released him, Leander sank to the ground. He was barely conscious. I spent the next few seconds in complete astonishment. I couldn't crouch down no matter how badly I wanted to. But if could, would I dare touch him again?

Now I felt tiny pins, like needles, sprout from every pore in my skin. My senses heightened to an extent I didn't think was even possible. My hearing, my eyesight, my sense of smell, they all suddenly doubled in strength. There was a commotion coming from the other side of the door, and yet my transformation continued undeterred. The sides of my face bulged, my arms twisted awkwardly and my toes felt like they were being ripped apart. I felt heavier, yet lighter at the same time. My nose and mouth hardened as they were forced together into a beak. And as for my neck, it seemed as though someone was removing the docking clamps, making it capable of turning beyond human capabilities.

As I felt my body turn into the direction of the exit, my eyes remained locked on Leander. Despite my concern for his life, there was nothing I could do. When he finally looked up, his eyes grew even larger than mine felt. They were bulging and his eyelids were quivering in disbelief. His lower lip was cold blue, like a little kid's who had just climbed out of an outdoor swimming pool. He looked completely drained. Satisfaction for his well-being coursed through me. At least he was alive. And, judging by the look on his face, there was no way he was going to give up on life before he could tell someone about this experience.

The door burst open. Voices exploded. Then, in quick succession, my head snapped back, my wings opened, and my claws pushed off. Faster and faster the inside of the temple flashed by. No matter what I tried, the hypothetical safety belts would not release me from the passenger seat, and I was forced to watch the unknown driver piloting my body.

Pockets of wind slapped against my face. It felt amazing and incredibly frightening at the same time. Corridor after corridor blinked past. I could only hope they were as empty as before; my head still hadn't fully recovered from the collision with Lycomedes' chest and felt like it would crack like the shell of a hard-boiled egg if it had to suffer another.

I had passed the double front doors before my brain had even time to interpret the sight of them. What my eyes did capture – and the sight remained burned on my retina for a few seconds afterwards – was a cascade of black hair from a girl I didn't quite recognise.

Straight on I ploughed, buffeting the air with my wings, until, after a few yards into the square, a wall of wind practically stopped me dead. With a quick glance at the sky above and a forceful stroke of my wings, I rocketed upwards, my tail feathers acting like a bioengineered steering device.

Despite my lack of autonomy, I felt so unrestrained, so alive. The wind whistling past my feathers, the complete silence except for the howling wind, it was exhilarating. There were no voices, no questions, no one telling me what to do, nothing. I loved every second of it. The only thing missing was being able to determine where to go, a fact that was rapidly overriding my sense of ecstasy with every yard I climbed.

Soon I was high enough to look down upon the entire island of Eresa. Except for the central square and the two large, adjacent temples, tree canopies cloaked most of the island in mystery. There were only glimpses of granite structures here and there, and after a little while I could discern a road network.

It surprised me how large the island actually was, which made me sad that my relationship with the druids wasn't running as smoothly as I had hoped. I would have loved to see more of the Sanctuary and made a mental note to, once this whole Shepherd situation was resolved, ask Leander for the rest of the village tour he promised me. Although, after what happened just now, I probably needed a time machine to make that happen.

Still higher I climbed, and now my head turned to the much larger island of Delos, where the temple of Isis stood on top of the hill. Or what I thought was a hill, as I could clearly see the roof of the temple protruding from the treetops about half way up a small mountain. Its shape was similar to that of Mount Cynthus, which was the name the Greeks had given it back in my own world. Only this version was covered with forest.

I was so focused on the islands' topography, that it was only when I was able to look around the mountain and observe the acres of fruit orchards stretching beyond it that I realised I had already travelled quite far off the coast. A blanket of water stretched under me, a sea of blue that appeared uninvitingly cold. There, like a caterpillar inching across a sheet of azure silk, I saw a ship braving the open seas. It had clearly just exited the docks where Selena and I had borrowed a boat yesterday. From this height it seemed to barely move at all.

Who could that be? I asked myself. This simple question seemed to trigger something. It was like my curiosity, my desire to know who was on that ship, was fighting against whoever, or whatever, had taken over by body. The change in control was there only for a split second. It was like I had grabbed the helm – or perhaps the one invading my mind had passed it over to me – and I had given it the tiniest of turns, just to see if I could.

I could ask to go with them, I thought as I felt my confidence rise. *Would that be an option? Would they take Denise and me with them? Just the two of us? And what about Ouranis? Would she be willing to let us go?*

The possibility that there was another way, that I could be once again the author of my own fate, acted as a powerful catalyst. I didn't even know if I wanted to go wherever that ship was going, but the mere thought that I could leave the mess we were in behind, and Denise and I could go somewhere else to gather our thoughts and get our minds straight, was incredibly enticing. It conjured an image of Denise and I standing at the bow of the Greek trade ship, freedom beckoning.

Yet the image shattered when the Denise's sorry excuse for a body entered the picture. From there, everything started to go downhill. The idea again came to me that there was a real possibility that Denise's body was still transforming, that her mind might well be underway, even now, to becoming another pawn of the Voidshapers. And, finally, my dreams of an escape were trampled on for a second time as I remembered Ouranis' claim about her being able to provide a cure for her. There was no way. We were stuck here.

The sinking feeling, which dropped into my stomach like a stone, splashing acid against my innards, hit me harder than it probably would have had I been standing on solid ground. It made me feel the wind rushing through my feathers as I imagined myself plummeting down, like the figurative stone was real.

My eyes shot open in horror. The wind *was* rushing through my feathers! I *was* plummeting down!

A curse formed in my mind, one that surely would have left my lips were it not for my bird body. The horned owl's body I inhabited now felt like a sack of potatoes instead of the light, hollow-boned bird it had been moments earlier. My feathered cheeks were being pulled up to my temples by the rush of air. My wings were now held above my head by the wind, immobile. My tail, unable to steer or slow my descent, was similarly useless. Inside I felt empty, alone, as though whoever had been playing with my body had left me to the mercy of the world once more.

Soon I reached terminal velocity, when gravity became unable to drag me through the air any faster. My speed was still incredible. But the fact that the force of the wind became a steady rush and didn't increase any further helped me, over time, regain the tiny amount of focus I needed. It helped me to form the words that I began to yell at my body. *Wings! Come on! Move, dammit!*

With a desperate effort I tried to actively reach any and every muscle of my body with my mind. Nothing worked; the rush of air had completely immobilised me. I felt like a droplet of water, frustratingly streamlined, as I was continuously being squeezed into that very shape by the whistling wind. The sea of blue was coming closer and closer. Hitting the surface at this speed would be like hitting concrete. Nothing but a bundle of feathers floating out to the open ocean would be left of me.

Again I focused all of my attention on my wings. In my head I was screaming louder than ever. *Why don't you move?! Bloody move!* My final curse ignited sparks of liquid fire in every fibre of my being and I felt my beak thrust wide. Out came a screech that I was sure would easily have carried to the people on the ship.

Moments before my body hit the surface, I felt a wave of tingling butterflies fluttering up the length of my wings. I pushed them downwards. The wind ripped off a good number of feathers, pinching my skin, but I didn't care. It felt as though I had finally found the cord to my backpack and the torn, but still useable, parachute had just shot out to save my life.

There was a clap like thunder. Water, icy cold, began gnawing at my skin like a school of piranhas. Judging from the pressure on my ears I was already at least five or ten feet under water and I immediately began thrashing my claws and beating my wings to prevent my momentum from carrying me even deeper.

My claws were more adaptable to a marine environment than I would have believed and pushed me upwards with remarkable ease. My wings felt a lot less heavy now and moved through the water like sea snakes. Upon breaking the surface, I gasped and my lungs filled with oxygen. Only then did I realise I was back in my old body, its control had been handed to me again and, perhaps most surprisingly, I was dressed once more like any of the druid apprentices in Eresa. Even my druid sandals had found their way back to me, and were secured tightly around my ankles.

I didn't have the time or the right state of mind to worry about how my clothes had survived the metamorphosis. As I wiped the blanket of water from my face, the island of Delos was right there, stretching across the horizon. But there was no way I could swim that far. This was the worst time to lose the ability to fly.

The dread of drowning saturated my brain. I was so confused. I began to whip my head left and right for any coastline close enough to swim to. There was only water and the occasional hill dotting the horizon. Soon I couldn't even tell which one was which anymore. All islands looked the same. Some larger, some smaller, but all demoralisingly far away.

I need to transform again, I told myself, as if the thought alone would spur my body into action. *It is the only way. Please work.*

Like a digital photo album that was being controlled by a house cat sitting on the remote, pictures of dozens of potential sea animals I could turn into flickered past, right up to the image of a great white shark. Everything inside me stopped. My hands and feet kept treading the water and the soft sloshing of the waves kept my ears occupied. But inside, everything was locked onto the image of the shark.

'The Voidshapers,' I whispered out loud. Slowly, the image of the great white shark turned to ashy black and its eyes began to shine blue light onto its imaginary environment.

I felt beads of sweat mixing with the salty seawater on my face. I could hear my own breathing become laboured. I began whipping my head more frantically this time. Left, right, left again. Behind every passing wave I expected a triangular-shaped fin to be lying in wait, black in colour and oozing its magical oil onto the water's surface.

In my frantic state I hadn't even noticed that the ship I'd seen earlier had turned and was coming straight for me. In my panic I hadn't even noticed it. It had noticed *me*, however, and was tacking its way steadily towards me.

Instinctively I raised my hand above my head and began to yell at the top of my lungs, waving one arm madly, while other one kept me from gulping down too much seawater. I was exhausted and could practically hear my legs groan from the effort. Still, the hope of rescue kept me buoyant; literally. It coerced my exhausted legs into further effort and staved off despair. I even forgot the fact that sharks, whether black, white, or even transparent, were attracted by floundering motions as well as the smell of blood. And that, due to my frantic efforts, I was only making myself look even more appealing.

The bow of the ship was cutting through the water like a waiter adroitly moving through a crowd. With every passing second, the vessel grew larger. Soon I felt my waving hand slow down and my elation disappear; not only did the ship's path lead straight through me, but at this speed there was no way I was getting on even if the crew threw down a rope ladder.

I was already beginning to move my weary body out of the ship's way with frenzied strokes when a familiar face appeared at the bow. Sophia was leaning over the railing with a determined look on her face. When she found me, her eyes opened wide in astonishment at what she was seeing. Then she turned back her head, pointed at me, and called, 'Father, turn port! I told you it was him!'

I was so glad to see the teenager's face, that my eyes remained locked onto her during the next few seconds. As she turned back to me, she brushed her hair from her cheeks and lips, throwing it into the breeze. The bundle of black hair had an odd, almost overwhelming, sense of familiarity about it. It triggered my memory of when I had flown through the double front doors of the Phoenix Hall minutes earlier, though I was sure she couldn't have been there. There was no way she could have made it to the docks in time.

The single wooden mast squeaked and the sheet of canvas flapped in the wind as the ship veered off just in time. Its wake waves pushed me away and prevented me from knocking my beleaguered head against the hull.

'Aaron, catch!' said a male voice I recognised as Pelegon Linard's. A splash followed as the rope he had thrown down met the water next to me. I quickly grabbed it and looked up, but the man had already vanished again.

'Thanks, Pelegon,' I said when Pelegon dragged me over the railing a soon after. 'Both of you.'

While I took a moment to catch my breath, Pelegon said, 'Not a problem. Are you hurt?' Judging by the tone in his voice, it appeared he wasn't sure whether he was doing the right thing.

I sighed. 'No, I don't think so. But that was... intense. How did you find me?'

'Sophia,' he said rather curtly. Marching away already, he commanded, 'Sophia, start untying the ropes! We need to keep moving.'

'Sophia? Hey, you aren't alone on this ship, are you?' I said as the lack of bodyguards caught up with me. With only the three of us here, one of which was a teenage girl, I felt incredibly naked and exposed. In fact, considering what Pelegon told me about what happened to their prison transport, coming aboard was arguably even more dangerous than being on my own, since the trading vessel was an even bigger target to the Voidshapers than my treading body.

I put a hand on Pelegon's shoulder to get his attention. 'What about the Darkness? Are you insane?'

'We're not staying here, Aaron. And neither should you if you know what's good for you.'

'What are you talking about? It's too dangerous out here. You know that better than anyone.'

Pelegon stopped working on his rope and took a deep breath. He closed his eyes for a bit. 'Tell me, how long've you been living with these people?'

'Uhm, almost two days.' I felt even more surprised by the answer than Pelegon appeared to be. I couldn't believe that around this time yesterday, Denise and I were about to arrive at the temple in pitch blackness.

'Listen to me, Aaron,' said Pelegon darkly. 'I don't know what's going on around here, but I do know it doesn't concern us. And it's plain you have no idea who these people are.'

'You mean the druids? Who cares about who they are? Think about your daughter.' My finger was aimed at Sophia, who was trying to adjust the sail on her own, without much success.

'She's exactly who I'm thinking about, my friend.' He continued untying the rope. When he had it untied, he coiled the rope around his wrist a few times to increase his grip. His muscles were bulging from the strain.

'These people,' he went on through clenched teeth, 'these *druids* as they call themselves, some of them are criminals, murderers, even. Or other scum you don't want to mess around with. I've seen some of their faces on drawings before, and others I know only by name and reputation. But trust me, Aaron, they are not your kind of people. Especially this Captain Kriton fellow. He's probably slit the throats of more people than you've shared a conversation with, ever.' With that he stalked off, shouting orders to Sophia, while making sure to keep the sail filled and smooth from his end. I didn't know much about sailing, but judging from the angle of the occasionally flapping canvas, Pelegon was getting ready to head for open sea again.

The truth in his words, for I knew in my heart that Pelegon wasn't lying, left me standing there uncomfortably for a few moments, unsure as to what to do. Then the reality of the situation came floating back and I followed Pelegon to the other side of the ship. 'So what? You've decided to take your chances with the open sea? Do you honestly think this Darkness is any more merciful than the druids?'

'I've seen our future in that hellhole, Aaron,' he said. 'And it's not looking bright. I left the decision up to Sophia and she wants to leave. So that's what we'll do. What about you? Will you come with us?'

'I can't say I'm not tempted to, but I'm not leaving Denise, Pelegon. And she can't leave. I'm sorry.'

'No worries, it's only a friendly offer. You're free to make your own choices. That's what life's all about.'

'So, can you drop me off on Ouranis' island? It's where your ship crashed.'

'No can do, sorry,' he said with a cordial shrug. 'We didn't exactly leave on the best of terms, so we're kind of in a hurry.' While my mind pondered the meaning of his words, Pelegon added, 'You'll have to wait until we're within swimming distance of some other dry land.'

I walked over to one side of the ship and watched the island of Delos becoming smaller by the second. To my right, a small peak rose from the sea, one in which Ouranis was probably going about her day. It was looking like a grey, floating buoy from this far off.

I swallowed as my already heavily-taxed brain laboured to find a solution. Transforming again was one possibility of course, no matter how remote. Because for one thing, I had no idea how to do it on demand. Nor did I have a clue how to contact the person, or entity, who did it for me last time, and I was quite sure I hadn't done it myself. Neither was there any way in this world or mine I was going to jump overboard and hope my instincts would kick in before I hit the water.

No, I needed something to take me over there, another ship or a raft of some kind. It just had to float, that was all. Float… or swim.

Trionyx! My entire brain lit up. *Yes, that's it!*

I closed my eyes, breathed in the salty air, and used every ounce of willpower and imagination to project my thoughts into the watery depths. I imagined casting my tendrils of thought into the water like fishing lines, trying to hook the great turtle and establish a mental connection. My mind was a complete mess. It was a chaos of one visualisation after another, each one contradicting the last. I tried every trick I could think of to contact Trionyx, but with each one the chaos only became worse, addling my thoughts.

My nerves were taking over, I could feel it. I needed to calm down. But how could I as the green disc representing Eresa was drifting away from me at such a frustrating pace and I found myself imprisoned, not by walls, but by the dark and mysterious depths running in all directions. Again and again I telepathically called out for the giant turtle, hoping he was still within reach. I focused solely on visualising the "fishing lines", trying to put my mind at ease by thinking of the aura of peace and serenity that radiated from a seasoned fisherman. It seemed to be working remarkably well, until…

Pelegon's voice suddenly boomed down the length of the ship. 'Bloody bastards! They're on to us!'

When I found him he was standing at the bow, peering into the same direction I was. His gaze, however, instead of being focused on the waves, was directed at the sky.

There, above the mass of green that represented Eresa, a massive blue and silvery cloud was congregating like an alchemy experiment gone wrong. I couldn't see what type of creatures it housed as of yet, but it was clearly a druid's doing, and a very strong one at that. In nervous anticipation the three of us watched the shapeless mass grow in size as it started to close the distance.

'Sophia, in the water, now!' said Pelegon the second his survival instinct kicked in. He was whipping his head left and right in confusion. He then sprang to one of the ropes, unsheathed his knife – the vessel was apparently not the only thing he had snitched from the druids – and began cutting. His knowledge of some of the Eresans' savage backgrounds was dripping from his face.

Sophia shot me a curious, knowing glance. *Is she blaming me for this?* Then the girl stepped back from the railing, her face turning suddenly anxious, and said pleadingly, 'No, father...'

'There's no time, Sophia!' Pelegon snapped at her, running to a second rope. 'Hide underwater till they're gone!'

When the second rope was cut, the sail dropped and both ropes made a loud whipping noise. Sophia and my eyes met once more. 'Go, I'll get your father!' I told her.

She nodded, bolted back to the railing, then hesitated to see if I kept my word. Pelegon was looking at the murder of azure crows that was coming for our flesh with purpose radiating from his profile. His mind was set, but so was mine. I dashed towards him, took a handful of cloth and dragged him with me. 'Don't be stupid, Pelegon! She needs you!'

'What in the...!'

The feathery beating of the wind of dozens of crows reached a noise-drowning crescendo, swallowing Pelegon's voice with ease. There had to be only a few yards left between their deadly beaks and our flesh, though I dared not look up. Sophia still hadn't jumped, which meant that Pelegon and I were about to crash into her.

'Jump, go!' I said, waving my free arm in panic. There were two yards left to go.

These few seconds of confusion were exactly what Pelegon needed. I received a sharp pain to the wrist and was forced to let go. The sudden decrease in weight sent me flying and I collided with the poor girl. Sophia was propelled off the deck, uttering a scream that lasted all the way until it was smothered by a great splash of water.

As my knees crashed into the railing, a waterfall of blue feathers descended upon the deck behind me. I was just in time to look over my shoulder and see Pelegon waving his hands and running to the other side of the ship, acting as a distraction.

As ethereal and mesmerising as the murder of crows was, their eating habits were gut-wrenching. It was like nothing I had ever seen. Through the chaos of translucent crow bodies and glinting eyeballs I watched the outline of Pelegon's body writhing on the deck. Within seconds, the poor man was lifted off his feet as if on strings, then ripped apart like a rag doll. And as the crows parted, an unrecognisable lump of meat met the deck and kept sliding until it thudded wetly into the railing on the other side.

The fear of death, of my life being snuffed out in such a quick and horrible way, was suffocating. I slapped a hand to my mouth as the irresistible urge to vomit washed over me. Fearing that the crows would switch target if I made too much noise, I let myself tumble over the railing. The crows targeted the sailcloth instead, and I could hear them rending it apart as if it were tissue on my way down to the water.

The rush of cold induced a shiver which, combined with the lingering image of what was left of Pelegon, made me vomit after all. With my legs keeping my chin above the water to the best of their abilities, I splashed my stomach contents away from me as quietly as I could. It didn't help much. I felt sick, exhausted.

'Sophia,' I whispered as loudly as I dared. I hadn't seen her since I had shouldered her into the water.

Meanwhile the crows were enjoying themselves up on the deck, making a cacophony of ripping noises, though the momentum of the ship was continuing to carry the vessel forwards. I was already drifting beside the aft section by now and, without a rope or anything else to hold onto, the ship would soon be out of reach. There was also still no sign of Sophia and desperation was starting to set in. What if I had knocked her unconscious when I pushed her overboard?

At once the whole world fell silent. The abrupt disappearance of the crows was such a switch, it was like Sophia had come from behind and had played a joke on me with a pair of earmuffs. Instead of throwing earmuffs, however, she threw a call, making me twist around with a gasp of relief. 'Thank God. Sophia, over here!'

And, at that moment, the very second I spotted the helmet of gleaming black hair bobbing up and down on the waves, my legs were pushed upwards as something huge and solid emerged from the depths and raised me out of the water: Trionyx had come at last.

Chapter 9

Physically and mentally drained, yet surprisingly calm, Sophia hopped from Trionyx' shell and landed with a crunch onto the beach of Ouranis' island. I was amazed by her mental strength. Not once had she brought up the death of her father during our trip back to the island. I attributed her lack of tears to shock, as I had witnessed people dealing with traumatic events by temporarily blocking it out before. And I knew she must have had a fair idea of what had happened to Pelegon, seeing that she had seen the crows coming. But since she didn't bring it up and I, of course, knew that there was no sense in looking for him, we had gone straight for Ouranis' island.

Like Sophia, I had remained silent all the way here. What did you say at a time like this, when the poor girl had barely showed any emotion herself? Denise, in her original form, would know. But I certainly didn't. So I decided to stave off the inevitable flood of emotions Sophia was sure to face for as long as possible, not least since I could never bring myself to tell her the details of Pelegon's death. Not to her. She was so young.

With the threat of the Voidshapers nagging at me like a horsefly waiting to sting, I was eager to leave the shore as soon as possible. I waved and thought my goodbyes to Trionyx, hoping he would understand, and then led Sophia into the cave. Only when we had made our way deeper into the tunnel did I stop to think what I was about to do.

'Hold on for just a moment, Sophia.' Sophia halted, but had no eyes for me. Instead she kept staring intently down the tunnel. 'I'm not so sure this is a good idea. Maybe you'd better stay here until I've talked to Ouranis, all right? I'm not sure what her energy will do to you.'

'You want me to stay here?' Sophia asked, a hint of anxiety in her voice. She looked back the way we came, through the tunnel to the pebbled beach and the waves beyond. There was something in her eyes that made me swallow, and yet I welcomed it at the same time; she was at least still capable of feeling something.

'I won't be long. And I promise I will keep an eye on you the whole time. I just don't want you to get hurt.' The moment I had said it, I regretted my words. I could only hope that the mention of pain wouldn't uncork the torrent of emotions that had to be bottled up inside that frail-looking body of hers.

She looked at me questionably. 'Then where are you going?'

'I'm... going to see a friend of mine. I need to ask her something, something important.'

Sophia puffed up her cheeks and stared at me for a moment. Then with in a voice bordering indifference, she said, 'Okay.'

My eyebrows climbed my forehead at her light-hearted response and I uttered a sigh of relief, though I tried to keep it subdued. 'Thanks. Stay here, all right? I'll back soon.' Then my eyes fell on the two puddles of crystal fragments where Selena had touched me that morning. Absentmindedly I started rubbing the back of my wrist, which was still a bit sore. The crystals incited an idea, but one I would never have voiced in a composed state of mind. 'If you want you can try to find a nice piece of crystal in there.' Sophia looked up at me with an almost pitiful expression on her face. 'Or not,' I added quickly. *That was stupid*, I added in silence. *Please have a solution, Ouranis.*

Sophia uttered a sigh of her own, went over to the opposite wall, pressed her back against it and slid all the way down along its smooth surface. I had no idea how to respond and felt so out of place, the only thing I could think of doing was to walk away and hope Ouranis was in a good mood.

'Back again,' said Ouranis, as her silky voice found its way into my head.

Yeah, uhm, can I come in? I thought, scanning the chamber. There was no sign of the Phoenix anywhere. Instead there was someone else waiting for me. A black figure, with the body of a hyena and eyes like tiny flashlights, appeared. She was leaving a trail of black ash behind her as she approached. At a few yards distance she halted and eyed me with those shiny blue marbles of hers.

'Hey, Denise,' I greeted her, trying to sound as friendly as I could. The sense of awkwardness that remained from my last conversation with Sophia suddenly exacerbated. I could feel a distance between Denise and me, one that was greater and more profound than the few yards of crystallised cave floor between us. Again it startled me how monstrous her appearance had become, though I tried not to let it show in my expression.

'You may come and go as you please,' said Ouranis. 'I have never forbidden anyone to enter.'

Only to leave, I commented before I could help myself.

'Fortune does not favour the foolish,' said Ouranis. 'My warnings have been clear.'

Right, I thought, still undecided as to whether to approach Denise or not; she did nothing to show her appreciation of me being here. *So, I haven't come alone. And I was wondering what would happen to Sophia if I brought her in here. It's too dangerous for her to stay outside.*

'What will happen to her hinges entirely on her actions, young Shepherd.'

I meant your energy. She's not a druid, so I'm not sure how she will be affected by it.

'Being a druid does mitigate the effect energy has on a person's body. It does not, however, provide much protection against mine. That said, if it is not my will, the human will not be harmed.'

The memory of Selena sitting on her hands and knees, fighting against the energy pressure Ouranis was inflicting on her came to me. *Do you mean you attacked Selena on purpose?*

There was a great ruffling of feathers and a flapping of wings as the giant Phoenix descended onto the chamber floor behind Denise. Upon touchdown her claws dug into the crystal coating with the sound of knifes on glass. Denise jumped up in shock.

'Very sharp.'

'Wha...?' I began to say before my voice faltered. The mesmerising beauty of seeing Ouranis in full glory, with her wings outstretched, her head arched proudly and splinters of crystal jumping from her muscled claws, was awe-inspiring.

She brought her wings back to her flanks. 'Your companion, young Shepherd.'

Oh, right. And with that I ran back to get Sophia.

As Sophia and I headed back to the chamber a few minutes later, moving as quickly as the slippery floor would allow, I figured it would be best to leave Lycomedes out of the conversation this time. It did take some effort to restrain my curiosity, for I would have loved to learn what Ouranis had to say about him. But considering how the mention of the old man's name had put an abrupt end to our previous conversation, I figured it couldn't be anything positive.

Instead of being struck by wonder, Sophia's reaction to seeing the Phoenix was one of a mixture of surprise and curiosity. Upon seeing her expression I thought for a second she might connect the blue and silvery body to the spectral crows with which the druids had punished her father for stealing the ship. But if she did, it certainly didn't show.

'Are you here to listen to the rest of my tale, young Shepherd?' Ouranis asked when the three of us, Sophia, Denise and I, had found a place to sit. 'If you are, I am willing to narrate it to you.'

Actually, I was hoping to ask you about something else, I thought, giving Sophia and Denise a glance. *Not that I'm not interested in what you have to say, of course. But you see, things haven't gone exactly our way and I don't think any one of us is welcome in Eresa any longer. It's pretty definitive this time.*

'You are the Shepherd. They must listen to you.'

I tried not to let my annoyance at Ouranis' naivety show too much; I figured that sitting in a cave on a deserted island had its limitations when it came to keeping up to speed with the zeitgeist of the druidic community. *Even if that's true, I don't think their Council sees it that way anymore. I don't understand how exactly, but suffice it to say I sort of ran out on them before they could question me. And after the breakout yesterday, and all that's happened with those Voidshapers, I'm not so keen to go back there, to be honest.*

As with the subject of Lycomedes, I decided to leave the way I transformed into an owl out of the conversation for the moment. That is, if I had any choice in the matter; just because the Phoenix only commented on thoughts, rather than memories, it didn't mean she couldn't read them.

'This is a troubling development, young Shepherd. And one that needs to be resolved as soon as we can make it so.'

I am very sorry. It wasn't all my fault, though.

'Hey, Aaron,' said Sophia suddenly, her voice curious, 'are you going to say something or are you two just going to stare to each other?' It was then when I realised how bizarre it must have looked to see man and a 3000 year old giant mythological beast staring intently into each other's eyes, saying nothing.

'We're talking to each other with our minds,' I said, fully aware I was probably making the situation worse, not better. I moved a finger between my forehead and Ouranis' beak to emphasise my point, then quickly withdrew it again when Sophia produced a satisfied smirk. If I hadn't known better, it was as though she already knew and had asked the question merely to tease me.

'Where did you find this human, young Shepherd?' Ouranis asked, seemingly amused.

She found us, to tell you the truth. She and her father Pelegon had stowed themselves away on a prison transport. It's the ship that crashed into your island. I assume you know about it, considering it's gone now. Pelegon was executed by the druids only an hour ago, and only because he was trying to make a life for himself and Sophia. I paused for a second, then thought, *I think she's in shock. She hasn't cried once.*

'Who sent the transport?'

I think his name was Arcturus. Selena said he is one of the lords around here. Sophia is part of the reason why I'm here, actually. She's lost everything now her father is gone too. Her mother was sacrificed to the Voidshapers.

'Hmm.' As the sound entered my skull, it felt like she was actively trying to shake my brain loose to see what would fall out.

Have you heard of him?

'Certainly. I have seen many of his people lose their lives,' she said solemnly. 'Lord Arcturus' desperate response to the Voidshapers' nest now located inside his borders is callous and ill-advised.'

The nest? That doesn't sound good.

'He has been feeding the nest with the lives of his people for over a year,' she went on. 'I have recently witnessed one of these offerings you spoke of. It is a deed born of despair. A wiser course of action would be to evacuate his people and leave the Hive alone. Yet, for some reason, he never did.'

Then why don't you tell him? He will surely listen to you.

'The Shepherd is the only one who can interpret my thoughts, young Shepherd. There is no way I can communicate with him directly.'

Then you should've asked a Shepherd, I thought in exasperation. *You just said it's been going on for a while.* A realisation hit me. *Is that the favour you wanted from me? If so, I can tell you the answer is yes. I'll tell him whatever you want if that's the price of the antidote for Denise. We can go together.*

Ouranis suddenly appeared highly uncomfortable. In the corners of my eyes I saw both Denise and Sophia draw back their heads in anticipation for the Phoenix's response; where any human female would simply twist in her seat, Ouranis shifting in discomfort was rather frightening, particularly from up this close. 'It is not that simple,' she chose to say.

Sure it is, I replied bluntly. *I mean..., sorry about that. I'm still not used to speaking in this way, using the telepathy.* Another realisation revealed itself to me. *Does it have something to do with the fact that none of the druids knew about the Voidshapers' existence until yesterday?*

A moment of silence followed, then, 'That is a tale for another day, I am afraid. You will know when you are ready.'

Great. Before she could dismiss me again, I tried to swing the conversation off the sidewalk and back onto the road. *Then what about the three of us? Do you know of a place where we can stay for a while? Like I said, we can't go back to Eresa.*

For what seemed like minutes, Ouranis remained silent. With every passing second I became more convinced my efforts to continue the conversation were in vain. The Phoenix was so different to any person I had ever talked to. I was used to people who simply said what they wanted to say, especially if they had the urgent desire to tell me something that I could sometimes sense coming from Ouranis. If I were to hazard a guess, it almost seemed like she was nervous as to how I would respond to her request. I took it to be a testament to her lack of understanding of human relationships, and of the lengths I would go to in order to save Denise.

Ouranis? I thought, in a way a mouse would tap the claw of a lion to find out if it was asleep.

The Phoenix's head gave a little jerk and a rustle of feathers swept through the chamber. 'There you are,' she sighed. Those three words induced a powerful wave of relaxation that soothed my muscles; somehow this time, she had not only passed on the words, but the emotions she was feeling as well. Now excitement flared from the great Phoenix and she added excitedly, 'I found him again.'

Found who?

'Quiet.'

After a minute or so, during which time Ouranis' eyelids had been squeezed together, she stood up and turned her feathery behind to us. Sophia and I looked at each other. Sophia shrugged. Neither of us said a word. When Ouranis finally turned back, there was a disarming presence in her eyes, an extra twinkle in addition to the ever-present glow.

'You need to be ready, young Shepherd,' she said at once. 'Your training starts tomorrow.'

Uhm, okay... I had no idea what to make of this. *It would help if I knew what I needed to be ready for, if that's not too much to ask.*

'Very true,' said Ouranis and she took a moment to consider. 'Do you remember everything I told you about Akhenaten?'

Of course. Well, I think I do. You said he was the first person to come to your world and he tried to create a Sphinx using Isis' powers. But then Isis put a stop to it and as a result, her energy was divided into seven pieces. Those pieces formed the seven Celestial Beasts.

'Correct,' said Ouranis, evidently pleased with the summary. She reseated herself, drew a deep breath and resumed her tale as though no time had passed since our last conversation. However, this time her voice had a sprightly feel to it, as though recent events seasoned the words with a diverse collection of spices before they left her skull. 'After his ritual failed, Akhenaten went back to the world you and your mate came from. He did not take his followers with him, however. They were left to create a new society of their own. For years we lived in harmony, side-by-side with the abundance of flora and fauna that inhabited this world prior to our existence. It was a time of peace and prosperity, and Akhenaten's followers were quick to explore and populate these lands. They were remarkably efficient at it. Then one day, a day none of us were prepared for, word reached us of creatures created through negative energy.'

The Voidshapers.

'Indeed,' she said, her zest diminishing as her words became overshadowed by sorrow. 'They were all-consuming, remorseless. By the time I learned about their existence, four of my siblings had already been absorbed into the Hive. They struck with precision, with purpose. My siblings and I were targeted first, before the rest of the animal life fell prey to their consuming nature.'

I'm very sorry. What about Akhenaten's followers?

153

'With the exception of those foolish enough to seek out the Voidshapers' destruction, they were left alone. I have yet to discover the reason why, yet they were. On occasion some of the Voidshapers were sent to feed – and still are as you have witnessed yourself – but never have the Voidshapers sought to absorb the human population completely.'

That's odd.

'Indeed. It was as though the Hive wanted them to continue to exist, perhaps to breed and supply a more permanent source of food. The answer could be as straightforward as this. But although I am careful not to underestimate the Hive's intelligence, I have yet to see any sign of restraint during the Voidshapers' raids. Everywhere they go, they devour what they can. To me it seems that the only reason why the human population has managed to survive is because the Hive has yet to send its Voidshapers to their cities, since the Voidshapers themselves have no conscience.'

And you are the only one of the Celestial Beasts who has managed to keep out of their grasp? I asked her without thinking. The moment it left my mind, I recalled the reaction Ouranis had given me the last time I mentioned her brothers and sisters' fate. I bit my lip in regret. *Whoops.*

'I did not,' said Ouranis mournfully. 'This body,' she lifted up her head and showed me the inside of her wings, 'has not always looked like this. My feathers once shone bright with colour, brilliant in the sunlight. They became collector's items, even objects of worship for Akhenaten's followers when I still shed them once in a while. What you are looking at is but a remnant of how I once appeared.'

I can't imagine you being any more beautiful, I thought truthfully.

'You have nothing to compare me with.'

I have to disagree, I thought with a small smile, glancing at Denise, whose mind seemed to be floating somewhere I couldn't follow. *I miss her so much.*

'In time, young Shepherd.'

Why? Why can't you just help her now? I've already promised I will do whatever you ask of me. Please. I'm afraid that what's happening to her may become irreversible if nothing's done soon.

Ouranis eyed me inquisitively. I could see her bulk expand and contract every few seconds. 'Very well,' she said at length. 'Your determination is admirable. And I can see that continuing to withhold this from you will only hinder your training, which is something we cannot afford. Not now he's this close,' she added, in what could only be described as a mental whisper. 'Yes, let us continue. The answer will follow.'

'Several centuries before you drew your first breath,' she went on, 'the Voidshapers managed to empty this world of all life except for the vegetation and, as I mentioned, many of Akhenaten's followers. It was on this fateful day that the world changed once again. For the Hive became suddenly dormant, waking only when it needed to feed or defend itself. This is how it has remained until a few days prior to your arrival.'

'For how long I was joined with the Hive after I had been absorbed is impossible to tell. My senses still worked, though differently. I found myself floating in a dark place. It was as if I had faded into another state of existence, one in which I wasn't concerned about trivial things like the smell of the sea or the warmth of the sun. The only things that mattered were to prolong my life as long as possible… and to rejoin my siblings. I yearned for them. I knew I had to be close, for they too had been absorbed into the Hive. And since I had not died, I knew they shouldn't have, either. There were other spirits there too, millions of them; all earlier victims of the Voidshapers. It was no way to live.'

While listening to Ouranis' story, a movement in the corner of my eye distracted me. I turned to my right and my eyes fell on a naked belly. Sophia had untied the rope binding her dress, had carefully exposed her belly, and was in the middle of prodding her belly button with upmost curiosity. To my amazement I beheld a tattoo of a black sun imprinted on her skin right around her navel area.

'It's pretty,' I lied to her. Although it was evidently applied by a delicate hand, I had never liked tattoos. And seeing one on a girl of Sophia's age was not only a first, it was also quite repellent. I couldn't help wondering whether it had been her choice to be left with such a permanent decoration. And even if it had been, was she old enough to make such a decision?

'And new,' Sophia said with a queer edge to her voice.

'Excuse me?'

'It wasn't there before,' she said. My mouth fell open. Sophia's hands, with which she was still preventing her dress from sliding back, suddenly froze. Then she gave a resigned shrug, adjusted her clothing, and watched me close my mouth again. 'Can I play with the dog?'

'What?' I felt so confused, it surprised me even a single word managed to pass my throat. Since Pelegon's death I had been so focused on the here and now, not once had I considered Sophia's almost otherworldly indifference to Denise's appearance. Now, however, after hearing her ask to take Denise out for a walk in such a casual manner, the whole situation caught up with me.

'Her,' Sophia added, pointing her finger unnecessarily.

I looked at Denise to try to gauge her reaction. The little of her body language I could discern made me wonder if Denise even understood what was going on; the black fog that had accumulated during my conversation with Ouranis prevented me from seeing whether she was wagging her bottlebrush tail or bearing her fangs. 'I don't know, Sophia,' I said guardedly. 'I don't think she's up for it.'

'Yes she is,' said Sophia with confidence, springing to her feet. 'What's her name?'

'Denise.' By the time my girlfriend's name had passed my lips, Sophia was already dashing across the crystalline floor, slipping and laughing as though surrounded by friends on a frozen lake.

'Come, Denise!' she called, her voice echoing around the chamber. 'Catch me if you can!' Denise gave a yapping laugh that only hyenas can produce and went after her. A few paces in she crashed to the floor.

'Denise!' I said. But she didn't care about the discomfort. She shrugged her lean body, got to her feet and continued, though at a slower, more tentative pace. Her toes were spread wide to offer her claws the maximum amount of traction, while her nails tapped across the crystal layer with each careful step she took.

'Oh, crap,' I cursed when I noticed Denise's posture. From my perspective it seemed like she wasn't just following Sophia, she was actually stalking her. 'Denise!' I called after her, aiming for something between a warning and a command.

'She means her no harm, young Shepherd,' said Ouranis, injecting the words directly into my head like she always did. 'She is simply interested in the human girl's movements. Because of her metamorphosis, your mate's eyesight probably works differently than before. It did for me during the time it took for my body to convert. If you doubt my words, look at her tail.'

That's what I'm concerned about. It's swishing. O'Connor, my parents' cat, does that all the time when it wants to attack, but can't get to its target. It's a sign of frustration.

'Your mate does not have the body nor the mind of a cat,' said Ouranis, as if I needed any reminding of that. 'Look more closely. She keeps her tail low and her wag is broad, which means she is being submissive. You can trust my judgement. No harm will come to the human, or your mate.'

If you say so.

'I would like to draw your attention to the fact that your mate has not tried to alter her shape once since you left her with me. It is a positive sign. For as you must have deduced from your encounters with the Voidshapers already, they are indeed able to alter their shape if they so desire.' A memory unfolded of a cloud of bats arriving at the beach of Delos before black panthers dropped down onto the grass like inky hailstones. 'But let us move forward and go back to my tale. There remains a great deal to cover.'

Sure. When I turned back to the giant Phoenix, my eyes fell on a shelf of rock protruding from the wall high above my head. It looked like some kind of roost. I deemed this was where Ouranis had sat when I entered the chamber.

'We shall continue the tale from the final years I was forced to spend absorbed by the Hive Mind,' said Ouranis. 'As I said before, my mother's abilities were split between the seven of us. The energy that carried the power which enabled her to pass between worlds, the same one with which she was able to offer Akhenaten and his followers a new home, was the one that created me. It is the most dangerous one for the Hive to possess, as you can imagine.'

To possess? Do you mean those Voidshapers can use your ability for themselves if they capture you?

'That is correct.'

But you said they already captured you once.

'And I escaped. It took me many years before I regained control over my ability. Though once I did, and found my way to the surface of the Vault, my abilities allowed me to link my thoughts with the world outside the Vault. My thoughts, my memory, my being, my entire consciousness was then transported into the vessel you see before you. I believe my own energy was used to create this body. Unfortunately, however, I had never been able to find any of my siblings inside the Vault. I had to continue my efforts from here.'

So what did the Voidshapers do with your ability before you regained control of it?

'Oh, the Hive tried to cross over to your world,' said Ouranis, sounding more playful now. 'And tried, and tried some more. And curiously enough, every time it did so, my location inside the Vault was altered. I cannot say I fully understand this process myself,' she said to my questioning look, 'perhaps the tremendous amount of energy it requires to access my abilities has something to do with it. Though every time the Hive used them, I was transported somewhere else inside the Vault of Spirits. Eventually I managed to reach the surface and got out. Now I think the reason why the Hive tried to cross over to your world must have been because my abilities enabled it to sense the almost infinite amount of bodies that reside there. Yet I had taken measures against the Hive crossing over, and it never managed it.'

She suddenly fell silent. It took me a moment or two to realise Ouranis was actually waiting for another one of my 'sharp' comments. My love for mysteries kicked in and I sank into thought. *She'd taken measures against the Hive crossing over?*

A great scratching noise came from far into the chamber. I turned around to see Denise lying belly up in her pool of black ash, and Sophia standing beside her, shrieking with laughter. The sight of Denise brought me right back to the day before, when she and I were plucked from the original island of Delos and deposited here like some bizarre melding of *Homer* and *The Wizard of Oz*. Then it struck me. *The Shepherd's blessing! That's it, isn't it?*

Ouranis bobbed her head, birdlike, in acknowledgement. I could actually feel the wind generated by the movement wafting against my face. 'I had foreseen the time when I might fall prey to the Hive, and so I passed on a portion of my energy to one of the druids. In doing so, the first Shepherd was created.'

And this is why I was transported to this world yesterday? Because I received the Shepherd's energy, your energy?

'I see no other reason. Although again the energy behaved most strangely once it entered your world; I cannot say I fully understand why the energy formed the pair of azure globes I can read from your memory. Nor do I know why you, of all people, were chosen as the gift's new vessel, particularly since there were several strong druids present at the time of the ritual. Indeed, the existence of the Shepherd is the reason why the Hive could not gain full access to my ability. It needed both parts, both components of my mother's ability. I knew it could only be a matter of time before the Shepherd would be captured and absorbed, of course, which greatly hastened my efforts to escape.'

'So, yes, at least part of the reason why you crossed over to this world must be due to the fact that you absorbed the Shepherd's portion of my mother's ability,' she went on. 'That said, it does remain a mystery to me why my ability activated when you received the energy. It should not have happened without my consent. The strange behaviour of the azure globes that you saw might contain a clue. But if so, it is one I cannot decipher at this time.'

'Another question I have yet to find an answer to is why, after I was absorbed by the Voidshapers, the Hive went into hibernation instead of immediately sending its Voidshapers after the Shepherd. The Hive must have been able to feel the connection that continued to exist between us. I am confident of this. Perhaps the reason is as simple as the Hive being confused about the new ability it had obtained and it was, as yet, unaware that it needed both components. I am confident the Hive knows this now, however.'

My mind went back to Denise and me crossing over. *Just to be sure, I am still capable of going back, aren't I? Now that I have the Shepherd's abilities, I mean.*

'There is no reason to think otherwise,' she said, to which I uttered a sigh of relief. 'When you have successfully passed on your Shepherd abilities to your successor,' she added.

And you can teach me how to do this, safely?

'That depends on your efforts, young Shepherd.'

All right, no pressure then. Please continue your tale, Ouranis.

'Very well. After my escape from the Vault of Spirits, I sought refuge in the very chamber we are standing in,' the Phoenix went on. 'It was a bleak place and I was forced to live here in solitude. There was not a single animal alive outside the Hive, nor was there a place you know as Eresa.'

There were no druids?

'Naturally there were,' Ouranis said, sounding a little offended for my dull-wittedness. 'There was a Shepherd. And only druids are supposed to carry the gift.'

Oh, right. Sorry. But wait a minute. If there were no animals, how could there be any plants? They need them, don't they? They're part of the circle of life.

Ouranis appeared pleased with my comments. 'As I said, it was a bleak place, the world in and outside my den. Humans, the descendants of Akhenaten's followers, had a hard time surviving, though not all was lost. Nature has a way of surviving in the direst of circumstances and she can bounce back from the deepest crevasse. She had me to aid her as well. To this day I have worked tirelessly to steal back the millions upon millions of spirits from the Hive Mind and bring them back to the light. It is a slow process and I probably could not have done it, or not as efficiently, were it not for the fact that the Hive had captured me and thereby supplied me with the experience I needed.'

You've been stealing back their spirits? How does that work?

'It is part of my ability. I am able to connect with the Hive Mind, search through the many spirits that are imprisoned in the Hive's Vault of Spirits, and pull them back to our world. As I said before, the spirits inside the Vault exist in a different state, a different phase if you will, and my ability allows me to change this state. I am confident it is the reason why I am the only one who has managed to escape thus far, even among my kind of whom some are much more powerful than I am.'

That's incredible. But still, being powerful seems to be a matter of perspective, then. I mean, if you are the only one who has managed to escape, then what is the use of having more power? I scratched my head for a bit and thought, *It was meant as a compliment.*

Ouranis bowed her head again in acknowledgement, though I wasn't sure if the meaning of my words had had the impact I was aiming for. And, by the sound of her voice as she spoke next, it was evident she wasn't prepared to suffer any further distraction. 'To my great regret, my ability to single out entities within the Vault of Spirits becomes increasingly difficult the deeper I dig. As a result, I have to free the spirits one at a time for the ones further in to be revealed to me. It is why I have been focusing mostly on marine and aerial animals; to save others I would have to leave my den. It is something I have been trying to avoid, since when I move, it is difficult to maintain focus on the Vault.'

'I have also refrained from freeing human spirits, since they are a superstitious race,' Ouranis went on. 'Many know about the Voidshapers, although they call them by different names, and they have become used to the animal life looking the way they do. As I am sure you can deduce yourself, they cannot remember a time when the animals didn't. However, it is something else to see their ancestors coming back to life, in their eyes. We know they aren't actually dead, or not in the way I understand death, yet the humans in this world do not. And remember, they too will appear transparent, which, due to the humans' religious background, will make them think their absorbed ancestors have returned from the realm of the dead. In addition, since the Voidshapers have absorbed the bodies the humans were born to, by pulling their spirits out of the Vault I would make them essentially immortal.'

I think that was a good call, Ouranis. I haven't yet met anyone beside the druids and Pelegon and Sophia. But if people in my world are in any way comparable with the people living here, they would definitely have a problem with their ancestors returning as ghosts. But, it is true that people here are already used to seeing animals that look like ghosts.

I thought about it for a moment and tried to imagine how I, or my friends and family back in my world, would react to see a deceased family member return in spectral form. It dawned to me that my view, and that of Ouranis, might be too pessimistic. *Although,* I thought at length, *as long as you don't drop a few translucent humans unceremoniously in their midst, I think there are a lot of people who would be overjoyed to see their ancestors returned to them. We would have to think about how to confront people with this reality, though. I'm not even sure how I would react.*

A smile curved as my mind showed me an image of Ouranis and I delivering a host of fifty ethereal humans to a settlement, one which entrance was pouring out cheering villagers. The sight of them reunited with their lost family prickled something in my memory. *So is that what you were so relieved about earlier, because you found someone you were looking for in the Vault of Spirits?*

Over the next half a minute or so, Ouranis stared at me, her eyes blank. Then she rose to her feet and turned her back to me, sweeping a great bundle of see-through tail feathers across my face. Tilting her beak upwards, she began to stare unfathomably up at the patch of sky that was visible through the vent of the volcano. In a voice laden with emotion, she said, 'It is. I have caught glimpses of my brother before, so I knew I had to be close to finding him. Now I have. After all those years…'

Her emotions affected me like a virus. I found myself at a loss for words, for nothing I could think of to say or do seemed appropriate. Of course I wanted to do anything I could to help, I had promised her that. But, again, what did I really have to offer such a magnificent creature?

'Tonight we will begin your training, young Shepherd,' Ouranis said, snapping me right back. There was no doubt in her voice. It was not a question. It was simple fact. And I went from feeling helpless to being focused solely on my upcoming training in the span of a pirate's cannon blast. 'Together the two of us should have no difficulty extracting my brother Flego from the Hive Mind. It is his spirit that I have located. When we have succeeded, I promise I will see what I can do for your mate.'

Any doubt I may have had for taking the road Ouranis suggested was wiped away by the Phoenix's promise. *I only hope I can actually do something to help,* I told her. *I'm not Selena or any of the other druids. But I do promise I will do my best not to let you down.*

'It is all I ask, young Shepherd. And in saying that, I think I am finally ready to answer the question you posed earlier, since you have now learned enough to be able to understand my position. You see, the reason why my abilities do not allow me to help your mate at this point in time is because in order to do so, I am required to disconnect my mind from the Vault of Spirits. And due to the fact that the many spirits imprisoned there are in constant motion, I risk not being able to find Flego again soon once I let him go. And time is, I am afraid, in short supply. As I told you, the Hive is no longer dormant. Something has changed, and I cannot see or sense what it is. All we can do is to prepare ourselves.'

Something bumped against the inside of my knee. Looking down I saw Denise staring up at me. She opened her mouth wide in what was evidently a yawn, closed her jaws, and curled up beside me. Soon most of her body was covered in black fog and I figured it wouldn't be long before only her brightly burning eyes would be visible. With Denise now enjoying a late afternoon nap, the silence inside the chamber began to creep up on me. I glanced over my shoulder, fully expecting Sophia to still be playing on the crystal floor. But the floor had turned into a still life of sparkling beauty.

'Denise, where's Sophia?' I felt another strata being added on the mountain of worries that was weighing me down. Momentarily, Denise looked up, sniffed, then her head disappeared into the fog. Whether she had understood my question or not, her patience with Sophia had clearly run out.

Have you seen her? I thought, aiming for Ouranis.

'The human girl is your responsibility, young Shepherd,' said Ouranis simply.

The sound of crystal shattering broke across my eardrums. *Sophia!* Within seconds I was already at the inner mouth of the cave, where the sound had come from. 'Sophia!' I said, firing her name through the tunnel like a heat seeking missile. 'Are you all right?!'

When my eyes found her, Sophia was standing over the joint craters filled with crystal shards. She was eyeing one of the larger slivers with interest, holding it up against the light that flooded in from outside. 'I like this one,' she said, squinting her eyes as the bar of light passed her face.

'You've got to be kidding me,' I said exasperatedly, after I came to a slipping halt. My hands were clasping my knees. 'Don't scare me like that, Sophia. Now, come on. Let's go back inside.'

Sophia gave me a reproachful look, snatched a good handful of fragments from the ground and walked right past me back to the chamber. I was quite gratified with the severe tone in my voice, though its effect on Sophia still came as a surprise. Then I remembered the firm hand with which Pelegon had treated her and I figured Sophia might be used to obeying people who felt this much concern for her. I quickly went after her.

Chapter 10

My stomach growled in discomfort. My eyes were drinking in the high chamber wall that ran all the way up until it was funnelled into the relatively narrow mouth of the volcano; no matter how long I looked, the sight's magnificence did not diminish. The three of us, Sophia, Denise and I, were sitting at one end of the chamber, waiting for the landscape outside to be gently bathed in moonlight. Ouranis had adjourned to her roost – probably to contemplate the remaining trapped spirits, and one in particular.

As my eyes hopped from one crystal dagger protruding from the glassy coating to the next, an odd, unfamiliar sound attracted my attention. It took me a moment or two to find its source. There, to my amazement, I watched a fifth crystal come into being in a cluster of four, like a hand growing an extra finger. At first it appeared like the glassy spike was being thrust through the chamber wall from the other end like the tip of a sword. Then I realised the crystal was actually being created on the spot, as tiny, pearly white orbs were floating in, condensing and congregating on the crown of a slowly growing, crystal stump.

I sat up and spoke softly, for I felt as though I was intruding on something miraculous, 'Sophia, look over there.'

Sophia turned and followed my finger to the growing crystal. 'Whoa,' she breathed, her eyes appearing disproportionately large in her delicate face. 'It's beautiful. Is Ouranis doing that too?'

'I think so.' I looked up to the Phoenix's roost. After my conversation with Ouranis, Sophia had displayed such a sudden and intense interest in the crystals that I had told her my view of them. From what I could gather, Ouranis, in an effort to extract more and more spirits from the Hive, was continuously channelling energy. And it was this energy that formed the foundation for the crystal coating we were sitting on.

Sophia's face suddenly drooped. Even the growing crystal didn't seem to retain her tiny adolescent attention-span any longer. 'I'm bored,' she said in a drawn-out voice.

'Bored? I thought you liked it here. Look, there's another one.'

'And I'm hungry.'

'I know, but it won't be long now, I promise. It's almost dark and Ouranis said she would take us somewhere else when it was safe to do so, remember? I'm sure there is plenty of food wherever we're going.'

Uttering something between a grunt and a sigh, Sophia stood up and marched, defiantly, over to Denise. Denise had been lying there for a while now, which meant that the black fog had obscured every feature of her body except for the tiny torches of pale light.

Upon reaching her, Sophia slumped like a petulant toddler, causing the half-dozing Denise to jerk her head up, startled. The fog responded a split second later, to the extent that Sophia was obliged to waft it away to prevent it from entering her mouth. The action also caused Denise's head became fully visible, first her soft pointed ears, then her snout, which now slowly descended onto her overlapping front paws. Without a moment's hesitation Sophia began stroking Denise between the ears, displaying a level of open affection even I would have been hard-pressed to show the hyena in her current condition.

'Denise is my girlfriend,' I said, without thinking. Sophia gave me a hard-to-read glance. 'She hasn't always looked like this,' I added, my cheeks burning. 'She was once like you and me. And very pretty.'

Sophia turned back to look at Denise. As she spoke, a shadow cast over her eyes. 'She's not the same as the ones on our ship. Her eyes are different.'

At the mention of what happened on board the prison transport, any thought of a reply vanished. I kept watching Sophia anxiously, chewing my lip. After suffering a blank mind for a few seconds, I frantically began thinking of a way to steer the conversation into calmer waters. Then, as slowly and inexorably as an iceberg breaking off into the flow, Sophia's grief overtook her: her eyes swam with tears, her head bowed, and she sank to the ground as though suddenly exhausted.

I rose to my feet, headed over and put my hand around her. 'It's okay, Sophia,' I said consolingly, pressing her against me. 'It's nothing to be ashamed of. Just let it out.' A wet sniff escaped the girl's nostrils. 'You're safe now.' At these words Sophia looked up, her eyelids quivering. There was no sobbing yet, but I was expecting it any second now. At the sight of her grief, my heart threatened to shatter like one of the chamber's crystals.

Sophia suddenly appeared to steel herself with every ounce of willpower she could muster. Her eyes became hard, focused. The shadows were back, darkening the white of her eyes. But it could also have been my own imagination. 'You promised me,' she said in a stony, granite-like voice, one that made me soften my grip and look down at her with mixed shock and remorse. She gave my arm a fiery glance. It made me withdraw it completely. Then she added in that same, flinty manner, 'On the ship. You told me you would get my father. Where is he?'

I was on my feet again in the span of a splintered second. My mouth refused to close or speak. Sophia didn't move. She continued to stare up at me like a doll taken straight out of a high budget horror movie. Her grief was gone. All of a sudden, she was like a completely different girl. How could she not know Pelegon was dead? She was in the water before the druids' crows descended on the deck, but, surely, she must know why we didn't go back for her father. It was obvious to me that the full ramifications of her father's death had not sunk in, but had she been in a state of complete denial all this time? She had seen the translucent crows, the danger. What was going on?

'He's... I don't know.' I continued to stammer as I staggered backwards. I had so hoped to avoid mentioning Pelegon, not indefinitely, but until I had summoned the needed courage and proper words to talk about his fate.

Silence fell between us once more. Sophia still had her hand on Denise's neck and, for the first time, Denise produced a groan of pleasure. She even pushed her head against Sophia's palm, clearly reluctant for the physical contact to cease. As Sophia stood up, slowly and deliberately, Denise went with her. It was almost as if Denise's neck was actually shackled to the girl's wrist by invisible handcuffs.

When she had drawn to her full height, which wasn't all that impressive, Sophia's free hand clenched into a fist. Even from a few yards away I could see it trembling and turning white from the strain. Then, after filling her lungs with air, she screamed in overwhelming rage, 'WHERE IS MY FATHER?'

At that moment, a great gush of wind swept my legs from under me and a sharp pain in my back followed as I hit the crystal floor; Ouranis had descended to put a stop to the conversation. I kept sliding for a few yards until I found myself lying in almost the exact same spot as when I drew Sophia's attention to the growing crystal.

Ouranis' smooth-as-silk voice came seeping in. 'It is time, young Shepherd. The darkness of the night will conceal our escape enough for none of the druids to notice us leaving. If any at all, I am confident there will be very few druids outside Eresa tonight. Trionyx hasn't ferried anyone over the last few hours.'

I didn't respond. My mind was still spellbound by the image of Sophia's anguished profile. I quickly pushed myself up again to see what had happened to the other two. Denise was on her feet, shaking her head to get rid of the fuzziness that had been knocked into her; she had been thrown against a wall by Ouranis' gush of wind. Sophia too had been blown across the crystal floor. She was lying on her side a few yards away, her belly facing the rock face, with her arms and legs sprawled awkwardly. She wasn't moving.

'NO!' I sprang up. And as the word bounced through the chamber, I felt my eyelids filling with salty water. I practically launched myself to her side and, mindful that she may have broken something, carefully rolled her to her back.

Sophia's eyes were closed, which I deemed was a good sign. This way she could just have been knocked unconscious. I took her wrist, which felt lifeless, and attempted to check her pulse. I had witnessed people do it before, but had never had the misfortune of needing to try it myself. There was no sign of life.

'Come on…,' I said, pressing her skin a little harder. There was still nothing, and I felt an unbearable tense of frustration ripping through my body. 'I don't feel anything. I must be doing it wrong. How do you do this?' I asked helplessly, as though there was anyone around who could explain it to me.

I switched to her neck; hoping to feel any sign of life, be it breath or heartbeat. Finally I managed to detect a pulse, faint but definitely rhythmic. 'Thank God,' I breathed in relief, for what felt like the hundredth time in two days. A salty droplet of sweat made its way into my mouth. Only now did I notice the bruise on Sophia's chin.

'If this is my doing, I do apologise,' said Ouranis. 'I wasn't aware the human girl was on her feet. She's so tiny.'

It's okay. She's still alive, I thought, ignoring the fact that Ouranis only mentioned Sophia in her apology.

'I am aware of that. Her energy has not changed.'

I think she's unconscious. Can't you do something for her?

'Perhaps I can. I may be able to give her some of my own energy to speed her recovery. Come, lay her down before me. I will see what I can do.' Delicately, I scooped up Sophia's body and put her down before Ouranis. Sophia's neck seemed barely able to hold her head in position, and it lolled to one side as soon as she touched the floor. It was almost too painful to look at the poor girl. She looked so serene; utterly different to how she looked a few minutes earlier. 'Now please step back.'

I did as she asked and the great Phoenix reared up, then ducked her head towards Sophia. Before her enormous beak even touched Sophia's body, I could feel a tingling sensation starting at the front of my knees, chest and face, then running all the way to the back of my body. It felt pleasant and warming, like a soft summer breeze. I figured it was Ouranis' energy.

The moment the tip of Ouranis' beak touched Sophia's belly, I saw something silvery white igniting in the Phoenix's eyes. It was there only for a moment, for the next was filled with a chaos of translucent feathers, combined with a birdlike screech that made me clench my teeth together in pain.

Now another, even more forceful, gush of wind cannoned into me, and I was launched backwards, my feet sliding across the crystal floor. Sophia was incidentally blown my way as well, and in mid-slide I squatted down to catch the still sleeping eleven-year-old before she could knock me over like a penguin on a frozen lake.

When I found her again, Ouranis was standing in the middle of the chamber, dumbstruck. I imagined steam rising from her nostrils; she was looking angry, confused, and her great wings were spread wide like a swan's, as though she was unsure whether to fly off or come closer.   I glanced down at Sophia to see if she was all right. Her eyes were closed. Her lips had become a thin line. Meanwhile, Ouranis had recovered. 'Grab the girl!' she said. 'We have been discovered! I cannot touch her again.'

In shock I looked up, seeing nothing but blue and silvery feathers streaking past. The crying call of a hyena followed from behind; Denise was the first to be snatched. The next second I felt one of Ouranis' claws grab me around the waist as well. My mind echoed Ouranis' voice. *Grab the girl.*

I did the only thing that made sense to me. Using both arms and legs I lifted Sophia off the ground and secured her against my chest and Ouranis' claw. With a few forceful strokes of her wings, Ouranis was already at the centre of the chamber. There she hovered for a moment to prepare herself for the climb.

I was hanging from one claw with an unconscious Sophia dangling lifelessly under me while, on my right, Denise hung. She looked petrified with all four legs stiff as branches, claws out, and her tail rigid like a bee's stinger. As we rose, wind pushed my chin into my chest and I saw the chamber floor becoming smaller and smaller. Meanwhile my abdominal muscles were being squeezed together by Ouranis' claw. My stomach felt like it was being left behind.

The walls of the vertical exit flashed by, while we kept soaring upwards like the molten rock that had once formed the chimney in the mountain peak. A moment of weightlessness followed as the four of us popped our heads and bodies out of the vertical tunnel. It seemed like time had slowed down as Ouranis turned to the east and I looked down the mountain protruding from the ocean's surface.

Then I saw it. Ahead of us, in the moonlight, something gigantic was slithering through the water. The elongated creature, whatever it was, consisted of multiple, pitch black humps that moved as one in an elegant, synchronised fashion. A ridge of toothed spikes ran across the monster's back. And in a rhythmic manner, a black, dragon-like head with shiny blue zircons as eyes kept diving in and out of the water like a dolphin. The creature was heading straight for Ouranis' island.

'Young Shepherd, you need to watch your grip,' said Ouranis. 'When I touched the human girl, the Hive must have sensed the connection I was trying to form in order to aid her recovery. I cannot explain why as of yet, but it might be due to the Voidshapers' proximity to my den; they are close. Do not allow the human girl's skin to touch mine, or they will continue to track us.'

At the mention of "Voidshapers", I looked down at the black serpent that was about to come ashore. I could clearly see the inky trail of blackness it was leaving behind on the water's surface.

The moment of weightlessness turned into one of near freefall as we began plummeting down one side of the mountain. Wind was pushing back my cheeks with such intensity that I literally had to press my lips together to prevent them from flapping uncontrollably against my teeth. My eyelids were forced together during the entire glide down to the water, which made it all the more difficult to keep Sophia's body from plunging into the dark depths when Ouranis suddenly pulled out of her dive.

The droplets of salty seawater came first, then the wind released its firm grip on my face. I knew we were flying level with the open ocean. I opened my eyes and found myself utterly dumbfounded. The rush, the anxiety, the thrill, it was all gone and replaced by an entirely new world. It was a world of silence, peace and beauty.

As I watched, my eyes feasted on a myriad of stars reflected in the waves. Directly ahead, the softly rolling surface of the sea was scintillating in the moonlight. It was a beam of light that, as we followed it, brought us to our new home.

Chapter 11

'You are not closing your mind,' said Ouranis, repeating the same comment she had thrown at me several times over the past half an hour. The impatience that underlined her words during the first few attempts was now bordering on frustration.

I had my eyes closed and was sitting on a boulder, back straight and hands folded in my lap. I had spent many an hour in the past few *days* in my efforts to develop my Shepherd abilities. Unfortunately, judging by my progress, I probably would have had better success at teaching Christmas songs to the frogs that were watching me from the periphery. The beasties had been there for the entire afternoon, sitting on a pair of lily leaves with their spectral bodies lined up in choir formation. At least they were quiet.

You only said I needed to open it, I thought. I was becoming rather annoyed myself, for Ouranis turned out to be even worse at teaching than Denise's grandfather was at acting his age. *So which is it?*

'I was under the impression you had something to show me. That is what you told me, is it not?'

A wave of embarrassment washed over me. *Yeah, well, I really thought I was getting somewhere. I thought I heard whispering, but it was very far away. Or very faint, I don't know. And I was hoping you could point me in the right direction.*

'I have been doing exactly that, young Shepherd. Several times now in fact. Yet you continue to meander the other way.'

I can't open and close my mind at the same time, Ouranis. It's impossible.

'Nothing is, and certainly not that. You merely need to learn to focus on one thing and exclude all others. It is the only way you will be able to separate the animals' thoughts from your own imagination, and, in a further stage of your evolution, single out specific voices. Before you manage to do that, it serves no purpose explaining anything else, and we stand no chance in our upcoming task.'

Can't you do something to guide me? Maybe something to visualise, like, "Think of a river and let its cool waters wash your mind clean". Or, "Let the voices of the fish melt on the surface of your brain like droplets of syrup dissipating in clear water".

An eerie silence fell, like a joke gone wrong. 'You deem it helpful if I would repeat those lines?' Ouranis asked, mirth dancing in her voice.

Yeah, never mind. It's just that I've tried several different visualisations and nothing has really worked for me, as you can see. I don't know what else I can try.

'You would be surprised by what I can see, young Shepherd. For now, I suggest you rest and have some nourishment. I have something different in mind for tonight.'

I suddenly realised I still had my eyes closed. The realisation came as a surprise, since I could have sworn I had been looking at the great Phoenix during our last conversation. I opened them and the underground lake on which bank I had been sitting and meditating for the first half of the day came into view.

My knees ached and so did my buttocks, despite my many attempts at different postures; mixing them up turned out to be the best thing for me if I wished to remain as relaxed and focused as possible. And, according to the few pointers Ouranis had given me since I started her little training programme, being relaxed and focused at the same time was the key to unlocking the Shepherd's full potential.

The sight of the blue water of the lagoon stretching before me was mesmerising in the afternoon sun. When we first arrived three days ago, it had looked like only a small pool with a semi-circular strip of grass on one side, hemmed in by a high rock face. When Ouranis put us down, however, Denise and I found ourselves gazing into the gaping entrance to a natural cave system, while the lake's surface had suddenly doubled in size; the lagoon outside turned out to be the tail end of an underground river that ran straight through the northern part of the island. The entire scene seemed to be plucked straight out of some fairy-tale utopia, one that would have been just that if it hadn't been for the building amount of doubt and fear brewing on the inside. The latter was potent enough to coat any scene of wonder with a layer of grease.

My world had slowed down considerably over the past three days. So much, in fact, that after the chaos of events that had followed our first arrival at the temple, it was like time hadn't moved at all. No word had reached us from the druids, nor was there any way to contact our loved ones back home. Not even with my mobile, which for all I knew was currently lying somewhere lost and forgotten in Denise's old prison cell.

The fact that we didn't know what was going on in Eresa was continuously gnawing at my brain, especially since I had left Selena, Lycomedes, and everyone else to the mercy of the Council without the any explanation. It wasn't like I had had much choice in the matter, of course, since, for a lack of a better description, my own body had flown me out of the Council's temple before I was able to do anything about it. Leander had probably told everyone as much the second he had come back to his senses.

For me the most frustrating thing was that there was no way of letting Selena or Lycomedes know that I hadn't acted out of my own volition, nor was I particularly keen to go back there and tell them. I didn't want to think about what Selena and Lycomedes had had to go through after my disappearance, not to mention Leander. They undoubtedly had to face all the charges, and were each held accountable for at least some of them. This included being involved with a "spawn of Darkness" called Denise and in extension, sharing some of the blame for the disappearance of most of the ritualists, staging a prison break when Denise and I were awaiting the Council's verdict, as well as allowing me to escape the Council's clutches a second time when I was supposed to wait until the time of my questioning.

Not that they could all be held fully accountable, of course. Leander wasn't present at the scene when Selena unlocked the door to our prison cell the night we escaped. And both Lycomedes and Selena were undergoing an interrogation when Leander saw me transform into a horned owl and choose freedom over questions. That said, if I put myself in the Council's sandals and looked at all that had happened since my arrival, the whole situation reeked of bad fish. In some weird way it was all connected, and Lycomedes was at the heart of it. Either he or his students were present in every single event. Peleus was an apprentice of his as well, and Leander told me Peleus had defended me before the Council, like he himself had done.

So for three days now, while they were being punished in ways my imagination could only guess at, I was sitting on rocks and lying in the grass doing the very thing Selena had been chosen for. I was the real Shepherd, while she was acting the part to the world outside our lagoon, fooling the only family she had left. Granted, she was doing it out of her own volition, but I had a lot more to gain than she did if she continued to protect us. In fact, by defending Denise and me she was setting herself up for the druids' purification ritual, which if Leander's expression was a reliable guide, wasn't a pleasant prospect. I, therefore, had already made my peace with the notion that they might have given up on me like they must be thinking I had given up on them, and told the Council the truth. If they had, I wouldn't hold it against them.

Then there was Sophia. Casted out by society, orphaned at eleven, and now balancing on the precipice between life and death in a wet cave with only bats and near strangers to watch over her. I could only hope the situation wasn't as dire for her as it appeared, and that the druids were willing to look past the act of thievery by her father and give Sophia another chance at a life. If she could find it in her heart to forgive them for what they did to Pelegon, that is.

To me, the situation with Sophia, who was clearly in my charge for the time being, added to my desire to make this whole Shepherd thing happen. If either Selena or I were truly accepted as the new Shepherd, we would have the opportunity to assist Sophia, cure Denise, and, hopefully, be on our way back to a world we actually understood. I had also decided that, if the druids wouldn't take her, Sophia was more than welcome to come with Denise and me to our world.

I looked up towards the mid-afternoon sky. It was a circular patch of clear blue, bordered by rock faces covered with moss and overhanging thicket. The sky looked freshly painted, dotted with tiny sheep drifting past in a leisurely pace. Despite the soothing feeling its beauty invoked, I felt miserable. Why wasn't it working?

There was no need for me to channel energy or to be able to transform, or even to summon an animal projection with teeth and claws. I just needed to master this one ability, to communicate with animals, and we would be good to go. We would go forth, detach Ouranis' brother from the Hive Mind, Ouranis would then turn Denise back to her normal self and it would all be over. Or would it?

What would actually happen to Denise when Ouranis were to turn her back? The Phoenix had already told me she wasn't sure whether Denise could regain her normal body, even if she banished the Voidshaper bit out of my girlfriend. And what if she couldn't? What if what would be left of Denise would be nothing but a ghostly reflection of how she once looked, a silvery projection of the woman I had fallen in love with? What kind of life would she be able to live in our world? Would she even want to go back?

Despite the surreal environment I found myself in, a subterranean jungle habitat displaying Mother Nature's best, my heart was in turmoil. My eyes travelled along the bank to the overhanging part of the lagoon. There, in the shade, Denise lay curled up against the still unconscious Sophia. It had been three days now since Sophia lost consciousness, and Denise had been by her side the entire time.

For obvious reasons, Ouranis hadn't tried to revive Sophia a second time, and neither had the girl shown a single sign of improvement. I had heard stories about people staying in comas for years, but I doubted any of them could have survived on a cold cave floor with only some moss and leaves as bedding and without any form of sustenance. Yet Sophia was going to have to if she still desired to cling to the life she had left.

The flat line in Sophia's improvement was mirrored in Denise's as well. On occasion I thought I could glimpse signs in the hyena's behaviour that reminded me of the girl I knew, but I could just as well have been wishing it to be so. In almost every element she had become a kind of house pet, driven by instinct and friendly to those who did no wrong to her, and quite unlike anything I would expect of a hyena – especially one looking like her. Denise's behaviour, as well as the knowledge that Voidshapers were able to choose and change their shape according to their needs, proved to me that her hyena shape was simply there for show. It had nothing to do with her mind or her appetite. In fact, I had yet to see her eat anything.

I was rather surprised at first that Denise had lost most of her interest in me so rapidly, and had offered it to Sophia instead. But I knew animals – again, not hyenas – sometimes did that if they thought someone else had a particularly strong need for their love. And, at this time, Sophia stood at the front of the queue.

That night, dinner consisted of the usual fruit and vegetables, a combination of olives, dates, pomegranates, apples and avocados. It had become routine for Ouranis to drop me off on top of the cliffs to gather my own meals, before she returned to the water's edge and continued to sit there, quietly.

Over the past couple of days I hadn't asked her once what she was actually doing, though I thought I knew. What else could it be than trying to clear the way to her brother, Flego, by detaching as many spirits from the Hive Mind as she could until I was ready? After all, it was what she said she had been doing for centuries before our arrival in this world. But even if it was something else, I still figured it would be best to preserve her privacy, as she had confided in me so much already. And knowing her, if she deemed it prudent for me to know, I was confident she would tell me, regardless.

I had been watching her for three days now and it still amazed me how her powers worked, the distance from which she was able to penetrate the Voidshapers' collective mind in particular. I knew these powers of her did actually work, because I had found myself staring at the evidence the first morning here. I had sat bolt upright, bearing witness to a group of frogs suddenly materialising out of thin air in front of her. I could clearly remember how I had gaped at the sight of them, appearing first as tiny, white orbs of energy, then forming translucent frog bodies and landing in the grass, as though they had simply hopped from one place to the next. The whole event had reminded me of a scene in some high-end science-fiction movie, and I had to resist the urge to look up and search for the spaceship that had beamed them down. After the frogs, I had seen many insects and birds been given an immortal body by Ouranis, and even heard occasional splashes of fish diving into the blue water of the lagoon.

I had already finished one of my apples and was tending to my pomegranate, trying to pry it open with my nails, when Ouranis finally came to pick me up. She had never left me on the cliff this long, which was odd by itself, and there was something distinctly funny in the way she snatched me up and put me down into the grass. Not to mention the manner in which she stalked away to the other side of the bank directly afterwards. Instead of the composed and rather serious Phoenix I had known her to be, she looked more like an overgrown ostrich whose mate had just messed up his tenth attempt at an enticing mating ritual. I only had to shoot a single, sweeping glance at the cliff wall to see why, however.

'Lycomedes!' I said when I spotted the old man leaning against the rock face.

While rubbing his chest, the old man said in an almost exact copy of my voice, 'Bishop!'

I quickly withdrew my waving hand, feeling awkward. 'What's wrong? Are you all right?'

'Not sure, my boy.' He was readjusting his shoulders with a concerned expression on his face. He then checked his chest for broken ribs before he breathed in deeply and added in mild surprise, 'It does appear so.'

'What happened? Why are you here?' To me there was no question how Lycomedes had gotten down here, as there was no way the old man could have managed the climb down with only a sore chest to show for it. And I had never seen crocodiles climb down a rock face, so he couldn't have summoned one of them to help him.

'She's a large creature, that's what happened. And she has quite the grip, I have to say.' He now began tapping his chest in multiple places. He winced when he reached his sternum. 'Oh, yes,' he said wryly, 'and my chest is still a bit sensitive from a certain collision with a giant horned owl.'

'Oh, right. Sorry about that.' *But quite the grip?* I added inside my head. *Ouranis has been nothing but gentle to me so far, at least from a physical point of view.* 'What's going on? Why did she bring you here?'

'Your guess will probably be just as bad as mine, or better,' said Lycomedes, as one of his usual attempts to be as vague as possible. 'And mine is that you're not doing as well as she would like.' Lycomedes' answer reminded me that it had been he who had prepared Selena to become the new Shepherd, which judging from the fact that she had been chosen by the ritual, had worked.

'I'm still a bit surprised she brought you, though, to help me with my training. Not that I'm complaining, of course,' I added quickly. 'I like the company and I can definitely use the help. It's just that I thought, you know, you weren't the best of friends.' The moment the last part of my sentence left my lips, I was already regretting them.

A crease appeared on Lycomedes' forehead and he puffed up his cheeks like a child trying and failing to blow out his birthday candles. He then turned to look at Ouranis, who was sitting in her usual absent, swanlike manner at the water's edge, and released the air from his lungs with a fleshy flapping sound. 'It's the first time I've seen her from this close up,' he said. 'So I can't say I know what you mean. Well, Zeuxis wasn't particularly fond of me, I admit, but to think he would throw a handful of dung onto Ouranis' image of me does come as a bit of a shocker.'

'I didn't say that.'

'There's no need to,' said Lycomedes, shrugging. 'If you've lived long enough among druids you understand how to read between the lines.'

'But it was me who said it.'

'And you're no druid?'

'Not that I am aware of.'

'Hmm,' Lycomedes uttered disbelievingly, nodding with pursed lips. 'It depends on how you look at it, doesn't it? One could argue you are one now.' A few moments passed before he snapped out of his trance and he beckoned me over. 'Let's get on with it, Bishop. Oh, just to warn you,' suddenly all I could see was a finger inches from my face, 'I won't be as lenient as your little friend over there.'

'You mean you're actually going to say something that could help me,' I said, shooting a reproachful look at Ouranis. She, of course, wasn't paying attention to anything but the contents of her own mind. 'I hope for all our sakes you won't be, Lycomedes. I have every intention of giving these powers to Selena as soon as possible, believe me.'

Lycomedes stared at me for a moment or two, then quickly recovered. 'Yes, well, let's all hope we'll get that far, shall we? Now enlighten me, what have we been doing?'

'Before we start, how exactly did Ouranis get you away from Eresa?'

'Oh, there was no need for her to come to the Sanctuary,' said the old man. 'She would never have done that... Or, I don't think so. I was out in the orchards helping with the gathering.'

'Out?' I repeated incredulously. A mental picture of the gigantic black serpent floated past. 'With those void... those dark things still out there? You won't believe what kind of creature they've mutated into this time.'

'You don't say?' Lycomedes' eyes narrowed to slits as he stuck out his jaw pugnaciously. 'Their existence didn't stop you and Selena from planning a little boat trip together, or from taking my crocodiles for a ride.' As I didn't know how to reply, Lycomedes quickly ploughed on. 'And what did you think was going to happen? We'd let those aberrations starve us to death? It's no wonder you haven't made any progress.' He paused, gathered himself, and folded his arms.

'If you must know, I was accompanying Kriton and his team to work on the provisions,' he said. 'Naturally it was me who had to do most of the picking. That's what you get if you volunteer. Never bother, if you know what's good for you. Anyway, we were almost done and many of us had their full baskets already on their backs when your big-beaked friend showed up. All of my work,' he made a slicing movement with his hand, 'wasted. Then, as you can imagine, there was lots of blue and silver everywhere,' he made a movement as though opening a pair of curtains, 'and the next thing I knew I was here. Well, almost.'

His story, combined with the image of Captain Kriton, Lycomedes and a host of other druids walking through an orchard, made a connection to my conversations with Pelegon moments before his execution. 'Lycomedes,' I said in a guarded, serious voice, 'have you heard about what happened to Pelegon?'

'I've seen it,' Lycomedes barked at me before shaking his head. 'That dung brain. I told Pelegon to be careful. The both of them, twice! Twice I explained how thin the twig was that separated forbearance and intolerance in the minds of the druids, particularly towards outsiders. People that haven't yet been accepted,' he added in explanation. He took another deep breath before he continued. 'Much can be said about our community, Bishop, good and bad. Yet lies and deceit have no place among us, neither do people who practice these arts. There are exceptions, perhaps, but apparently I hadn't been clear enough. And it has cost those two dearly.'

'Well, there's no doubt about that,' I said tentatively, still considering whether I should go on, even as the words were rolling from my lips, 'but one of them is still alive.' Lycomedes' eyes, which had been lowered for most of his diatribe, suddenly shot upwards. I felt something in my throat wriggle uncomfortably. 'It's not Pelegon.'

Without visibly moving any other part of his body, Lycomedes' eyes performed a quick survey of our surroundings. When he spotted Denise and Sophia lying in the cave on the other side of the lagoon, he turned towards them and shielded his eyes from the sun. 'The girl,' he said, peering into the distance.

'Sophia, yes,' I said, emphasising her name to remind him of the fact that she was, in fact, a person. 'I rescued her.'

Lycomedes dropped his hand and turned back to me. 'This ought to be some tale,' he said, unable to disguise the curiosity in his voice.

It took me a second or two to realise why the old man was looking at me like that, and then I remembered how Pelegon had gotten his hands on a boat. 'I had nothing to do with it,' I said defensively. 'I came aboard only after they had already left the docks.'

Lycomedes frowned, doubt filled his eyes.

'Look at the timing,' I said, annoyance building inside me for the fact that I had to work this hard to convince one of the few people of whom I had been sure would be behind me. 'Pelegon and Sophia had already stolen the ship when you were being interrogated by the Council. And I was waiting on the other side of the door, remember? I was with you and Selena all the way until you were asked inside. So how could I possibly have helped them?'

'Indeed you were.'

'Well, you must have heard what happened from Leander. I transformed again.' Lycomedes give a quick nod, but didn't say anything, and merely waited for the next part. 'So I ended up in sea and Pelegon and Sophia picked me up. I climbed aboard, then your crows attacked us, I managed to escape with Sophia and brought her before Ouranis. That's all, really.'

Lycomedes stared at me for a moment, then. 'That makes perfect sense. Now, let us forget the whole issue of how both the girl and I are able to survive being this close to Ouranis, because the explanation is probably going to be lengthy. The whole issue of Ouranis' aura supposedly being too strong to approach is obviously a lie. And a convenient one at that, now that think about it.' He paused, evidently to make sure I wouldn't start explaining. 'The girl is still alive, isn't she?'

I nodded. 'She's been unconscious for the past few days, though. I can't wake her up.'

'I see. She can do a while without food, I think. I would try to keep her hydrated, however, or she won't survive for long.'

'Yeah, I know.'

'Anyway, let's not continue to dwell on it and hop on to more important matters, Bishop. When you escaped Pelegon's ship, did you see any of the Piscines?'

Yes, why would the life of a little girl be important? I thought, feeling slightly put-off by Lycomedes' lack of empathy. 'No, I don't think so. Who are they?'

'Fish heads. Members of the fish clan. They were sent to retrieve the ship and see if there were any survivors.'

'I didn't see anyone. But I must admit, with the Darkness still out there, I was rather focused on getting to Ouranis as fast as I could. And after what happened to her father, I didn't want Sophia to focus too much on what was going on behind us. Trionyx took us there, actually. He was amazing. So maybe these Piscines didn't notice us sitting on his shell. He's quite large.'

'It wouldn't surprise me.'

'So what about you and Selena? What did your Council say?' My curiosity easily outweighed the dread I felt for the upcoming answer.

Lycomedes took a deep breath. 'They are divided. As it stands, the state in which you left Leander corroborated much of Leander's story, for most of the Council deemed it unlikely he had willingly subjected himself to the treatment you gave him. Then there were some who saw you leave, although of course, they didn't know it was you before Leander told them so. We brought Leander to the healers afterwards. He still hasn't recovered.' I clenched my jaws in shame. 'Yes, he is not doing well,' said Lycomedes, apparently keen on rubbing it in. My escape evidently hadn't impressed him, probably because it was at the expense of his student. 'The other way around, the Council deems it to have been unnecessary for you to drain Leander of his energy, if he was really intent on helping you escape the interrogation. He could have just allowed you to walk away.'

'Is that what I did? I drained him of his energy?'

'It appear so, yes.'

'So that means the Council believes I am the only one responsible for my escape,' I said, relief coursing through me for the fact that Leander was exonerated and wouldn't have to bear punishment on top of what I did to him.

'They believe Leander,' said Lycomedes. 'Now about their final verdict, if you're still interested,' he added in a voice that pushed my chin up and made me look at the old man, 'we've been given twenty-nine days. Twenty-six now, to be exact.'

'Until…,' I said, for Lycomedes had fallen silent again.

'Till the Council has to make a decision whether to bring Selena before Ouranis or not,' finished Lycomedes, as though it was as obvious as the beauty of the private piece of paradise we found ourselves in.

'To bring her before Ouranis? Does that mean they are not going to go through with the purification ritual? Leander told me about it.'

'That is yet to be determined. However, the Council does want confirmation from Ouranis first. They fear that if Selena truly is the one destined to be the next Shepherd, they might anger Ouranis. Additionally, the purification ritual which Leander spoke of carries great risk to both the recipient and Ouranis' gift itself. The gift is supposed to jump to the next most worthy candidate, but forcibly removing it is not something that is considered lightly.'

'Now, traditionally,' he went on, 'the inauguration of the new Shepherd, the one where they'll receive Ouranis' blessing, can only be held at the night of a full moon. This only occurs once a month.'

'That's odd, isn't it?' I asked. 'I thought Ouranis was called a sun beast, not a creature of the moon.' Why this fact interested me at a time like this was beyond me, but it did.

'She is. And at this particular night the sun shows its true power over the moon. It sets the moon ablaze and so illuminates the path the new Shepherd must walk. Also, because Ouranis can be thought of as the sun, the Shepherd, at least for some druids, refers to the moon. Together these two celestial bodies regulate the natural world, as do Ouranis and the Shepherd, in a way. They aren't my words,' he added to the incredulity I imagined dripping from my chin.

'No, I wasn't thinking of your words per se,' I said. 'I was thinking back to what Pelegon told me about the, uhm, attitude you have towards each other and the type of people you invite into your circle. I mean, your traditions all sound so spiritual, while at the same time you watch each other play gladiator in that arena of yours. And Pelegon was pretty vocal about some of the druids' backgrounds.'

'Are you suggesting we should judge people by what they were like and have done in the past?'

'Well, yes. To some extent at least. It does say a lot about a person, doesn't it?'

'Only if you expect someone to repeat the same mistakes.'

'And you don't believe that?'

Lycomedes shrugged. 'That depends on their motive for staying in Eresa. Once you become a druid and discover the potential of the synergy between man and animal, it changes you. And for most of us, for the better.'

'So you're not concerned at all that some of the people you are hanging around with are convicted criminals?' I asked bluntly, throwing all caution to the wind. I felt like I just had to know, since I was confident my journey would one day lead me back to Eresa.

'Pasts are wiped clean once the new apprentice has been set on a new path,' said Lycomedes dogmatically. 'Or they are forgiven. The method has never failed us.'

'Never?'

'Never. Some rotten apples have been revealed, that is true, and they had to be discarded. Not everyone has the right mind-set, the endurance, or the love to become a druid. If one doesn't have the right mind-set, they will fail to generate the passion needed to establish a proper connection with the type of animal of their choice. And without the mental link, they will have a difficult time summoning a corporeal image of their animal. They are easy prey.'

'So just to be clear, Captain Kriton does possess this passion you are talking about,' I said, grinning sceptically.

'Oh, most definitely. His love for bovines and the incredible destruction their stampedes can cause is one of the greatest among all druids in Eresa. "Bovine" here refers to any land animal that fights by charging its enemy,' he added to my dubious expression. Again it surprised me how the druids of Eresa emphasised the fighting capabilities of animals, and chose to use those features in particular to categorise them. 'His real strength lies in his love for training and his thirst for battle, however,' said Lycomedes. 'That is how he became captain.'

'Right. I think I just had something else in mind when you mentioned the word "love". But I guess it's not really important right now.'

'There are many kinds of love, Bishop. And the numerous different reasons to part from their old life and turn a new leaf that are represented in Eresa, as well the huge variety in the druids' backgrounds among its inhabitants, has resulted in a very diverse community. But,' he paused portentously, 'all druids share and treasure the same passion.'

'Some of us live very secluded and peaceful lives, and actively avoid the double-dealing and backstabbing that's become so ingrained in clan politics,' Lycomedes went on. 'Others, as you pointed out, do like to test their strength, some even daily. Within this more belligerent group there are those like Kriton who live only to fight and to hone their abilities, while others are more concerned with the laws and the structure of our society. You've already met a few of them too.'

I thought back to the turbulent first two days of my stay in this world and one image bubbled up in particular. It was an image of Lydus screaming wildly that he would tell his captain about Selena's unshepherdly efforts to free Denise and me from our prison. 'Lydus,' I said.

Lycomedes nodded. 'As well as his captain, Helios, the day before. The man nurtures Eresan law in a way you would only expect a wild pig to care for its wallow.'

'And in which of these categories do you see yourself fitting in, Lycomedes?' I asked with a small smile decorating my face.

There was a pause, then he answered with a nod of approval, 'In between.'

In a fleeting thought I felt that whatever had happened between Ouranis and Lycomedes must have been quite severe; I imagined they would be fairly compatible had things turned out differently. We both fell silent and our gazes turned to the frogs in the lagoon playing tag across the lily leaves. Their croaking and splashing sounds put small smiles on both our faces. My mind started daydreaming. I thought about what it would be like to link my energy to those frogs like the druids were able to with their animals.

In view came an imaginary, man-sized frog standing in a field of flowers. In the daydream I was standing behind it with my hands pressed together in a praying position. With a wet, fleshy sound, the frog opened its mouth and whipped its tongue around a black, ash-covered snake and swallowed it whole. A great burp escaped its mouth, one that made the earth beneath my feet vibrate.

Lycomedes' voice suddenly shattered my musings and my fantasy scene faded. 'Twenty-six days and two hours, give or take,' he said as he watched twilight starting to re-dye the sky.

'Sorry?'

'That's how long we have to convince the Council that either Selena or you is the Shepherd.' His voice betrayed he had just experienced a daydream of his own.

'Oh, right. Do you think that's enough time?'

'It better be. The fact that Selena's animal is a Phoenix might conceal her inability to perform the feats a Shepherd should be able to for a while, I expect. But it certainly won't last, not after she's sent to receive Ouranis' blessing. And even before then, we can do nothing but hope that the Council won't lose their patience with her. She's lied before.'

'What happens if they do?'

'They will force her to perform the ritual that ends the cycle of the Shepherd and transfers Ouranis' gift to her successor; the purification ritual we spoke of. However, since not her but you currently possesses the gift, the ritual will inevitably fail. And, given that she survives, she will be held accountable for not being willing to part from it, if such a thing is even possible. There has never been a Shepherd who hadn't been willing to pass on the gift, if the Council wished it. No matter the Shepherd's influence, it is their duty to obey, for the Council's word is final. Selena knows that. After that, more debate will follow, I am sure.'

Lycomedes looked away. A few extra lines appeared on his face. 'Regrettably, the purification ritual will probably take Selena's life, because the fact that she is linked to Ouranis instead of to an animal we have experience with, will work against her. But if they indeed think Selena has become her own counsel, purification is the only way for the druid community to regain possession of the gift.'

'There's no way she'll let herself be killed over me,' I said incredulously. 'She mustn't.'

'Selena has been training to become the best she can be, and someday perhaps become the Shepherd, for all of her life in Eresa, Bishop,' said Lycomedes. 'You have only seen a tiny glimpse of her determination and the sincerity with which she has cherished her connection with Ouranis.'

Their connection wasn't strong enough to prevent her from collapsing when she approached Ouranis, I commented in silence, *or from Ouranis giving her a free ticket into her home.*

'And I can tell you she doesn't care as much as a crocodile's behind about what you think she must or mustn't do,' Lycomedes went on. 'She will do exactly as she sees fit. And if she wants to give up her life to let you keep yours, she will.'

'But why? I don't understand. She barely knows me. And to tell you the truth, she didn't seem too upset when she realised it was me who received the gift, not her.'

'Sacrificing an innocent life to save her own is not what a real Shepherd should do,' said Lycomedes. I wanted to say something in return, but my throat refused to produce anything. 'To a Shepherd, all life is sacred. This purity of thought is one of the key components to become eligible to receive the gift, something most druids share. When Selena suspected you may be the one who received the gift, she was more concerned about your life and what the Council would do if they discovered the truth than to fulfil her ambition to become the Shepherd. I must admit I, too, was surprised by her indifference at first. But now I've had time to take step back, I can understand why she did what she did. She felt responsible for you and your girl, partly because she thinks she might have been able to stop that one dark hyena to bite Denise if she hadn't allowed her confusion to overtake her. We talked about it quite a bit, mind you.'

'Now, going back to the gift, our fear of losing it prevails over all else. If it is a choice between your life and the gift, to the Council there is no choice, unfortunately. So if word reaches them that you indeed possess the Shepherd's gift instead of Selena, they would come after you no matter where you ran. They would even follow you to your world if they could manage it. And once they caught you, you would undergo the same fate I have just drawn for Selena. The Shepherd's gift is that important to us. Ouranis is that important.'

'But what if, before those twenty-six days are over, I gave myself up and proved to the Council that I am the real Shepherd?' I asked. 'I know I can't convince them otherwise. Not unless Ouranis comes with me.'

'I will not lie to you, Bishop. It would be difficult. After what happened during the Shepherd ritual and Selena's concealment of the Darkness's existence, even Selena would have a difficult time as the Shepherd, and she does. Yes, they know,' he added in response to me chewing my lip. 'Aristion's story made it hard to deny that Selena knew about the Darkness before Aristion returned to the Sanctuary. She even brought one back there herself; they identified Denise as one of these dark entities using Aristion's description of them.' He sighed. 'People are already wondering whether Selena is worthy, but many choose to withhold their judgement until she is brought before Ouranis.'

'That's… I didn't think about that,' I said in a defeated voice. 'I also didn't think that keeping a few secrets would be that big of a deal. She only did it to protect Denise and me. Why is that such a bad thing?'

'If it were up to me, it's not, Bishop.' He put a hand on my shoulder. 'Our leader Xenocrates, however, would say, and he does, that Selena's actions nearly cost Aristion his life. Aristion is a highly accomplished druid and, in fact, Captain Cyrene's husband. And as a captain, she is a member of the Council.'

'I still can't believe Selena put that much on the line for us.'

Lycomedes turned away. 'For the Shepherd.'

Chapter 12

I was standing with my claws in the dirt. I was at a square, a familiar one. On both ends the Phoenix Hall and the Arena of Repentance stood gazing down at me like a pair of gargantuan behemoths. The sun stung my disproportionately large eyes. My body felt different, yet familiar. With every tiny movement I made, I heard feathers rustling.

There was no one around. With the exception of the soft howling of the wind that blew overhead, the silence was absolute. Then out of nowhere, druids clad in white with sashes in a rainbow worth of colours appeared on the scene. In quick succession they materialised out of thin air, first appearing as white, shapeless blobs of mist, then quickly gaining mass and colour. Their bulk made me realise my size was considerably smaller than I remembered it being the last time I had metamorphosed. But druids couldn't teleport. Was I dreaming?

The druids were excited, and spared no eyes for me. Wherever they appeared, they hit the ground running and started pelting towards the Arena of Repentance. It was as though the yearly circus had arrived and there were only a limited amount of tickets to be distributed. I watched in amazement how they queued up before the entrance as a single great, jostling crowd, each trying to muscle their way to the front.

After the last one had disappeared inside, the chaos of intoxicated voices became reduced to a susurrating background hum. Finally, only two voices could be heard, one of which sounded familiar.

'Pitiful,' said one of them, a composed, male voice. It had a condescending air about it, as though he was doing the listener a favour merely by speaking. 'The boy is not even a druid.'

'What're you yappin' about?' another, more gravelly voice asked. The man seemed to have difficulty containing his excitement. I instantly recognised the voice and spun around to see Captains Kriton and Helios, the Bovine and Vespine clan leaders, descending the steps to the Phoenix Hall. 'As long as it fights, I'm game. That old crook Lycomedes signed him up, didn't he? I suppose that woman'll give the kid a good beating.'

'The arena is not meant to be misused as a place to exact punishment, Captain Kriton,' said Helios, in the manner of a schoolteacher rebuking a wayward ten-year-old. 'As a captain, you shouldn't encourage this kind of conduct.'

'Yeah, I see you're doing everythin' you can to stop them,' said Kriton sarcastically. 'Or are you just goin' to watch like the rest of us?' He gave a raspy chuckle.

As they strode past, two towering giants, every single one of my muscles froze so my feathers wouldn't betray my position. They could easily see me if they just stopped squaring up to each other, yet they didn't. My eyes followed their every move, my breath having taken up a defensive position in the back of my throat. It was trying to replace a lump of bile, which was being pushed up into my mouth. I figured they only needed the tiniest prickle, the tiniest rustle of feathers, to take a step sideways and dig my owl face into the earth with the sole of one of their sandals. Why was I so small?

'Again you exemplify the exact reason we've changed the conditions to become a captain, Captain Kriton,' said Helios, his foot landing only inches from my face. 'It is a shame the decision can't be applied retroactively.'

'I'd like to see them try,' Kriton uttered through a sneering smile, cracking his knuckles.

When Kriton and Helios had gone out of earshot and began ascending the steps to the Arena of Repentance, more questions began to rise up inside me. *Lycomedes had signed someone up to fight? Who could it be?*

As if my own will had called it into being, a piece of parchment came drifting down. I neatly impaled it on one talon and looked down at a picture of an owl, captioned, "The False Shepherd". It was opposite a rough sketch of a young woman I vaguely recognised as Phoebe, a member of the Feline clan I had met on this same square with Leander. Underneath the title it declared, "Match of the Month: Leopard versus Shepherd".

The moment I was finished reading a thick droplet of water pecked the parchment. One more followed, then another. And as I looked up, an entire swimming pool worth of water was coming down from the sky like a sheet. They had been released by a mattress of grey thunderheads that was clouding the world into shadow.

I opened my eyes with a start. Raindrops were hitting my face with such relentless vigour, they forced me to close them again. Before my hands could shield me, however, the rain stopped.

I was lying on my back. Carefully I opened one eye to see what was going on. Ouranis' giant beak entered my view. It turned out to be the perfect substitute for an umbrella. Because of its translucent nature, I could see the raindrops impacting its bony top from the other end, leaving streams of water flowing copiously down the sides. It was a spellbinding sight, until Ouranis tipped her head and brought the tip of her beak down to only inches above my face.

Having the same effect as putting my head under a tap, my face, neck, and most of my chest became soaked. Sputtering madly I dived out from under the localised waterfall. Without thinking I crawled until I found the only spot where the grass wasn't glistening as much. Everywhere else continued to be attacked by the heavy downpour.

I sat down and wiped my face. To my left and right, massive claws were digging into the grass. Above my head, an impressive collection of see-through feathers were shielding me from the rain. Following the belly of the Phoenix, my eyes fell on Ouranis' head. She was looking scathingly down at me, inducing a shiver that not even the cold of the storm was able to.

I heard the claws on either side push off, my convenient cover disappeared, and once again I found myself falling prey to Heaven's wrath. Before I had time to react, however, I felt a tug on my toga and was snatched up like a naughty wolf cub.

'Hey!' I tried to wrestle myself loose. It was hard to breathe with my druidic garments constricting my windpipe. The next thing I knew I was flying twenty yards through the air.

I hit the surface of the lagoon, belly first and with jabs of pain shooting in every direction. It felt like it took me a second or two before I began to sink into the lake's depths, so shocked was I when I saw the blue carpet of water coming at me.

'You fell asleep again, young Shepherd,' said a disappointed Ouranis, her smooth voice entering my brain even as my body was sinking rapidly. I could feel the pressure on my ears building. There was nothing but a sea of blue everywhere I looked.

Only for a minute.

I gave a good series of kicks and broke the surface. When my eyesight returned, Ouranis was peering down at me from the bank of the lagoon, the continuous downpour cascading off her domed head like flowing locks. She had her head held high in a patronising sort of way, though I couldn't help but notice a twinkle of amusement in her cobalt eyes.

'Perhaps, perhaps not,' said Ouranis. 'But a minute wasted is a minute my brother Flego does not have. Our time is coming to a close, young Shepherd. I can sense another change in the Hive Mind, one that is quite different from last time. It has grown more resistant over the past hours. I cannot say for certain, yet I believe the Hive has come to realise what I have been trying to do. Perhaps it is because it has been focusing on my siblings, and has therefore not cared about the animal spirits I have freed thus far. Now that I have linked my thoughts with Flego's, however, it must have become aware of my presence. I believe it has started to actively thwart my attempts to free him.'

By the time I arrived at the shore and hoisted myself onto the bank, the downpour had turned into a soft drizzle. *You tried to get him out by yourself? Why? I thought you needed my help for that.*

'It would make it easier, yes. But unfortunately your progress has not been encouraging, and recently I found that the link between my brother and me had strengthened. I decided to chance it.'

You said "had", I observed. *Does this mean it no longer does?*

'That is correct,' she said sorrowfully. 'This is not the first time, either. I am confident, however, that I would have succeeded had the Hive not interfered. I believe that somehow, the Hive Mind managed to block my mental probe with another spirit, or perhaps multiple ones.'

Ouranis turned her head sideways. I followed it and my heart gave a jolt. I didn't even realise I was already on my feet until I began stumbling backwards. A disbelieving cry escaped my lips as I beheld a shimmering tiger sitting a short distance away. It was gazing longingly up the vertical cliff face that was trapping it.

The animal's broad back was turned to us. As the sun broke through the clouds, the stripes on the tiger's back began to glisten in the sunlight like the trail of a comet. Their twinkling beauty was only matched by that of the whiskers protruding from the sides of its face. But the thing that amazed me most was its size; it was at least twice as large as any of its non-translucent cousins I had seen in a zoo or on television.

The tiger's appearance was not the only thing new in our private paradise, however. The shoreline behind it was covered in a thick, crystal coating. Four giant, catlike paw prints were imprinted in the glassy plateau.

Ouranis?

'It happened when the Hive Mind interrupted my link with Flego with the spirit of the tiger,' she explained. 'The amount of energy I had reserved for Flego's new body formed one for the tiger instead, causing it to grow larger than it should when I pulled the tiger's spirit out of the Vault. The excess energy spilled onto the ground and formed the crystal layer where the tiger materialised. Normally when I free an animal's spirit, I operate much more efficiently and the effects are less… dramatic.'

Did the same happen to Trionyx too when you freed him?

Ouranis took a moment before she answered. 'The one the druids call Trionyx was an accident. He is the first spirit I have ever freed from the Hive.'

Really? That's incredible. Then he must be hundreds of years old. Thousands, even.

'No animal in the Land of Aten has aged for centuries, young Shepherd. The ageing process disappeared along with our corporeal bodies. I told you this already. Neither can we reproduce.'

My mind went blank for a moment. Ouranis had indeed mentioned before that the spirits she freed from the Vault became essentially immortal, but with all that had happened since then I hadn't yet stopped to think what this implied. *But if that's true, it means you don't need sustenance, either. I talked to Selena about the fact that she couldn't eat meat, since the animals here have, as you say, lost their corporeal bodies. But the same holds true for the animals too. They can't eat anything either. Or they don't need to, not if they are immortal.*

Now I remembered Lycomedes telling me that the animals had no need for lungs either, quite in contrast to a metamorphosed Shepherd. This too hadn't resurfaced till now. *But then, if they don't eat, hunt, or have children, what do they do all day? I mean, it's what animals do.*

Another realisation struck me. *And you're a Phoenix. Legends in my world talk about the Phoenix as being an animal capable of regeneration and rebirth. But you...* My thoughts trailed off, as Ouranis looked away. My words seemed to pain her. *That was you before you were taken by the Voidshapers, wasn't it?*

'It was a long time ago.'

Well, if it helps, I'm here if you want to talk about it some time, Ouranis. I feel like I have only scratched the surface of your incredible past, but I am willing to learn, and aid you where I can. Of course you would rather talk to Flego instead of me, I added as an afterthought.

'It is a tale for another time, young Shepherd,' said Ouranis. 'However, if it still interests you, I would like to tell you what I think happened with Trionyx.'

Please.

'Being young, you must understand I was very inexperienced – and too rash to be allowed the responsibility my abilities placed on me. Once I had discovered my ability to penetrate the Hive, I felt such a need to not only help my kin, but also free the other spirits that had been absorbed by the Hive, I tried to link with too many spirits at once. The unfathomable amount of spirits imprisoned by the Hive, combined with the knowledge that I was the only one who could get them out, got the better of me. I have no excuse.'

I would probably have done the same thing if I were in your position. So as far as I'm concerned, you've nothing to be sorry for, Ouranis. Did this happen before or after you were absorbed by the Voidshapers?

'After. Before that time I had no idea that I was capable of such a feat. And as a result of my ineptitude, an unknown amount of spirits was fused together and formed the creature you know as Trionyx. Unfortunately, I do not have the knowledge or the skills to undo my mistake.'

Well, why would you? He seems happy, doesn't he? At least you got him out.

'My only wish is to do what I can for the Hive's victims, young Shepherd. I am aware I can never change the world back to the way it was, but I can try. That said, I have never wished for the power or the responsibility to decide on a creature's fate. The fact that I do is something I have learned to accept, yet not enjoy.'

You don't want to play God.

'Neither did my mother.'

No, no, of course not, I thought quickly as the realisation stabbed me that her mother was a God too, or she was known as one. *It's just… It's an expression.*

Ouranis turned her massive body, saying, 'We will depart in two days, Shepherd. Be ready.' And with that she pulled herself off the ground, gave a few forceful strokes of her wings, grabbed the tiger in her claws and took off. Befuddled though it was, it was obvious the tiger had a certain amount of trust in Ouranis, which prevented it from struggling. Together the two of them shot skywards and disappeared behind the line of trees sprouting from the cliff's edge.

Later that night, the storm culminated in a display of its full fury, which it unleashed on the underground lagoon with deafening results. I was forced to retreat into the cave. Ouranis still hadn't returned yet and I was starting to feel hungry. With her not there to taxi me up the cliff and the storm coating the rock face with slippery liquid, there was no way for me to gather my dinner without risking my neck in the process.

My stomach wasn't the only thing that concerned me, though. Ouranis had never left us alone for this long. The Phoenix had been at our side as a steady – and for the most part silent – presence for the past week. And now that my biological clock told me she was well overdue, the loneliness was beginning to hatch unnerving daydreams, with the downpour continuously drilling into the surface of the lagoon.

As I approached the bedding on which Sophia still lay comatose, face up and both hands on her belly, Denise's hyena head shot out from the cloud of ash around her. After spotting it was only me, her head disappeared again. I shrugged it off – I had become used to the lack of interest she was giving me nowadays – and went over to the boulder I had sat on for many an hour, watching our unconscious eleven-year-old and wondering what more I could do for her.

Sophia had barely shown any sign of life since she collapsed back inside Ouranis' den. The only reason I knew she was still alive was her almost non-existent breathing and a weak, but steady, pulse. It had now been a week and she hadn't eaten anything I would count as actual food. On occasion I had managed to get her to swallow a few drops of water when I wetted her mouth and lips, for cracks began to appear a few days after we arrived at the lagoon. Before that time, even that was too much to ask for.

Her swallowing reflex gave me the idea to try some fruit juice I had squeezed from apples and apricots, which indeed worked, but I knew it wasn't enough in itself to keep her alive for long. The human body could only survive for three to five days without water and the same amount in weeks without food. Even I was beginning to long for something of substance, since those juicy vitamin bombs, as well as the occasional olive or avocado, were hardly protein-rich. The only upside about her lack of appetite, if you can call it that, was that I only had to clean her clothes in the lake a few times over the past week.

My desire for variety and sustenance had invoked dreams of hunting and roasting the various forest animals I had seen. But there was no way I could actually act on them; my moral conscience, as well as the knowledge that Ouranis had invested time and energy into saving them from the Hive, prevented me from doing so. Not to mention the fact that hunting one of those boars I had seen churning up the forest floor would mean that I would be killing a creature that was untouchable by time. And frankly I wasn't sure if my taste buds, deprived as they were, were ready for a slab of meat through which you could read the morning newspaper.

Tonight there were not even apples to squeeze, or the aroma of fresh apricots. There was nothing except for a dark cave, the din of the rain, and wet, cotton robes that glued to my skin like cheap wallpaper. I looked away from Sophia's peaceful face. It did nothing to clear the picture of her dark hair rippling down the bedding of leaves she lay upon, with her closed, unmoving eyelids, her pointy chin, and her slightly sunken cheeks.

I felt a tear trickle down the side of my nose. *What more can I do for her? What has she done to deserve this, to slowly wither away until death takes her? Where did I go wrong to end up in this situation?*

I could see no way out. Ouranis had already made it clear she couldn't do anything for Sophia without the risk of giving up our position to the Voidshapers. I had mentioned the subject several times, but to no avail. She was adamant about the fact that we needed this hideout, that we mustn't jeopardise it. For some unknown but all-important reason we couldn't risk being forced to leave, despite having the entire planet's worth of hiding places we could fly to at our disposal, at the expense of this one little girl.

I knew that what we were about to attempt was important. But wasn't it worth the risk to help Sophia? For all we knew, she might only need a tiny push, a nudge over the edge, and she would return to the waking world. Or, if not Ouranis, perhaps the druids would be able to save her. From what I had learned so far they were quite proficient at messing with other people's energy. Perhaps one of their many rituals could help her. But Ouranis didn't want to debate it. She said it would only endanger the druids even further if they tried to help Sophia.

When it became clear Ouranis couldn't be swayed even to try to open a telepathic link with the girl and send energy that way, as she was essentially doing the same thing with the Hive Mind, I switched my concern towards Denise. My hyena girlfriend still hadn't shown any sign of change in looks or behaviour, be it for good or ill. I was beginning to worry that we were taking too long, that we were giving the Hive too much time to reel her in and devour her mind completely.

As for my abilities, the ones Zeuxis had so graciously burdened me with, there had barely been any change either. I had had no success whatsoever in opening a dialogue with the creatures around us. It made me wonder what had actually happened back on the island of Delos with Selena when the dozen or so squirrels came out to greet us. Had that really been my doing? Or was it just a case of the squirrels' curiosity winning the battle over their fear, and had they simply come to investigate?

Animal telepathy was, according to Ouranis, the easiest of my Shepherd abilities and the most important one for me to master in preparation for our trip. Ouranis had invited Lycomedes over a few times more to lend me some encouraging words. He couldn't stay, obviously, since that would incite questions, with questions came lies, and lies would lead to a decrease in trust if discovered. Or so he told me. Neither was Lycomedes willing to abandon Selena just yet, not until proper arrangements could be made.

His criticism might not be as constructive as it could have been, but his visits did strengthen my understanding of why Selena chose him as her master. Sadly, Selena couldn't join us herself as she was being watched like an earthworm in a chicken coop; the Eresan law had become her prison and her druid family her guard.

The two instances when I had shapeshifted into the form of an owl had been discussed repeatedly. More often than was strictly necessary, really, since Lycomedes and Ouranis were still not on speaking terms. It was becoming increasingly annoying to have to repeat the separate conversations, especially since both Lycomedes and I didn't have a clue as to what made the Phoenix so wary of the old man – and she wasn't ready to tell us.

Despite their differences, Lycomedes and Ouranis were still able to supply me with some useful information. After my first flight during our prison break, Lycomedes told me about Leander's link with owls, which was the reason why he thought I had to have made some kind of connection with Leander that caused me to choose that shape. Now that he heard about my flight from the Phoenix Hall and my seeming possession, however, it suddenly dawned to him that Zeuxis had a great fondness for owls as well.

This hadn't occurred to him before now, because Zeuxis, as the Shepherd, had a connection with many types of animals. And due to his decades of experience, Zeuxis had been able to transform into many different shapes. Creating a mental and energy-based link was, after all, a great deal easier if one could actually communicate with animals telepathically rather than through endless meditation.

Interesting though my predecessor's background story was, it still didn't explain what had actually happened at the time of the Council meeting I missed. In the case of our escape from Denise's prison, we thought that my subconsciousness had probably reacted to Lydus' deadly swarm of bees by transforming my body. But, that time, it happened so fast, I couldn't tell whether I was still in control as I rocketed towards Lycomedes. Because even if I wasn't, my mind and the one that was in control at the time were probably thinking the same thing anyway.

As for the second incident, there was no question about me not being in control of my own actions: my voice was quite different when I told Leander that I wasn't going to be questioned, and my flight through the corridors of the temple was most definitely piloted by someone with a lot more skill than I had shown thus far. But who was it?

The rain was still coming down hard on the outdoor part of the lake. The rivulets of water that were continuously streaming into the mouth of the cave had turned into gurgling ropes. By now, the cave entrance had turned into a toothless giant's mouth with threads of saliva connecting its pockmarked lips. A shiver ran through me. Lacking fuel, the fire had dwindled to embers. I would have brought some with me along with tonight's dinner, but obviously that had to wait. There was nothing else for it than to take off my toga, wring it out and put the damp, sticky piece of cloth back on or suffer the cold night air in my underwear.

As it had done many times this past week, my mind was going over the incident at the Phoenix Hall. The look on Leander's face when I drained him of his energy was as vivid as it had been the morning it happened. I could almost feel myself transform again, feel the feathers pinching every square inch of my skin except for my legs. I imagined myself whistling through the corridors like some guided, airborne projectile. Then, just when I passed through the front doors of the temple in my mind, my attention switched to the bundle of black hair that had appeared in the corner of my eye. It looked so familiar.

I looked down at Sophia again. Her hair, which grabbed the bedding of leaves beneath her head like some alien moss, reminded me of the near-identical one I had seen during my escape. *No, I've been over this*, I confirmed in silence. *She couldn't have been there. She was at the docks with Pelegon. It's got to have been some other girl. There is bound to be one with hair like Sophia's.*

A pair of tiny blue lights blinked on inside the constantly moving cloud next to her; Denise was awake and gazed at me. I stared back and tried to produce the friendliest smile I could under the circumstances. Then her hyena head appeared in full as she stretched stiffly. The shapeless nimbus immediately started to collapse into itself, reducing to a pool of magical ash which was continuously being fed by the grime from her skin.

Denise yawned, stretched again, then doubled back to Sophia. There she lifted up her head as though she was listening to something and stared at the ceiling for a spell, muscles rigid. I watched in silence. At length Denise bowed her head, put her front paw onto Sophia's chest and nudged the girl's cheek with her snout.

'Denise, what are you doing?' I said in a whisper, my eyes growing wide.

The hyena gave no response. Instead, she retained her contact with the girl and froze once more. I was on my feet and had my arm outstretched, but was so perplexed by the unexpected turn of events, I couldn't think of anything to say or do. In addition, my desire for something to happen, anything at all, wasn't helping.

After what seemed like minutes, Denise finally looked up again and withdrew her paw. The ashy secretion that had been cascading down her paw and head oozed away before it dissipated completely, leaving the girl unchanged. Then, to my utter amazement, Denise looked me straight in the eyes. The back of my neck prickled. There was a connection, something that wasn't there before. A soothing wave of warmth entered the top of my head.

'Denise?' I asked tentatively. The hyena bowed her head submissively and for some reason I had the impression she was smiling at me. But before I could act on it, Denise gave Sophia a quick glance, then loped away, shaking her head as though dazed. The blissful moment popped like a bubble.

'Denise! No, stay. I just want to…' My breath caught in my throat; Sophia's eyes had suddenly shot open. In a state of all-devouring shock I stared down at the girl. I watched how her tiny pink tongue appeared and started to lick her upper lip. Then she swallowed, pushed herself up into a sitting position and began smacking her lips. I shook my head to get rid of the veil of confusion that had wrapped itself around my body.

Quickly I hustled over to support her back and said, 'Sophia, thank goodness. You're awake. But… how?'

Sophia's dark eyes looked up at me. 'Water, please,' she said in a wheezing, raspy voice.

'Of course.' I hurried over to the bucket Lycomedes had left me, the rest of my body moving almost too fast for my legs to keep up. When she had taken a few good mouthfuls, I asked, 'Do you feel any pain?'

Sophia shook her head and took another measured swig from the bucket. If I were in her position I would probably have drained it completely. She, however, appeared satiated and was already looking more alert.

'Can you move your toes?' I asked, considering she had appeared limp as a ragdoll since the accident. I was hoping it hadn't paralysed her. In response, which took some time, she looked over to the tips of her sandals and played with them a bit. I uttered a sigh. 'Good. I'm so glad you're awake. I can't believe it.'

Sophia looked up at me for a bit, then glanced over her shoulder at Denise, who was staring at the sky through the continuous downpour.

'Denise!' I said excitedly. 'Look who's finally joined us!'

Probably due to my excitement, Denise did look back at us, but it took a few moments before the sight of the blinking Sophia had made its way into her legs. Despite the rapid reaction of her ears, it struck me how utterly exhausted she looked, with the light beaming from her eyes at only half strength and her tail dangling dully between her hind legs. When she finally did come over, her mouth was hanging open and her tongue flapped with the motion: something had evidently drained her to the point of near-coma.

It took the storm about an extra hour to pass and Ouranis an hour more to return to the lagoon. Sophia and I spent this time mostly in silence, for she still seemed weak, but I couldn't help asking what she remembered about what happened in Ouranis' den. Unfortunately, she barely remembered any of it. Neither could she recall anything of the past week, which, I deemed, was probably a good thing. Not that it seemed to make much of a difference to the girl; the only thing Sophia seemed to be concerned about was the return of Ouranis. As a matter of fact, Ouranis' return was almost like an obsession to her. Denise appeared more jovial now too, even towards me. It made me all the more happy to see the Phoenix; finally I had some good news to share.

There you are, I thought in relief, as the cave spit us out.

'Young Shepherd.' Ouranis dug her claws into the bank and folded her wings like a goose returning for spring. 'I see you have solved one of your worries. I am pleased. It makes two of us.'

It took me a moment to realise what she was talking about, then Sophia passed me with Denise following at her heels. *Oh, yeah, Sophia. She woke up a couple of hours ago. I'll tell you all about it. But first, where have you been? It's been hours since you left.*

'Indeed. As I mentioned, I went to solve one of our problems.'

Just the one? I quipped.

'As was the case with Pelegon and Sophia's ship, there are many more empty vessels currently roaming the seas, young Shepherd,' said Ouranis sombrely. 'The Voidshapers have devoured many of Arcturus' crews, leaving the ships adrift. Tonight I intercepted one of them and brought it ashore for when we leave for the Hive.'

Yes, about that. Look, I understand why you want to leave as soon as possible, I do. But I really don't know how much I will be able to help you. It's been going really poorly. Even Lycomedes said I don't have much talent for spiritcraft.

'It is unfortunate, but I am afraid we cannot risk delaying our journey any longer. I have made my decision. We will depart the day after tomorrow and you will have to continue your training on board the ship. I do not know how long our journey will last. It might be as short as a day, or as long as seven. I see no other way, however, for even now I can feel Flego's spirit slipping away from me. The Hive continues to push him deeper into the Vault by bringing lesser spirits to the surface. Thus, by thickening the layer of spirits between him and the outside world, the Hive attempts to cloud Flego's spirit from us.'

All right, I will do what I can, I thought resolutely, despite still having difficulty envisioning this so-called "Vault of Spirits". *Will Lycomedes come with us?*

'That will be his decision. I have no objection if you feel that you need him.'

I can barely feel anything anymore, to tell you the truth. I've only been here for a week or so and I'm already carrying more responsibility than I'm comfortable with. This whole Shepherd thing, Denise, and now Sophia. I'm glad Sophia is awake and seems to be all right, but I don't know, maybe we should bring her to Eresa after all. She asked me to request it, actually. So I thought, maybe we should. If the druids accept her, she'll at least be safe there.

'I do not think that is wise. Not after what happened in my den. I would rather not give the Voidshapers any incentive to enter Eresa. Until I understand what happened in my den, she will have to stay with us.'

If you say so. And what happens if we get there and I can't help you?

'Believe in yourself, young Shepherd. Two days.'

'There is a crease on your forehead,' a gruff voice informed me around noon the next day. The ambience was pleasant, with Sophia's mirthful voice and Denise's playful cackling bouncing between the rock faces in the background.

'So?' I asked in a whisper to prevent me from losing my concentration. I was sitting in the grass with my eyes closed, legs outstretched and my back resting against a smooth spot at the foot of the circular cliff. I hadn't heard Lycomedes' voice for over fifteen minutes, and had forgotten he was even there.

'It means you're trying to force the connection.'

'Of course I am,' I said. 'How else am I going to be ready?'

'A druid's abilities have nothing to do with force, or mental strength, Bishop,' said Lycomedes. 'You have heard all this before. Summoning an animal guardian is about acceptance and allowance. You must accept the animal. You take a step back and let the guardian step in. It's that simple. Communicating with their consciousness follows the same principle. You're not foraging for food, you're dealing with living entities. So you must first accept they can use you to convey a message, and then allow them to do so. They must come to you, not the other way around. And for this to happen you have to make yourself attractive and tempt them into using you.'

I opened my eyes and looked sideways to Lycomedes. In response he inclined his head and gave me a lofty look. It would have been more effective had he worn spectacles, though the message came across nonetheless. 'I have to make myself attractive?' I asked. Lycomedes' look turned serious as he nodded in acknowledgement. 'How am I supposed to do that?'

'Acceptance and allowance,' he repeated.

I let out a sigh and closed my eyes again. *Acceptance and allowance*, I thought irritably. *I've been doing that for days.* Even as I thought it, something felt weird. *Or... or haven't I?*

As I sat there, pondering, I could feel my insides churning uncomfortably. Had I actually accepted my situation? What about Denise's situation, Sophia's? I felt drained. The fear of the day after tomorrow, the odds of success of our mission, the communication gap between Denise and me, they were all laughing at me, mocking me. Things had indeed improved after Sophia's return to reality, and I was glad to see Denise finally happy again, but there continued to be a giant barrier between us, both verbal and emotional. The hyena continued to show signs of my girlfriend's personality, but the majority of the time her animalistic features seemed to have precedence. It was almost like the Voidshaper was playacting to try to fool me into thinking there was still hope.

'That's it,' said Lycomedes, a rising tone of encouragement underlining the words. 'Let it go. Empty your mind so others can fill it up.'

I didn't care anymore. What was the use? What could I do? Convince a couple of squirrels to swim over to the Hive and poke the Voidshapers in the eyes? The great Ouranis, an elephantine Phoenix with an entire army of druids ready to rally behind her if she just said the word. Yet she chose me to help her. Me…

Then, in the span of a lightning bolt scarring the sky, a black veil was pulled over my eyes. I already had my eyes closed, yet this darkness, this emptiness I was looking at, was all-consuming. Just peering into it gave me the sense of losing myself, as though I had lost the connection with my body.

A high-pitched, inhuman voice spoke directly into my brain. 'Where is she?' It sounded like the question wasn't meant for me. 'Find her. More!'

As I kept watching, I thought I could see movement in the distance. Something enormous, like a pitch-black mountain, was swaying back and forth against a background of the darkest grey. The difference between it and its background was barely noticeable, yet it was there nonetheless; there was something else there with me, something alive, and it seemed not to have noticed me yet.

'Disperse. Wings. Teeth.' The thing, whatever it was, made the words sound like the days of the week, which it counted on its fingers. I had a sense of great distance between us, rendering it safe to keep watching and listening in. Suddenly I felt my throat contract as though garrotted. A great tug followed and I was pulled forwards, racing towards the black mountain with impossible speed. I came to a spine-jarring stop while, at the same time, the voice pounded its next words directly into my brain.

'Weakness spawns folly. Weakness,' there was a long pause, 'spawns folly. You know, do you not, *young Shepherd?*' The voice paused again and I felt like being strip-searched. A chuckle filled the dark void around me. It sounded empty, mechanical. 'So entertaining. Come, bring her to me and together we'll play.'

Coughing and spluttering, I opened my eyes. My mouth was full of black ash mixed with saliva, between my teeth and dripping from my chin. Blots of it stained the grass too.

'Bishop! Great Circle,' said Lycomedes.

We'll play? I repeated in my mind, watching the magical filth seep into the ground. There was no doubt in my mind that the "her" the thing had mentioned was Ouranis. But the link had been severed. I hadn't even been left the time to reply.

I looked up. Lycomedes was bending over me, his hands on his knees, his eyes screwed up. Instead of looking at me, however, he was examining the products of my coughing. Then the old man's face started to swim before my eyes. My brain felt as though injected with helium. I quickly turned away, too quickly in fact, and the kind of drunken stupor I was experiencing intensified instantly.

'Fascinating,' said Lycomedes' voice from somewhere to my right. I paid him no heed, for my mind was still in the process of recuperating.

The sun was casting half of the lagoon in shadow. I could see the rim of the cliff painting a line on the lake's surface, though the line was moving constantly because of my intoxicated haze. My heart skipped a beat; my eyes had fallen on the frozen figure of Sophia. She was standing at the very edge of the bank, her face rigid, her eyes piercing, and every bit of her attention aimed at me. She was soaked to the bone, her dark hair glued to the sides of her face and chest. There was something in her eyes that reminded me of the moment just before she collapsed in Ouranis' den and had screamed at me about her father.

As I watched her standing there, the stupor slowly evaporated, leaving me with only a mild headache. Now my attention was drawn away yet again. The ground beneath my hands and knees was quaking in a rhythmic fashion, one that was growing in intensity with every beat. With all I had experienced, the creative side of me was fully expecting to see a translucent tyrannosaurus, raised from a time long past, coming at me in full charge. Instead, it was Ouranis.

'There is no time left,' the Phoenix said, pumping the words into my skull with an amount of ferocity I hadn't seen or heard her display before. 'We have to leave this instant.'

Why? What happened?

Ouranis came to a scraping halt, sending grass blades flying everywhere like throwing knives. Lycomedes and I had to use our arms as shields or risk a facial scrub. 'I am not certain. I felt a dramatic spike in the number of imprisoned spirits, which can only mean one thing: the Hive has become desperate. In its attempt to thwart my progress, it must have opened the attack on the human population. Despicable though it is, it is working. It may even have discovered my reluctance to touch human spirits, which has put me at a disadvantage. Tell him.'

Her words sent a jot of adrenaline through my muscles. 'Lycomedes, Ouranis just told me we can't wait till tomorrow,' I told the old man. 'Something has happened with the Darkness and we need to go now.'

'Aristion!' said Lycomedes, whipping his head back to Ouranis. The shock of his gaze made the great Phoenix twitch her neck. 'Take me back to Eresa, quickly,' he said, appearing to forget to whom he was talking. 'He can help us… Please,' he added as an afterthought.

I repeated Lycomedes' words in my mind and asked, *Will you do it?*

'How does this druid, Aristion, know about the Hive?' Ouranis asked in return.

Aristion was one of the druids who helped perform the ritual that brought me here. Lycomedes must have talked to him about our mission, I think.

There was a moment before Ouranis inclined her head and said, 'So shall it be. I see no reason to hide the Hive's existence any longer. Now the Hive is targeting humans, the druids must prepare for what is coming, for they *are* coming. Young Shepherd, when I return, it is your responsibility to make sure Sophia and Denise are ready to depart. Do you understand?'

Of course. And thank you, Ouranis.

As I watched her grab Lycomedes and take off, I pondered for a moment on what possible reason Ouranis could have had to hide the Hive's existence from the druids in the first place. She had asked me not to discuss the Voidshapers with Lycomedes or anyone else. And because of my wish to maintain a healthy relationship with Ouranis, I had complied without question. But I never really stopped to wonder why she deemed it necessary. Wouldn't it help the druids to prepare if they knew what they were up against? Ouranis said Eresa was in danger and she had known about the Voidshapers for a very long time. So why keep the truth from them?

I thought of Zeuxis, the previous Shepherd. He must have been in the same spot, since Ouranis had said she had told the story about Akhenaten and the fate of the Celestial Beasts to most of, if not all, the Shepherds before me. And seeing that none of the druids knew about the existence of the Darkness before Denise and I came to this world, let alone their real name, I figured Zeuxis must have kept quiet as well. Had he known why?

After Ouranis and Lycomedes had vanished behind the cliffs, I looked back at the spot where I had last seen Sophia, albeit a bit more hesitatingly than I normally would have done because of the weird, steely look she had given me earlier. She was gone. I found her again in the cave, flapping her shirt above the smouldering coals to bring out the last bit of residual heat.

Like every night, I had made sure the fire would keep burning throughout the morning hours, not only to keep the cave at a comfortable temperature, but also to keep the bugs away. Because translucent or not, the buzzing those pests produced was as annoying as any of their corporeal cousins. And we had found out the hard way that sleeping next to still water was definitely not a good idea without a good mosquito repellent. Luckily for us, however, the years the insects had spent inside the Vault of Spirits had rid them of their thirst for blood.

We were still busy wringing out and drying Sophia's hair and clothes when Denise noticed the tell-tale wing strokes of Ouranis. She looked up with a jerk, straightened her ears and opened her mouth, her tongue rolling out like a red carpet.

'Are you prepared, young Shepherd?' Ouranis asked me before I could spot her.

We are. Where are you?

'Come forward and grab the human girl.'

The next thing I knew the entire mouth of the cave was covered by a blanket of blue and silver feathers. I was lifted up effortlessly by the waist. Denise underwent the same fate, and she let out a cackling growl that lasted all the way until we had traded the underground lagoon for the pocket of air above the island's jungle.

Only when Sophia stopped screaming did I realise she had been voicing her excitement too. I had been so focused on Denise, I hadn't noticed the squeal her tiny throat was producing. Judging from the way my ears throbbed, I figured that the human ear might have been incapable of hearing the first part of her scream. This also meant that Ouranis may actually not have been the reason for the sudden scattering of the colony of translucent bats when she picked us up.

Blots of brown and green flashed by in waves of colour. I had Sophia secured around the waist. And, since we were flying against the wind, I had to constantly readjust her body to make sure the damp octopus that was her hair wouldn't grab me by the face in some undesirable mating ritual. After a series of futile attempts I gave up and rested my chin on my shoulder, so that the tentacles had to settle for my left ear and the back of my neck instead of my face. I did so just in time to spot a cluster of apricot trees bearing the juiciest looking specimens I had seen thus far. That being the last thing I saw of the island, we sped away towards the horizon.

Chapter 13

The moment we hit the deck of Ouranis' procured trading vessel, Denise disappeared behind my legs. I felt her dark secretion push against my ankles like a kitten starved for attention. Ouranis had just put us down between the four that were already there: Aristion, the only survivor of the Shepherd ritual, Lanike, one of Lycomedes' apprentices, a woman I wasn't familiar with, and finally, Lycomedes. All except Lycomedes stood gazing up at the giant Phoenix, eyes shining blue.

It was quite obvious from the fact that their profiles weren't completely stricken by shock from seeing the great Phoenix up close that Ouranis must have brought them here. I also figured Lycomedes must have told them his view on why they weren't squashed by Ouranis' powerful aura the second the Phoenix approached them. It was evidently still a treat to see Ouranis this close up, however. Her coming had put an abrupt end to their conversation.

'You must be Aaron,' said Aristion, finally meeting my eyes and inclining his head.

I did the same. My hand was itching to grab something to shake, but I knew that the druids didn't share that customary greeting. 'And you Aristion. I'm pleased to meet you. This is Sophia, and Denise.'

Denise moved out in the open, one paw at a time, her body still oozing ash. The parts of her body that had been visible behind our legs had probably been drowned by Ouranis' magnificent presence. Because now she showed herself in full, Aristion as well as the unknown woman jumped backwards and slammed their palms together in response. Neither of them uttered another word; they were too focused on their energy and their own survival to speak.

Lycomedes, Lanike and I all leapt forwards to create a living shield between both parties.

'My mistake,' said Lycomedes, holding up his hand apologetically. All eyes except those of the woman focused on him. 'I should have warned you she was coming. You two,' he indicated Aristion and the woman with a flapping finger, 'release.'

At Lycomedes' command, Aristion increased the distance between his hands by an inch or so, his face turning from vexation to befuddlement. The woman wasn't as easily convinced.

'Althea…,' Lycomedes warned her. Only now did the woman called Althea move her eyes towards the old man, albeit cautiously; until now they had been flicking between both of our group's flanks, the expectation of the black hyena advancing from behind our backs burning in her eyes.

'She's not with the Darkness. She's my girlfriend,' I said, trying to convince the woman.

Althea switched to me. 'Preposterous,' she said, the rest of her mind evidently still focused on her hands.

Lanike took another step forwards. 'If Master believes him, we should too, Althea. Please, you know why we're here.'

'I'm not so sure that I do,' she said.

'Then why did you come with me?'

'You said Lycomedes asked for your help,' said Althea. 'He is the reason I'm here. You said nothing about these two. He's a fugitive.'

'I can explain everything,' said Lycomedes. 'There is no need for violence, believe me.'

Lycomedes' words soothed Althea. She sighed and let her arms drop. The second they parted I beheld a slither of blue light, which vanished into nothingness. 'It's been too long, Lycomedes,' said Althea, inclining her head to the old man. He returned it graciously.

'Then let's hear what he has to say before we start accusing people, shall we?' said Lanike, relief coating her words. This seemed to do the trick and even Aristion eased his shoulders.

The party broke up and we were all brought up to speed as to who we all were and what we were doing here. Apparently, Althea, now in her mid-thirties, had once been a student of Lycomedes as well. After earning her druids sash it became clear she hadn't just learned how to defend herself from the old man. She had also incorporated some of his philosophies into her own views on society, which resulted in her decision not to join any of the seven clans of Eresa. Instead, she had taken up residence in one of the more open-minded and free-spirited districts of the Sanctuary.

Despite his similar views, this was not where Lycomedes spent his days. He had chosen to stay with the clans to teach the less experienced, and in most cases younger, generation of druids what it meant to be one. He would rather do this without bothering with the division between the druids, but apparently this was impossible, or at the very least, impractical. This impracticality was largely due to the fact that the Council consisted mostly of clan captains, and they kept the druid masters on a tight leash. In addition, to become a druid one is required to choose an animal and link with it. And occasionally, druids in training required outside help to create the connection with their animal, which was supplied by members of their future clan.

The head of the Council, Commander Xenokrates, as well as Megara, his second-in-command, were clanless however. It would have disturbed the balance of power otherwise. As Lycomedes had explained to me back in the lagoon, his good standing with them was the main reason why Lycomedes had been allowed to keep his position as a druid master without joining a clan.

Aristion appeared to have a great deal of respect for Lycomedes. It was he who had "given him his eagles", to use his own phrase. But his respect for the old man wasn't the reason why he wanted to come. Instead it was his quest for revenge on the Darkness for the atrocities it had committed during the ritual that had prompted him to join. As one of the ritualists himself, he not only grieved for the lives of the druids that had been lost that day (for he had known several quite well), but held the Darkness responsible for the nightmares that followed every time he closed his eyes.

As it was, he was the only actual witness of what happened during the attack beside Selena, Denise and I, and we had seen only little. The attack had occurred a little over a week ago and by the look in his eyes it was clear that Aristion could barely think of anything other than what happened that day. For one as traumatised as he was by the event, it was a true testament to his respect for Lycomedes not to attempt to exact his revenge on Denise.

As it turned out, Lycomedes had informed him, and only him, of what we were about to do so he could cover for Lycomedes when the time came. But once he heard about our plans, he insisted in coming with us. As for Lanike, fate had willed it for her to overhear the conversation between Lycomedes and Aristion, which led to her insistence to come with us. From what I could gather, she too had lost someone dear to her during the Shepherd ritual.

'What is on your mind, young Shepherd?' Ouranis asked a few minutes into Lycomedes' explanation of the purpose of the journey we were about to embark on. I was amazed to discover that Aristion, Lanike and Althea had all answered the call of our quest without even knowing exactly what they were up against, or what the purpose of our trip was. Basically, all they knew was that it was to help Ouranis and that it involved the Darkness. 'I can see something is troubling you.'

I'm not really sure, to be honest. I turned around and watched her trying to find a comfortable place to sit on the deck. No matter how she twisted and turned her massive rear, her large bulk was doomed to occupy the entire quarterdeck at the ship's aft. I had to brace myself not to laugh. *Can't you read my thoughts?*

'I am not continuously reading your mind,' she said, her voice sounding almost offended. 'You are allowed to keep some of your thoughts private. In addition, I am also trying to determine what the changes the Hive has recently undergone. At first I thought its increase in power was the result of the absorption of more spirits. Now, however, I am not as certain. Something seems to have happened in addition to that.'

I think I may have the answer, Ouranis. Or part of it. Maybe you should probe my memory if you can. Because when I was training with Lycomedes this morning I had some sort of vision, I think. I don't know how else to describe it.

'Please bring it to the surface,' said Ouranis. 'I will observe.'

As my mind did a retake, the black veil and the even darker mass came floating by. The memory was definitely a lot less invasive as the experience itself, though the creature's voice was as loud as it had been that morning. 'Weakness spawns folly. Weakness… spawns folly. You know, do you not, *young Shepherd?* So entertaining. Come, bring her to me and together we'll play.'

Ouranis didn't speak again for a long while, a time during which I tried to keep my mind as calm as possible to give her the peace she obviously needed. I figured she was probably checking the new information against the facts she could gather by probing the Hive Mind. Finally, she said, 'You should not let the Hive's words trouble you, for they are of minor significance in light of what is happening. Neither do they change our position, for I do not believe it is capable of truly harming you at a distance, unless, perhaps, you allow it to do so.

'Not capable of…?' I began to retort exasperatedly, then continued in thought. *Not capable of harming me? That vile ink was coming out of my throat!*

'It is merely attempting to scatter you mind,' Ouranis pressed, 'and I need you focused. I have never been closer to rescuing my brother Flego, and the Hive knows it. I need you, young Shepherd. And for that, your mind needs to be clear.' I swallowed. 'We will discuss this further when we return. Now, do I have your full attention?'

Yes, Ouranis.

'Thank you. Then I regret to tell you that it is as I feared. I believe the Hive has become capable of relocation.' Even as she spoke, I thought I could feel her mind slipping, as though she was going back into trance.

Relocation? You mean the entire Hive is on the move? Ouranis didn't say anything more, and after a minute or so it seemed like she had fallen asleep. *Ouranis?* As I looked into her eyes, I saw a wispy tendril of energy, like a slither of smoke, leave the corner of her eye. Something had gone very wrong. She was crying. But instead of tears, pure energy was leaking out.

I didn't dare say or think anything more. The only thing I seemed capable of was watching the Phoenix's eyes, which acted as floodgates for her emotions. Finally she blinked the access energy away and said, 'It must have taken her ability. It is the only explanation.'

Whose ability are you talking about? I asked tentatively.

Ouranis straightened up again and looked out over the sea. 'My sister, Krixi. The Gryphon,' she added quickly in an attempt at an explanation, before she sank back into her previous, contemplative state of mind. She breathed in through the slits in her translucent beak. 'Thus far I have been able to use my ability from a distance because I knew in which direction I had to aim my mental probe. This is evidently not the case anymore. Previously, the enormous number of spirits made the Hive incapable of moving as a single unit, or I deemed it so. Its core, for lack of a better description, had become shackled to a single location by the Hive's insatiable gluttony.'

'It has become more important than ever that we succeed in separating Flego from the Hive Mind, young Shepherd, for his abilities will be paramount in pinning the Hive Mind to a fixed location and keeping it there. If we allow the Hive to roam free, it will make it nearly impossible for me to find the remaining Celestial Beasts. That said, the fact that the Hive Mind has discovered a way to utilise my sister's ability, Flego alone might not be able to counteract my sister's ability, which means we will have to attempt to get her out as well.'

So your sister, the Gryphon, has an ability related to movement?

'That is correct. Krixi has inherited the Sphinx's legendary speed. When she was still among us she could make her tiny body move so fast, she almost appeared to be in several places at once.'

That sounds incredible. But what about the Hive? How are we supposed to catch up if it moves that quickly?

'We will have to find a way to free her before the Hive finds out how to utilise the full potential of her ability. It is my belief the Hive has not been able to as of yet.'

I glanced over my shoulder. Without my conscious direction, my eyes were counting the heads present on the ship. *I don't understand. Don't we need more manpower for this? From what I've seen of the Voidshapers and the druids so far, we're going to need a lot more muscle if we want to take on the Hive. Why don't we go back to Eresa and ask more of them to join us? If we can get a few captains to join us...*

Lycomedes' voice interrupted my thoughts. 'Bishop.' When I found him he was beckoning me towards him and Aristion.

'Just a second,' I called back. Lycomedes gave a nod and continued his conversation.

'It is a risk, I admit,' said Ouranis, 'although I am confident this is the way it should be. If we opened a direct assault on the Hive with the help of the druids, we might have a better chance of staying out of the Voidshapers' grasp. If nothing else, we could use the distraction the druids would provide. But we cannot afford losing too many druids, not at this time. In addition, if the Hive moves around too much, we will have no chance of locating my brother and sister. Thus, I believe our journey can only be one of stealth. If we succeed, only then should the druids be alerted.'

Be alerted? I repeated in silence, more to myself than to the Phoenix. The odd choice of words seemed significant somehow. It reminded me of the fact that Ouranis had been the one responsible for the creation of Eresa. She had also refused to talk about the reason why the druids didn't know about the Voidshapers' existence until a week ago, and had yet to give me the reason why I was supposed to keep their real identity secret as well – and this while she had been extracting spirits from the Hive Mind for hundreds of years. Now, however, after knowing Ouranis for over a week and witnessing the druids' thirst for battle, the answer suddenly seemed almost comically obvious.

Ouranis, this is the reason why you've kept the existence of the Voidshapers a secret, isn't it? I told her. *You were afraid they would head out and go look for a fight.* Ouranis remained silent and my train of thought continued. *Then that's also why you've never asked a Shepherd to warn this Lord Arcturus and his people. You didn't want the clans asking questions and finding out about the enemy the rest of this world has been fighting.*

'You are correct,' Ouranis said softly. The three words were practically drowning in trepidation, as though she had pictured this moment in her mind and was now waiting to see if I would react the same way she had been hoping I would.

It's your private army, my mind blurted out, feeling excitement for the fact that the truth finally hit me in the face. Thinking it out loud made it seem so obvious, I could slap myself a second time for not seeing it sooner. *It's true, isn't it? You created Eresa. You taught the druids how to utilise their magic.* I paused for a moment to think, then thought, *So basically, without them realising it, you raised them to one day help you rid the world of the Hive.*

Ouranis said nothing. My mind started spinning. Names began drifting by. Helios, Kriton, Vespines, Bovines, the Arena of Repentance, and several more until one came along that didn't want to give up its spot to the next in line. It was that of Lycomedes, whose owner, I now realised, had approached me.

In the corner of my eye I could see Ouranis' head give the tiniest twitch; she had seen Lycomedes too. Behind the old man, Althea, Lycomedes' clanless ex-apprentice, was emerged in conversation with Lanike. The three elements, Ouranis' reaction to Lycomedes' presence, the old man himself, and Althea, all fused into this one revelation.

'You,' I told Lycomedes, pointing vaguely at his chest.

'Me?' he asked, his eyebrows fusing together.

'Of course.' I closed my mouth and said to Ouranis, *That's why you don't like Lycomedes. He thinks the division between the clans is a mistake. And he teaches this to his students. Althea is living evidence of that. But you want the clans to be there, don't you? It helps the druids prepare for the upcoming war. It helps them hone their skills in battle.*

'Are you finished, young Shepherd?' Ouranis said, her voice even softer now. It ignited a sense of compassion inside me that I didn't think was still there after my experiences with Denise and Sophia. I thought I had spent it all.

I... I'm sorry. I got a bit carried away, I thought, meaning every word. *It wasn't an accusation, though. More like an observation.*

'I bear no grudge,' she said, 'so long as you keep this to yourself. If our mission is a success, the druids will know everything about the Voidshapers soon enough. They must have learned about their existence already, of course, after the attack on my mother's temple. It is the way of things.'

I will, Ouranis. Just one other thing, though, if you don't mind. Eresa is a sanctuary for people who seek a fresh start in life. So how come none of the newcomers have told the druids about the Darkness? Pelegon knew, so others must have too.

'Zeuxis...' Ouranis paused, then said in a concluding fashion, 'My mother's ability is not the only thing a Shepherd is required to protect, young Shepherd.'

After our conversation and everyone's agreement that they wanted to stay and help, Ouranis grabbed a bundle of ropes Aristion and Lycomedes had fastened to the bow, and we were on our way. Our speed easily exceeded any our single sail would have been able to provide.

Despite her desire for haste, the giant Phoenix made sure she stayed low to the water's surface and used the islands we encountered as cover, so we had the best possible chance of reaching the Hive unnoticed. As we had no idea where the Hive had gone off to or even in which direction it was travelling, its previous location was the only lead we had. What happened from there on out was a bridge we could not see, let alone know where it would bring us.

'Lanike, wasn't it?' This was the first opening I had seen since we met on the ship, as Althea had only left her side a minute ago. I had just finished my conversation with Lycomedes, which turned out to be little more than a concise strategy briefing. I had also asked him about the pretext under which he and our druid companions had left Eresa. With a smirk I would only have expected from someone one third his age he told me there was none since, again, Aristion was supposed to cover for him. He told me they would deal with the consequences later.

'Hello,' Lanike said with a fleeting glance at Althea, who didn't have the necessary eyes in the back of her head to notice us.

'Am I making you uncomfortable?' I had stopped halfway between squatting and standing. 'I can understand if I do.'

'No, no, it's okay,' Lanike said hastily, although not very convincingly. 'Please.' She indicated the empty spot next to her and I sat down, my back leaning against the ship's railing.

'All right,' I said, and an uncomfortable silence fell. Lanike seemed to be lost in thought and I wondered what she and Althea had been talking about. 'So,' I said after a pause I deemed I had allowed to last for way too long, 'I wanted to thank you for helping us.'

'I haven't done anything yet.'

I chuckled. 'Same here.' She looked at me in full and I could see her face ease up and her eyes narrowing a little. It forced a laugh out of me and made me ask, 'What?'

'You're different. The way you carry yourself. You're from the homeland, aren't you?'

'I guess I am. You've got no problem with that?'

'I think it's fascinating. I don't know if you remember, but I was the first one who saw you enter Eresa a week ago. Althea was there too, but we were having an argument and she didn't...' At that point, a jolt of shock went through her muscles. She simultaneously started backwards, shielded her face with her arm and took a forceful, hissing breath.

Her conversational tone and her reaction clashed so radically, I knew immediately it couldn't have been me that made her jump. And sure enough, looking sideways, Denise had made another one of her impacting appearances.

The way people reacted to her presence was starting to grow so tiresome, I had to make an effort not to utter a heavy sigh and appear like some insensitive prat. This was made even more difficult by the fact that I did remember my first visit to Eresa, and that Lanike was the one who had uttered the scream that summoned the entire plaza to our location.

'You don't need to be afraid, Lanike,' I said, feeling a bit annoyed to have to explain it once more. 'She won't do anything. She's harmless.' Another look at Denise made me want to snap the words back out of the air with my teeth and swallow them. 'I mean she's with me, and I trust her.'

Lanike's hands had already made contact with each other. Her eyes shifted from me to Denise and back again. Then she nodded and slowly her palms parted. Denise, on the other hand, didn't seem to want to back off. She was staring at Lanike as though hungry for a limb or two. As I looked at her, the rest of the world seemed to disappear. *Jealousy? Ha, I knew it! I can see it in her eyes, she...* Denise turned to me. Her nostrils flared and at once, the sliver of hope I was holding onto bloomed like a tropical flower. *There you are. That's my girl. Now I know you're still you.*

I felt my lips curl into a broad smile. Denise sniffed, stuck her nose in the air, and briskly stalked off. An idea occurred to me. It was one born both out of curiosity for how Denise would react, and from a sense of longing for more proof that Denise's mind was indeed still hers. So I called across the deck, 'Sophia, can you take Denise for a walk?' Denise froze for a moment, paw hanging suspended in the air, then began to act as though she hadn't heard me.

Sophia was standing on the other side of the ship, staring motionlessly at Lycomedes and Ariston, who both seemed fired up about something. Due to the high winds I could only make out the words "snakes", "risk" and "ash cloud". In response to my call, the girl switched to me and spent a second or two considering her answer. Then her eyes swept from left to right to take in the entire length of the vessel, which wasn't great. When she found me again she held up her hands as if saying, "Take her where?"

'Please?' I added. There was no need to say anything else; she was already coming over. Denise, with black ash continuously dripping from her chin, had now completely turned and was looking at me again with a granite expression. She had evidently spotted Sophia and I figured she must have linked it with my voice; even if she couldn't understand my words, she clearly had no trouble deciphering their meaning. Her mouth was closed, her face unmoving. Upon meeting her eyes, something welled up in my chest right around my heart area. *Sorry for that, Denise, but this confirms it. You may not be fully able to understand me, and we need to do something about your appearance before I can take you to another Christmas party, but you've got to be still in there somewhere.*

A small hand with dirty nails entered my field of vision, one that began stroking Denise behind the ears. Except for a few involuntary jerks of her ears, Denise gave no acknowledgement. Her steely gaze remaining locked onto me until Sophia finally managed to draw her attention.

'I see our Shepherd has competition,' said Lanike as we watched Sophia and Denise walk off, Sophia muttering something that sounded rather harsh.

'Excuse me?'

Lanike turned her head, pulled up her knees and placed her folded arms on top of them. Then she shrugged. 'Not that it's any of my business, but I can't see any other reason why Selena would protect you. You must have done something right with her.' Her eyes found me. 'And she is a difficult one to please.'

There was a curious edge to her voice and I wondered if Selena's love life really was none of her business. 'She does? I mean, you spoke to her?'

'Not in person, no. She's been too busy with the Council and Lycomedes. But news travels fast in Eresa. As do rumours. And according to them, Selena has been trying to convince the captains to leave you alone. Supposedly, your arrival and the incident during the Shepherd ritual was a simple coincidence. What do you think?'

'I... I'm not really sure, to be honest. After Denise, nothing really made sense anymore.'

'How so?'

'Well, she's human,' I chose to say, deciding on openness. 'Denise is a victim, like those druids you lost at the temple. The Darkness turned her into, well, you know...'

Lanike gave a slow nod and glanced over at the black-haired girl and the even darker coloured hyena standing next to her. Sophia and Denise were like statues, peering at a small island moving across the horizon in the distance. 'Aristion's story is true, then. They *were* attacked.' She fell silent again.

'You didn't think it was?'

Lanike produced a small smile. 'I figure you know quite a bit about us already, don't you, Aaron? Otherwise you wouldn't be so surprised when people doubted his story. And you must know all about the story considering the company you enjoy.'

'I haven't spent that much time in Eresa yet,' I said, 'but Selena and Leander were quite open about your customs.' I almost wanted to include Ouranis, who I wasn't supposed to be able to talk to, obviously. 'And Lycomedes can barely stop talking when we touch the subject.'

'That I believe.' She chuckled and said, reminiscing, 'Master taught us his rules of engagement. We were at the orchards with the entire group, Selena, Leander, Briseis, Peleus and me. It was one of our first trips together. Fun times, you know? Captain Kriton had just been made clan captain. Or he had scared the Council into making him one, I'd better say.' A smile appeared on her face. 'That was some battle, I tell you that. Anyway, one of his rules reads: doubt raises questions, questions supply answers and answers enable correct reasoning. It may not work for many of us, but it does for me.'

'I bet it does. And your Council? What do they think of Aristion's story?'

'Oh, they have no choice. They have to believe him, or at first. The founding principles of Eresa are honesty and integrity, aren't they? And Aristion is a druid. So they have to believe he is telling the truth.'

'But what about Selena's story? She's your Shepherd after all.'

'True. But the thing is, Selena and Aristion's stories don't necessarily contradict each other. Selena confessed she saw Adrastus change into one of these dark entities, just not much more. She couldn't find the other ritualists, which Leander, Briseis, Peleus and Lycomedes all confirmed. End of story, basically.'

'She has to have said more than that. She has helped us escape and everything. Your Council surely wouldn't have settled for that.'

'She is the Shepherd. And as I said, you must have made a good impression on her.' She eyed me with the practiced look of a seasoned journalist. I had to think of something quickly to steer the conversation away from gossip and back to the facts.

'How is Leander, by the way?' I was considering not bringing this up out of fear of the questions that were sure to follow, but nothing else sprang to mind.

Lanike's expression changed in an instant. She took a moment to search my eyes before she answered. 'I will tell you,' she turned to Ouranis, who was gliding smoothly in front of the ship, claws clutching the ropes, 'in exchange for your story. It is plain to see by your reaction to her presence that you have met Ouranis before. You were even less intimidated by her than we were. What happened to you after you fled from Eresa? And how did you end up with the great Ouranis?' It was clear these questions had been on her mind since we first met, but she had chosen to wait for the right opportunity to ask them.

'I thought it was sort of obvious, actually. Selena took us to her. You must have heard about our break out.' Lanike nodded. 'Well, in order to prevent anything bad happening to us, to Denise and me I mean, Selena brought us to Ouranis' cave. It was the only place the Council didn't dare enter, or so she told us.'

'Because they would be crushed to death,' said Lanike. 'Or so *we* were told,' she added with a smile.

I couldn't believe how refreshing it was to talk with another person again after a week of having only Lycomedes and Ouranis to talk to. I had grown fond of them both, but they were always so business-like, so focused on progress and the future. Sophia wasn't very talkative no matter what subject I brought up and Denise, well, a simple tail wag or flick of her ears just wasn't enough to satisfy my need for a good conversation. But with Lanike, everything seemed so easy. Her personality sparked something in me, something people who shared the same wavelength often did. And reluctant though I was to admit it, her unquenchable thirst for information reminded me of Denise. *Perhaps that's why she acted so jealous earlier*, I thought.

'Yes, about that,' I said. 'It seems that Ouranis doesn't necessarily share your need for honesty. Apparently, she can switch her energy off if she wants to.'

Lanike narrowed her eyes thoughtfully. 'Lycomedes had a similar explanation.' She breathed in deeply, then said, 'She's quite different from what we've been led to believe.'

'Trust me; you haven't seen the last of it yet. You should have seen my first encounter with her. Anyway,' I said quickly to throw Lanike off the scent of my Shepherd abilities, 'wasn't Selena once brought to Eresa by Ouranis? How could that have happened if no one can get close to her?'

'We always thought it was because Selena linked with Ouranis the moment she touched her,' said Lanike. 'It is supposed to have protected her. Now I'm not so sure.'

Lanike was on the right track. Selena linking with Ouranis had indeed nothing to do with her supposed immunity to Ouranis' energy. I was just about to tell her this when I had to physically force my lips together, since I almost let it slip that Selena had been responsible for a certain double crater filled with crystal shards inside Ouranis' den. And that shouldn't have happened if Selena had inherited Zeuxis' abilities, regardless of how Selena had survived being picked up and carried to Eresa by Ouranis as an infant. After all, the Shepherd ritual happened several years *after* Selena joined the druids and our first meeting with Ouranis occurred *after* she became a Shepherd.

'Who knows,' I chose to say. 'It is a reasonable line of thinking, though. Ouranis may even have wanted Selena to link with her. So, um, one of the reasons why I wanted to talk to you was because of Leander. How is he doing?' Before the question had even left my mouth, my muscles tensed.

Lanike sighed through her nostrils. 'He'll have to make do without his owls for a while, but the healers think he'll recover. He's strong, Leander.' She hesitated, then added, her voice dripping with a surprising amount of emotion, 'And Aaron, he asks for your forgiveness.'

Chapter 14

Confusion took my head for a spin. For a while we sat there and didn't speak again until Lycomedes asked me to come over.

Leander was sorry? Did he actually think it was he who had made it happen? I had transformed into a horned owl, that was true. And horned owls were Leander's specialty. Selena and Lycomedes knew about the real reason for my transformations. Leander, of course, did not. As far as he was concerned, I was just a young man from the druids' home world with no ability to spiritcraft, no link with a spectral breed from the animal kingdom, and an innocent victim of fate.

I felt amazing. It was like a burden had been lifted from my shoulders and I could stand tall again, head in the wind. Because if Leander truly thought it had been he who had forced his energy on me, the Council must as well. Still, it seemed too easy, too convenient. Was this Leander protecting me again? Had Selena, perhaps, got to him first and explained the situation? Had she asked Leander to twist the truth?

Over the last two minutes, Ouranis had slowed down considerably and our speed had suffered as a result. My mind eased into the rhythm of the soft pounding of the waves against the ship's hull. The silence seemed to thicken the air. It was as if the trepidation we all felt clogged the atmosphere, the same way heat makes porridge of milk and oatmeal.

After every stroke of the Phoenix's wings, several long seconds of muteness followed, broken only by the whispers of my companions and the splitting of water. Ouranis remained so close to the surface, her translucent body almost blended with the ocean. She was perfectly camouflaged. The only thing that would make our approach even more unnoticeable was if she took us onto her back and hid us behind the clouds above. I would have loved her to do so, and wondered if she didn't because of Sophia and Denise. This in turn also made me wonder if we had done the right thing by bringing them along and not giving in to Sophia's suggestion to leave her with the druids.

When I joined them, Lycomedes and Aristion were discussing the black dots that had popped up on the horizon. They appeared too small to be islands. As we moved closer, Aristion's observation that they could be ships turned out to be right.

There were no islands to use as cover. There was no storm to mask our coming. There was barely a cloud in the sky and the sea was calm, allowing us easy access to the drifting fleet. Whoever was on those ships only had to glimpse our way and we would be spotted. Our options were twofold: go straight for them or try to go around.

Do you know who's out there? I asked Ouranis.

'I believe I do, but I did not expect there to be this many,' she said, injecting the words directly into my brain as she continued to glide us forwards. 'If the human male, Pelegon, was telling the truth about the human sacrifices, either Arcturus has changed his mind since Pelegon left or he has grown desperate. For this is over three times his usual offerings.'

Are you saying all those ships could be here as a sacrifice? There must be dozens of them. But wait a minute. Is this the reason why the Hive is on the move? I mean, the ships must have looked like a floating feast waiting to be devoured.

'Or his army,' said Ouranis. 'Yet your comparison of the Hive to a mindless beast is a result of your ignorance, young Shepherd. The Hive would never succumb to such banal temptation. It thinks the way its puppets move: fluidly like a droplet of water.'

I see. I apologise. What do you want us to do?

'Not be intimidated, no matter what your eyes behold.'

'Girls,' Lycomedes whispered over his shoulder as we approached the ships, his hand tapping the air behind him. Lanike and Althea fell silent immediately. The world seemed to do the same.

A large trireme, sails down and devoid of life, passed our bow. Or we passed it, for the ship's only movements were caused by the slow rocking of the waves. Another ship came up at our starboard side, and the next thing we knew we had entered a graveyard at sea, the many vessels acting as tombs for the memories of their lost crewmen.

I couldn't even hear my companions breathe. Our heads swayed left and right while Ouranis continued to pull us in deeper. There were no living spirits left to tell us their tale, no bodies to recover. Whatever had transpired here, and Sophia had perhaps the best idea out of all of us, it must have been a horrific event.

Sophia! The name struck me like a carpet beater. And when I found her, my body felt like ready to crumple like the beaten carpet itself. The poor girl was sitting with her knees pulled up and her chin buried between them. Only her eyes were visible between the lines of black hair and the shaggy dress her father had left her with. She wasn't shaking, but cramped up, stricken by the continuous repetition of her memories. She was forced to watch them, eyes open or closed.

I heard my own footsteps pounding the planks as I ran towards her. 'It's going to be okay,' I said, kneeling beside her and pulling her head against my chest. 'It's all right. Ouranis will protect us.'

'Pelegon,' whispered Sophia.

'I know, shh.' I moved my fingers through her hair and began caressing her crown.

There was a moment of silence, then, 'She's here.'

Moving away from her slightly I looked down into her dark brown eyes. I opened my mouth to speak, then closed it again. I figured she must have meant to say, "He's here", but if she had, I still had no idea how that could be; her father was dead.

A small, loving smile creased the corners of her mouth. A sense of peace emanated from them, which eased each of her features in turn.

'What do you...? Are you sure?' I asked. She nodded and her teeth showed. 'Where?'

Slowly Sophia moved her chin to her chest. At first I thought she indicated her heart in an effort to explain that her father was with her in spirit. But when I was about to confirm this idea, and perhaps add a few comforting words if my sense of compassion inspired any, she spoke again. When she did, her voice was sharp like the tip of a spear. It reminded me of the change in personality she had shown back inside Ouranis' den. 'Below.'

My legs gave a jerk and the next thing I knew I was on my feet. It was as if my survival instinct had engaged of its own accord, though I had no idea why. It wasn't because of the little girl, I was sure. It was something else. Everything tingled, my skin, my brain, even the marrow in my bones. I knew I had to say something, do something. I had dreamt of this moment before: it felt like a nightmare waiting to be unleashed, one that I had already lived through in my sleep.

'Lycomedes,' I called in a hoarse whisper, my eyes still locked onto Sophia. She was looking up at me, expectantly and inquisitive. My voice easily carried to the other side of the deck where the druids stood. 'I... We're not alone.'

From the other side of the deck, four people and one black hyena were staring back at me, their faces hard and mouths closed. Nobody understood what was going on.

'Bishop, get over here,' Lycomedes whispered back. It was clear by the sound in his voice he was wondering why, after all this time of acting the stealthy predator, I was letting my enthusiasm get the better of me. But I didn't care about that anymore. Something inside me told me it didn't matter. We had been spotted.

'What are you talking about?' Lycomedes said when I was within normal whispering range. My eyes were still on Sophia, head turned over my shoulder. The girl, refusing to move, followed me with her gaze.

'He's right,' said Aristion, his voice reduced to a fraction. 'Quiet, all of you.'

All sound ceased. Then a gentle sloshing conjured an image of something or someone being lowered into the water on the other side of the trireme a little off our port bow. I thought the whispers I heard was just the wind singing in the masts and the ropes around us. But a short grunt from Denise, who had stayed with Sophia, told me she had heard it too. And sure enough, without even noticing us, a small, wooden lifeboat with a pair of men at the oars emerged from behind the stern of the ship. Seeing them trying to escape whatever their memories fed them made me realise how large the ship they ventured from actually was. It could easily accommodate a crew of over a hundred and fifty people.

'They might be able to tell us what happened here,' said Aristion. 'We need to halt.'

For me this was no reason to panic. I simply had to reach out with my mind and I could ask Ouranis to act on Aristion's suggestion. This was obviously not the case for the others. While the women lined up at the port side of our ship, Aristion moved further up the bow to attract Ouranis' attention. Lycomedes turned to me instead. It was safe to do so since no one was paying any attention to us anymore. I gave him a nod.

'You may be able to see through my eyes, but I am not blind, young Shepherd,' said Ouranis when I had conveyed Aristion's wish to the Phoenix. 'And in contrast to what you might think, I cannot simply stop and turn.' She paused briefly. 'I can, however, do the same to you.' And with that she released the ropes, twisted her massive body in mid-air, reversed course with a few strong strokes of her wings and dug her translucent claws into the bow of the ship.

A wave of commotion went through the party, starting with Aristion and ending with Sophia. Many fell to their knees and hands while the ship bucked like a horse gone frantic. Ouranis then flew back up again and, after the ship levelled, landed elegantly on the aft section.

The men in the lifeboat had noticed us now too. They were struck by a moment of indecision and gaped at the overgrown, see-through chicken wrestling with the seemingly insufficient size of her drifting roost.

'Do not be afraid,' Lycomedes called out to them. His knees were still a bit wobbly. 'We've come to look for survivors.' This, of course, wasn't entirely true. In fact, the aim of our search was to look for this massacre's predators, not their prey. But since the Hive was nowhere to be seen, its victims were our only lead.

The two men found Lycomedes because of his waving hand. Due to the old man's tiny size in comparison to Ouranis they had difficulty adjusting their eyes to their new target. Now they turned to each other, silently discussing their options.

One of them raised a hand, a trembling one, and his companion did the same. They were utterly spent and I wondered what they could have possibly thought of doing with that small lifeboat of theirs, since the closest shore was miles away. Even if the weather remained the same, they couldn't possibly hope to reach dry land before their muscles gave out. Their decision to try it anyway was testament to the fact that fear of the most intense kind can make even the strongest and most valiant of men go mad.

We helped the men aboard and Aristion handed them each a piece of fruit to sustain them. They were both bare-chested and wore simple woollen garments bound around their waists. Considering how the Eresans looked, I thought they might be slaves or prisoners at the very least. Both men were traumatised beyond the point of speech.

In silence we watched the fruit disappear, while Aristion descended to the vessel's lower deck to fetch a pair of cloaks. The weather may not have suggested they needed them, but this little extra comfort appeared to put them more at ease. One of the men's hands was still trembling as he put another piece of fruit into his mouth when the other found enough strength to start talking.

'We are very grateful,' he said. His eyes remained locked onto Ouranis, who had aimed her senses at the open sea. He then looked at our empty mast, swallowed, and stated, 'We cannot stay. How...?' Something seemed to be hurting him internally, and the man winced in pain.

'Easy, now,' said Aristion. 'Who are you? Where did you come from?' The man didn't reply and Aristion glanced at Lycomedes. 'What can you tell us about your attackers?' he tried again.

'Let him breathe for a moment, Aristion,' said Lycomedes.

'No, we cannot stay,' repeated the man, his voice stronger now. His mind seemed confused and he suddenly remembered Aristion's last question. 'Attacked... It were the Mindless.' His eyes slid out of focus. He wasn't able to see us anymore. 'They were everywhere. There were... so many.' The sentence ended in a breathless whisper.

The sincerity of the man's speech caused uneasiness in all our hearts, something which showed in our eyes. Althea gave a startled breath and in the corner of my eye I saw Lanike's hand move towards hers. It was carefully done so nobody would notice it.

'The Darkness,' said Lycomedes, nodding.

'The man's right,' said Aristion. 'We can't stay here and wait for these creatures to attack us too. They are bound to be on the watch. We need a plan.'

Lycomedes held up a hand to stop Aristion from continuing. 'First, tell us why you came to this place,' he asked the man. 'Who sent you here?'

The man evidently had no problem giving this information. On the contrary. His eagerness showed as he gritted his teeth in anger. 'Our Lord, Lord Arcturus.' As had been the case with Pelegon Linard, the name seemed to leave a bitter taste. 'His men took us here against our will. We were today's dinner.'

'Lycomedes, they're like Pelegon,' I said. Aristion's eyes narrowed at the mentioning of Sophia's father, yet he remained silent. 'Or close enough anyway.' I turned to the man and asked, 'Are you from the resistance too?'

'You've heard about us?' It was difficult to say whether he was pleased to learn this, but he was certainly surprised.

'We've met one of you before,' I said. 'Two, as a matter of fact.' I indicated Sophia. The girl seemed to be lost in thought with her face turned the other way and her arm dangling in a mound of billowing ash. Denise had to be somewhere within the ash and, by the looks of it, was probably getting her ears scratched.

At the sight of them, the man let out a sudden scream of horror and almost pulled the second man's arm out of its socket. The second man joined in, eyes wide, and both crawled away in fear until there was nowhere else to flee but the open ocean.

'Easy, easy,' said Aristion, using his voice to calm them. The men's heads twitched in unison, the movements quickened by their adrenaline. Their senses seemed to have doubled in strength as they took in each of Aristion's features. 'I know how unsettling this is,' Aristion added. 'But she means you no harm.'

'She?' one of the men said, his voice shaking and realisation dawning in his eyes. 'You're in league with them!' He actually placed one hand on the railing behind him and seemed ready to jump at the slightest movement from Denise. 'You can't trust that thing. It's one of the Mindless!' His throat raw from a lack of moisture, he choked on his next words. '…ruthless.'

'She's not one of them,' I said, unable to keep the exasperation out of my voice. 'She may look the same, but she isn't. Lycomedes, tell them.'

'I second that,' said Lycomedes, his mind only partially in the here and now. Where the other part was, I had no idea. 'As long as you stay calm, no harm will come to you. I give you my word.' The man's face loosened slightly.

'This is wrong,' the other man said hoarsely, his back still pressed into the wooden balustrade behind him. 'The Mindless cannot be trusted.'

'You are not the only ones who have suffered by their hands,' said Aristion, his voice dark. 'We call them the Darkness. Please, tell us what you know. It might help getting us all out of this place safely.'

'Tell them about the woman, Alphaios,' said the man who had spoken last. 'Do it.' The colour of his voice told me he was curious as to how we would react.

Alphaios looked at his companion with doubt etched into his profile. He was shaking his head slowly while he considered his friend's suggestion.

'This place gives me shivers,' said Althea, stroking her upper arm.

'I agree,' said Lanike. 'Lycomedes, we shouldn't hang around for too long. We need to do something.'

Lycomedes gave her a quick glance, then turned back to the men. 'What woman?' he asked.

'She called herself "the druid", but everyone knows they are just a myth, a legend,' said Alphaios, for his friend remained silent.

'*She* wasn't,' said the other.

'She had a few tricks, perhaps,' agreed Alphaios. His face drooped. 'The sad thing was, many believed her. They were scared. And Lord Arcturus was one of them.' While Alphaios was speaking, the five of us shot each other looks ranging from confusion to disbelief.

'Where did you meet this druid?' Aristion asked.

'In Lord Arcturus' capitol, Chalandros,' said Alphaios. 'Some say she appeared out of nowhere, just popped into existence.' He shook his head. 'She played her part well. As legend holds, druids are able to command lesser creatures and even summon them back from the grave.' His lips twisted into a sceptical grin. 'When the woman appeared, there was indeed a bear by her side. She seemed to have trained it well.'

'A bear,' Aristion said thoughtfully. 'When did this happen?'

Alphaios seemed to struggle with the fact that Aristion believed him so readily. It took him a moment to answer. 'A little over a week ago, if memory serves me. The story about her coming spread through the city like a disease. Only a disease would have been more humane…'

'You've heard of her,' interrupted the other man, reading Aristion's expression. It was like a statement and a question at the same time.

'Only in passing,' said Aristion, softening his words with his hand. 'Now, please continue, Alphaios. I don't wish to use more time than is necessary. What does this druid have to do with all this?' He indicated the eerie graveyard around us.

'Everything. She came to us bearing a message. She gained access to Lord Arcturus' court and told him about a portal to the south. The Mindless were supposed to be looking for it. And if Lord Arcturus managed to bring the Mindless close enough to the portal, she said they would leave our world forever. Our Lord believed her,' he added as though even listening to the druid woman was a sin.

None of us said anything, probably all for different reasons. The thing we had in common, however, was that none of us was able to think of a satisfactory reply that would not imply we knew more than we should. Not if we were indeed here as a rescue party. What did surprise me was that none of the men had said anything about our druid robes if they really had seen or heard about this lone druid.

Ouranis, are you following this? I asked the Phoenix.

'I am, young Shepherd. I have read your mind.' She paused, then said, 'I have heard enough. If you take the human girl, I will take the ship.'

The human girl? Oh, right! I had completely forgotten about her. I looked around and found Sophia bent over the ship's railing, peering into the water. My mouth and my legs reacted instantly, and both at the same time. 'Sophia, no! What are you doing?'

Time appeared to have slowed down. All my attention was on the girl's back. Upon hearing my words, Sophia pushed her body away from the edge, straightened up and turned to face me. When I caught sight of her face, the corner of her mouth, which was pulled up into a smile, changed into a flat line. And by the time she was looking fully at me, both corners were drooping and her entire face was contorted with sadness.

I half expected her to scream again like she had done inside Ouranis' den. She didn't utter a word. But even if she had, I wasn't sure I would have heard her. Because behind her sad, pretty face, a pair of pitch-black humps, each the size of the average automobile, emerged from the watery depths. My eyes were transfixed upon them. Even Sophia's face had become a distorted blur.

The double figure was so otherworldly and yet it sparked a sense of recognition inside me. I knew I had seen something like this before, perhaps in a different colour or size. The answer was on the tip of my tongue.

Everything was happening in near silence. None of my companions were looking my way. Behind the humps, a colossal, pitch-black island pushed the water aside. The island featured a pair of small mountains, one on either side and was connected to the humps by an enormous, scaly loaf of bread.

A powerful bird's cry suddenly battered my eardrums. With Ouranis' voice, a pair of enormous eyelids opened, pupils blazing; what appeared to be black mountains were actually the eyes of a monstrous creature. And the humps turned out to be its nostrils. If someone was holding me at that moment, he would surely have been thrown overboard. The shock of fear that went through me at the sight of the vast eyeballs set in the snout of an impossibly large crocodile sent me flying backwards across the deck.

Everyone was screaming. There was chaos everywhere. The amount of people on the deck seemed to have tripled in a matter of seconds. Next thing I knew, Sophia collided with my legs and belly, hugging me tightly and making it impossible to move. Denise bumped into my other leg; she too was terrified.

Ouranis had recuperated and her voice pumped into my brain. 'Tell them to hold on!' Looking up, I watched her initiate her dive. With the sound of yielding wood she came down on the bow of our ship, tilting the ship almost to the point of wheeling end over end. With a series of powerful wing strokes, she just barely managed to keep us from going the way of the Titanic.

It was total bedlam. People were tumbling, desperately groping for something solid to hold onto. I had yelled Ouranis' instructions to the others moments before she landed, but nobody needed telling; everyone had looked up at the sound of the Phoenix's cry and their instincts had taken over.

Sophia was still holding fast. It felt as if all my organs were being squeezed. Together we hit the deck like a single, inseparable entity and slid across it with the rest of them. Denise too, her nails scraping across the planks. Water was continuously gushing alongside the hull, not because of our speed, but because of Ouranis' battering wings.

Ouranis finally managed to pick up speed, which thankfully levelled the deck. We still had trouble standing up, with the wind pushing down on us and the ship riding the waves. Nevertheless we were off through the graveyard at sea, our leg muscles repeatedly countering the hull ramming the water.

Chapter 15

When I finally got used to the rhythm of the ship, the memory of the monstrous head we were fleeing from seized control of my mind. One hand was on Sophia's shoulder. I used the other to keep my balance. I couldn't help myself; I just had to look at the thing that had emerged from the deep.

I was positive I had to have been dreaming; this creature could not be true, not even in this world. As I looked back, all I could see was a mountain of black filth obliterating my view of the horizon. But at least it was stationary. It didn't seem to be pursuing us. *What was that thing?* I asked Ouranis, still trying to find the giant eyeballs within the dark cloud. *Was that a Voidshaper?*

'I cannot say for certain,' she said, her voice stressed. 'Judging by its size, it might even be the Hive itself. I have been trying to locate it, yet my desire to find my brother and sister must have befuddled my senses. I thought the Hive may have split up, since I sensed its presence in multiple directions. I still do. But I did not think about the possibility of an entity this large to be contained in a single shape, let alone to be submerged.'

Submerged..., I repeated.

I looked at Sophia. Had she known? She had said there was something below us, but I thought she meant Pelegon. I didn't understand. What was I missing? Pelegon wasn't with the Voidshapers. He wasn't turned into one of them. He was executed by the hands of the druids, punished for stealing their ship. Why, then, had Sophia said he was there? Or did she mean something else, or... someone else?

Ouranis brought the ship about and we all stood on the deck, watching the dark, shapeless mass in the distance. Alphaios' voice came from behind. 'What's going on? Why aren't we moving? Anybody?' Nobody paid him any attention. All eyes were focused on the Hive and our minds bonded in thought, trying to see the best course of action through the dark path ahead. 'Danaos, what's wrong?'

'It's come back for us,' whispered his companion named Danaos, his eyes quivering. 'To finish us.'

'Lanike, Althea,' said Lycomedes, 'remember what we've discussed. You need to be ready. Aristion?'

Aristion turned and nodded. He then put his hands together in a praying position and a blue sheet of energy ignited between them. He had his back turned to Alphaios and Danaos so they had no idea what was about to happen. I did and, in anticipation, waited for Aristion's animal of choice to leap from his chest.

In utter silence, three birds shot from Aristion's chest like cannonballs. The eagles immediately began circling the ship. Alphaios and Danaos swore in unison and jumped backwards. Their eyes shone with both shock and reverence at what they were seeing, even more so than when they saw Ouranis for the first time. A druid of legend was standing before them in the form of Aristion, whose previously invisible aura was now slowly turning blue as he pumped more and more energy into his limbs.

Another eagle followed, then another. And before long, as many as ten translucent birds were circling the ship. Meanwhile, Lanike and Althea had joined Sophia, Denise and me as they were supposed to. Lycomedes had given them the task of minding us while he and Aristion would keep the Hive busy. This would give Ouranis the best chance of fulfilling her mission. As for how Lycomedes knew about Ouranis' mission in the first place, he simply said that the Shepherd had passed it on. Apparently, this explanation was enough for Lanike and Althea and they had not pressed the matter further. Little did they know that their new Shepherd was with them every step of the way.

Something was happening over at the dark cloud. I could see it in Lycomedes' reaction when the old man's body tensed up. Like a gush of wind blowing from behind, the dark cloud expanded, then collapsed into itself like a house of cards. Seconds later there was nothing left but rings of spreading water, which pushed the drifting fleet away from its broiling vortex.

Ouranis, the Hive is gone again, I thought. *Have you been able to do anything yet?*

'I am trying, young Shepherd.' Ouranis was circling the pocket of air above our ship. 'I was hoping to have more time. Flego has to be near the surface of the Vault of Spirits, which the Hive evidently carries with it, but for some reason I cannot find him. If the Hive continues to move, I fear I may need my full ability for this.'

You mean you need me.

'I am aware you are still young,' she said, having read the trepidation in my voice. 'This is not a question of strength or skill, however. When combined, my abilities should amplify yours and yours should strengthen mine. It is why I brought you with me. You are not alone.'

It's okay. I'm prepared to do whatever it... Before I had time to finish my sentence, Lycomedes' voice boomed across the deck.

'It's coming!'

A sudden hard impact sent another wave of commotion through the group. It was accompanied by the sound of splintering wood, but one that was oddly muffled as it came from under the water. I heard running footsteps, then, 'We're making water!'

'Everyone, group up!' said Lycomedes. He was standing next to Aristion, who was still concentrating on his eagles. I wasn't sure what he was trying to do with them, but whatever it was, it didn't seem to be working. 'You too, Sophia!'

'Go, do as he says,' I said, pushing Sophia along. I was trying to keep my voice calm, but it was difficult to do under the circumstances. 'Denise, stay close.' Denise may or may not have been able to understand me, but neither did she need telling; she remained glued to my leg no matter where I went.

When we had all banded together on the deck, the flock of eagles began to close in on us. They were moving so fast, it was hard to tell one from another. Only now it dawned to me what Aristion was aiming for; he was using the eagles as a shield as well as a distraction. The problem was that none of us knew what exactly he was protecting us from, including him. And it certainly hadn't stopped the Hive from ramming us. To the enemy, it had now become a simple waiting game.

'We can't lose the ship!' said Alphaios, pressing his back against my shoulder. 'We are lost without it. I've seen it happen. The Mindless… they will come for us!' Again, nobody cared. The druids had their own style of fighting and judging by their reactions, losing the ship would be nothing more than a minor inconvenience. It may even be a calculated loss.

'Whatever happens, whatever you might see, do not leave our side,' Lycomedes told the group in a commanding voice. And for a while we stood there waiting in silence, eight people and a black hyena, with nothing but a cocoon of blue feathers and beaks to look at. Was the Hive actually just waiting for the ship to sink?

A muffled noise, a mixture between a whale's song and an earthquake, made all of us whip our heads to the sides of the ship. There, a pair of massive jaws shot skywards, one on each side, rising from the water like giant pincers.

'Hold your positions!' said Lycomedes, might anyone have forgotten his last command.

My knees were shaking and yet their trembling was a far cry from the fear Alphaios and Danaos were displaying. The jaws rose higher and higher. There seemed to be no end to them as fang after jagged fang made its appearance. One of the jaws featured a huge, bulbous tongue reminiscent of a great octopus arm.

My thoughts reached out desperately. *Ouranis…* There was no response. Where was she? What was she doing up there? Everything inside me screamed. My body was frantically trying to convince my mind to send the command to move. My skin prickled, my muscles felt cramped, and Lycomedes' face retained its look of unshakeable determination. I felt a great deal of admiration for the man well up inside me and couldn't help but feel inspired by his courage.

'Lanike and Althea, stay put!' said Lycomedes suddenly. 'Aristion, now!'

The moment his last word left his mouth, Lycomedes rammed his palms together and from both his back and his chest sprouted two large crocodiles. At the same time as the crocodiles landed on the deck, Aristion's cocoon of circling eagles lost cohesion, split in two, and shot towards the enormous jaws. Lycomedes' crocodiles followed the eagles in mad pursuit, legs flailing, jaws opened wide.

'Follow me, all of you!' said Lycomedes and he started pelting towards the bow of the ship.

We were not even half way there when an indescribable noise made me look over my shoulder. The concentrated attacks of both Aristion's eagles and Lycomedes' crocodiles bored holes into the black pillars of teeth – as though they were made of butter. Our enemy seemed little more than smoke, a sight that went against anything I was expecting. The Hive couldn't possibly be this frail.

With their foundation compromised, the massive jaws toppled over. With only little density left in them, the jaws still threatened to bring down the ship as they fell. But before they had the chance to do so, the disconnected jaws broke apart. And, out of the falling pillars of smoke, a writhing mass of giant Void scorpions rained onto the deck. Their number combined with their weight tipped the ship forwards, causing us to grip the railing tightly so as not to slide down the tilting deck and come within reach of the vicious pincers.

I grabbed one of the railing's balusters, body sliding. *Ouranis, where are you?*

Finally, she answered. 'I found him, young Shepherd. He is close.'

That's great, I thought, feeling annoyed at her priorities. *Can you help us out first? We're getting swarmed over here.*

People on both sides of the ship were imitating me, hanging on for dear life and desperately trying not to fall into the frenzied swarm of scorpions. The scorpions, in turn, were climbing the tilted ship like black flames.

I looked away to stop my knees from shaking. My eyes fell on Sophia. She had her arms wrapped around one of the railing balusters higher up on the deck and her legs around Denise. How she was doing it, I had no idea. Poor Denise, lacking hands and feet, she had no choice but frantically scrapple against the rough planks. A wave of gratitude for Sophia washed over me.

'Denise, I'm coming!' I said while I tried to find a good foothold for my sandals.

Denise yapped anxiously and slid down a few inches. Sophia's legs seemed about to give out. Her entire body was stretched to the limit and her face was locked in a grimace of agony. I could almost touch her. Black grime from Denise's hide was making its way into my right sandal. Then, with a shriek from Sophia, Denise lost her grip and collided with my chest. I was just in time to wrap my arm around her ribs and keep her from disappearing into the sea of advancing scorpions below.

From up the bow, Lanike and Lycomedes were encouraging me to continue my climb. But the shock of having my girlfriend suddenly back in my arms again – something I had dreamt of but not dared do because of her cold treatment of me – made me unable to respond to their yells.

Denise's jaw was hanging open and her tongue was dangling from between her teeth. Black filth dripped from her chin and from the tip of her tongue. Her glowing eyes, lacking pupils, gazed into nothingness, or perhaps they were turned to me. I couldn't tell. I pushed the thoughts of her appearance away. I needed to climb. *She* needed me to. It was all on me now.

As I continued to pull myself up and follow Sophia to the others who had gathered at the top, a series of powerful gushes of wind battered down on us. Then a pair of giant claws dug into the planks next to me and the entire ship levelled, propelling handfuls of scorpions off the ship's stern; Ouranis had come at last.

Meanwhile, on the other side of the railing I was holding onto, the waterline was rapidly closing in; we were still sinking. And now that the vessel was level once more, we had only seconds to abandon ship.

'Faster, let's go!' said Lycomedes. When I found him, battling gravity, he was the only one still standing there. The others had probably already jumped overboard. At his words, Denise started pelting towards him. The old man pointed and said like a seasoned dog trainer, 'Jump!'

Following Denise, Sophia and I launched ourselves into the water with Lycomedes close behind. Next thing I knew we were pulled out of the water and onto a raft by Alphaios and Danaos. 'Thanks,' I said before I realised what I was sitting on.

As it turned out, just before leaving the ship, Lanike had used her spiritcraft to summon a slither of sea snakes. To my amazement they had entwined to form a blue and translucent raft. Lycomedes, however, chose one of his crocodiles instead.

Ouranis, who was keeping the scorpions occupied to give us time to escape, pushed off the second the deck became flooded. Only an empty mast and a sea of drowning scorpions remained. One after another, the scorpions then dissolved into plumes of black smoke, which disappeared beneath the surface.

That was close. Thank you, Ouranis. How is Flego? Are you still in contact with him?

Before Ouranis had time to answer, Lycomedes said, 'Lanike, Althea, make your way towards one of the vessels! We will keep those creeps busy. Bishop, if you two are going to do anything, I suggest you hurry up. I don't believe we've seen the last of these things.' I gave Lanike and Althea a concerned glance, but Lycomedes had been discreet; they didn't realise he had been referring to my telepathic link with Ouranis.

Ouranis?

The great Phoenix was gliding through the air many yards above our heads and again, didn't respond. Meanwhile, Sophia was doing her best to isolate Denise from Alphaios and Danaos with her body, since the two men were evidently still ill at ease in her presence. And the raft was uncomfortably tiny. The two men had taken position on the opposite side to her, while Lanike and Althea were both lost in concentration.

The atmosphere felt thick with energy, almost like a sauna. Standing this close to a pair of working druids was a curious experience, but, despite the danger, fascinating too.

There was a splash of water and the rest of us looked up, fully expecting something black and monstrous to break the surface. Instead, the familiar shape of a dolphin's snout emerged. The animal was so beautiful and friendly, our tension instantly began to dissipate. Then Althea's outline flashed blue and a second translucent dolphin dived into the water. The dolphins quickly started pushing the raft away from the rapidly disappearing mast.

Lycomedes and Aristion were standing together, each on their own summoned crocodile. Several more crocodiles had been summoned by Lycomedes and they were acting like bodyguards, while above them, Aristion had called in the support of his eagles. The two druids seemed to be protected from all sides, yet danger lurked. Now shaped like killer whales, the Voidshapers popped their domed heads above the water and began closing the trap.

Ouranis, please answer me, I thought, more to myself than to the Phoenix. I didn't want to disturb her, but at the same time, the desire to do something, anything, was overpowering. I couldn't sit idly by when the druids were fighting for our lives. I wished I brought some kind of weapon with me so I could swim over there and help.

For a moment I thought the solution had come to me. A moment of desperation, need over desire. Maybe a situation like this was exactly the springboard my abilities needed to bloom. I could shapeshift. But how? It seemed so long ago.

While Lanike kept the raft in one piece and Althea's dolphins put more and more distance between us and Lycomedes and Aristion, I felt my confidence shrinking like an ice sculpture on a beach. Why was it so difficult to act when you so badly wanted to? Why did I always have to overthink a situation instead of simply act on instinct? I had done it before.

Ouranis' voice came as a blessing and a curse. It wiped the image of the horned owl I was trying to shapeshift into from my mind's eye. Instead of feeling light and feathery, I again felt big-boned and useless. 'Young Shepherd, there has been a complication.'

A complication? Another one?

'Yes. Flego's spirit is attached to a burden I cannot identify. I suspect the Hive has somehow chained him to the other spirits around him. I fear this confirms my suspicions. The Hive has realised what I am attempting to do and is fighting back. We will have to hurry.'

Maybe I can help. I'm ready, Ouranis. Just tell me what to do.

'I am not certain that is wise.'

What are you talking about? Why not? I thought you said you needed your full ability for this. That's why I'm here. Let's go, I'm ready. During the short silence that followed I could sense Ouranis' hesitation. Had she changed her mind at the last hurdle?

When she finally spoke again, I felt goosebumps run all the way up my arms. 'Very well. First, I need you up here with me. Find a way to distance yourself from the others so I can pick you up.'

This is it, I told myself. *This is what I've spent the past week training for. I can do this.*

'Young Shepherd,' Ouranis added, 'I suggest you touch as little of the water as possible.'

No kidding, I thought, then said, 'Lanike, please, I need a favour.'

Lanike turned, her palms still glued and her face hard in concentration. 'What is it, Aaron?'

'I... I don't know how to say this, but I need to leave this raft for a minute.'

There was something about Lanike's eyes that told me she wasn't as surprised by this as I thought she would. The timing of my request seemed to bother her more than anything else. Althea next her appeared not to have heard me.

Lanike gave Lycomedes and Aristion a quick look, both of whom were locked in a violent struggle against the ink-covered killer whales. From this distance it looked like a battle of black versus blue and silver, as one summoned creature after another was ripped to pieces by the opposition. Knowing that both druids had only seen the Voidshapers in action once, it was incredible to watch them. They displayed nothing other than intense focus and a will to survive, hardened by years of battle experience with their comrades.

'Can't you wait until we get to the ship?' Lanike asked. 'We're going to use that one over there. It shouldn't be too far for Lycomedes and Aristion to reach once they find a way to do so.'

I glanced over my shoulder at the ship behind us, then at Ouranis. I could almost feel the Phoenix's gaze boring into the top of my skull while she waited for me to make my move. 'I'm sorry. I can't. If there's anything you can do… I'd hate to have to swim.'

This was evidently too much for Althea. She gave Lanike a searching look. 'Lanike…,' she said warningly. Lanike looked up at her. Althea was quite a bit taller than she was. 'You can't let him go out there.'

'Let me?' I asked her, frustration boiling.

'Why not?' said Lanike, her voice inflected purposefully. 'I thought you said he was only a fugitive.'

Althea shot me a look. This was obviously not for my ears. 'Lycomedes is partial to him, and that is enough for me.'

'Then what is your problem?'

'That Lycomedes is partial to him,' repeated Althea. 'If you send him out there and he dies… Lycomedes' orders were clear. We were to keep them safe. Why do you want to go anyway?' she added to me.

'That's… I can't tell you that.' I recovered quickly. 'But it's not your decision, it's mine. And I'm going out there with or without your help.'

Althea shot me a look of contempt, but I thought I could detect a hint of admiration as well; druids generally like people who stood up for themselves. And my motivation was clear: help Ouranis, help Denise.

'It doesn't matter,' said Lanike with finality. 'Aaron, I need to conserve my energy for the possibility that we need another raft. But you can take one of Althea's dolphins.'

'What?' Althea sputtered.

Lanike sighed. 'Lycomedes told us to give him all the support he needs, remember?'

'This is not what he meant,' said Althea exasperatedly.

'Well I think it is. Now, Aaron, you said you were in a hurry?'

'Oh, right. Thanks, Lanike.' I turned to Althea. 'So how about it? Are you going to help me?'

'Fine,' she said mutinously. 'But you better make sure you don't waste it.' And with that one of the dolphins remained behind, its domed head bobbing up and down expectantly.

I spared one final look at Denise and Sophia. They were both sitting, Sophia with her arms wrapped around Denise's neck. Denise was almost entirely cloaked in black fog and I could only guess as to whether she understood what was going on. From a far corner in my consciousness, voices were telling me not to go, not to leave her. They implored me to think it through and the longer I looked, the louder they became. At last I used the thought of Ouranis and our mission to push them away, and I jumped.

Chapter 16

'Young Shepherd!' My jump had propelled me into the air. When Ouranis' voice reached me I was still flying, with the raft behind me and a translucent dolphin waiting patiently below me to grab hold.

I thought it had been me who concentrated on the Phoenix's face, but instead it was she who had penetrated my mind. In that instant, Ouranis and I were closer than we had ever been. Her concern for my well-being, stronger than any emotion of my own, was permeating my soul with astounding force.

The second my feet left the raft, however, I immediately sensed that something was wrong. The blue surface below me turned black as pitch, and yet there was nothing I could do to alter my course. I was in the air and the ocean's surface was about to hit me in the face. A dome, impossibly large, emerged from the depths below me; the giant Void crocodile had come to investigate. I landed, belly flat and limbs sprawled, on its soft surface.

The shock of the crocodile's sudden appearance made me unable to move until I saw Althea's dolphin slide out of sight. I tried to push myself up with my hands. It was a difficult ordeal because of the inky substance the dome was continuously producing and I had to fight the downward flow of oozing grime so I wouldn't slide down as well.

A screech came from above. Ouranis was on her way, but she was intercepted by a swarm of something unidentifiable. The swarm was composed of the oily remnants of the killer whales Aristion and Lycomedes had defeated. The whales that were still intact were continuing their attack to bring down the two druids and enslave their spirits. More cries filled the air, human ones this time, and I wheeled around to witness the final seconds of the raft's life; Lanike's slither of snakes was balancing on the snout of the gigantic crocodile that was the Hive. I appeared to have landed on its crown.

The raft's six passengers were glued hip-to-hip in teams of two, Denise and Sophia, Alphaios and Danaos, and Lanike and Althea, all trying to prevent the other one from falling off. All except for Lanike, that is. She still had her palms together in a desperate attempt to save the raft. I called out to them, but the rush of water flowing down the sides of the crocodile's head drowned my voice. Then the raft gave way and I watched my companions – along with an entire host of blue snakes – tumble into the water and out of sight.

'No! Denise!' I cried. There was no helping them. There was nothing I could do except hope that Ouranis would hurry up so we could begin the extraction. With any luck, the Hive would be too distracted by us to worry about six tiny figures fleeing in fear.

A dark cloud drifted overhead and cast my surroundings into shadow; the swarm that had attempted to thwart Ouranis had masked the sun. It was like the world itself blacked out. Below as well as above, there was nothing but blackness; cold shivers made their way into my bones. My mind was with Denise. I imagined how she was frantically treading the water, trying to move away from the giant maw of death with Sophia beside her, doing breaststrokes. It was too much to take.

I was about to jump down onto the crocodile's snout and look for them when I was engulfed in a beam of light. It blinded me and I used one arm to shield my eyes. I could hear the beating of giant wings above me; Ouranis had managed to penetrate the swarm. Then a pair of giant claws encircled my chest, tightened around my ribs, and we were off.

I was still dangling and about to voice my gratitude when Ouranis said, 'When I release you, spread your legs.' And the next thing I knew I was somersaulting through the air. My heart was in my throat. My head was filling with blood.

Ouranis' words kept bouncing against the inside of my skull and I had no choice but to act upon them, widening the crease between my legs. The action went against any instinct I had as a man, but my trust in Ouranis won the battle. Then with a gentle, yet still slightly nauseating bump in the family jewels I landed onto Ouranis' neck.

Instantly, my entire world changed. It had gone from near utter darkness to nothing but light, blue and white. The open sky was extraordinary. With each of Ouranis' strokes we climbed closer and closer to the world's ceiling, my hands clasped around bundles of see-through feathers.

The rush of wind and excitement was exhilarating. She had taken me for a ride over a dozen times now, often to transport me from the lagoon to the fruit trees up on the cliffs and back again, but seeing the world from between her claws was nothing compared to the top seat. It was a breathtaking experience.

Denise and the others, I thought as I peered down at the giant crocodile's head within the fleet of ships. The empty vessels looked toyishly tiny in comparison. *We need to go back for them.*

'We can do only one thing at a time, young Shepherd,' said Ouranis. 'It is the nature of singular beings.'

Then go back. They're in the water.

'I apologise. I cannot. They knew about the risks of coming with us. As soon as we have extracted my brother, we will go back for them. For now, they are on their own.'

What? No! The druids came with us to help, not to sacrifice themselves. And what about Denise and Sophia? They didn't agree to anything.

'You are correct,' said Ouranis after a moment's pause. 'It does not change the fact that we should focus on our mission, however. With the Hive this close and distracted, it is the perfect opportunity.'

My girlfriend is not bait! I snapped at her. *None of them are. What am I even talking about? The Voidshapers might see Denise as one of them! They will take her from us!* Ouranis didn't respond, so I tried again. *Wasn't it you who taught the druids that all life is sacred?* This comment may have been a gamble, but one that I thought might just work, since I had heard Lycomedes as well as Denise's guards tell me this. And I knew that the Shepherd, and in extension Ouranis, had taught the druids the principles they abide to.

'I am going to regret this,' said Ouranis. And without warning she flipped her body over, folded her wings and let gravity take over.

The blanket of blue dotted with white clouds changed into a smooth ocean with several deceptively peaceful-looking landmasses. My ears felt like they collapsed into each other as the air pressure began to live up to its name. While Ouranis' body remained firm, steady and controlled, my mind did the exact opposite. It was spinning so much; I had no idea of her destination, and no interest beyond hoping we reached it quickly.

Soon I was forced to shut my eyes due to the buffeting wind. We plummeted through several layers of air before Ouranis spoke again. 'Hold tight, young Shepherd!'

What do you think I'm...? Before I could finish, Ouranis flapped open her wings and began beating the air with her corded limbs. We became stationary almost instantly.

My body collided with her neck and my face dug into the carpet of feathers as my momentum continued to pull me downwards. Everything ached. My thighs felt like mush already. While my mind was catching up with what was happening, I could feel Ouranis' powerful muscles in her neck, shoulders and wings labouring to maintain her position. The wind howled obediently with each stroke of her wings. Somewhere in the corner of my mind a distant, female voice was saying, 'Down. Go back to your master, you foul, wretched... Flego, I am coming!'

I peered around Ouranis' neck. Below us I beheld the black swarm, which I now realised were bats, fighting the onslaught of ripping and cutting winds. The swarm was massive and was relying on the power of numbers. But individually, their tiny, fleshy wings were no match for the giant Phoenix. As they continued to climb closer and closer, screeching in hunger, each slash of wind tore the wings of the front runners to pieces and ricocheted them into the swarm below. There they dissolved into smoke, of which a great column was already retreating back to the ocean's surface.

'Be ready, young Shepherd,' Ouranis told me. 'We go in one,' she gave another powerful stroke, 'two,' she gave another, 'three!' And as she sent a final gush of wind towards our attackers, she used the backward force to initiate her next dive.

Faster and faster we raced past the swarm and the thick pillar of smoke extending all the way to the ocean's surface. I could only hope Ouranis could still see where we were going, because I couldn't. In my mind's eye I beheld the trail of black bats behind us; I was sure they were pursuing the second they saw Ouranis make a break for it. My fear provided any detail my eyes would have been able to pick up if I still used them.

Ouranis' wings flapped open once more and I felt the angle of the wind change. I pressed my body into her translucent feathers to prevent the howling wind from tossing me off her back. My eyes ached from the dehydrating effect of the wind and I still couldn't see where we were going. My ears weren't much help either; the air pressure still prevented them from doing their job. They felt like they were about to pop. Only when Ouranis pulled up was I able to open my eyes and appreciate what was happening. The pressure on my ears eased with it.

The sound of a pair of impossibly large jaws snapping close came from behind. I looked down and, as Ouranis continued to climb, the enormous crocodile that was the Hive fell back into the water. Upon making contact with the surface, the fleet of ghost ships around us rocked with the waves like toy boats in a bathtub.

It's working, I told Ouranis, realising what she was trying to do. *It's after us now. Keep going.*

'Unfortunately, the Hive is not our only concern,' she said. And she was right. The swarm of bats had abandoned their pursuit, taken a moment to regroup, and were now approaching us from above.

Have you seen any sign of Denise and the others? I asked as I swept the area around the monstrous crocodile.

'I am not certain.'

What do you mean you're not...?

She twitched her neck and I fell silent. 'And I would appreciate it if you sat still, young Shepherd,' she added. 'I am not accustomed to carrying humans.'

Right, sorry.

Ouranis dodged the swarm, then dived again. Hanging upside down I took in the crocodile's body and wondered where the millions upon millions of enslaved spirits were actually located. Did they make up the crocodile's body itself? Or was there a special area, like an organ, where the spirits resided? Perhaps they weren't even physically here at all and only materialised when Ouranis extracted them and gave them a translucent body.

Despite her enormous bulk, Ouranis moved through the air like a ballerina. Each swipe she took at the Hive, raking her claws across the ink-like skin on the crocodile's body, infuriated our enemy even further. It in turn used every weapon at its disposal, teeth, claws and tail, to get rid of the annoying horsefly that was us.

Speed was on our side and Ouranis used it to lure the Hive further and further away from the place where I thought the others were supposed to be. There was still no sign of them and I wondered how far they could have travelled. With each attack, the Hive generated additional tidal waves, each powerful enough to sink ships and swallow the average coastal village in one go. Doubt poisoned my mind; could anyone survive such chaos?

Ouranis, I hope you have a plan, I thought as the swarm and the Hive came at us for another go, hoping to sandwich us between teeth and bat wings. *I doubt the others can hold on much longer.*

'Look ahead, young Shepherd. That is where I am taking us.'

The island? Why?

'As expected, I have lost connection with Flego again. The Hive is moving around too much to maintain the link. And I agree, we will have to make our move soon or the druids will be lost to us. It is a loss I rather prevent. I am confident, however, that they have not yet been absorbed by the Hive. No new spirits have been introduced to the Vault for some time. Of that, I am certain.'

Then why are we heading for the island?

'Two reasons. Like I mentioned, we will have to work together to get Flego out, and you are not able to concentrate while you are on my back. You should not be ashamed about this. It is only to be expected. You are still young. As for the second reason, you will find out soon enough.'

Either our speed was so great, or I figured the island must be incredibly tiny, but I barely noticed it when the small landmass shot past. Looking back over my shoulder, it turned out the island was nothing more than a clump of trees bordered by a circular, white beach.

Ouranis doubled back and said, 'Release your hold, young Shepherd. Do not be afraid.'

When she felt me release my grip with my legs, she shook me off her back. Weightlessly I hung in the air four a second or two, then she caught me in her claws. She brought me down and I started skimming across the beach, my legs running frantically to keep up with my momentum. Buckets of sand were making their way into my sandals, while my druid robes flapped with the motion. Ouranis let go and flew off. I came to a panting stop and watched Ouranis as she continued on, following the curved shoreline, until she bent around the trees and disappeared out of sight.

Silence fell. With it, everything appeared to come to a halt. I felt the adrenaline, which had been present while we had been fighting the Hive, ebb away. I sighed deeply. The excitement had tensed my muscles. And, as the rush faded, the soreness kicked in.

Only seconds passed until Ouranis' voice came again. 'I need you here. Come quickly.' With her voice, the adrenaline, the excitement, everything came flooding back in an instant. Immediately I started running, an act made difficult by the thick layer of loose sand that covered the beach.

Then I saw it. The Hive, still in its crocodile form, was heading straight for us. It was still about a mile away, but ploughed through the water with incredible haste. The black smoke that oozed from its hide was like steam issuing from a Victorian train. Its black eyes with blazing pupils were devoid of emotion, purposeful, merciless. Numbness spread through my body. *Ouranis, I could use some help here.* The voice of my thoughts sounded distant; the sight of the advancing giant sucked almost all of my attention away.

When Ouranis answered, her voice was soft and made my ears twitch. 'It is I who needs your help, young Shepherd.'

I turned around and there she was. She had circled the island to maintain her speed. Remaining low to the ground, the sand beneath her whipped into a spray by the power of her wings. In addition to her usual magnificence, a nimbus of blue light surrounded her, leaving a trail of silvery blue in her wake. My jaw dropped at the sight of the Phoenix and for a moment or two, nothing else existed but her.

Then a bang snapped me out of my trance. Her aura had flared up like a Roman candle. Out of thin air, a blue and translucent monkey materialised and landed agilely on the beach. It gave a loud screech and fled into the woods. Another bang followed, then two more; one by one, extracted animals of seemingly random shape and origin began dropping onto the beach like some strange weather phenomenon.

'I need you to contact Flego and show him the way out,' said Ouranis, her voice sounding preoccupied. 'I will continue to extract spirits to keep the surface of the Vault of Spirits clear for you. Can you do this?'

Yes, of course. I will try, I answered, even though I still wasn't sure I knew exactly what was going on, or what to do. But I didn't want Ouranis to worry, and kept my thoughts as resolute as I could manage.

In the distance, the Hive had arrived at a submerged sandbank. For the first time since I had seen it, I realised its crocodile body was nothing more than convenience. Unlike any crocodile I had seen in a zoo or on television, it had pushed itself up onto its hind legs and began gazing around confusedly. Seeing it like this, with its front paws hanging awkwardly like the claws of a tyrannosaurus and its broad head twitching every time Ouranis extracted another animal spirit, gave the creature an almost humanoid appearance.

'Now, young Shepherd!' Another bang followed Ouranis' voice, along with hooves running across the beach.

I closed my eyes. The Hive's open jaws and humanoid appearance occupied my consciousness and I had difficulty focusing on anything else. I tried to think of Ouranis, but her predicament, combined with the continuing bangs and animal sounds, sent my strings of thought into a tangled mess. I knew I had to think of something else. I needed my mind steady and composed, like Lycomedes had taught me over the past week. I had to use some type of conduit, some kind of picture to calm my mind and think past the menacing exterior of the Hive.

I thought of the underground lagoon, of Denise and Sophia playing under the waterfall in front of the cave. I thought of sitting in my underwear and drying my clothes over the fire with Ouranis perched on the small strip of grassy bank, meditating on the images of her brothers and sisters. From there I thought of the seven Celestial Beasts, the Phoenix, the Manticore, the Cockatrice, the Gryphon, the Chimera, the Hippocampus and the Pegasus. I had at least a general idea of what the creatures looked like, or what the legends of my world had taught me. Flego, I knew, was a Manticore, a cross between a lion and a scorpion. But unfortunately, Ouranis had never taken the time to provide me with a detailed description and, as it was, I had never asked for one either.

The thought of penetrating the mind of such evil as the Void Hive and search for Ouranis' lost brother seemed so far from what I was capable of, I didn't think Ouranis would leave it up to me to actually connect with him. I thought she just needed me to supplement her own ability; perhaps put a metaphorical hand to her back while she fished for her brother. To make this work, I knew I needed an image of some kind to lock onto. Selena's teachings, or, at least, the few pointers she had given me during our exercise on the beach of Delos, were foremost in my mind.

'Try to see nothing but this single animal and examine every one of its features,' Selena had said. 'Take them in as if you had to draw a picture of the animal into the sand once you open your eyes.'

How was I supposed to do this when in my mind, a lion and a scorpion were locked in a cross between a cage fight and a mating ritual, battling for the right to be the front end of the Manticore's body instead of its rear? In the end I decided to focus on Flego's name instead of his appearance and simply tried calling out for him in the hopes that he would hear me, like I had done with Trionyx.

There was no reply. Again and again I tried, but then a great splash of water slapped me back to the waking world. Over at the sandbank, the Hive had apparently overcome the nuisance that was Ouranis. It was back on all fours, ready to charge. *I can't find him if I don't know what to look for*, I thought desperately, my eyes remaining locked onto the giant crocodile.

'You need to be his beacon, his guiding light,' said Ouranis, most of her mind evidently busy. 'Flego will come to you.'

Why would he? He doesn't even know me.

'You are the Shepherd. You are part of me. Trust in my abilities and he will come. In a way, you are his brother, his family.' Another bang came from my left and I heard the snarl of a big cat; Ouranis had saved another animal spirit. 'Trust in that Flego will see my mother's light burning within you. You merely have to let it shine.'

A soothing wave of warmth washed over me. *I merely have to let it shine*, I repeated softly. *Isis' light is in me.*

'Yes. Use it.'

I indeed felt something burning within me, although I wasn't sure it was related to an Egyptian goddess. In the meantime, the monstrous creature that was the Hive was moving forwards, getting ready to slip back into the water. Its head still twitched every time Ouranis extracted another spirit, yet its pace remained steady. Meanwhile, it was like my mind and body were fighting for dominance. Part of me wanted to try it again, yet another part was more concerned with my mortality – which seemed about to be tested.

The black crocodile left the sandbank, slid beneath the surface and vanished from sight. A weird prickling sensation made its way up my body. My feet started shifting through the sand, away from the shoreline. I could hear nothing but Ouranis' bangs. My eyes continued to search the calm, ocean's surface.

There was a disturbance in the water half way between the shore and sandbank. I saw several eddies form in the distance, signalling that something large was travelling my way. My druid robes were glued to my skin; salty droplets were being squeezed from every pore in my body.

My legs kept staggering backwards until with a sudden bump, I found the treeline. At that moment a fountain of water spewed forth, a cocktail of black and blue; the crocodile was already here and it had launched itself out of the water. As the water retreated, in sight came a giant maw and a pair of massive claws, the latter pounding the muddy beach with an earthshaking ferocity as it landed.

'It is confused,' said Ouranis as though she just realised this herself. I could do nothing but gape at the crocodile towering over me, most of my body now shielded by a tree. 'It desires to alter its shape, but it cannot due to the fact that I am continuously changing the Vault of Spirits' configuration. This is our chance. Young Shepherd, while you carry on trying to find Flego, I will continue to keep the Hive distracted. Together, we may yet succeed.'

I turned away from the beach and pressed my back against the tree trunk I was hiding behind. My breath was high in my chest. My mouth was open to allow for the much needed oxygen to pass into my lungs. *Okay. I will*, I thought, panting.

I didn't dare look back at the beach. I needed to do this. I blinked the sweat from my eyes. My imagination fed me image after image to accompany the chaos of splashing, stamping and snapping noises coming from behind. The Hive might be confused, but its size and erratic behaviour must be making Ouranis' job a difficult endeavour. I wondered, if only for a moment, what would happen to the extracted animal spirits if the island perished. Could immortal beings be harmed?

I realised my mind was trying to distract me from the task at hand. I didn't want to try it again, but I had to. Ouranis needed me to. I closed my eyes and tried to focus solely on Flego's name. Instead of shouting like last time, I took up on Ouranis' suggestion and imagined myself as a lure. I continued to call out his name, although this time, my wish was not to find him, but for him to find me.

With my eyes closed, I saw nothing but darkness in every direction. It allowed the first imagery that entered my mind to paint a picture. The memory of the beach behind me made me think of a lighthouse radiating its light through the dark mist that surrounded me. I visualised seeing a Manticore, as big as Ouranis, follow the light that I sent out for him. It was working, or it felt that way.

The image was like a vivid dream and the longer I stood there, looking out into the foggy darkness with my mind's eye, the more the imagined environment increased in clarity. Soon I lost all sense of where my real body was. Time appeared to slow down.

Slowly the picture increased in detail and I found myself standing on a high cliff. Dark mist clogged up the horizon. To my left and right, a ragged cliff face was ceaselessly battered by the waves below. The rhythm was soothing. There was a hint of salt in the air, carried by the moisture the waves added to the wind with each pounding. Next to me stood a lighthouse, tall and undoubtedly familiar. Somehow I had the feeling it belonged with me. We were there together, acting as one. Heat was beaming from the metal exterior and I thought of Ouranis' gift, which the Phoenix herself had said was burning inside me.

The fog on the horizon crept closer and closer. Soon the sea vanished and all I could see below me was a clean drop-off ending into nothing but dark mist. I felt alone, with nothing to hear or see but my own voice and the lighthouse next to me, which felt like part of me as well.

Was this the Vault of Spirits inside the Hive Mind? Had I done it? Had I made my way inside? Or was this nothing more than a dream world created by my own consciousness? I couldn't tell one way or the other, but there was no time to ponder. I had to act, for the quicker I got out of here, the better.

'Flego!' I called out once more. My voice ebbed away, devoured by the silence. There was no surface to reflect it. There was only fog, which acted more like a pillow than a carrier. I tried again and again, but to no avail. I looked down the cliff. *What do I do now? I could turn around and go that way, but the mist is so thick, even the lighthouse might not be able to guide me back.*

My clothes were wet, probably from a mixture of sweat and the humid atmosphere condensing on my warm body. I was beginning to feel cold and wondered about how to get back to my real body back on the island, if this was indeed real.

More questions arose. What if Flego couldn't find his way to me? How long was I supposed to wait? What if he did come and we were stuck here together? Had I willingly become one with the Hive? Was I part of it now? And what was happening to my body? Had the crocodile already snapped it in half and changed it into a hyena like Denise's had? Or would I become a different animal? An emperor penguin perhaps, or a flesh-eating maggot? *Or*, I thought, *a horned owl.*

The inside of my skull lit up. I felt lighter somehow. The realisation had struck me that I was here in spirit, not in body. Would it work? Was I still in control of my spirit body? Could I shapeshift?

I thought of my legs as claws, my arms as wings and my clothes as feathers. The experience of the two times I had metamorphosed aided me. Like the ability to talk to animals, the ability to change my shape was part of Ouranis' power as well, even though I had never seen her use it. Perhaps her abilities worked differently in combination with a human body. Whatever the case, I needed her power to be the lure. So why not here? Why not now?

The world around me felt tiny and distant. I could easily push off, spread my wings, and fly wherever I wanted to. It was no more difficult than walking. The ability to fly was an integral part of me. It was easy. And yet, no feathers appeared and the joints in my neck didn't offer my head the freedom of turning a near 360 degrees. I was still human, or appeared that way.

But my feet were standing on the cliff no longer. They had left the ground and I was now drifting freely through the air, effortlessly. The cliff and the lighthouse below me were slowly fading into the gloom below. As I was floating there, aimlessly, I became disorientated. The cliff and the lighthouse were gone. Panic washed over me, like I was suffering from agoraphobia. I had never thought I was susceptible for a fear of open spaces, but then again, I had never been in place this alien before. *What is this place? There's no way this is just a dream.*

Like a newborn kitten seeing the world for the first time, my eyes tried to make sense of my environment. I peered dazedly around for any object, anything at all, I was able to name and identify, and still I saw nothing but fog. The act reminded me of a few summers ago, when my twin brother Keith and I took a well-deserved break on top of a peak while hiking. I remembered us cloud gazing together, each trying to make the other to see what they were seeing.

I imagined the fog around me to be a cloud. It was like I was back on that peak with Keith. It gave me a sense of peace, of security that I didn't expect the thought of my brother could induce. I imagined he had just given me the first turn. But no matter where I looked, the fog was impenetrable, its wispy contents ever-changing. There was no making sense of it, until…

Slowly my surroundings began to take shape, strangely, eerily. It was like my time in the Void had convinced the fog that I was eligible to see its real identity. My eyes began picking up different features belonging to the animal kingdom. I blinked. *Surely it must be my imagination running wild.* But it didn't stop there. There were humans too, half naked people, and I quickly looked down at my own body to see if I was still wearing my druid robes, which I was.

My environment continued to increase in detail and before long I found myself floating amidst all kinds of animal and human spirits. Unlike the ones Ouranis had saved, however, these spirits were darker of colour, set against an even darker background. They didn't seem able to notice me, or one another. They were simply there.

I did the only thing that made sense to me. Calling out for Flego certainly didn't, for I would have hated to wake these zombielike spirits up and have to deal with them first. I had no idea how they would react, or if I could wake them up at all. But I didn't want to chance it. Among them, somewhere, was Flego and I needed to find him. Until then, I decided to remain silent and leave the others spirits in peace.

There was also no telling how much time had passed since I arrived here, if time had any meaning in this place. And every second I took felt like an insult to Ouranis who, as I was floating there, awed and dumbstruck, was probably using every effort to keep the Hive away from my body in order to buy me a few extra minutes.

Having nothing solid to push off from, I willed myself forwards. It was then when I realised I couldn't. I wasn't in control anymore and thinking back, I hadn't been in control of my body since I got here. I had been able to yell, but that only happened in my own mind like my conversations with Ouranis. I hadn't physically moved my mouth. And before, had I actually used my muscles to push off from the cliff?

I felt stupid. Of course I couldn't move. If this was the Vault of Spirits, if this was the same place Ouranis visited with her mind when she fished for spirits to extract, there was no way I would able to fly around and dig for the Vault's deeper layers. Otherwise Ouranis would certainly have done it herself. She would have come in here and searched for her brothers and sisters instead of asking me for help. She would have reunited with them in spirit and simply pointed the way to the surface. It could never be that easy.

I was here, yes, but that only meant I had successfully connected my thoughts with the Vault. And the spirits around me probably formed the top layer from which Ouranis was extracting prisoners. But then, where was she? Why wasn't her mind in here with me, freeing spirits? And where was Flego? Ouranis had said her brother was relatively close to the surface. She only needed me here as bait.

My train of thoughts ended. Something else popped up. *Could Denise be in here as well? Could her spirit be cast adrift, as listless and desolate as these poor wretches? Ouranis said Denise was different from the Voidshapers, and she said she may be able to help her after we get her brother out. But I never asked her where Denise's spirit actually resided. On the other hand, I've seen evidence of her presence, her personality, haven't I? Doesn't this mean her spirit is in there as well? This is all very confusing.*

My eyes jumped from one solemn face to the next. Lion, gazelle, shrimp, fish hawk, an old Greek with a white beard, a Greek woman of the same age, a Bluefin tuna. Every creature belonging to the animal kingdom was represented, each as translucent as the next. Then out of the blackness behind the tuna fish, a tiny figure came streaking towards me. Despite her incredible speed, her squeaky, girlish voice was quicker. 'Ouraniiiiiiiiiiis!'

My instincts told me to blink my eyes, but my eyelids refused: I still had no control over them. The tiny creature, whatever or whoever it was, was on a collision course with my face and yet nothing I tried could move me out of her flight path.

There was a beak, opened wide as far as it would go, and a head full of feathers. Her two large, oval eyes were full of joy and beamed with the thought of being reunited with her big sister at last. The creature stopped dead inches from my nose, her large eyes comparable to those of an eagle fledgeling. Her beak snapped close, which made the eyes only larger, and for a few seconds we floated there, staring at each other. Neither of us blinked.

'You're not Ouranis,' said the creature at length, her voice girlish. She seemed quite surprised by this. While she spoke, her beak remained closed, which made me wonder whether the scream she uttered earlier had actually come from her mouth. 'Who're you?'

I'm Aaron, I thought back, my mouth still inoperable. It was an answer born out of habit, for every single ounce of my attention was focused on the Gryphon hatchling drifting in front of me. The hind part of her body was that of a lion cub, while the front looked like that of an incredibly fluffy, adolescent eagle. The entire body was, like everything else in this place, dark and transparent.

The young Gryphon let out a gasp, beat her wings once, and leapt backwards. 'What did you do with our sister? You hided her, you did, you did!' she screeched in bad English, although I knew it was Ouranis' gift that was translating the Gryphon's speech. Before I could answer, she puffed up her chest in anger and said, her voice injected directly into my brain, 'Fleger!'

Fleger? I repeated. *Did she mean Flego?*

I hadn't even seen him approach. From the direction the Gryphon had come from, a giant Manticore came flying towards us, his bat wings at half power. His lion face, which was almost as big as that of Ouranis, looked like that of a high school teacher after a gruelling week of camping in the wild with his students. The way his scorpion tail was dragging behind him only added to the picture of utter exhaustion.

The moment his eyes found me, a jolt of shock went through Flego's enormous body. The rolling wave made its way through the connecting sections of his tale until finally, with a flick of his stinger, the tail bent upwards and came to rest above his impressive mane.

I attempted to throw my hands into the air in a gesture of good intention, but my body was still paralysed. *I mean you no harm*, I told him, my experience of conversing with Ouranis aiding me well. *I swear.*

'It's not us we're concerned about, human,' said Flego, his nose uncomfortably close to mine and his voice heavy. 'You carry something that belongs to our sister. I can feel it.'

I can explain, please.

Flego drew back his head and began to eye me questionably. His voice turned quizzical. 'This ought to be good. Krixi, are you listening?'

'Oh, I am. I am,' said the Gryphon playfully.

Krixi? I asked myself. *This tiny Gryphon is Ouranis' sister, one of the great Celestial Beasts?*

Flego ignored my comment about his sister. 'Well?' he demanded.

I... I'm the Shepherd. I'm here with Ouranis. We came here for you. The both of you, I guess. My eyes fell on Krixi. *Wait a minute*, I added to myself. *Didn't Ouranis say that another spirit, a strong one, was weighing Flego down? It must have been her.*

'Shepherd? What's a Shepherd?' Flego asked, interrupting my train of thoughts. At first I couldn't believe he hadn't heard of the Shepherd before, but then I remembered the unthinkably long time Flego and the other Celestial Beasts had been cut off from the outside world. Also, Ouranis told me Eresa was founded *after* she managed to escape the Vault of Spirits, which meant Flego and Krixi had never set foot inside the Sanctuary.

The Shepherd is a druid who has inherited part of Ouranis' powers, I explained. Flego looked doubtful. *It's the truth. It was your sister's own choice to divide her powers*, I added quickly.

'So now you're a druid too.'

Well, not exactly.

'Fleger, what's a druid?' Krixi asked, her head tilted to one side.

'They don't really exist, Krixi,' said Flego impatiently. 'Humans often bend the truth. It's in their nature.'

Krixi shook her head disappointedly. 'Too bad, too bad. They sound like fun.'

No, they do exist. They live in a sanctuary not that far from here. You have to believe me.

Krixi looked hopeful. Flego screwed up his eyes. 'Have to? And why is that, hmm?'

Because I've come to take you out of here. Ouranis is keeping the Hive busy to give us this chance.

Flego scanned his surroundings with a quick sweep of his eyes. 'Did you hear that, Krixi?' he said, an obvious note of scepticism in his voice. 'This human is going to show us the way out. How's that?'

Sending her wings into a fluttering frenzy, Krixi let out a shriek of laughter. The gale of wind she produced – or I thought she produced – made me topple over backwards. And, with my body still beyond my control, she sent me spinning end over end through the sea of spirits behind me.

Lines of distortion suddenly blurred my vision; Krixi had propelled me straight through the backside of a bull elephant. Flego was quick to catch up with me. Half way through my next somersault I smacked, face first, into his fleshy bat wing.

Flego looked down at me with curiosity. Finally something dawned to him, his lion eyes grew wide, and he said, 'You're not really here.'

Figured it out, have you? I thought, feeling rather disgruntled with the slow wittedness of my companions.

'I think I have,' said Flego in surprise, looking back at the elephant spirit. The elephant didn't appear like it had noticed me passing through. And curiously enough, nor did Krixi's gust of wind seem to have had any effect on the other spirits.

'The other spirits don't appear to be dense enough to ward off your thoughts,' said Flego. 'Interesting.' His face steeled. 'But the only thing it proves is that you do indeed possess some of my sister's abilities, not how you got them.'

I told you. I'm the Shepherd. She gave them to me.

'Krixi don't think so, oh no,' said Krixi. 'Our mother made us this way. Ouranis is proud of who she is. She is.'

I know, Krixi, I thought, aiming my mind directly at her. She started in response to my gaze. *I've been living with your sister, with Ouranis, for the past week. She is here, I'm telling you. She wants to save you. Flego, please, you must have felt something. Ouranis has tried to connect with you specifically for quite a while. She told me she almost succeeded in getting you out at least once, but we think the Hive must have realised what she was doing. So Ouranis asked me to help her. And we're not alone in this either. There are others who came with us and...* I fell silent again. The fate of Denise and the others was such a heavy weight on my mind, it made the rest of my thoughts too incoherent to make sense of.

'Let us assume this is true,' said Flego.

How else would I know about her attempts to contact you? I interrupted him.

'You have her abilities. You can read minds. It's only a small step to think that you have her memories as well.' As I didn't have an answer ready, nor could I think of any, I remained silent. 'Assuming you are telling the truth,' he went on, 'which is unlikely, how do you suppose you'll get the two of us out of here, hmm?'

My mind went blank. As such, the truth was the only thing left for my mind to behold. And because I wasn't using actual speech, it was virtually impossible to conceal anything from someone who was reading directly from my thoughts. Finally, I thought, *I don't even know how to get out myself.* This simple act of honesty, the bare truth, made Flego and Krixi look at each other in mutual understanding. They could taste my vulnerability in my words. I knew they could, because I was able to do the same. It tasted empty.

'Leave that to me, human,' said Flego.

You know of a way to get me out? But you just told me I'm not really here.

Flego produced a smile. 'Your thoughts are here. If your spirit were here too, now that would be tricky, wouldn't it?' He indicated the floating spirits around us with a nod of his head. 'It's obvious that your mind still thinks like that of a human, or Krixi wouldn't have been able to blow you away. It was merely your mind thinking she was blowing you backwards.' Even though his voice was quite sincere, the look in his eyes made me wonder if Flego himself knew what he was talking about.

All right, I said, unconvinced. This was hardly the time to think of the minutiae, and I decided to leave it be. *So what are we going to do?*

'What do you think? Shall we trust him?' Flego asked his little sister as though asking her if she fancied an ice cream cone.

'I do, I do,' squeaked Krixi, her eyes mirthful. 'Make it a good one, Fleger! Whohoo!' She punched the air with her eagle fists, each one accompanied with a playful whoop.

'Good enough for me,' said Flego, turning back to me. 'Aaron, was it?'

Yes…, I thought hesitantly. I couldn't pinpoint what it was exactly, but something in his eyes put me off. There was definite excitement. Yet it touched upon a near unholy glee you didn't want to see in the eyes of a creature this large when you had no motor control to speak of.

Flego lifted one of his lion paws and slowly clenched it, visibly savouring the moment. 'Hold perfectly still. And remember, we're counting on you to save us.' Then he drew himself up, paw drawn backwards, gave a forceful flap of his wings and all went black.

Chapter 17

The ground was groaning in discomfort. Repeated forceful impacts sent waves of tremors into my body. I was lying on my back and something heavy was pressing down on my stomach. I could barely move because of the weight. When I opened my eyes, there was a green blanket covering my face.

An odd kind of grunting was mingled with the sound of stamping feet. A pair of giant jaws snapped closed overhead. Instantly, the scene I had left behind when I penetrated the Hive Mind came rushing back and I distinctly picked up the sound of flapping wings. *Ouranis! Where are you?*

'Young… Shepherd…' Her reply was distant and her voice fatigued. *What's wrong? Where are you?*

I wiped away the blanket of leaves from my face. A clear blue sky came into view. I tried to push myself up with my elbows. A small tree was using my body as a mattress. I squeezed myself out of the fallen debris – there was more covering my legs – and finally I was able to discover how the island had fared during the time I was away.

Barely anything of the small forest was left standing. A black crocodile sharing its size with the average skyscraper was standing triumphantly in its midst. The Hive had abandoned all pretence of being an actual crocodile and was again standing on its hind legs, swiping its massive claws at the comparatively tiny Phoenix. A group of translucent animals, among which were the ones Ouranis had extracted from the Hive, had congregated on the beach to my left; despite their presumed immortality, they had sought safety in numbers.

Ouranis, I met Flego and Krixi. They are waiting for us to get them out.

'Flego…,' said Ouranis, her voice barely audible. 'And Krixi too? He must not have been willing… to leave her behind…'

While listening to her voice, I followed Ouranis as she circled the giant crocodile. We had no time to waste. I was desperate to get Flego and Krixi out of in the Vault of Spirits. But as it turned out, because she was flying so fast, I hadn't really noticed how she had fared since I had been gone. And now that my concern for her well-being really kicked in, I felt my heart crumple like a tin can.

For lack of a better word, Ouranis, the most extraordinary creature I had ever laid eyes on, was bleeding badly. One of her hind legs was ripped off, as was a large chunk of the flesh on her flank. The aura of energy she had generated around her body was still present. It appeared to act like an energy shield, a bandage; where everywhere else the aura was but a thin ribbon of light, at the place of the torn-off body part it was thicker and burned white hot. Still it didn't prevent a trickle of blue sparkles to leak from the gaping hole, reminding me of blood.

My eyesight went blurry from tears. Her image slowly faded. I blinked the tears away and instantly, my view of her started fading again. I could do nothing but watch as she twisted and fluttered through the air, dodging the crocodile's groping claws with increasing difficulty. Inside I screamed, my organs wept, yet my mouth didn't comply; either because I was terrified of the black beast towering over me, or deep down I knew it was no use. There was nothing I could do for her.

'Young… Shepherd…' Her voice was urgent. She was trying to tell me something. Then with a final downward slash, the tip of one of the crocodile's nails clipped Ouranis' wing. It raked through her blue aura as though it was made of liquid and sparkling droplets sprayed from her body like blood from a shotgun wound. Her cry of pain tore my soul.

Ouranis, no! Save yourself. You've done enough. You're injured, please.

'Get… my brother… out,' she said as she swooped to the ground and pulled up just in time. She stayed low from now on to make more difficult for the Hive to catch her, being as large as it was. Ouranis' wounded body was continuing to rain droplets of energy onto the trampled forest.

But how? I only talked to them. I don't know how to take them with me.

'You do not have to. I will… keep the Hive in one place.' Ouranis reversed course and again started circling the crocodile. It in turn smashed its giant tail onto the beach in anger, displacing sand and water with frightening ease. When Ouranis reappeared at the crocodile's other side, she said, 'Your body… is the lure. When you make contact, your mind is… split. Let your body be the beacon and…' Her sentence was cut short by the crocodile landing on its front claws. On its way down, the crocodile had struck at the Phoenix with one of its claws, showering the island with another spray of blue sparkles.

Cushioned by the forest litter, Ouranis smacked to the ground, her only hind leg bent outwards, and kept sliding until she came to a halt a few yards in front of me. As she lay there, motionless, the ribbon of energy behind her slowly dissipated into the ground.

The rest of the world seemed to disappear. Her eyelids quivered and slowly she opened one of them. She found me standing there, at a loss for words or action. She gazed at me beseechingly. Her pupilless eye dripped with horror. It was too soon. She wasn't done yet. She still had so much to do, so much to teach me. And yet, starting from her tail feathers, her entire body began losing cohesion. The same way I had seen the crystals in her cavern take shape but in reverse, her Phoenix body disintegrated until there was nothing left but her imploring features.

'Young Shepherd, it is up to you now.' The last of her neck evaporated. 'Have faith in your abilities, and in mine. Your instincts will guide you.' Only one eye and her beak were left. 'Goodbye...'

Her last word was still echoing around in my skull, with the last bit of her beak about to leave this world, when her fading image was suddenly replaced by a pair of giant, black nostrils. They were tilted sideways and were placed next to the vertical line of a closed mouth. Behind them, in the distance, I saw a pair of crocodile eyes squint in delight; at the very last second, the Hive had thrown itself onto the ground, snatched Ouranis' spirit from the road to the afterlife and recaptured her. Ouranis was theirs again.

The sudden gale that the snapping jaws produced blasted me off my feet. I fell backwards onto the blanket of leaves and grass, my mind immune to the pain.

With the sound of breaking branches, the crocodile dragged its massive head back through the forest debris. It drew itself up to its full height and took a moment to savour Ouranis' spirit. A small sliver of energy trickled down its lips like raw egg white turned blue.

As of yet, I wasn't sure whether the Hive knew I was even there. It might have thought the meddling with the Vault of Spirits had been solely Ouranis' doing. My mind racing, I looked around for a hiding place and found one in a fallen log, which was just large enough to provide cover. I crouched behind it and slid most of my body out of sight, hoping the debris the log was resting on wouldn't yield.

With my breath high in my chest I looked up into the face of the crocodile. It was still savouring its latest snack. Slowly the crocodile, standing again on its hind legs, brought its jaw to its chest. Its eyes fell on me, a puny ant in comparison. Then its jaws parted and out came a low, continuous grunt, wiping all hope for avoiding becoming lunch from my mind.

I gulped. My trembling legs began shifting me backwards once more. But this time, there was no treeline left to run to, no one to turn to. I was alone, again.

Despite my predicament, or perhaps because of it, I could barely think of anything other than Ouranis. She was the light in my head that shielded me from my own fear. Her beautiful beak, her crystal-covered cavern, her blue feathers, the images acted like wards against the monster that towered over me. The beauty of my thoughts was mingled with sadness for the Phoenix's fate, and both amplified each other, steeling my thoughts.

Part of me wanted to fall down on my knees and mourn, but another part wanted to act. She wasn't dead, somehow I knew this was true. I could feel it. And she needed me. She needed me to be strong, to fight, to fly. Yes, I needed to fly.

The gigantic maw of doom looking down at me began to increase in clarity. The black teeth became sharper around the edges, the droplets of greasy ink that continuously oozed from the crocodile's body became more distinct, and I thought I could even discern scales covering the beast's hide.

My skin prickled, then sprouted feathers. My eyes grew. My nose and lips came together into a beak. My bones hollowed, my neck joints unclamped, and my toes grew apart; my body was shapeshifting and my desire to survive was making it happen. My pointed ears twitched as they detected something coming from behind. There was a flapping of a thousand wings and, without moving the rest of my body, my head turned effortlessly over my shoulder.

A black cloud was moving towards me. There was something in front of it too; pursued by a swarm of Void bats, a raft made of blue reptiles came speeding my way. Lycomedes, Aristion, Lanike, Althea, Sophia and Denise were all on it. Only Alphaios and Danaos weren't there. My heart performed a victory dance, tossing my fears into the wind. They were all right, they were all fine. Denise too. She and Sophia standing next to her were gazing at me with blank expressions.

Behind me, the Hive dragged its tail through the forest litter. The sound of it made me snap back my head and launch myself into the air at the same time; before the Hive had the chance to attack, I took flight.

When I cleared the beach, the raft sailed under me. It was about to hit the shoreline and I wanted to warn them. 'Don't come too close, it's quicker than you think,' I tried to say. Everyone looked up, even though my beak hadn't uttered a single word of my warning; evidently, I had traded my vocal chords for wings.

A jolt of panic went through the druids on the raft. 'No!' said Lycomedes, his hand on Aristion's arm. 'Don't hurt it. It's friendly. Focus on the swarm.'

I didn't understand what Lycomedes meant at first, for my eyes were on Denise and Sophia, both of whom were following my every move. But then I noticed Aristion standing in a praying position and holding his ground, watching what he thought was his nearest enemy: me.

'Zeuxis?' Aristion said to no one in particular, something dawning in his eyes. As it was, Aristion had only ever seen a real flesh-and-blood animal when Zeuxis, the previous Shepherd, had shapeshifted. Naturally, when he looked closer and saw I was no Voidshaper, he thought I was him.

'Of course it's not him,' Lycomedes barked at him. 'The bats, Aristion! Focus on the bats!' Aristion snapped out of his trance at once. And from his chest shot a series of blue eagles, beaks and claws ready to defend their master.

I figured the Hive must have received quite a shock when it saw me flying off like that. Otherwise it would have acted before now. Whatever the case, it had obviously recovered and with earthshaking ferocity, landed on its front paws. Then for the first time, it let out a dragon-like roar no crocodile should be capable of.

With the bats and Aristion's eagles behind us locked in frenzied aerial combat, the group scattered across the beach, Lycomedes and Aristion going one way, Lanike, Althea, Sophia and Denise going the other. His display of spiritcraft had probably made Aristion the prime target. Without a moment's hesitation, the Hive went for him and Lycomedes.

My breath became stuck in my throat as I watched the Hive charge our way, causing the island to groan with each thundering stride. Meanwhile, Lycomedes had emulated Aristion, and was preparing to summon. A second later, Lycomedes' raft crocodiles vanished into thin air, while fresh ones separated themselves from the old man's body. They were barely large enough to nibble on the giant one's toenails though, and it was obvious they would do little damage to the immense mass.

I had only one solution, one small chance to save Lycomedes and Aristion; I navigated into a convenient gust of wind and initiated a counter charge. The Hive didn't appear to notice me until I had passed over its nostrils and was half way down the snout. The ridges above the Hive's eyes creased and the next thing I knew I was tossed into the air by the snout, my wings flapping uncontrollably and the island flashing in and out of sight.

Tumbling vertically through the air, I heard someone yell my name. My eyes found the island again and I flapped open my wings to steady myself and regain my bearings. In a haze I watched a huge, black figure push off from the island, going straight up. Then the Hive's jaws snapped closed inches from my tail; I was too far up to reach. On its way back to the ground, the crocodile blew forcefully through its nostrils and I was propelled upwards again, the wind pressing on my head and back.

The view was incredible. The figures of Lycomedes and the others were barely discernible from this height. In the distance I could see a large landmass, which I figured must be this world's version of the mainland of Greece. I quickly made my way back down again, but made sure to stay out of biting reach of the Hive.

In the meantime, at the shoreline opposite my companions, many of the rescued animals had entered the water in an attempt to take control of their fate. Most seemed barely able to swim, yet still preferred braving the open seas over rejoining the Voidshapers. And even for those that had the ability, their frantically paddling paws stood no chance against the current anyway. Watching them made me again wonder what they were actually afraid of. They couldn't drown, surely, for they had lost their mortal bodies when they were absorbed by the Voidshapers. But as for the ethereal bodies Ouranis had offered them, once they had sunk to the bottom of the ocean, would they be able to withstand the enormous pressure generated by gallons and gallons of seawater? Would they be able to move at all?

Looking at the Hive, I now wondered if my distraction attempt had really been this annoying to keep it from going after the others, and then it struck me. Ouranis was theirs again. And I was the Shepherd. I was the other half of Ouranis' power. So for the Hive, catching me was the final step, the last hurdle, before it could leave this world and go to mine, where a buffet without equal was waiting to be devoured. It must know this to be true. It must be sensing it. It must be sensing me.

Sure enough, with the key it so desperately desired dangling above its head, the Hive Mind was fixated solely on me. While I was looking down, it was gazing up with a stare so entrancing that it was hard to look away. But the Hive's crocodile feet had no way of taking its jaws within reach. I was too high up.

Slowly the Hive's jaws opened and out of its throat, a column of smoke began billowing upwards. Seconds later, a pair of great bat wings emerged from both sides of the pillar, reminding me of both the swarm of bats that was continuing to fall prey to Aristion's eagles, and of Flego.

Upon seeing the giant bat wings emerge, a weight lifted from my feathery shoulders; an idea had surfaced. My head felt suddenly lighter, while my heart began to pound more rapidly. The sight of the Hive opening its mouth, the wings appearing, I knew this was it. This was the exit. By belching out another one of its creations, the Hive was opening its gates.

Everything was tingling. Waves of exhilaration flowed through my body. It was like my mind was taking a deep breath in preparation of a yell. Then I called out with every ounce of willpower I had left in me. *Flego! Krixi! This is your chance! Follow my voice! It will guide you to me!*

My yells were directed at the giant crocodile beneath me. I felt so close to it, so connected, it was like I simply had to step sideways and I could slip into the Hive Mind again like I had done earlier. For a second I imagined this was how Ouranis must have felt when she connected with the Hive all those times.

My thoughts felt as though they were in two places at once. It was split, just like Ouranis had said it would. I couldn't actually see the spirits inside the Vault like I did before, but I could sense them. My mind was cast back to their lonely vigil, as well as their blank and unheeding faces.

My real eyes, however, saw something entirely different. A head, a flat nose and a broad mouth full of jagged teeth appeared in the pillar of smoke. And soon the only things not fully formed were the Void bat's hind legs and the membrane that extended between them. It was almost as large as Ouranis had been, large enough to swallow me whole.

Again and again I yelled Flego's name. This had to work. It just had to. I didn't dare move out of fear of losing the connection. We were so close, and there was no telling when the next time would be that the circumstances were this favourable.

Then something clicked. A connection spawned between me and a spirit so powerful, it startled me. The difference in strength between this one and the others I could sense floating inside the Vault of Spirits was staggering.

The feeling was comparable to someone grabbing my tongue and pulling himself up. I physically felt my body moving downwards against the upward pressure of air under my wings. It brought me dangerously close to the emerging giant bat, and almost within biting range. Its hind legs were nearly finished and now the bat, still tethered to the pillar of smoke, began to snap at my tail feathers with rabid ferocity.

Pond-sized droplets of inky grime were flying everywhere as the bat continued to wriggle itself loose from the pillar. It was trying to speed its creation, which was still underway and mere seconds from finishing. Meanwhile, Flego, for I knew it was him, was continuing to inexorably pull himself free. I couldn't actually see him, nor did I need to, for my mind was painting the picture of him using the connection between us like a rope ladder.

The bat was free, its black eyes gleaming. It gave a forceful stroke of its wings, black liquid spraying everywhere, and came to hover next to me, watching the dying breaths of its first ever morsel – which was me.

A lionlike roar filled the air. The bat didn't even have time to look down.

What actually hit the creature I couldn't tell, because the next moment, the bat exploded into a puff of black smoke that clouded my vision. It could have been a rake from his claws, a bite, or perhaps Krixi had had something to do with it. But Flego was free at last, which he announced to the world using a throat any male lion would die for. Krixi was at his side, a Gryphon hatchling cute enough to break any girl's heart and adding a screech of joy to her brother's deafening roar.

Seeing them together, twisting playfully through the air, was blissful, but at the same time, left a bitter taste on my tongue. I swallowed it away, thinking, *I'm so sorry, Ouranis. I wish you could be here.* My mind steeled and I went after the two Celestial Beasts. *And you will. I will make sure of it.*

Chapter 18

'This feels good,' Flego told anyone who was reading his mind. 'Krixi, do you taste it?'

'I do, I do,' said Krixi.

'Freedom. Finally.'

Flego came to a stop in midair and breathed in through his nostrils. Krixi, on the other hand, wasn't able to contain her excitement as well as her brother did. Sharing her speed with a peregrine falcon, she continued to zip circles around the Manticore until Flego looked away, blinking dazedly.

Something was happening below. Perhaps it was the disappointment of seeing two of the Celestial Beasts out of its belly, or the physical trauma caused by Flego and Krixi's escape might have something to do with it. Whatever the cause, the Hive appeared like it was suffering from severe haemorrhage and a bad case of stomach ache at the same time. The crocodile collapsed onto its back, ground shaking. It writhed in agony, limbs convulsing, and its jaws opened wide in a guttural scream.

The three of us looked down, surprised. None of us knew what to make of this. Lycomedes and the others had retreated as far away as the beach let them. Both Lycomedes and Lanike were hastily summoning rafts to facilitate their escape. Sophia was evidently trying to calm down Denise, but the latter had no intention of waiting for Lanike's snakes. Upon seeing the Hive convulsing in pain, Denise turned tail and jumped into the water. Seeing her aversion to the giant crocodile pleased me greatly, for it again proved to me that her mind was still ours.

I only looked away from Denise when something that shouldn't be possible attracted my attention. The Hive's jaws began to move beyond their physical limits. It was a sickening sight, as though invisible hands had grabbed the crocodile's nose and chin and were tearing them apart.

As was the case with the pillar of smoke from which the giant bat had spawned, the crocodile's throat belched up more of the familiar black grime. This time, however, it seemed rather due to a sickness instead of an effort of will. Finally, while the image of the overstretched jaws continued to haunt me, the entire crocodile's body dissolved into fog.

'There are humans down there,' said Flego in mild surprise, injecting his words into my brain directly. 'And you,' I looked over at him, 'you look different.' I couldn't believe what I was hearing. Did he only just realise I looked like a bird?

'He does,' said Krixi. 'He looks like me now. Fleger, is this what a druid is?'

'This isn't how he's supposed to look, Krixi,' said Flego, sounding impatient but also a bit insecure. He looked at me for the answer.

No, it's not. But never mind that. We need to get the others out of here. Meanwhile the black fog was spreading across the island like the contents of a smoke grenade.

'You know these humans?' Flego asked.

Yes, I do. I tried to keep my voice polite, but inside, everything squirmed with the desire to grab Flego and Krixi by the neck and make them save my friends. *They are the ones who came with us. They are the ones who helped free you.*

Krixi had lost interest. She had flown off and was scanning the island hopefully. 'Ouranis? Sister? Where you go?'

Flego made to go over to her and join her in her search. I had hoped not to mention Ouranis before the others were safe and cursed in silence for the way this was going. About half way there, Flego turned. There was no question he had heard me. 'You know something, don't you?' he asked. We both fell silent for a spell and Flego looked around, his eyes squinting. Then he added, the thought startling him, 'She's not here. Ouranis, she's gone.'

I'm very sorry, Flego. It only just happened.

'That's impossible.' He looked down at the growing cloud of smoke. 'She is Ouranis. She can't have fallen prey twice to this... this thing.'

I followed his gaze. Half of the trampled forest and a large portion of the beach were hidden behind a layer of dark mist, while the small portion that was yet untouched was populated by my companions and the few animals that had been too scared to enter the ocean. The swarm of Void bats was gone, probably vanquished by Aristion's eagles. As we watched, curved tails and pincers emerged from the mist. They were attached to gleaming, black bodies of Void scorpions which, after making their appearance, began to spread out across the island.

Flego was still in shock. His voice was barely audible. 'It can't be. Ouranis. How did it happen, human? Speak up.'

She was badly wounded by the time I got back from talking to you inside the Vault of Spirits. It happened so quickly, I... There was nothing I could do, I'm sorry. The Hive recaptured her. But please, Flego, can you help me get my friends out of here?

Flego didn't answer. Whatever he was thinking, he kept it to himself. And over the next few seconds, I watched the fury in his face build. When he spoke at last, his voice induced a flashback to Kriton, the druid captain with an insatiable hunger for battle. 'Krixi, you remember last time we fought the Voidshapers, don't you?'

'I do,' said Krixi mirthfully, taking her body for a spin. 'Yep, yep.'

'Then do it again. Reveal them for me, like you did last time. Your brother is going for the ground shaker.' Krixi let out a joyful whoop for Flego's choice of attack.

Watching them prepare for a combined assault reminded me of the fact that before the Celestial Beasts were captured so long ago, they had fought the Hive and the Voidshapers for months, perhaps years, until their enemy proved too much in the end. Seeing the seven divine children together, protecting the gate to this realm, would have been a sight beyond my imagination.

Krixi's speed was incredible. Her body was so small and light, gravity barely seemed to have any control over it. This meant that any speed she gathered on her way down was the same speed with which she flew up again, arced through the air, then initiated another dive.

Again and again she swooped in and out of the fog and over the confused heads of the scorpions, blowing more of the mist away and out across the water. Some of the scorpion bodies were only half finished when Krixi's gale reached them, and upon breaking connection with the fog, their bodies disintegrated. Krixi's attacks slowed the scorpion army down considerably, but it wasn't enough to keep them from going after Lycomedes and the others.

Flego nodded, half in appreciation and apparently half in reminiscence of their previous battles against the Voidshapers. When he was satisfied with the results, he uttered a continuous growl, tucked in his wings and allowed gravity to take over. As he plummeted to the ground, the upward air pressure forced his translucent mane into the shape of a flickering fire, while his scorpion tail fluttered bonelessly behind him.

I raced after him, furiously beating the air with my wings. Then, with impossible force, Flego hit the ground and lightning-shaped fissures shot into multiple directions. The island split apart like a birthday cake being mutilated by an overenthusiastic toddler.

Fed with the image of Lycomedes and the others tumbling like dominoes, I made to stop my descent at once. But I was flying so fast, it seemed to take ages, especially since most of my attention was gobbled up by the ocean taking advantage of the cracks in the earth and the long fingers of water rushing in from all sides.

A few seconds in, the rent island was still in upheaval, torn into multiple pieces by the power behind Flego's attack. Animals, humans and Void scorpions alike fought their hardest to stay out of the water.

I figured that, after seeing the Hive transform, Lycomedes had told the others to stay on the beach instead of risking the open water out of fear of what was hiding beneath the surface. Escaping on a raft was out of the question now anyway, since the majority of the fog had already disappeared into the water. And we all knew the Hive was just as capable in the water as out.

While Flego and Krixi busied themselves with the scorpions, I hurried over to the druids. They were discussing their options in frantic voices. But since there was no way to communicate with them, I turned to Flego instead. *Flego, I'm with the others. What do you suggest we do?*

While we communicated, Flego continued to thrust his stinger into the backs of one Void scorpion after another, tossing them into the air where they dissolved into smoke. 'How many of you are there?' he asked, then added while stabbing at another scorpion, 'Get back here, you phoney spawn of ash and bile! You too. There you go. Ha!'

I did a quick headcount. *Four adults, one girl, and Denise and I. So seven in total. Denise is the… I know what she looks like, but she's not really a Voidshaper. She's my girlfriend. Your sister trusted her,* I added just in case.

'Well I can't ask her that now, can I? Very well. Can you change back?'

You mean to my normal body? I'm not sure. I think so. In the meantime, Sophia was helping Denise back up the chunk of earth that was ours.

'Then do it,' said Flego. 'I'll take care of the rest. Krixi, the human whelp with the black hair is yours, got it?' Krixi was probably too far off for me to hear her thoughts, because the answer never came.

'Aristion, behind!' Lanike screamed suddenly.

Aristion was watching his flock of eagles, which he had been busy re-summoning ever since the first scorpion appeared. In his blindspot, a tentacle, black as pitch, had emerged from the fissure behind him. It continued to shoot into the air like a flower reaching for the sun. And before Aristion had time to react, it slashed through the air like a sword.

Upon hearing Lanike's warning, Aristion dived to safety, the blue slither disappearing between his palms as they parted. He was only able to do so in time because he wasn't the intended target. The tentacle, instead of landing on Aristion's head, stopped dead inches from his scalp. It bent double so the top part continued its way towards me.

A sharp pain inflamed my shoulder. The tentacle hit me with such force, when I slammed into the ground, my right wing felt like it had been torn off. Inside I screamed in pain, a scream which left my throat and beak as an earsplitting screech. Through squinted eyes I could see hands shooting upwards to protect their owners' ears. Denise gave a yelp that could just as well have been caused by the stinging of her eardrums as possible concern for my safety.

'Check if he's injured,' said Lycomedes. 'Quickly!'

'No, it's not possible,' said Althea, sounding awestruck. 'He can't be him…'

'The Darkness. We mustn't let it enter his bloodstream,' pressed Lycomedes. 'Check his skin.' Before anyone had time to reach me, I felt my body change again. I was sure I hadn't commanded it to, yet my body was slowly turning back to its human proportions. Both Lanike and Althea let out a simultaneous gasp.

'The Shepherd,' Althea whispered breathlessly. 'It's true. But... that's not Zeuxis...'

'It *is* Aaron,' said Lanike in confirmation of her earlier suspicions.

'Yes, yes,' said Lycomedes impatiently. 'We are all here. Now what are we going to do about that?'

'Flego, he's coming,' I told the group in a weak voice. My shoulder was still throbbing horribly. *Please, hurry up*, I added in silence, projecting my thoughts outwards, hoping Flego would catch them.

'Aristion, your eagles!' said Lycomedes. 'Call them back. There're two of those tentacles now. Watch it!' Aristion let out a curse and a fluttering of wings announced that his eagles complied with Lycomedes' wish.

I was lying on the ground, my belly glued to the white sand. I tried to turn my head and watch what was happening, but I couldn't. It felt like one of my collarbones was broken. It hurt even to breathe.

'Here he comes,' said Lycomedes. 'All of you, stand together.' His words were followed by a giant claw pressing in on my rib cage, emptying my lungs and injecting my body with shots of pain.

My mind was too fuzzy to fully appreciate what was happening. There was shouting, a few shrieks, and the next thing I knew I was in the air, hanging from one of Flego's claws. I looked sideways and saw Aristion dangling from the other one, his face drained. He was surveying the scene below. By the sound of it, Lanike and Althea were hanging from Flego's hind ones. Where Lycomedes and Denise were I had no idea.

Sophia's fate, on the other hand, was clear to any soul within several square miles. She was having the time of her life with the lightning-fast Gryphon hatchling. Her screams were like an echo bouncing through a mountain range, fading in and out every time she zoomed past.

Thank you so much, Flego, I thought with relief soothing my brain. It was incredible how much being saved did for my burning shoulder. *That was close.*

'Hey, it's us that have to thank you, human. We've been trapped in that deadening place longer than I care to remember.'

Without meaning to, I thought back to Ouranis. It was impossible not to, as the way I was travelling was exactly the way Ouranis had handled me until today. In spite of her distant personality, I had grown so close to her that losing her caused me more pain than those black tentacles would be able to inflict. She represented safety, a home, something Eresa had, without question, failed to offer. And there was something else too, almost like a family connection, which I had barely even noticed before now. With our friendship severed, the link between us broken, the split ends sparkled as though the electric current that was supposed to pass between us had nowhere to go. I knew this feeling had to have something to do with the fact that part of her was in me.

'Don't beat yourself up over it,' said Flego, who had glanced down and read the expression on my face. 'She's tough, my sister. We'll see her again.'

Yes, we will, I thought, my mind hardening like concrete. *We definitely will.*

'That's the spirit. We'll just take a moment to patch you up and once you're good to go…' His sentence was interrupted by a short yell, and then a series of screams from Althea.

'Lanike, no! Lanike!'

Flego's grip around my chest intensified and I was treated to more waves of agony. 'What's happening?' asked the Manticore. 'What are those two…?' He let out a growl of anger when we simultaneously spotted a tentacle at least ten times the size of the one that had struck me. It was reaching out from one of the fissures in the island below us and had coiled itself around Lanike's legs.

'I can't breathe!' Aristion uttered through clenched teeth.

Flego, your grip! I thought. But Flego had no time to comfort his passengers. He was locked in a tug-of-war with the tentacle, which seemed moments away from taking another victim. Lanike's screams of pain were bone-shivering.

I thought we had have left the island behind us by now, but apparently we hadn't. Flego had mostly concerned himself with remaining out of reach, and had flown up rather than away. As it was, below us there was a final strip of beach coming up with a carpet of giant, black scorpions waiting to catch whatever snack rained down on them.

'Lanike, shake it off!' said Althea. 'Shake it off!' She was trying to put her hands together so she could use her spiritcraft, but in his haste, Flego had trapped one of her arms against her body.

'I can't. It's…' A great ripping of fabric drowned her voice. Lanike cried in pain. Her robe was torn, revealing part of her naked belly.

'Krixi, get over here,' said Flego inside my head. 'I can't hold the human. If this goes on any longer, she'll be ripped to pieces.'

A second tentacle joined the first, then a third. They moved through the air like giant water snakes before suddenly shooting towards Flego. With the first tentacle still binding Lanike's legs together and us weighing him down, Flego only barely managed to dodge the first few attacks.

It was mad chaos. Flego was darting this way and that, trying to avoid the slashing tentacles, sending wave after painful wave into my injured shoulder. Krixi did her best to reach the tentacle that was holding Lanike, but with Sophia slowing her down and the pair of Void tentacles keeping both her and Flego busy, she had yet to land a single swipe. Then Lycomedes' terrified voice sounded from above. He was apparently sitting on Flego's back. 'Look down below! That's where they're coming from!'

What I saw next was so horrific that I couldn't even feel the pain from my shoulder anymore. Everything had gone numb. Below us, a little off the coast of what was left of the island, an octopus-like creature over twice the size of the giant crocodile rose to the surface.

The beast was massive. Its balloon-like body, which easily dwarfed the wrecked island, created tidal waves each time it moved one of its tentacles. Its limbs were definitely more than the usual eight. I could see them branch out beneath the surface of the water like the roots of a tree. The creature had no eyes as far as I could see, and yet it was able to pinpoint our locations with the accuracy of a chameleon shooting its tongue at a fly.

'My legs. My legs!' cried Lanike. Her face was gleaming with sweat and tears.

'Do something!' Althea screamed at anyone who would listen, her voice raw. She was crying too, yet her pain wasn't physical. 'Lanike!'

It was almost like it happened in slow motion. Lanike slipped from his grip before Flego had even opened his claw. Her legs still bound together by the tentacle, Lanike's body kept shrinking and her shriek fading. Althea's cry of helpless abandon, cursing the injustice of what was happening with every ounce of strength in her lungs, followed Lanike all the way down to the beach.

Just before hitting the sand, a black spike penetrated Lanike's back and pierced her naked belly; one of the scorpions had caught her. Lanike's limbs and neck went limp instantly and her head lolled backwards. Then, as though being coated with chocolate, black ink began to spread rapidly from the stinger protruding from her belly.

'Althea, no!' said Aristion. 'Save your energy. It's too late.'

Althea had freed her arm and had her palms pressed together. Blue energy cloaked her body and I thought I saw a tiny version of a dolphin's tail fin appear and then vanish in one of the slithers of energy that licked her outline. She knew it was no use, but she needed Aristion's words to refrain from sending a school of dolphins at the Void scorpions.

'If I hadn't released her, the Hive would have torn her in two,' Flego told me, his voice low and apologetic. 'I had no choice.'

I know, I thought. *No one blames you. It's… it's just hard.* Finally I managed to look away from Lanike, who was thrown into the sand like a sack of potatoes and was well underway of becoming a Void scorpion herself. *Will her spirit remain intact?* I asked when Flego had flown well out of reach of the Hive's tentacles.

'It should.' His voice had a curious edge to it.

You're not certain? His response took too long. *There is something else, isn't there?*

'The truth is,' said Flego at length, 'new spirits, fresh ones, need time to get used to existing inside the Vault. It's not easy to explain, and I don't fully understand it myself. But suffice it to say that new spirits do not appear the way we did to you – and still do, apparently. Not at first, I mean.'

'It doesn't appear to be following us,' said Lycomedes from Flego's back. 'Aristion, how is everyone?'

Ignoring the conversation between Lycomedes and Aristion, I thought, *So what are you saying? We can't save Lanike until she is ready to be saved?*

'That about sums it up.'

Then what about Ouranis? Does the same thing apply to her?

'I can't say,' said Flego. 'But we're not going to try it now. I need to get my strength back first. That first attack was pathetic. It should have meant the end of the island, not just split it into a few pieces.'

Oh, you mean the ground shaker? I asked in mild amusement despite the severity of the situation. I regretted it soon after, for the chuckle that followed made my shoulder hurt.

'I only said it because it would help Krixi remem…,' said Flego before he realised I was only pulling his tail and tightened his grip in annoyance. 'Very funny, human.'

Aristion's voice came again. 'Lycomedes!' He didn't seem able to utter anything else. He was looking out into the distance where, as I followed his gaze, three more massive octopi emerged from the ocean's depths.

My mouth fell open. My mind was trying to reject reality. *This can't be. It just can't.*

Krixi's shrill, panicked voice entered my mind, wiping it clean. 'Fleger!'

'Yes, Krixi! Fly! FLY!'

Chapter 19

That's Eresa. That small island over there.

'Then that's our heading,' said Flego, the morning sun glittering in his mane. With the scene featuring the monstrous Void octopi playing on repeat in the back of my mind, we had travelled all through the night. Flego's bat wings were ill-suited for long journeys – and he had as many as seven passengers weighing him down – which resulted in our speed being but a fraction of what Ouranis had managed to achieve. On our way back, we had picked Alphaios and Danaos up from one of the abandoned ships.

Wait, you're not seriously thinking of going there, are you? We can't do that. We have no idea how the druids will react.

'It seems my sister, Ouranis, did all right, considering the company she brought with her,' said Flego. 'Those other humans are from this place, Eresa, too, aren't they?'

I knew he was talking about Lycomedes and the others, as I had told Flego about their involvement in his and Krixi's rescue. Not only did I want to be as forthcoming as I could towards the Manticore, I also thought it best to put the Eresans in an as brightest light as possible as far as Flego was concerned, since I needed their help in convincing the Eresans of Ouranis' capture and the danger the Voidshapers posed.

Yes, they are. Or most of them are. But Lycomedes and the other druids are not exactly representative of the druid community. By the lack of a reply I knew this wasn't enough to convince him. *Look, the situation is a lot more complicated than it seems. That's your sister's den. That volcano over there. We'd better go there first so I can bring you up to speed. You'll understand what I'm talking about once I've explained everything.*

'I'm not going to shut myself in there,' said Flego, clearly exasperated. 'I'm terrible with tight spaces.' He paused for a moment, then, 'You're not afraid, are you, human?

What? No, of course not.

Flego halted and remained stationary: it was time to make a choice 'Then what's so terrible about seeing these humans off,' he said. 'They can't hurt us. Not them.'

No, that's not what I meant. Look, part of Ouranis, part of your sister, is in me. That means I am their Shepherd, but they don't know that yet. I'm supposed to keep it a secret.

'Why are we stopping?' Aristion asked. Of course he had no clue about the conversation that was going on between Flego and me. I looked from him to Althea and Alphaios, who were both dangling from Flego's hind talons. Althea appeared barely conscious, while Alphaios was gazing upwards through Flego's transparent body to Danaos, Denise and Lycomedes sitting on the Manticore's back. Through this much body mass, we could only see their blurry outlines.

'We better not go straight to Eresa,' said Lycomedes. I was grateful for not inserting my name in his suggestion, for the whole issue about my shapeshifting had so far remained miraculously undiscussed. I figured Lanike's death might have something to do with it. Whatever the case, I liked to keep it that way for now. 'Delos will do. Trionyx can take us the rest of the way. He'll have to because I don't think I can summon even a tail, let alone the whole thing.'

'I thought these humans had agreed to help you and Ouranis,' said Flego, going back to our private conversation. 'And now you're telling me you need to keep your identity a secret? Says who?'

Your sister did, actually. It will really make a lot of sense once you've heard the whole story. And Lycomedes just said they'll be fine if you put them down on the main island, I added hopefully.

'He did, did he? Good for him. But it's not his decision, is it? It's yours.'

Mine?

'It's clear by the way you're acting you've been living under my sister's wing for some time, human,' said Flego. 'Perhaps a bit too long, considering what's good for you. She's always loved secrets, my sister. But she's not here anymore, is she? We are. And her way of doing things probably made sense when she was here. Now it's up to us.'

For three creatures born from the same divine energy, it struck me how different Ouranis, Krixi and Flego were. Their personalities were nothing alike, which told me there might be truth in Flego's words. Ouranis wasn't with us anymore. And she was an object of worship for the druids. With her gone, who knew what destiny had in store for the druids of Eresa? Would the clans come together, united against a common foe? Or would the capture of Ouranis be the crushing blow, the scissors that would cut the link between the clans and pit them against each other?

With this in mind, and with the Hive on the move, did it actually make sense to go to the Sanctuary and tell the Council everything? They needed to prepare, they needed to be ready. Because judging by the Voidshapers behaviour up till this point, it was only a matter of time until they would arrive at the Sanctuary and plunge the druids' world into darkness. *Will they even stand a chance, prepared or not?*

265

I took my time to consider my answer and was glad that Flego acknowledged my need for it. As it was, I was the only one who could convey Flego's thoughts to the druids, and vice versa. Without me coming with them, Flego and Krixi had no business in Eresa, for they had no means of communication. I figured this was probably why Flego said that the decision what to do next was ultimately mine.

And what about Lycomedes, Althea, Aristion and the two sailors we had saved from the scavenged fleet? What would become of them after we dropped them off in Eresa? They would be questioned, surely, for they hadn't told anyone but a chosen and trusted few about the journey they were about to embark on. The Council would want to know where they have been. Would they be able to keep the truth about me from the Council? Lycomedes probably would, but the others too? And like Flego said, was there any purpose to it? Why keep up the facade any longer? Come the time of the Shepherd initiation ritual, Selena's lack of the gift would be revealed anyway – as would Ouranis' disappearance. So why wait?

Flego, I need a word with Lycomedes, I thought finally. *He's been with me from the start and I need to know what he thinks.*

In response, Flego landed in the flowerbed close to the path that led up the mountain to the temple of Isis. We all disembarked, some more spiritedly than others. Sophia and Denise instantly reunited like a pair of magnets, Sophia leaving Krixi alone with the translucent crickets that had leapt for safety when the Gryphon hit the ground. Krixi played with them for a bit, hopping from one cluster of flowers to another, but didn't seem to have an appetite for spectral bugs.

Aristion looked at Lycomedes, clearly wondering what we were doing here. The old man turned to me instead. He considered me for a moment, then said placidly to the group at large, 'Aristion, Althea, meet your new Shepherd.'

Both Aristion and Althea froze. Behind them I saw Sophia stare at Lycomedes for a second or two. She had evidently heard him. Then she returned to Denise, who appeared completely disinterested.

'Don't tell me you haven't guessed, because I know that's not true,' Lycomedes told Aristion. Althea beside him nodded in silence, but Aristion still seemed unable to give a response. He seemed to be travelling down memory lane to see whether every curve, turn and twist that fate had taken after Zeuxis' death added up.

'The ritual, Selena, Ouranis…,' Aristion muttered. He glanced over his shoulder to Denise and began shaking his head. 'The Council… This is bad, Lycomedes. You know what this means, don't you? There are rumours going around Eresa that something went wrong with the ritual. But it was too soon to tell, like you said at the hearing. And the Council believed you. Or most of the captains did. But this…' He shook his head again. 'This is bad. Remember, they already know about her.' He indicated Denise. 'Whatever evidence there is to the contrary, the Council thinks she is part of the Darkness. And with her at Aaron's side, they'll think Aaron stole the gift. They'll strip him, Lycomedes. They will never agree to this. They will never accept him.'

'They will have to,' said Lycomedes matter-of-factly. 'I'm not going to let them strip Aaron.'

'Let them?' Aristion asked, taking Lycomedes by the arm and turning him away. 'You know that, after what happened last time, you have no influence over the Council anymore, don't you?' he continued in a lower voice. 'You'd be lucky if you don't get stripped along with him. I know you don't agree with many of their decisions, but this is going too far. Does Selena know?' Lycomedes nodded. 'Great Circle. All this time… It does explain a few things, though.' Aristion sighed and fell silent.

I took a step towards Althea. 'Are you okay?' I asked her. She hadn't once diverted her eyes from my chin. Upon hearing my question she found my eyes. 'Althea?'

'I knew it from the moment I saw you change back,' she said. 'Back there, on the island. But I still don't believe it. Did… did Lanike know?'

'If Selena didn't tell her, I don't think so, no,' I said. Althea looked away, her eyelids drooping. 'I'm really sorry about what happened. Ouranis arranged the whole thing and I… I know that's no excuse.'

'It was her decision to come,' said Althea. 'You shouldn't blame yourself. But I wish she never had. I wish I hadn't.' Her pupils went out of focus and a hint of shame for her confession fell over her face.

'I understand. If it's any consolation, we are very grateful. Flego, Krixi and I, I mean. Without you, there's no telling whether we had been able to get them out of there.'

'Those are their names?'

I nodded and turned around to see Flego and Krixi standing on the path, peering into the forest. I wondered whether Flego actually knew it led to the temple of their mother, where a basin supposedly stood with their mother's tear inside it. Or perhaps the real tear had dried up long ago and the druids had been refilling the basin with ordinary water for millennia. Of course, the story of the basin could also have been a fabrication, something Ouranis believed to be true. She had never taken the time to check, never deviated from the task at hand, never let go of her obsession with the imprisoned spirits.

'Are you done talking?' Flego asked when he noticed me staring. 'This waiting is giving me itches.'

Just a little longer, Flego. It would help if I knew what you two are going to do if we're not going to Eresa.

'No.'

No? What do you mean?

'It means it won't happen.'

Why not? I thought the decision was up to me. Doesn't that mean I have a choice?

'Not necessarily, no.'

That's just silly. Then why did you agree to land here?

'Because you said you needed time to understand your decision.'

No, I said I needed more information to make the decision.

'In your case, that's the same thing. Because, one way or another, we *are* going to the druids. That volcano is too small and this place doesn't seem all that interesting. Look at my sister. She's bored already. I can't have her badgering me all day, now can I? So hurry up. If those druids are as strong as you say they are, there are bound to be one or two worth fighting. And if those ash-spawns attack first, all the good ones might be gone.'

Is that what this is about? You want to go to Eresa to pick a fight? This is serious, Flego. Once again I experienced how easy it was to overstep your mark when conversing telepathically. Luckily, the Manticore wasn't easily offended.

Flego flew up and landed in front of me, front paws digging into the flowerbed on either side. 'I'm aware of that, human,' he said, his broad lion snout inches from my nose. 'So how about it?'

His efforts to intimidate me only made me smile; I was too used to Ouranis to be browbeaten by her brother. Glancing over my shoulder, I saw that everyone except for Lycomedes had jumped away in fright. With Aristion having leapt out of earshot, the old man began scrutinising me with a calculating stare and waited patiently for my next question.

'Where would Selena be right now?' I asked him, our eyes locking.

'At her home, probably,' said Lycomedes.

'What do you say? Shall we go and see her?'

The old man's face lit up with an almost disreputable amount of excitement. 'In style?' he asked, his bad teeth showing.

I looked up into Flego's massive face. The Manticore's eyes glinted expectantly. 'In style.'

Chapter 20

As we made our way around Eresa, we were careful to ensure no druids saw our approach. The thick forest in and around the Sanctuary served as the perfect camouflage. With Lycomedes as our guide, Flego and Krixi brought us to an opening in the forest on the east side of the island. The path was painfully reminiscent of the one where Lycomedes had been waiting for Selena the night she saved Denise and me from the prison cell. Unlike the path where we had fended off Lydus and Aerope, however, this one was narrow and seemed to be seldom used.

Lycomedes and Aristion were in front, our two Celestial Beasts brought up the rear and the rest of us stayed in the middle. The atmosphere around our fellowship was tense; Lycomedes had warned that the success of this trip would hinge on which of his fellow druids we would meet on our way to Selena. The possible scenarios were endless. It would all depend on which clans they belonged to, if any, and whether they would be willing to listen to our explanation. And there was no doubt in my mind we would meet someone soon, for Flego's bulk was so large, he generated a constant background noise of breaking twigs and yielding branches.

Because she was essentially still a student, at least until the time of the Shepherd initiation ritual, Selena shared her area of residence with Leander, Peleus, and the other students Lycomedes had agreed to teach. The mention of "other students" meant that Lycomedes did not have to call Lanike by her name, a wise choice judging from Althea's hesitation to take this route.

When the first houses came up, each suddenly appearing as though nature herself had provided them, I figured we couldn't be that far from the Phoenix Hall and the large square beyond. To my regret, the rest of Eresa was still a mystery to me, and I found myself often peering between the trees to catch glimpses of the Sanctuary I was still hoping to see in full someday. My shoulder continued to throb, though the ache was beginning to subside.

We arrived at a terraced house, the first of three homes linked together. Disappointed at the need for secrecy, Flego and Krixi hid themselves the best they could within the vegetation behind the building. Sophia, Denise, Alphaios and Danaos went with them.

The presence of our two sailors, Alphaios and Danaos, did pose a bit of a hindrance to our upcoming plans. Lycomedes thought it would be best to keep their existence hidden, at least from certain individuals, until the Council was apprised of the story around their rescue; allowing them access to the Sanctuary without going through the proper channels first was against Eresan law.

The other option was to leave them at the island of Delos, but Lycomedes didn't want to take the risk of them being discovered by other druids. Over the past twelve hours they had barely said a word except uttering their consent to any suggestion we made to them. And judging by the way they marched into the forest after Flego and Krixi like a pair of pickled penguins – as well as the cocktail of wonder and dread that had been present in their eyes ever since they saw Ouranis for the first time, pulling our boat – I knew it would take them at least another twelve hours to collect their thoughts and tell us their full story. In any case, with the Voidshapers undoubtedly desiring back the two powerful spirits we had taken from them, the island of Delos was too dangerous a place to be without proper backup.

The house the four of us entered was dark and displayed an air of neglect. A musky odour hung in the air, which was odd considering the animals in this world had no sweat glands to produce it. Perhaps it was simply a combination of dust and resin.

The room, a living room by the look of it, was small and sparsely furnished. A large, wooden box stood against the wall with a bowl of fruit placed on top. Despite the gloom I noticed that the box was beautifully decorated, featuring a carved out image of a Phoenix on the front and folded wings at the corners. I wondered what was in it, but I obviously had no intention of going through Selena's belongings without permission.

We proceeded to the back where, in a room barely large enough to support a bed, we found Selena. She was lying on her back with her eyes closed and both hands on her belly. The faint light was reflected by her cheeks. With a start I realised her face was wet with tears.

'Aristion, Althea, maybe you'd better wait outside,' said Lycomedes in a small voice. 'Bishop, you stay.' He approached the bed and squatted, his skinny calves stressing. He didn't say anything for a spell, then, 'Bishop, come closer. She's awake.'

Before I had time to comply, Selena became aware of her visitors. Her eyes shot open. 'Master? You're alive?'

'I can't remember a time that I wasn't,' Lycomedes said in reply, smirking guilty.

A visible wave of relief went through her. 'Bless the Goddess. I was so afraid.' Her eyes found me and they grew even larger. 'Shepherd! Uhm, Aaron…' Appearing flustered, she put her hand through her hair, but stopped halfway through when she realised she was doing it while I was watching.

An awkward moment passed, then I said in an attempt to shift the attention from me, 'It's not just us. We're all here. Or…' My breath faltered as Lanike and Ouranis' faces popped up. I couldn't go on.

'What happened to you?' Selena asked Lycomedes, turning away from my face with obvious difficulty. 'Is it true…? Ouranis?'

'I fear it is, my dear. Ouranis is no longer with us.'

Selena gasped and put a hand to her mouth. Her other hand was on her belly. Her eyes filled up with tears again. 'I knew it. Yesterday, I… I felt her disappear.'

'What about your spiritcraft?' asked Lycomedes. 'Are you still able to use it?' The tone in his voice told me he had been wondering about this for a while. Selena shook her head and Lycomedes looked away in anger. 'I thought you wouldn't, with Ouranis lost to us. This certainly complicates things, particularly with Aaron back here.' A moment of silence fell, then he placed his hand on Selena's and said, 'I am confident it will come back, however.' Selena shot him a hopeful look, but Lycomedes didn't elaborate.

'I'd like to know how it happened,' said Selena, sitting up properly. Talking seemed to return purpose to her eyes. 'How did you survive? And where are the others, Lanike and Aristion?' To me, she added, 'You said you were all here.'

'I shouldn't have said that.'

Lycomedes folded his arms. 'How do you know so much about our mission, Selena?' he asked sternly. 'It was supposed to be covert.'

'What?' Selena looked taken aback. 'The girl, Sophia Linard, told us. You sent her back, remember? You told her to convey a message.'

'A message? I did no such thing.' Lycomedes was evidently confused. Yet, for some inexplicable reason, Selena's words didn't seem so far-fetched to me. I felt the hair on the back of my neck stand up like antennae, tuning in to the truth. Somehow her words made sense, yet at the same time, they didn't. Sophia had been with us the entire time. In fact, with regard to this message Lycomedes had supposedly passed on to her, I couldn't remember Lycomedes saying a single word to Sophia, ever.

'According to Sophia, you did,' said Selena simply, her eyebrows raised. There was no proof of trickery in her eyes.

'When did this happen, Selena?' I asked, because Lycomedes wouldn't talk. He was too busy perusing his memories.

'Yesterday morning, when you left her behind,' said Selena. 'She was half in shock when she arrived. She's had to walk all the way here across Delos. Do you know what kind of danger you put her in?' she told Lycomedes. 'It's a miracle those dark things haven't found her.'

I put a hand on Lycomedes' shoulder to stop him from interfering. 'And what did she tell you, exactly?'

'That you had gone away on some special journey with Ouranis to see the mother of the Darkness,' said Selena. 'Many thought it was just a story to get rid of Sophia. Not me, though.'

'And those were her exact words?' I asked. 'The mother of the Darkness?'

'I believe so.'

Lycomedes and I looked at each other. Our minds were like blank sheets, hoping to be painted with whatever the other person was thinking. Lycomedes shook his head slightly, telling me he had no answer. But he didn't have the same information I had. He hadn't experienced the same events.

Lycomedes had not been with me when Sophia broke down and screamed for her father inside Ouranis' den. He had not been with me when Ouranis touched Sophia's unconscious body and, in doing so, alerted the Voidshapers to our position. He didn't know about the black tattoo on Sophia's belly.

My insides writhed like a snake pit. Had I been a fool for trusting the girl? Had I been blinded by her innocent appearance? Had I really been this naive that I didn't see the truth that was right in front of me? But if so, how could Ouranis not have sensed the connection between Sophia and the Voidshapers after hundreds of years of being immersed in the Hive's consciousness? She was one of the Celestial Beasts, a being of immeasurable power. Surely she would have said something if she doubted Sophia's allegiance. All this time, I had convinced myself that if anything was amiss, Ouranis, no doubt, would have known. She would have seen. She would have told me.

Being with Ouranis had been so comfortable, it had felt so secure, so safe, now that she was gone, it was like veil was pulled from my eyes. Without it, every single thing I had experienced in the past two weeks appeared senseless. I began to doubt everything that the druids, as well as Ouranis, had told me.

'Are you saying you honestly don't remember sending her to Eresa?' Selena asked Lycomedes, tugging me back to reality with her words. Lycomedes began to stare at the ground. Even he seemed lost.

'He didn't send her, Selena,' I said. 'Sophia has been with us the entire time. Actually, if I'm not mistaken, she's standing on the other side of this wall.'

Lycomedes stood up. His mind had apparently returned back to the present. 'Let's get her in here. There has to be some kind of misidentification at play here. For all we know, Sophia could have a twin sister who's been on the boat and is either trying to joke us, or perhaps hoping for some childish form of revenge for leaving her behind. Or...,' he began to add, looking away in thought again. 'I suppose the twin wouldn't know about us leaving for the Hive, would she? Hmm, it makes you wonder why Sophia wanted to come with us in the first place, or why Ouranis wanted her there.'

'She didn't,' I said. 'Sophia wanted to stay.' With my mind still racing, I went to stand in the doorway to block the way for Lycomedes.

'Bishop?' inquired the old man, halting in front of me.

I looked around him at Selena and asked, 'Are you confident it was Sophia who told you all this? It's been a week. You could have mistaken her for another girl.'

'How many girls with black hair like hers do you think there are in Eresa, Aaron?' she said, sounding insulted. I stayed my ground and her face hardened. 'Yes, I am certain it was Pelegon Linard's daughter, the girl we saved from the wreckage.'

'Then please sit down, both of you, and hear me out first before we do anything,' I said.

In the shortest and most concise manner I could without cutting out anything essential, I told them about every event concerning Sophia's weird behaviour, as well as Ouranis' volatile reaction upon touching her. Selena and Lycomedes listened with rapt attention. I was half way through the fact that Sophia and Denise had grown closer than any child of eleven should want to when Aristion's voice entered from the living room.

'We're wondering what's taking so long. Lycomedes?'

'We'll be right there,' I called back.

It took a few moments before Aristion was confident this was all he would get and I heard him leave the house again, muttering to himself. Judging by the old man's vacant expression, Aristion's visit hadn't registered on Lycomedes' wall of thoughts at all. No matter how we viewed it, there didn't appear to be a simple answer to Sophia's ability to be in two places at once except for the presence of a twin sister borrowing her name. And however unlikely this theory was, it was one that was easily verified once we made our way to the heart of the Sanctuary.

If there was one thing I was sure of, however, it was that Sophia wasn't going learn about my suspicions of her being connected to the Hive until I had no choice but to tell her. Whatever game she or her sister were playing, for whatever sinister reason, she needed to think we were playing along. And if she was merely a victim of some grand, manipulative plan orchestrated by the Hive Mind – something that was possible considering that the Hive had been able to penetrate my mind and even open a personal dialogue before – it would only put us, as well as Sophia, in more jeopardy if the Hive knew I suspected her of something.

As for our present situation, the Council demanded truth and openness. We all knew this to be true. And Selena argued that without some kind of proof, the druids of Eresa would never accept that Ouranis had been captured. She was their idol, their God, which meant that if we did manage to convince them of her capture, it would leave a hole in their hearts that could only be filled with something just as profound. Another Celestial Beasts perhaps? Or maybe two?

'Remember,' Lycomedes said to me as we made our way back outside, 'the druids of Eresa have pasts many are not proud of. You know this. And shocking them with the capture of Ouranis without something to mend the wound could end in utter chaos. I've always said it. Creating the seven clans was a mistake. But it is one that was made long ago and we are many years too late to reverse it. Simply put, we have to give them something in return. They need it, or the clans will be at each other's throats before the sun rises again tomorrow. They will put the blame for Ouranis' capture on everyone but themselves, you in particular.'

'Because I am the Shepherd,' I filled in, as I felt the frustration of the first few days here rising again.

'Among other things,' said Lycomedes vaguely, his eyes flicking towards Denise. 'All I'm saying is that they need something to wow them. It is how they are raised. You'll understand it better once you've lived with us for a while. And you will have to in the near future, because the Darkness will come. I am sure of it. And they want you.'

'Because I am the Shepherd,' I repeated, rolling my eyes. 'Then let's do this,' I said confidently. 'No more hiding, no more lies. Too many people have been involved and I won't ask anyone else to lie for me and Denise.'

'It wasn't just for you,' said Selena, joining my other side. And she was right, of course. If she had allowed the druids to strip me of the gift like she was supposed to, there was a chance it would have been lost forever – and with it, the druids' connection with Ouranis. To the Council the risk of losing the gift might have been acceptable, compared to an outsider running away with it, but to Selena it wasn't. Ouranis meant everything to her, which I could see spelled out in her face as she drew beside me. The fire behind her eyes had dimmed. I felt the same. I missed Ouranis too. It made me all the more determined to, one day, relight those blue pearls.

Selena had stopped. I was looking over my shoulder and was about to ask her what was wrong. But now the entire scene froze, or it seemed that way. There was hardly a breeze in this part of the forest, so the leaves around us barely moved. And now Selena, whose eyes were treated to a sight only the great Ouranis could trump, became shocked to the point of paralysis.

'We might have forgotten to mention our new friends,' Lycomedes whispered in my ear, evidently amused. Selena's eyes twinkled blue as Flego emerged from between the trees.

'Whoops,' I whispered back, suppressing a chuckle. This was hardly a laughing matter, but Selena's electrified profile was so comical, it took quite an effort of will not to burst out laughing.

'Selena, this is Flego and Krixi,' I said. *Flego, Krixi,* I added in silence, *this is Selena. She's on our side. She has a special connection with your sister, Ouranis, actually.*

'My sister's got good taste,' said Flego, taking in Selena's voluptuous body. 'This human has a powerful build.'

Krixi, who judging by her crumpled face was about to lay an egg, suddenly burst out from her hiding place. She passed Flego at a speed only she was capable of, a speed which caused Flego's mane to fold over his face like a wet napkin. Flego shook his giant head and shot a severe look at Krixi, who stopped dead in midair within two feet of Selena's chest and buffeted her with a gush of wind.

Selena staggered backwards, yet Krixi's sudden approach invoked barely a change in her blank expression. She continued to stare at Flego, completely dumbstruck. Despite the many years of spiritual connection with Ouranis, save from the one short meeting inside Ouranis' den, this was the first time she saw an actual Celestial Beasts from up this close. And there were two of them.

'I no think she's so special,' said Krixi, landing in front of Selena. The top of her head barely reached Selena's orange sash. Krixi followed Selena's robes all the way up to her face. Selena peered down at her in return, her eyes still twice their normal size. 'Nope.'

'Aaron?' Selena asked without averting her eyes.

'She says she likes you,' I lied, realising she couldn't hear Krixi's thoughts. Without it, Selena had no idea what Krixi's intentions were.

'She has a funny way of showing it.' The initial shock had faded and was being replaced by a building sense of nervousness.

'Listen up, everyone,' said Lycomedes promptly. The severity in his voice made everyone look at him except for Krixi. Even Flego seemed interested, even though he needed my help to interpret Lycomedes' words. 'This is where it will all be decided. The future of Eresa may very well be determined in the coming hours, perhaps days.' The silence that followed seemed to thicken with every second that Lycomedes waited for his words to sink in. We formed a semicircle around the old man.

'All of us have witnessed first-hand the danger the dark entities pose,' said Lycomedes, his eyes jumping from one face to the next. I had never seen him so serious. 'However, what we weren't aware of was how significant and imminent this thread was. Until now. There should be no doubt as to what the Darkness's intentions are and to what lengths they are prepared to go to claim what they seek.' His eyes rested on me. 'I say "should", because I know you all well enough to guess your reactions,' Lycomedes went on. 'But I cannot stress strongly enough that this is a time when we need to stand united. We need the clans. And above all, I need each and every one of you.'

He breathed in deeply and pointed to the west where the square and the Phoenix Hall were located. 'A few moments from now, when we announce our return, we need to be as one in our resolve. If we cannot convince the Council of the upcoming threat, we will not be prepared when they arrive, and disaster will descend upon Eresa.'

'There is no telling how much time we have,' he went on after another pause, 'but I believe it is a matter of days, not weeks, if that. Our enemies already have Ouranis. This means that we have to assume they can sense Bishop's presence and are able to track it to Eresa. By a twist of fate, for good or much worse, he is our Shepherd and our only link to the Celestial Beasts. More importantly, by his own account, he is the key to the home world. Our enemies need him if they want to cross over and there is no doubt in my mind that they do. To them, the home world is a banquet of immeasurable proportion. And considering how powerful they will become might they succeed, we cannot allow them to cross over, no matter the cost.'

'Enough with the lecture,' Flego told me, boredom stretching his voice. 'Does that senile old human ever shut up? I thought we came to this place to mount some kind of defence. I tell you, if this goes on much longer, I'll go in by myself and give those druids of yours some target practice. That'll prepare them well enough.'

That might not go as smoothly as you think, Flego, I thought, mirth coating my words.

'Hmpf,' snorted Flego and he looked away.

Just a little longer. We all need to be on the same page here. If we're not, the three of us will probably end up fighting the Hive by ourselves.

'Fine. Take your time, human,' he said, sinking through his feet and lying down. 'It wouldn't hurt to give the Hive a warmup before the fun starts.'

Don't you think you're underestimating the druids a little? They are capable warriors. At hearing these words, Flego let out what was evidently meant to be a roar of laughter and slammed his front paw into the ground. The effect was so powerful, the earth beneath our feet roared with him.

'What's happening?' Aristion asked through the rapidly fading earthquake.

'It's okay,' I said. 'It's only Flego, he...' But before I could finish, Lycomedes interrupted me. He peered anxiously over his shoulder.

'Enough talk. Everyone except you four,' he pointed at Sophia, Denise, Alphaios and Danaos, 'get on Flego's back. It's time to make our entree. Althea, are you with us?' Althea shot a nervous glance at Aristion, then nodded. 'Aristion, can I count on you as well?'

'Of course, Lycomedes. I wouldn't have gone with you if you couldn't.'

'My gratitude,' Lycomedes said to the both of them. 'Bishop, you do the honours?'

There was no need to ask Flego for permission. The giant Manticore had clearly understood. And before the group had split up, Flego was on his feet again, excitement returning to his profile. 'Finally,' he breathed, lowering his scorpion tail like a portable flight of stairs.

No sooner had the five of us found a place to sit when Flego treated the forest floor to a powerful gale. He beat the air with such force, Lycomedes, Aristion, Selena, Althea and I had to hold onto each other for support. Lycomedes was in front, Althea near his tail, and the rest of us were squeezed between them. I couldn't see anything of our ascent because of Selena's blonde hair whipping my face and scores of branches and leaves hitting me from all directions. It was like sitting in the eye of a tornado. Below us, Sophia, Denise, Alphaios and Danaos should be retreating back into the house.

The canopy of leaves spit us out. We could already hear shouts coming from the scene below. The only words I could pick up were "Darkness" and "Ouranis", because they were repeated so often. Since none of them had ever had the honour of seeing the great Phoenix up close, I wondered how many of them only noticed the family resemblance between our flying mount and Ouranis, and how many mistook Flego as the real thing.

Behind us, I could hear Flego's scorpion tail flicking excitedly, like that of a dog having been shown a sausage. With each stroke of Flego's wings, treetops parted and revealed people pointing at us and yelling in surprise. As of yet, none of them dared to summon anything with wings to thwart us.

We picked up speed. Houses flashed by, many of which were partly camouflaged by layers of vegetation. There were empty streets and ones packed full of druids, all leading to different parts of the island. Then two temples popped up at the same time, large and white, with a plaza sandwiched between them full of druids and their summoned avatars.

At our approach, the spectral animals accompanying the druids vanished one after the other. Flego barely seemed to notice them. Or perhaps he did see them, but they only made him more eager to throw himself into their midst. He continued following his straight flight path until he came to a halt above the plaza's centre, trapped our legs with his folded wings and landed quite gracefully for a creature his size in the midst of the onlookers.

Probably out of instinct more than anything else, the druids around us kept or placed their palms together and took up defensive positions. Their eyes didn't show the fear people in my world would have shown, or the wariness of warriors startled by a surprise attack. Instead, and this could have been due to the presence of the friendly faces on the Manticore's back, every single one of them appeared awestruck by our sudden arrival.

Soon after we landed, a woman's voice reached us. 'What is the meaning of this?'

'It's Captain Cyrene,' Aristion whispered. Lycomedes gave him a quick look, and then fixed his gaze on the woman standing on the stairs leading up to the Phoenix Hall. She was of small stature, had a round, pretty face, and a white sash around her waist. This meant she was one of the Avians, the bird clan.

Lycomedes dismounted and raised his arms. 'Do not be alarmed,' he said loudly for all to hear, yet still seeming to address Captain Cyrene in particular. 'We have come bearing grave tidings.'

'This is going to be interesting,' said another unfamiliar voice. A woman with short red hair, a pointy face and a red sash binding her druid robes together exited the temple. She joined Cyrene on the stairs.

I looked at Selena. 'Captain Niobe,' she muttered, her face like a taut guitar string. Niobe, I knew, was the Feline captain and the one with whom Lycomedes had some kind of quarrel with since before I came to Eresa. I was yet to find out what it was about, but judging from the time it took for Lycomedes to find his next words, their argument was yet to be resolved.

'We've heard enough of your lies about your little journey, Lycomedes,' said Niobe, after performing a quick appraisal of Flego's body. If she was impressed, she did a good job of masking it. Everyone else, including Cyrene, continued to look dumbfounded. 'Clever, to send a little girl to spread them. You thought her innocent appearance would add to your tale's credibility, did you? Travelling with the great Ouranis... How gullible do you think we are?'

A powerful rumbling came from Flego's throat, which I could feel entering my legs and rattling my spine. It silenced Niobe, and she now seemed determined to avoid Flego's eyes. She simply continued to scowl at Lycomedes, who, by the way he twiddled his fingers, was nonplussed by Niobe's reaction. I, too, didn't understand why Niobe wasn't as awestruck as the rest of the crowd, but I was too busy placating Flego to think of a way to help.

I laid my hand on Flego's shoulder and thought, *Easy, Flego. Please, let Lycomedes handle this*. A realisation struck me. *You understood her, didn't you?*

'I've managed to commune with your thoughts directly, human,' he said, palpably calming down. 'I hear what you hear.'

Good to know.

'They are not lies, Niobe,' said Lycomedes, his voice gathering strength. 'We have journeyed to the place of origin of the Darkness, the enemy that attacked Zeuxis, Aristion, and their companions during the Shepherd ritual. The great Ouranis asked us to do so in an attempt to save her brother and sister, who, as you can see, are both here.' To anyone but Niobe, Lycomedes' introduction of Flego and Krixi was unnecessary. And Niobe still wouldn't look away from the old man's face, which, judging from her gnashing teeth, was becoming increasingly difficult.

If you were waiting for a chance to greet the druids, this is it, I told Flego and Krixi telepathically. I was sure Flego was about to do something to make his presence incontrovertible, even to Niobe, when Krixi went ahead and took the lead. She let out an ear-splitting screech, which in contrast to her speech *was* audible to the audience, and lifted off. Like a spinning top she began spiralling through the air, forcing laughter and shouts of appreciation from the audience.

'Ouranis never told us about any siblings!' Niobe said over the clamour, shielding her eyes from the dust thrown up by Krixi's aerobatics. 'And you expect us to believe that, coming from you?! This only proves you made some friends, nothing more!'

'I don't think Krixi here agrees with you, Niobe!' said Lycomedes , clearly enjoying the effect Krixi was creating. The wind died down and Krixi let out a cackle of laughter of her own, much to the pleasure of the crowd. 'And neither does the rest of Eresa. You're quite alone, I fear.'

Niobe gave the crowd a scathing look. 'If what you're saying is true, there is one way to prove it,' she said. 'And it shouldn't be too difficult, seeing that the Shepherd is with you.' Her eyes lingered on Selena for a second or two, and then returned to Lycomedes. Lycomedes didn't appear to like where this was going. 'Produce Ouranis.' Lycomedes didn't know how to respond.

'See?' Niobe asked the crowd. Only those wearing a red sash seemed to be listening. 'I told you he was a fraud. And his hapless students have to suffer because of it. Mind you, one of them is our Shepherd.' Niobe's voice was vice-like and seemed to have crushed all of Selena's sense of self-confidence. Sitting next to me on Flego's back, I had the impression that she would bolt for cover if possible. I pitied her, but at the same time wondered if this said anything about Selena's personality or more about the respect the druids had for their captains.

'Phoebe,' Niobe went on, feeding on the confidence she drained from Selena and the other druids, 'assemble your team. Find the other captains. We have to learn the truth.' Phoebe, who had been watching the scene from within the crowd with a vampiric smirk, acknowledged her captain's command and disappeared. 'What are you looking at?' Niobe snapped at Cyrene, who, if I wasn't mistaken, was a captain herself. 'Don't tell me you believe him? It's his usual web of deceit, as always.'

Cyrene gave no response. The Avian captain's eyes refused to leave Krixi's translucent body. By the way they shone with reverence, Krixi might as well have been the great Ouranis herself.

I looked away and found Aristion and Althea. Neither of them had said a word since we arrived at the plaza, and I couldn't help but wonder why neither of them felt the need to defend Lycomedes. It was then when I realised that Aristion was an Avian too. He was wearing the same white sash, which could only mean that Cyrene was his captain. Did this explain his dispassionate behaviour? More than any of us, he should be the one trying to convince Cyrene of the truth of Lycomedes' claims. She should be proud of what Aristion had accomplished in the past two days. He and his eagles had been a tremendous help.

A memory unfolded in my mind. Sophia had just jumped down into the water and a murder of spectral crows was descending down onto the deck behind me, pecking the flesh off Pelegon's bones. The sickening sight reminded me that it had been an Avian who had executed Pelegon that day, and all for stealing a vessel in an attempt to take control of his life. Had it been the captain herself? Was the person responsible for the death of Sophia's remaining parent standing mere yards away from me? Or had it been the Council's decision to condemn Pelegon to death and had the Avian, whoever it was, merely pulled the metaphorical trigger?

Shouts came from within the crowd. 'Lycomedes! Master!' Druids were pushed aside to make room for a pair that had apparently missed our grand entrance. They were Briseis and, coming up behind her, Leander.

My heart skipped a beat. This was the first time I had seen Leander in over a week. My last sight of him was through owl eyes when I had shapeshifted after he touched me inside the Phoenix Hall. On our way to the Hive, Lanike had told me that Leander thought it was he who did something to me that made me transform. It may have been a natural reaction from his point of view, but I knew differently. Now I had shapeshifted a few times, I was shamefully aware that my instincts must have changed my shape out of fear of the interrogation I would have been forced to undergo otherwise.

They are friendly, I thought reassuringly when I felt Flego's paws beneath me shift. *They're students of Lycomedes.*

Leander swept his eyes across the scene that opened up for him and found me sitting on the giant, translucent Manticore. He hadn't forgotten. And how could he? Along with his apology, Lanike had also informed me about his, hopefully temporary, inability to use spiritcraft. Unwillingly, I had sucked him dry of his energy and used it for my own transformation and escape. Why I had used *his* energy was still a mystery, because I had done fine on my own on the other two occasions. But the apology Leander had passed on to me suggested he didn't hold a grudge. Still, how long could he conceivably be a druid without magic? Or perhaps the knowledge that I, not Selena, was the real Shepherd would be enough for him to start hating my guts.

'What are you doing…?' Briseis began until Flego moved his gaze from Leander to her. She gulped and fell silent at once.

'It is quite all right, Briseis,' said Lycomedes in a calm, fatherly voice. 'I must ask you not to get involved, however. This matter is not one that can be resolved with force. Or it should be avoided, for we are at a disadvantage.'

Briseis looked at Niobe, who was discussing something with Cyrene in hushed voices. Their whispering was drowned out by the dozens of murmuring onlookers, who, judging by their faces, seemed to be drawing their own conclusions.

'Do I even want to know what "this matter" is?' Leander asked sardonically.

'Better not,' said Lycomedes. 'I'm not quite certain you should even be down here. How are you recovering?'

'Still nothing,' muttered Leander under his breath. If he had trouser pockets I was sure he would have hid his hands inside them.

Now Flego gave a sudden start and Selena and I had to hold onto each other to keep our balance. Unaware of my injury, Selena grabbed my shoulder and squeezed it hard, forcing a curse from my throat.

'I'm sorry,' she said. A shriek followed and she slid down Flego's flank. Before she had even hit the ground, the crowd responded and gasped in unison; their Shepherd was down.

'Selena!' I called out, but Lycomedes was already hoisting her to her feet.

Everyone fell silent; the reason why Flego had reacted in the first place stood before us. It was a twosome I was already familiar with and part of the reason why Lycomedes wished to keep our return convert. It was the Vespine captain, Helios, along with his vice-captain, Lydus.

After his first reaction, Flego's muscles had continued to move between my legs; his entire body had become restless and I couldn't quite figure out whether it was out of excitement or readiness. Whichever it was, there was no doubt he realised that what standing before us was not the average group of people. With Captains Cyrene and Niobe joining them, they totalled three clan captains plus Lydus, who I had been unlucky enough to see in action before. But it was probably the tension emanating from the crowd now Captain Helios had entered the scene that really put the Manticore on edge.

'Lycomedes,' said Helios, his voice patronising. His passive appearance was contradicted by his eyes, which continued to hop from face to face even after he spoke. Niobe was grinning; by taking over the conversation, her Vespine colleague acted exactly how she planned it.

'We are here to talk, Helios, nothing more,' said Lycomedes in a steady, clear voice. 'It is important that I speak to the Council as a whole. It concerns the very survival of the Sanctuary.'

'You are not in a position to make demands or to issue orders, Lycomedes,' said Helios, a patient, almost indifferent expression on his face. 'You have violated our laws by leaving the confines of our territory and consorting with outlaws.' His eyes didn't say as much, but there was no mistaking who he meant. 'And the list goes on.'

'What I have to say transcends laws,' Lycomedes turned to Niobe, 'or personal opinions. Allow me to explain and I am confident…'

'Nothing…,' Helios paused to make sure the silence that followed was absolute. His eyes flashed. '… and no one is above the law. Without it, there can be only chaos.' Hidden half behind his captain, Lydus smirked and nodded in appreciation for Lycomedes' discomfort.

'Captains Ione, Megare, Cyrene,' Lycomedes said, his voice higher now and near pleading. This was the first time I had heard Lycomedes address a captain by their title, directly or indirectly. Niobe's eyes narrowed, as though being called "Captain" by Lycomedes was, in itself, insulting. 'You must see reason. Ouranis has fallen. We are all that is left. The Voidshapers are coming. We have seen them.'

Lycomedes' last statements had fallen on deaf ears. Ouranis had fallen. It was all the audience was able to ascertain before their minds shut down. Everywhere I looked, slithers of blue vapour formed. It was like azure flames, barely noticeable, had begun to lick the crowd and slowly built in strength. The air became heavy. I could feel it as it passed my nostrils and entered my lungs. It was as though the atmosphere was beginning to turn into a liquid.

'Ouranis,' some whispered, clearly distressed. Others were looking at Selena, their eyes imploring her to refute this impossible truth. Yet it was possible. It was the truth. And Selena did nothing to convince them otherwise. Instead, her expression steeled and Lycomedes' supportive hand found hers.

'Shepherd, is this true?' Helios asked Selena, his eyes slow but piercing. 'Has Ouranis met her end?'

Selena looked over her shoulder and found me still sitting on the giant Manticore. With a start I realised what was going through her mind. I shook my head nervously. Yes, I had told the group I didn't want anyone to lie for me anymore, including Selena. And at the time, I meant it. But with this many druids around us preparing their spiritcraft and longing for us to admit that this was all Lycomedes' version of a practical joke.... Was this really the time?

Selena turned back to Helios. My eyes remained glued to the back of her head. When she spoke next, I watched her jaws move and heard her voice, and I still couldn't believe she was doing this to me. 'Why don't you ask Aaron Bishop? He is our new Shepherd, not me.'

Over the next second or two, all eyes found me. My brain was dazzled by them, as though I had been transported to a carnival's hall of mirrors.

'Fleger!' Krixi cried at once, a panicked edge to her voice. She had obviously seen them too. And her perception of energy was probably several times as astute as mine, which acted as a catalyst to her panic. His sister's cry was exactly the trigger Flego needed. His body, which was like a powder keg having just received a spark, jerked, before he pranced and cantered like a frenzied horse.

I was close enough to grab his mane. Althea wasn't and with a cry she slid off his back and fell to the ground. With Aristion having dismounted earlier, I was the only one left on his back.

There was a fluttering of wings and Krixi was up in the air again, screeching her discontent at the crowd. Nobody had any attention to spare, however, for Flego let out a roar that made my muscles scream with the desire to flee. Then something happened which instantly brought me back to the moment when Selena and I had gone to see Ouranis.

The very second Flego landed on his front paws, it felt as though a weighted blanket was placed on my shoulders and back. It was the crushing power of an incredible amount of energy – Flego's energy. I knew it was, for everywhere my body touched his, a tingling sensation began to attack my skin. And over the span of a few seconds, which many people, including the captains, used to press their palms together and connect to their spiritcraft, the weight of the blanket of energy continued to increase.

The energy pressed down on my ears. Krixi's fluttering became muffled and soon vanished. I could hardly breathe. The energy was as suffocating as a boa constrictor. My ribs felt like they were about to crack. My stomach became locked in a battle against the churning juices within. My mind called out imploringly. *Flego!* There came no answer.

With effort I lifted my head to the crowd. Many had managed to distance themselves from Flego; they too realised what Flego was doing. It was the same thing Ouranis did when any one entered her den unasked, which they had been warned about since first stepping foot inside the Sanctuary. To my astonishment, instead of kneeling and bending double like the rest of the druids, the three captains were actively fighting Flego's empowering aura of energy by summoning creatures from their bodies and sacrificing them to the building pressure like living shields.

A soft voice I recognised as Flego's entered my head. 'Too… tired…' The next thing I knew, the giant Manticore sank to the ground.

My ears popped when Flego's aura returned to normal and the excess energy disappeared. Slowly the atmosphere filled with groans and mutterings, some evidently disgruntled, but most sounding impressed. Some voices dripped with such reverence; if I didn't know better I would say they had just felt the hand of their personal God on their shoulders – which, of course, wasn't that far from the truth. Then a commotion went through the group and many straightened up, the clamour returning with a vengeance.

'What in the name of our Goddess is going on here?' asked a squeaky, fatigued voice. A small, elderly man had appeared in the doorway of the temple. He had a shock of white hair with a bald patch on top, a face that strangely reminded me of a gazelle, and a purple sash bound around his waist.

Are you all right? I asked Flego as the crowd regained its composure. I slid off his back to remove my weight as he was clearly not able to lift his own.

'My years of imprisonment must have drained more out of me than I thought,' said Flego. 'I apologise. I could have taken them.'

I know you could, I thought consolingly. *It's okay. I think they got the message. Krixi?* The Gryphon landed next to me. She gave her brother a long stare. If I wasn't mistaken I could actually read disappointment in her profile, but it was hard to tell with at least a whole chicken's worth of translucent feathers covering her face.

'It is Lycomedes, Commander Xenokrates,' said Niobe, a malevolent kind of eagerness in her voice. She had obviously held back her response for a more dramatic effect. 'He has come to tell us about his journey.'

Xenokrates looked at each of us in turn, then sighed and said simply, 'Bring Lycomedes and the Shepherd.' With that he turned on his heel and disappeared inside.

'You heard him, let's go,' said Niobe, approaching Lycomedes but stopping just short of touching him. By the way she looked at the old man you would think he was contagious. The other two captains, along with everyone else, eyed the scene with mixed emotions, but I was interested in Helios in particular. Thus far, his face had shown a lack of empathy, a level of blind obedience, I had never seen in a druid before. Even now, when many druids stared at Flego with concern, Helios merely seemed interested in whether Lycomedes would obey the summons. The sight gave me the chills.

'Lycomedes?' said Aristion, half questioningly, half warningly.

'I will be fine, Aristion,' Lycomedes told him. 'Don't do anything reckless until I return.'

'You too,' said Niobe when Lycomedes had passed her and began to ascend the temple stairs. 'Both of you.' Selena and I looked at each other in confusion. 'Yes, let's go. Either one of you has to be the Shepherd.' A grin appeared on her face. 'Not that your lies will last for long, though. Commander Xenokrates will sort you out.'

Chapter 21

Xenokrates turned away, his thoughts distant.

'It is the truth, as unfortunate as it is,' said Lycomedes in a voice much smaller than the one he had just used to report about the Darkness. Xenokrates nodded slowly in contemplation of the events following the Shepherd ritual.

As the silence stretched on, I looked around Xenokrates' study to get some idea of the man sitting behind his desk. In contrast to Selena's home, the room supported only a few less practical objects. Among them was a pair of potted, man-sized plants standing in both corners behind the desk. Xenokrates, still deep in thought, was gazing at one of the plants' branches placed in a stone vase on his desk. Behind us, I knew, was a statue of a prancing stag standing on a king crab, carved out of marble. I had taken a quick look at it once we entered. Beautiful though it was, I didn't want to examine it any further since it seemed impolite to physically turn my back on the conversation, which had started the second Selena had closed the door behind us.

'Devastating,' muttered Xenokrates. I thought I glimpsed a side of Lycomedes' personality in those beady eyes. 'Do you have any idea how unlikely this seems, Lycomedes? This man,' he pointed at me, 'Zeuxis' successor?' He shook his head. 'And this Darkness...' He closed his eyes and became lost in thought again.

Selena and I both looked at Lycomedes. He continued to study Commander Xenokrates' profile as though the location of some hidden treasure was written on it. As I watched, my shoulder gave an involuntary twinge and I hissed through my teeth. Now that most of the excitement had flowed out of my muscles, pain was there to replace it without mercy.

'We need to get you checked out,' Selena told me in a low voice, so not to disturb the commander. 'You should have said something.'

'To do what? So we could have stopped by a physician?' I snapped back at her. 'This is a little more important, don't you think?' Selena looked away and seemed to sink an inch or two into her chair, apparently embarrassed. *Sorry, Selena, but I already have someone in my life whose concern for my well-being trumps her need to breathe.*

'We need to prepare, Xenokrates,' said Lycomedes, urgency coating his words. 'Send word to set up defences around Eresa. These dark entities are unlike anything we've ever come in contact with. And that is not saying much, I'm afraid; I don't need to remind you that our spiritcraft has never been tested in real combat. Not like this. It is impossible to predict how the clans will react.'

Xenokrates considered this for a moment, then regained his composure and said coldly, 'Do not speak to me in that tone in the presence of the captains, Lycomedes.'

'I am talking to you *now*. There is no one around but these two,' he added with a glance to Selena and me. 'This is about our survival. That should be our only objective.'

Xenokrates gave Lycomedes a long stare. Finally his eyes narrowed as though he saw something he couldn't see before. 'I trust you, old friend. You know that. But if what you are saying is true and Ouranis is truly gone, we have gone beyond orders, beyond laws. We are talking about our people's hearts. I don't have to tell you what Ouranis meant to the druids, and that is without even mentioning Zeuxis. He has been our Shepherd for over three decades. I was relieved when I heard Selena was his successor, because I think she is worthy of the position. But even she would not have had an easy task of convincing the druid community of her right and ability to carry Ouranis' gift. The past week is evidence of that.'

'What is it, Selena?' asked Lycomedes, who had caught her straightening up. 'Do not be afraid to speak your mind.'

'I'm not, Master. I was merely thinking about Commander Xenokrates' words. I thought that perhaps there is some light to be found in the events that have befallen us. I, too, had envisioned the transfer of Ouranis' gift quite differently, particularly when I found out it was supposed to be me. But Aaron is the Shepherd now. And with his coming, Flego and Krixi, Ouranis' siblings, have found their way to Eresa as well. I say let these changes work for us and unite us instead of holding on to a past that will not come again. Aaron may not be used to our ways, but he has proven his courage by first seeking counsel with Ouranis, something very few would have dared try, and then aiding her in the retrieval of her brother and sister.'

I found it difficult to keep my mouth shut. I, of course, had had little choice in the matter in both occasions; it had been Selena who had, for all intents and purposes, thrown me in front of Ouranis on my first day here. And since Ouranis had promised me to try to save Denise if I helped her free Flego, consenting to go with her to the Hive had been a no-brainer as well.

Unfortunately, unless Ouranis could find Denise's spirit somewhere inside the Vault of Spirits and help her get out, given that she was actually in there, the Phoenix was not in a position anymore to keep her word. It only added more fuel to my desire to get Ouranis out of the Vault as quickly as possible, fuel to a fire that was burning my buttocks as I sat there listening to people who may well have Denise's fate in their hands.

'Well said, Selena,' said Lycomedes. 'And if that isn't convincing enough, Bishop has lived alongside Ouranis for over a week. There should be no question on anyone's mind that he has received Ouranis' blessing.'

'You make it sound a lot more courageous than it was, Lycomedes,' I said. I hated to be put on a pedestal like this, especially when all it did was handing me responsibilities I really didn't want to shoulder. I turned to the commander. 'It was Lycomedes and Aristion and the others who did all the fighting. As much as I wanted to help, I was mostly just there.'

Lycomedes cut across me. 'Just there, you say? Those two we picked up, Alphaios and Danaos, were also just there. Have you taken a good look in their eyes? I'm not certain they will ever be the same again after what happened yesterday.'

'That's different,' I protested. 'Their entire fleet was massacred.'

'You penetrated the Darkness' mind with your own. And it was you who got Flego and Krixi out of there, not Ouranis. You can downplay your part all you like, Bishop. In the end it is the druids who to decide who to either hide behind or fight for. On that note, I pick Krixi,' Lycomedes added with a smile. Selena looked at me as though saying, "You did all that and you're still not convinced of your own ability?"

Lycomedes was right. I, too, knew I had done my part. But it was difficult to admit it while being in the presence of people who possessed powers as amazing as that of the druids.

'These two, Alphaios and Danaos,' said Xenokrates, 'have they expressed any desire to become druids?'

'They've expressed a desire to stay alive,' said Lycomedes. 'Whether they want to become the "stuff of legend", to use their own vocabulary, is difficult to say. What do you think?' he asked me.

'Me?'

'Yes, Bishop,' said Lycomedes. 'Our point of view might be too biased to answer this question. Most of us will find it hard to believe there is anyone who would not want to become a druid if the choice is theirs.'

'Including you?' I asked with a meaningful smile.

'I leave that to your own judgement. Now, as a – forgive me for using the term – outsider, how would you define Alphaios and Danaos' wishes?'

'I haven't really had the chance to have a real conversation, but like you said, they want to stay alive,' I said. 'And as was the case with Pelegon, there isn't really a place for them in the world anymore. At least not anywhere where this Lord Arcturus can find them.'

Lycomedes turned to the druid leader. 'That is enough, isn't it?'

Xenokrates inclined his head. 'It is. And speaking of our neighbouring Lord, I must say I am a little bit concerned about this druid they told you about. They didn't give you a name at all?'

'Unfortunately, no,' said Lycomedes. 'It was a woman and she's linked with bears, but that is all they gave us. It is indeed a troubling thought that there are druids outside Eresa. And bears too... I don't recall there having been an ursine summoner before.'

'I don't remember anyone managing to leave Eresa alive,' said Xenokrates truthfully. The simplicity in his voice, just the bare truth and nothing more, was almost frightening. Pelegon may have had a fair idea of who the druids were, or who they were before. But considering his escape attempt, I didn't think he fully understood what he was up against.

'It goes to show, doesn't it?' said Lycomedes.

'It certainly does.'

After our conversation with Xenokrates – concluded with the commander's announcement that he needed time to consider how to inform the captains, and us sworn to secrecy – we were left to do as we pleased. It was the captains' job to tell the clans, and in a manner and at a time of their own choosing. Xenokrates said he would also tell the captains that, if anyone had questions about what happened or what they were supposed to do, they were to go to their captains for further instructions, not us. I in particular was glad to hear this, for I would have hated to become the kind of celebrity who had to walk around with bodyguards to keep the frantic crowd off his back.

To much astonishment from the audience, the three of us exited the Phoenix Hall as though the past two weeks had never happened. There were no guards to escort us out, no further orders. We were pardoned for everything we and the people we had dragged into our schemes had done in disagreement with Eresan law. I wasn't sure whether our exoneration was due to me being the Shepherd or the fact that Xenokrates had more important things on his mind than placating the likes of Captains Niobe and Helios, but we accepted it without complaint. I figured that, given that we survived, there was time and opportunity enough to ask about the details later.

'Time to move, everyone,' Lycomedes said to Flego and the familiar faces circling the Manticore. He had just shown Helios a piece of parchment signed personally by Xenokrates, to which the Vespine captain had simply nodded, turned around and walked off, leaving Niobe to stare after him. 'You too, Leander, Briseis. We're leaving.'

Leander and Briseis looked at each other, shrugged, then turned to leave. In response, the druids closest to them started and blinked at them confusedly. If I didn't know better they appeared afraid Leander and Briseis were about to attack them. Others continued to look at our group with their jaws hanging open or their faces turned angry, but all of them as shocked as the druid next to them by the ease with which we had dodged punishment.

'Oh, hold on.' Lycomedes held up a hand and took a quick perimeter sweep. 'Briseis, have you seen Peleus? Where is he?'

Briseis turned around again, as did Leander. 'I'm not quite sure,' she said.

'Can you find him?'

'I suppose, yes.'

'Good. Have Peleus and you meet us at my house. Leander,' Lycomedes added, 'can you arrange for some food?'

Leander looked, half amused, up at his master. He seemed to love the fact that Lycomedes couldn't care less about whoever was watching him organising the upcoming garden party. 'Sure. Do you need anything fancy, or...?'

'As long as there is enough,' said Lycomedes curtly. Leander nodded appreciatively. 'Bishop, have you asked our two friends what their plans are?' he went on to ask me. Meanwhile, Flego and Krixi were eyeing the scene with interest; they were both loving the attention.

'I will do it now,' I told him. *Well?* I asked Flego, knowing all too well he had already read Lycomedes' question from my mind. *Have you thought about what you want to do?*

'I'm sure we'll find something to entertain ourselves somewhere around here,' said Flego, aiming his massive face at the circle of druids around us. As though linked to a single mind they took a step back, but not necessarily in fear. There was something submissive about the way they inclined their heads as they did, which suggested there was really nothing to worry about.

'Fleger want show druids his "shatter",' said Krixi happily. 'He does, he does.' A hoot and a twitter followed, which put smiles on some of the druids' nervous faces. Krixi was obviously becoming more popular by the second.

You will be all right, I thought, nodding. *But please, be careful. We don't want any accidents, okay?*

Flego considered me for a moment. 'You really did spend too much time with my sister.'

Chapter 22

My world had changed once again. In contrast to Lycomedes' prediction, the Hive did not show any of its many faces over the next week and speculations began to form among the inhabitants of Eresa left and right. Were it not for Xenokrates' firm belief and continued assurance that we were indeed in grave danger, I was sure Niobe and the other Felines would have had been able to gather a lot more followers behind them as they did. The Felines didn't believe a word of Lycomedes' warnings, or so they made it appear, and over the following days I occasionally spotted a red-sashed individual prowling around, preying on any evidence they could use to discredit him. And all this while Niobe was a captain herself, and by extension, a member of the Council.

Fortunately there was only one opinion that really mattered, and that one belonged to Commander Xenokrates. From what I could see, the captains' function and influence didn't exceed that of the average advisory board. Even Megare, Xenokrates' right hand and a sort of chief of staff to the captains, was little more than a consultant to the man in charge. This meant that Xenokrates had a near presidential amount of power over the druid community. And, as a self-proclaimed "old friend" of Lycomedes, he was on our side no matter how far-fetched Lycomedes' claims may have seemed. So as long as Lycomedes managed stay away from the Arena of Repentance or any of its greedy-for-blood fight schedulers, we were confident we could handle Niobe and her pride of followers.

The clans, Felines included, were given guard duty by orders of the Council. They were to put up a defensive perimeter around Eresa by dividing the circular island into six sections, one for each clan except the Piscines, and each posted their druids accordingly. The Piscines, instead, were assigned to patrol the coast as their animals of choice were more effective in the water. As it stood, no one was to leave the Sanctuary until further notice. Even the orchards were out of bounds.

Needless to say, due to the heightened security, the fear of the Voidshapers was ever-present. It was noticeable every time the druids shot their heads towards a bush or tree because they thought they heard something, and the tense and drawn looks on their faces. Cutting through this tense atmosphere was the druids' profound trust in Eresa's defences, which they often felt the need to reaffirm when I overheard them talking to each other, if only to ease their feeling of insecurity. They were clearly unaccustomed to this kind of strict management.

As for me, there was only one thing on my mind: to take control of my Shepherd abilities and find a way to help Ouranis. I was fully expecting my worries about Denise to flare up again now that things had settled down a little. They did not, though this was probably because, in my mind, her fate and that of Ouranis were linked.

The path that was laid out before me, the one that represented my future, had but a straight route. Every minute the Hive postponed its attack was a minute I could spend training and honing my abilities. And given enough time, they could potentially lead to the rescue of Ouranis, who had the only known antidote for Denise in her Phoenix talons. I just had to stay alive long enough to get it and hope Denise would not succumb to the Hive's manipulative gaze before that time.

Naturally, and particularly during the times I was alone with Selena, I thought about curing Denise myself. The subject often arose in our conversations, as it was Selena who initially suggested it. She was keen to point out that part of Ouranis was in me, and since Ouranis possessed the ability to find spirits that were lost even hundreds of years ago, I would, in theory, be able to do the same.

Both Selena and Lycomedes knew about this now, as I had decided to tell them all about the Voidshapers and Ouranis' efforts to repopulate this world. I felt like they had earned it after everything they had done for me and Ouranis. But above all, with Ouranis gone and Denise still only sporadically responding to my attempts to communicate, I yearned to enhance my bond with them.

Unfortunately, theories sometimes remained just that, theories, as was the case with Selena's. Because no matter how hard I tried and how much grief it caused me, neither my tears nor my efforts made any difference. For some reason I simply could not connect with the hyena, despite my proficiency at mind reading with beings like Ouranis and Flego. Even Krixi's mind which, even after a few thousand years, was still childlike and dewey-eyed, was easy to penetrate. And I had successfully invaded the Voidshaper collective as well. So why not Denise? Why was she different?

Was it because of what Flego had mentioned about new spirits that arrived inside the Hive Mind? He did say that spirits needed time to get used to the Hive and that they didn't appear the way older spirits did. But if that was true and Denise's spirit was indeed inside the Vault of Spirits, not in her hyena body – something even Ouranis had not been able to tell – who was controlling her hyena body? And, anyway, what did this say about the other Voidshapers? Were they all merely empty shells, like puppets controlled by a ventriloquist? The times when I had seen Voidshapers transform a human body, the newly-formed Voidshaper did not seem confused at all. Did this prove these creatures were not really alive?

In the end, I didn't really matter; if Denise was really inside the Hive Mind and the hyena that Sophia Linard was keeping as a pet wasn't actually her, I had no way of connecting with her anyway. It was for this reason that I didn't want to brood on it too much, for my hope was all I had left. At times like this, when I was close to my girl and tried, once more, to listen to Denise's active thoughts, I imagined what she would say to me: to not stop fighting. And there was no way in this world or ours I would.

A week had now passed since our impressive homecoming and our conversation with Xenokrates, and I still hadn't tried to contact the Hive directly.

'It is too risky,' Lycomedes had said when we discussed the matter over dinner, which consisted of a healthy salad with avocado and various fruits. There were still no translucent steaks on the menu. 'Considering that the Hive has established contact with you once already, we must assume it is keeping an eye on you, or several. When it contacted you, it may have wanted to test the connection, or scare you. It might even have been hoping it could lure you to its location considering your proximity to Eresa and us. Whatever its objective was, it is clear the Hive has some degree of influence over you.'

'No, it doesn't,' I said defiantly.

'Which is why, I am confident, it is a mistake to keep prodding or you might get burned,' Lycomedes added.

'I'm not. And for the record, the Hive contacting me didn't change anything. I'm not letting the Voidshapers dictate my actions. I haven't yet and I never will.'

My eyes fell on Denise. She was passing our table on her way outside. She and Sophia were spending a lot of time in the garden these days. I missed their company, Denise in particular, but I was glad to see they were having fun together. I was grateful they at least had each other, which made me grow fonder of Sophia on a daily basis. I followed Denise with my eyes until the last bit of grime had vanished, but unfortunately, I received no recognition. I felt my heart sink; I would have sworn her mental health had been improving since Sophia woke up at the lagoon. And on the ship on our way to the hive, I was convinced I had glimpsed an unmistakable hint of her personality. *I wish I knew what is going on in that head of yours, Denise*, I thought.

Then my mind travelled to my conversation with Lanike on the ship Ouranis had procured for us, and how jealous Denise had acted towards her. *I hope Selena isn't the problem*, I thought. *I know we're training a lot, but it's for a good cause. If I ever want to get Denise back, I'm going to need those Shepherd powers. On the other hand, Denise probably doesn't know that…*

'Are you quite certain about that, Bishop?' said Lycomedes, commenting on my assertion that I wouldn't let the Voidshapers dictate my actions. It took a moment for my thoughts to tune in on the subject again.

'Hmm? Oh, of course I am.'

Lycomedes nodded in an almost condescending sort of way. 'Explain to me, what did you do after the Hive made contact with you?'

'I told Ouranis about it, of course.' Lycomedes continued to look me straight in the eye and waited. 'What?' I demanded.

'You told Ouranis. And what did she do?'

'Nothing. We didn't talk much about it because there was so much going on and we had to focus on the mission. I thought the Hive was just trying to intimidate me or something, and so did Ouranis.'

'I see. So Ouranis simply took you along, and allowed you to fight with her side-by-side?'

'She may have hesitated a little, but that's only natural, isn't it? I mean, I only just got my powers. And I told her more than once that I wasn't sure I was capable. She must have felt the same.' Lycomedes' look turned inquisitive. 'You think she hesitated because she didn't trust me?'

'We can't ask,' was the only thing Lycomedes had to say on the matter, his hands in the air, and I was left alone with my thoughts.

So much had happened over the past couple of weeks, I barely knew what to think. And frankly, I felt like I had done enough thinking for the coming two years. It was therefore a blessing that I had Leander, Briseis and, particularly, Selena to act as a distraction. They were druids. And if there was one thing druids valued above all else, it was the connection to their avatars, and – for some even more so – their capabilities in duels.

It so happened that I desired the same kind of personal progression, though not for the same reasons they did. Their priority was to connect more profoundly with their animal of choice than any zoologist, dog trainer or snake wrangler had ever managed to achieve. Mine was to become a tool, an instrument. I wanted to split open the Hive, take Ouranis and as many other spirits as I could on my way out, have the great Phoenix undo Denise's transformation, and go home.

'Is it bothering you again?' Selena asked the following morning, as I sat up and absentmindedly placed my hand on my shoulder.

'No. No, it's nothing. I was just… It's something I do when I'm worried. My shoulder is fine. It's been that way for a while now.'

Indeed it had been, which was as much of a mystery to me as it was to everyone else, Lycomedes in particular. He had been standing right next to me when one of the Hive's tentacles hit me on the collar bone. I was confident something had snapped inside, either bone or tendon, and to not even feel it anymore less than forty-eight hours later was something not even the Shepherd should be capable of. Or so I was told. And now, a week after we returned, the injury was but an afterthought.

'Good. Then, did you see or hear anything during your meditation?'

I sighed and looked around to be sure. 'No. And neither did they, apparently,' I said, with a nod to the cluster of trees. Judging from the chattering noise the translucent birds produced, they were clearly inhabited. But unless I went over there and shouted at them, they would not hear a thing I said, not even as the Shepherd. And that when I had been trying to have them do so for the past hour...

We were sitting behind Lycomedes' house as we had done on a daily basis since we got back from the Hive's location. Selena had just guided me through another one of her meditations in an attempt to contact the animals of the forest, with little result. Once again I wondered whether the success of that first try on the beach on the island of Delos, when the dozen squirrels had supposedly answered my call, had indeed been due to my efforts or the inquisitive nature of squirrels.

'Let's try again,' I said and I lay down again.

'What about your dreams? Have they changed at all?'

I looked up. 'Are you going to ask me that every day?' The fact was, ever since we got back from our journey, my dreams had been littered with owls. No matter what subject I dreamt about or where I went in my sleep, there was always an owl watching me from the sidelines, often multiple. They all looked slightly different, but shared that same penetrating stare. It was quite disconcerting, so I told Selena about it after our first night here. I knew it interfered somewhat with my training, but her daily reminding me of this fact wasn't exactly helping.

'It's what you asked me to do,' said Selena.

'No, I asked you to help me with my training. There's a difference.' Selena didn't respond. And as my eyelids began to droop to prepare for another attempt, hurried footsteps closed in.

'Leander, what is wrong?' I heard Selena ask and I sat up again.

'It's... Peleus...,' said Leander, panting. He had just appeared around the corner of the house. 'I can't find him.'

'Again? Have you asked Captain Ione? Maybe he is doing something for the Canines.'

'I've checked. She doesn't know where he is either. I didn't think much about it at first, and thought he might be practising for his test.'

'Maybe he is,' said Selena.

Leander finally regained his composure. It wasn't like him to be this distraught and I figured his continuing disability to use spiritcraft was largely accountable for his emotional state. 'Then he's doing it outside Eresa,' he stated.

'I thought you weren't allowed to leave the island,' I said. 'And wasn't Peleus under guard?'

As it was, Peleus had gone missing once before, at the time of our conversation with Xenokrates the previous week. Briseis had gone looking for him, but had returned empty-handed. Peleus turned up some hours later with no recollection of what had happened to him – and famished too. His future captain, Ione, had assigned one of the Canines to him for his own protection, as well as that of others.

'You're right, Aaron,' said Selena. 'There has to be another explanation.'

'You know how he is,' said Leander, his face screwed up. 'You know how desperately he wants to pass his test. Eresa isn't the best place to practice with his jackals. There isn't enough space. He's probably given his guard the slip.'

Selena shook her head. 'I doubt it. Peleus can act rashly sometimes, but he knows about the danger. Does Lycomedes know?'

'Lycomedes is not his master anymore, Selena,' said Leander, 'or he won't be soon. The man is about to become a Canine.'

'Do you think there is a connection with the other disappearances?' I asked. 'How many have disappeared by now? Three?'

'Four,' said Selena bitterly. 'Five if you count Peleus' earlier disappearance. There has to be some explanation. He is the second Canine too.'

'And the other two?'

'Piscines.'

'Have they started an investigation yet?' I followed up. Selena gave a nod, but she appeared too distracted to elaborate. Leander took a final, deep breath and wiped his brow. 'I can ask Flego and Krixi whether they've seen anything,' I suggested. 'They've been flying around the island a lot and none of the other druids could have asked them, obviously.'

'Yeah, you do that,' said Leander idly. He seemed to have calmed down a bit and sunk back into his usual nonchalant way of life.

I looked at both of them in turn. Selena returned my gaze, but seemed to look right through me as though my face was as translucent as Flego's scorpion tail. 'Wow, thanks for the enthusiasm. I thought Peleus was a friend of yours. Who cares if he's a Canine?'

'Hmm?' Selena murmured. She suddenly seemed to remember my suggestion. 'Yes, you should ask Flego. But don't be too long. We still have a lot of work to do. I'll go inform Master.'

I looked at Leander. 'I don't care what clan he's in,' he said. Either he was telling the truth or he was a very good liar. 'Peleus can do whatever he wants. He's a grown man.'

'And what if he can't anymore?'

'I don't know, all right? I know it's fishy, but there's not much more I can do.' Leander gave me a look as if saying, "And I have you to thank for that". With that he turned to leave. Seeing him do so made it clear to me I had misread his expression earlier; he wasn't distraught. Leander was simply surprised how taxing it was to sprint without the surplus of energy he was used to walk around with.

In the meantime, Selena had already gone back to the house. When she was half way across the yard, I called her name. She turned. 'I was just wondering. What clan will you be join...' My breath faltered; half way through the sentence it felt like someone grabbed my foot and stuck it as far as it would go down my throat. I completely forgot that Selena had lost her ability to spiritcraft when Ouranis was absorbed by the Hive. 'Nevermind. I'll go and see Flego,' I finished hastily.

Leander was about to disappear behind the house. I made to follow him, cheeks blushing. 'Aaron,' Selena said, her voice sounding curious, her eyes following Leander. A moment passed. When Leander was gone, Selena pressed her palms together and added, 'Ouranis will always be with us in spirit.'

Her last word had barely left her mouth when a pair of giant, translucent wings sprouted from Selena's back. In more aspects than I cared to admit, she looked like an angel who had glided down from heaven. The smile that appeared on my face made it almost impossible to speak. For a spell I stood there, watching Selena's wings, and memories of Ouranis came flooding to the surface of my mind. It was like drinking a concoction of mixed sadness and jubilation and I felt both emotions journey to every corner of my body.

'When did you...?'

'Only today,' she said. 'Master doesn't even know yet.'

'So beautiful,' I whispered, to which Selena's cheeks turned the colour of cherries. Then in a louder voice, I tried, 'The Avians?'

The wings vanished. Selena's smile faded and her face turned serious. 'They wish.'

When I arrived at the Arena of Repentance not ten minutes later, a great uproar made me pick up speed. It was coming from inside the building and by the looks of it I wasn't the only one interested. The entrance was blocked by at least six bodies from what I could see, all waving and shouting at the people who were obstructing their view of whatever was going on inside.

'Excuse me,' I said to a young woman standing in front of the stairs. 'Do you know…?' With a start I realised who the woman was. It was Aerope, the young woman who had been with Lydus during Denise's prison break.

She let out a gasp. 'Shepherd.'

'Yes,' I said awkwardly. 'I'm sorry to have bothered you.'

'No. No, it's all right.' Her gaze was as intense as it had been in the garden behind the Phoenix Hall. She continued to stare hazily at me for a bit, her eyes searching my face, then she blinked and turned back to the entrance of the temple. 'There's an interesting fight going on.'

'Now? Who is fighting?'

'I'm not sure.'

I looked at her questioningly. Her entire posture screamed the desire to go inside. 'Then what are you standing here for? Why aren't you inside?'

'I'm summoning the energy to get through that,' she jested, pointing up the stairs to the crowded entrance. Without applying some force there was indeed no way she could get in. 'Oh, it's not the druids who are fighting that are interesting,' she added, misreading the question written on my face. 'It's the audience. The Manticore is watching.'

'The Manti… Flego?'

'You don't get out much, do you?' said Aerope, evidently amused. 'Flego often comes to watch our battles. He usually watches from the top of the arena.'

Often, usually? We've been here for only a week and he's already made a name for himself. Look at that crowd. They are not here for the battle. They are here for him! I have to see this. 'Isn't there a back door we can use?' I asked hopefully.

'Why would you need a back door? You are the Shepherd.'

'So?'

Aerope considered me for a moment. 'Do you promise to take me with you?'

'Sure.'

Without further ado Aerope scaled the steps to the temple and tapped one of the druids obstructing the doorway on his shoulder. 'Menelaus, the Shepherd and I would like to enter,' she said in a polite voice.

'The Shep…?' Menelaus began. His eyes found me and grew to the size of kiwi fruits. 'Shepherd! Of course.' And with that he stepped aside. 'Let them through,' he told the others. 'The Shepherd has come to watch the fight! He's here!'

The crowd parted and let us in. I hesitated; on Lycomedes' advice I had mostly stayed out of the other druids' way for the past week, except for Lycomedes' students, of course. He felt it was better that way, and I agreed, since neither of us wanted to answer too many questions about our trip to the Hive. If there was anything they wanted to know, they were to go to their captains, who received their information from Commander Xenokrates directly. As a result, aside from those moments when I had seen them looking at Selena with reverence, this was the first time I saw the effect my Shepherd title had on the other druids up close.

My moment of indecision was noticed. Aerope grabbed my wrist, which in my astonishment had no strength in it to deny her, and pulled me inside. A few seconds of a lot of hair and many dutiful faces followed, then a wall of sound hit me with the force of a punch. Everywhere I looked, people were cheering and raising their fists in exultation, or alternatively banging their open palms against the marble pillars surrounding the courtyard in frustration. A pair of druids, both unscathed and breathing calmly, were standing on either side of the inner place in some kind of stand-off.

'What are they going to do?' I asked Aerope over the tumult. 'I mean, aside from the obvious. How does this work?'

'You'll see,' said Aerope. Her smile was so sweet and innocent, this druidic version of a cage fight was one of the least likely places I would expect her to want to spend her time. Yet here she was, beaming with delight. 'Look, didn't I tell you?' she said, nodding at the roof circling the courtyard. 'It's your friend.'

I followed her nod. There, with his massive, translucent head resting peacefully on his front paws, was Flego. The way he was lying there told me he had quite a few hours of watching the druids butting heads under his belt already. He gave an elaborate yawn and, almost instantly, the crowd fell silent.

Both druids inside the courtyard looked up at him and Flego took a moment to peruse their features. If my eyes weren't deceiving me, both men tried to appear just a bit sturdier than they did a minute ago. They straightened their backs and lifted their chins as though posing for a sculptor, whose job it was to capture them in their finest hour. Then Flego raised his paw, pointed at one of the fighters, and an explosion of enthusiasm mixed with utterings of disappointment filled the air: the bet was on.

Flego, can you hear me? I thought, feeling grateful for the ability to talk telepathically. If not, the only option I had that I could see was stepping out into the courtyard. And considering the stand-off that was about to turn into a proverbial cockfight, I figured that wasn't the brightest idea.

Flego jerked and lifted his head. He immediately began searching the audience. 'Ah, human, there you are,' he said, our eyes locking. 'You're just in time.'

I didn't come to watch, Flego. As tempting as it is, I added in order not to discredit his pastime. The Manticore produced a humming sound not unlike a cat's purr. I wasn't the only one who had heard him; several onlookers, particularly those positioned directly under him, looked up. *I was hoping to discuss something, something important.*

'Can't it wait?'

I'd rather not, if you don't mind.

Flego rose and shot a wistful look at the fight that was about to start. 'I hope I won't regret this. You better not let me down,' he added in a smaller voice, which might not have been meant for me.

Thank you. We'll meet outside.

'Where do you think you're going?' Aerope asked. I had barely moved my foot in the direction of the entrance. 'They haven't even started yet.'

'I'm not here for the fight, Aerope. I only wanted to talk to Flego.'

For a moment she looked at me as though I was mad. Then she said, slightly crestfallen, 'Fine.' She made to follow me and halted when she noticed I wasn't moving. Her eyebrows climbed up her forehead.

'I meant just him and me, actually. You won't be able to hear anything anyway. We're talking with our minds.'

Her face turned slightly angry now. 'You're not very good at showing your gratitude, are you? I brought you one of the best spots in the arena and now you're just going to leave me here?'

'No, of course not,' I said hastily, thinking quickly. It was indeed quite selfish to leave her standing here when it was she who had made the conversation possible. I merely thought that, because of her interest in the duel, she wouldn't want to leave. 'I'm sure Flego wouldn't mind if I brought you along,' I added.

When I was finished I thought I could read the question, "And you?", forming in her face, but she didn't voice it.

We made our way outside and found Flego on the edge of the plaza. There were a few onlookers, but since they merely stood gawping at the giant Manticore and didn't dare approach, Flego couldn't be bothered by them. Back over at the temple, Flego's prediction about the outcome of the duel appeared to have injected a near fanatical enthusiasm into the crowd; judging by the deafening pandemonium they were creating the druids wouldn't rest or eat again before they knew whether Flego had been right.

By Menelaus' absence at the entrance I deemed that the druid had capitalised on the opportunity to follow Aerope and me inside the arena. Aerope realised this too. She began shaking her head, her lips wrinkled; doubt about her leaving her prime seat to Menelaus or any of his friends was written all over her face.

'What's on your mind, human?' Flego asked as Aerope and I drew close.

You're doing well for yourself, I see, I thought, indicating the arena. *I'm glad to see you're on good terms with the druids already.*

'They're good fun. I think it adds something extra to their fights if I pick a winner beforehand. They are a lot more vicious if I do, because one wants to prove my point and the other is determined make up for their weaker appearance and prove me wrong. I can't imagine why my sister kept herself locked up in that volcano of hers, I must say. Life could have offered her so much more.'

I know what you mean. But Ouranis didn't have much of a choice. She was determined to free as many spirits she could, and more importantly, to find you and the other Celestial Beasts. She couldn't do that here. If she used her powers here, it would affect the druids. I know because Ouranis couldn't use her abilities when I was standing too close to her. And that is if she could find the time to do something useful among this many distractions. This last sentence I would never have said to Flego's face if the words had to pass my throat and lips before making them known. But once again the Manticore proved hard to offend. In fact, he nodded appreciatively as though coming here was the best decision he ever made.

Of course, aside from not being able to use her abilities as frequently as she deemed necessary, there was also the fact that Ouranis had special plans for the druids, whom she had raised to serve as her own private army against the Hive. And I had the impression she didn't want to become too familiar with the druids since it would have changed her relationship with them. She was a Godlike presence in the druids' lives and to be completely honest, I think she liked it that way. She communicated with the Shepherd and that was enough. Or it was for her.

Seeing that the secret about the Voidshapers' existence was out and that Flego had little partiality for secrets himself, I didn't think there was much to gain in telling him about Ouranis' plans for the druids. In the back of my mind I thought he already knew, or perhaps guessed, since Flego seemed to remember a lot about his sister. And even if he didn't before he probably did now, because I would be foolish to think he had not scanned my mind for anything I might be keeping from him. If this was the case, perhaps the fact that he didn't bring it up was because he didn't want to talk about it. Naturally, I had no objection.

'That's my sister for you,' said Flego. 'She's always felt responsible for what happened to this world and its inhabitants. She was like that before our capture. And apparently,' he looked over at the Phoenix Hall, 'even after years of solitude she hasn't lost her touch. I guess it's only natural. One among a group has to carry the weight, or no one does. And between my siblings, well…' His voice trailed off. He then suddenly seemed to realise who he was talking to and straightened up.

'I can see where she's coming from, of course,' he added hastily, steering the conversation away from his brothers and sisters. 'I, too, have to keep my energy in check when I'm close to humans. It's a given she had to do so as well.' He turned his gaze to the arena. 'It took some practice before I was able to be among this many of them. A couple of days, you know? But it was time well spent.' Had his facial muscles been more developed I was sure I would have seen a smile on his face right now.

I hadn't seen Aerope since the start of the conversation and I found her standing behind me, her face a little paler than I remembered it. Her hesitant demeanour stood in stark contrast with how she carried herself earlier. 'Are you all right?' I asked her, suppressing a grin. 'He won't bite, in case you're wondering.'

She looked at me, which took her eyes only the tiniest of movements. Then she withdrew her hand from my shoulder – I didn't even know it was there – and she showed herself to Flego.

'How long did you say you've been in this world?' Flego asked, looking from Aerope to me, then back again. There was something in his voice I didn't quite like and it took me a moment to recognise it.

For your information, I only just met her, I thought, my stomach contracting by the mirth in his voice. *We're not together or anything like that.*

'I can read your mind, *Shepherd*,' said Flego pointedly. 'And I can tell when you're lying.'

All right, fine. I met her before. But we were practically enemies back then.

'No you weren't. She's an Avian. She hasn't laid a toe on you. That was the other human's business, the one with the bees. On that note, you should practice closing your mind. I can read your memories and emotions as easily as though seeing a reflection in clear water.'

And yet you only just found out how to do it. But anyway, you know she is an Avian? You can tell? I thought, deliberately ignoring the comment on my mental strength, for I hardly needed reminding. *Oh, right, the white sash.*

'I can now,' said Flego. 'And not because of their garments. I can sense their energy. It doesn't work with everyone though, only with druids who have a distinct energy signature. My guess is that she's been a druid for quite a long time.'

I looked at Aerope, who seemed to have sparked a sudden interest in Flego's batlike wings. *Really? She is about the same age as me. I thought she might still be in training, like Selena and Leander. She does have a white sash, so I guess I was wrong. Apprentices wear orange.*

'This is all very interesting,' said Flego, 'but we could have discussed this during the fight. I hope there's another reason why you asked me here.'

You're right. There is.

'May I?' Aerope asked me, gesturing vaguely at Flego.

'By all means, go ahead,' I said, curious as to what she was about to do.

Aerope gave me a satisfied smile and advanced on Flego, taking care with each step. The giant Manticore standing before us suddenly looked a lot more menacing, especially with a skinny girl like Aerope approaching him. With her arms outstretched and her face blank like a painter's canvas, she gave me the impression of a zombie that was mindlessly following any stimulus.

Nobody but a member of the bird clan, a person with a profound understanding of bird physiology, could have done what Aerope did next. With a single touch to the crease of where the giant bat wing met Flego's flank, she brought the massive Manticore to his knees, literally.

Dust flew up as Flego slumped down and collapsed onto the ground, uttering a groan of pleasure. The groan caused a wave of awkwardness to make its way through my body as I watched how the translucent beast underwent a wing massage of the likes he had never experienced before.

'Where did you find this human?' Flego asked in a lethargic voice, his eyelids undecided whether to open or close. 'And why didn't you introduce us sooner? Much… sooner…' The fingers on his front paw flexed with delight, which made the claws dig into the earth. 'I didn't know you had such good taste. Oh, yes. This… is truly…,' Aerope gnawed on her bottom lip and pressed both her thumbs into the see-through muscles, '…extraordinary…'

Can you still talk, or do I have to give you a minute? I thought, suppressing a snort.

'Yes, please,' Flego said in a voice I wish I had never heard coming from him. Following his reply he made a hasty noise that sounded like he was scraping his throat, but it could also have been something entirely different. 'Continue.'

I got right to the point. *I wanted to hear your opinion about Eresa's defences. Lycomedes says the Voidshapers can attack at any moment. They are already quite late by his prediction, in fact. And now there have been some disappearances as well. I thought maybe you or Krixi know anything about that.*

'I haven't eaten anyone,' said Flego in all seriousness. 'Or not for some time.'

I meant, have you seen anything out of the ordinary, I said, doing my best not to comment on Flego's attempt at a joke. It was one that was probably forged out of the waves of delight that were resonating through his brain. *Maybe you have seen anyone leave the island.*

'Krixi!' Flego called without moving his lips. Then he fell silent again and continued to savour the treat Aerope was giving him.

I watched the clouds for a spell, then, 'Whohooo!' Something extremely feathery was plummeting from the skies. It tumbled, flipped, twisted and did everything else you would expect an off course and out-of-control projectile would do, until, inches from the floor, the fluffy cannonball came to a full stop. Fluttering wildly and blowing up dust, Krixi let out one of her playful hoots and screeched, 'Fleger, have you see that? That is at least a hundred feet.'

'I saw it,' said Flego, unimpressed. 'What took you so long? Where were you?'

Long? It was more like ten seconds, if that.

'I was looking in our sister's home,' said Krixi. 'See?' She kicked something glittering towards her brother.

Flego looked at it, his eyes suddenly hard. 'Where did you get that?' Behind him I saw Aerope step back from his wing; without any regard for his masseuse, Flego had jerked his wing back at the sight of Krixi's crystal.

'From the mountain, silly,' said Krixi. She was obviously under the impression she had told us this already and began hopping on impatiently on the spot.

'She's right,' I said, then repeated my comment inside my head. *I recognise the crystal from Ouranis' den.* Memories threatened to overwhelm me, but I remained resolute, at least outwardly.

'I told you I didn't want you to wonder off too far, Krixi,' said Flego.

'It's not far,' said Krixi. 'Oh, no. You can see it from up there.' She nodded to the sky.

'With your speed, I can hardly fault you,' said Flego. 'I'm not mad. Just don't go back there.'

'Oh, I won't,' retorted Krixi curtly. Flego nodded and his posture eased.

She hasn't told you everything, Flego, I thought, still looking at Krixi. She, in turn, continued to stare at her brother, squinting as though things didn't go as she had planned. *She's hiding something.*

'You heard the human. Spit it out,' Flego told his sister, his scorpion tail flicking in annoyance. 'Come on.'

Aerope, who had just returned her hands to Flego's wing, started once again and this time, actually jumped backwards in fright. This was the final trigger. She apparently had enough and came to stand next to me, but not before giving both Celestial Beasts a wide berth.

Krixi puffed up her feathery cheeks. *Why don't you want to go back there, Krixi?* I asked her.

'Because...,' the Gryphon paused for more dramatic effect, 'the evil creepers are there.'

Evil creepers? Krixi closed her eyes and nodded.

Flego and I found each other and said in unison, 'Voidshapers!'

Chapter 23

'Even you can't enter here without permission, Shepherd. Security has been tightened. You can state your business to me.' My mind was racing so fast, I had difficulty understanding the guard's words. I had just come to a halt in the entrance chamber of the Phoenix Hall. Flego and Krixi were watching me from the other side of the plaza. Aerope was scaling the stairs behind me.

'I need to speak with Commander Xenokrates,' I said. 'It's important.'

'That much is clear by the way you bolted in here,' said the guard. 'But this is as far as you go. I cannot let you pass.' The intense stare he gave me told me my Shepherd status had not yet been fully accepted by everyone.

'It is either that or you can ask the commander to come outside,' said Aerope, panting slightly.

'Easy…,' I whispered to her.

'No, let me handle this,' she said. Then to the guard, she added, 'What's it going to be, Baerius?'

The guard Baerius suffered a moment of indecisiveness. Only by the disgruntled look on his face, I wasn't sure summoning his leader was one of the options he was considering. 'My orders are clear,' he said.

'So are our duties,' said Aerope. 'The Shepherd is here with information about the Darkness. Now let us pass.'

I wondered whether she was making matters worse by including herself, but Baerius didn't seem to have heard Aerope's last sentence. At her mentioning of the Darkness, Baerius' eyes had widened and he muttered, 'Peleus…' Only now did I notice the brown sash around his waist, which meant he was a Canine and soon-to-be clan mate of Peleus. Evidently, they knew each other.

'I'm sorry. What did you say?' I asked in the most polite voice I could muster without losing too much of my directness. To Aerope, I said, loud enough for Baerius to hear, 'Peleus is one of the druids that disappeared.'

Aerope was quick on the uptake. 'That's right,' she said to the guard. 'And the next one that disappears will be on you.' The young woman's confidence in the face of a much larger guard was actually quite comical, and I had to force myself not to let my amusement shine through. I looked at her, frowning. She returned it with one of her own as though saying, "This is the way you deal with Canines".

As the silence stretched, I felt the tension in the chamber build. When I was sure the sound of snapping canine jaws was only seconds away, Baerius turned on the spot and strode off.

'We druids have a different way of doing things than you are obviously used to, Shepherd,' said Aerope as we watched Baerius disappear through a doorway in the back. 'We respond well to different stimuli. If you want things done, you need to say it as it is. Particularly with Canines. They aren't the brightest.'

'I'll remember that.'

I was just going over the required attributes for joining a clan in my head – which I was sure had nothing to do with someone's brain capacity – when Flego's voice entered my head. 'Krixi and I are going to scout the area. Do you think you can handle things here?' By the tone in his voice I knew he had at least some idea of the bullet we had just dodged with the guard.

We're going to have to, Flego. Scouting the area is a very good idea. We need to know what we are up against. Be careful, all right? Especially with your sister. If Lycomedes was right and the Voidshapers are coming, we're going to need every able body to defend Eresa.

'Defend you, you mean.'

I'm only part of what the Hive wants. It wants bodies, no matter where they come from. And those of the druids with their high amount of energy must seem extra tasty, so eventually it would have come here whether I was here or not. The only reason it is after me in particular is because of my connection with my world. But maybe this is a good thing. If the Hive itself is coming, we may be able to use this opportunity to try to get Ouranis out of there.

'Let's focus on our survival first,' said Flego. 'That means all of us. I never thought I'd say this, but the humans might be useful if we ever want to get rid of the Voidshapers completely. It's been a while since I met anyone to test it on, obviously, but I think I'm still a good judge of character. And I have seen the humans' warrior spirit. And if they end up as Void meat, it's going to get a lot tougher from here.'

Considering it coming from you, if I were a druid, I'd take that complement and run with it.

'I do have a heart,' said Flego. 'Or I used to have one, before the "evil creepers" took it. Now all that's left in its place is a big lump of energy overflowing with...'

Bloodlust? I filled in.

'... love,' he finished, and I watched him and Krixi take flight.

I let out a suppressed laugh, one that was I sure would reach the other side of the plaza. *Good luck. You too, Krixi.*

'You are certain you are not mistaken about this, right, Shepherd?' said Aerope as we continued to wait for Baerius to return. The entrance chamber was eerily quiet, particularly due to its contrast to the Arena of Repentance on the other side of the plaza, where it sounded like a duel had been won. The cheering had gone from encouraging to celebratory.

'Well, Krixi said she saw them,' I said. 'I don't think she would lie about something like that. She knew her brother was going to find out otherwise. Why? And please don't call me Shepherd. My name is Aaron.'

She gave a curt nod and said evasively, 'You'll see…, Aaron.'

Footsteps reached our eardrums and we turned to see Commander Xenokrates entering the chamber with an anxious looking Baerius on his heels. The old man's bald patch gleamed in the late afternoon sunlight flooding in from the entrance. 'Tell me what you know, Shepherd,' he said in an imperious voice, quite unlike the one he had used in our only other conversation.

I gave him an obedient nod. 'Sir, Krixi, one of the Celestial Beasts, has spotted the Darkness. It appears they have taken over Ouranis' den. Flego and Krixi are on their way there as we speak to see how many there are.'

Xenokrates acknowledged my words without question. 'Baerius, find Captain Cheiron. I want to know why the Piscines haven't reported in yet. No,' he said, grabbing Baerius' arm, 'that won't be necessary. Follow me.'

We exited the Hall, the commander taking the lead with a spring in his step that was quite remarkable for his age. The old man reached the centre of the plaza, where he jumped onto the raised platform, clapped his hands together and closed his eyes.

'Aaron,' said Aerope suddenly. I halted. She seemed content and began to stare at the druid leader. Baerius joined her on her other side.

Xenokrates was like an ancient statue having just received the spark of life. His entire body was rigid while his robes and his band of white hair fused with the wind, following its rhythm and joining in the orchestra of the trees that circled the plaza. The only sound to disrupt the wind's song was the distant chorus of yells and banging coming from the arena.

My skin began to prickle all over. The air smelt zesty all of a sudden, as though someone had seasoned the air with an assortment of spices before it made my way into my lungs. In contrast to what happened when Flego imposed his energy pressure on us, I felt lighter somehow, more inclined to do something, anything. Xenokrates' energy – for I knew this was what I was feeling by the blue aura that had just ignited around the old man's body – felt encouraging.

The blue coating around the commander appeared again different than those I had seen before. His seemed to bubble and froth, like boiling water before turning to steam.

The hubbub flooding out of the arena ceased. The people nearest to the entrance turned and once they saw Xenokrates standing on the platform, they elbowed one another to pass on the message. The people inside must have sensed something was up too, perhaps they had felt their leader's energy like I had, because the silence was so absolute.

While the druids inside the arena filed out, others arrived at the plaza from different parts of Eresa, each with the same amount of wonder etched on their profiles. Soon the entire plaza was filled with druids, each of them lured here by their leader and, by extension, the information I had given him. Now I understood why Aerope wished to make sure I was telling the truth. Druids hated liars. And to be called here for no reason, by their Shepherd no less, would not sit well with them.

Flego, can you hear me? I did my best to prevent the butterflies in my stomach from affecting my voice.

It took a while for the Manticore to answer, then, 'Yes, human, I can.'

Have you found anything yet? Commander Xenokrates has just summoned about all of Eresa. Or the part that belongs to clans anyway. I don't know about the rest.

'I am inside my sister's den with Krixi. The Voidshapers aren't here anymore.'

The butterflies turned into horse flies. *What do you mean they're not there? All the druids are here. What am I supposed to tell them?*

'The truth is best, most of the time,' said Flego. 'The Voidshapers must have seen Krixi leave the mountain and changed tactics.'

So you are confident they were there before?

'I see no trace of them, footsteps or otherwise, if that's what you're asking. But Krixi says she's seen them and I know for sure she isn't lying. This means they either were here and left, or Krixi saw something that wasn't an actual Voidshaper.'

Well, can't you see which one it is by reading her mind? Ouranis did so with me once, and you can read mine too.

'Only superficial ones. I am not my sister, human,' he said, his voice brittle. By the sound of it I was walking on thin ice. 'Are you capable of such a feat? If you are, I wouldn't recommend relying on it too heavily with Krixi,' he added before I had time to reply. 'She has a powerful imagination. Moreover, believe it or not, Krixi's consciousness is a lot more complex than yours. Her linguistic skills might not have developed as much, but she is still one of us.'

During our talk, the commander had begun his speech. I only noticed it when I looked up from the ground and saw at least a hundred pairs of eyes staring at me. They all conveyed different versions of, "Can we even trust this guy? He's not even a druid."

Xenokrates' was forced to double the volume of his voice, which now boomed over the heads of his audience. By the sound of it, he had read the same question in the Eresans' eyes. 'This information comes directly from the Celestial Beasts,' said the druid leader. 'We must prepare ourselves.' There was no response. Those looking at me continued to do so.

'Druids!' called the commander, finally grabbing everyone's attention. He paused for the most doubtful-looking to turn their heads towards him too. 'We are fighting the one enemy that has ripped Ouranis from our lives.' Eyes narrowed everywhere; this seemed to do it. 'We are fighting an enemy that will not stop until it has devoured every single living entity on this world. We are druids.' A lightning bolt cracked in the pocket of air above the crowd; the result of many minds tuning in. 'We are Eresans. We are the only line of defence that stands between our world and the homeland. We cannot fail.'

Now I beheld a blue sheet of energy around the group of druids. They were preparing for war. I could see it in their eyes. Xenokrates surveyed his audience from left to right; his eyes hopping from one face to the next. 'The great Ouranis has been reduced to a slave,' he said in a grinding voice. Another lightning bolt arced through the air, despite the semi clear sky. 'Let her suffering be your guide, like she has been... and will be again!' People began to mutter under their breath, clenching their fists and brewing a concoction of rage and thirst for revenge on the inside. 'She has taught us the ways of spiritcraft. She has been our mentor. She trusted us, cared for us, and now she needs us. This is our chance to repay her. This is our day. You have your orders. Go.'

At this simple command, the group dispersed. When it did, I found Kriton in the crowd. For a reason that was beyond me, the Bovine captain hesitated before obeying Xenokrates' words. Our eyes locked. But then a dwarf-like man with a beard and broad shoulders called back for him and they bounded off with the rest of them.

'Don't you need to go with them?' I asked Aerope, watching Baerius approach Xenokrates on the platform.

'And leave you here unprotected? I don't think so.'

'Oh, our Shepherd won't be entirely defenceless, Aerope,' said Xenokrates calmly, passing Baerius as though he wasn't even there. His ears had apparently remained unaffected by his age. 'He will be with us.' He joined us and added over his shoulder, 'Baerius, find your captain. She should be preparing the Canines to secure Delos.' Baerius gave a nod and left the scene.

'Uhm,' said Aerope, clearly unsure what to make of this. 'Commander, who is "us"?'

The commander smiled at this question and turned towards a small group of people standing nearby. They had apparently waited patiently until the stream of people had left the plaza, which finally allowed them to approach us. They were none other than Lycomedes and three of his students, Selena, Leander and Briseis.

'Lycomedes does not belong to a clan,' said Xenokrates. 'Neither do his apprentices. And due to their familiarity with the Shepherd, I asked them to accompany the Shepherd and me in the case of an attack. But considering the unfortunate circumstances that have led to Selena and Leander's lack of spiritcraft, perhaps it is best if you stayed as well, Aerope.'

Selena, who had just come within earshot, struggled for a second or two, then said, 'Commander, this is not entirely correct. I have, in fact, managed to regain control over my spiritcraft.'

Everyone except for Lycomedes and I raised their eyebrows, but it was Leander who voiced his thoughts first. 'You have?' he said, turning to Lycomedes for confirmation. Lycomedes closed his eyes for a moment, to which Leander breathed in deeply through his nostrils; it was a tough pill to swallow.

'Only recently,' said Selena, cheeks blushing slightly and avoiding Leander's eyes. Her wet eyes found me instead. I nodded, for I too felt that, in light of what we were facing, honesty was the right path to take. 'I haven't had the time to test it thoroughly, but I am nevertheless confident in my abilities.'

'Confidence is good,' said Xenokrates simply. 'I still think it is best if Aerope stepped in for Leander, however. Or do you have something to surprise us with too?' he added to Leander.

The answer was made obvious by Leander's discomfort to everyone but Xenokrates. The commander, however, had probably too much on his mind to notice it. Leander shook his head. When he did, there was no hint of anger in his face, not at me, not at anyone. It was as though he had accepted his fate and had moved on, which allowed him to inject his next words with a commendable amount of determination. 'There's bound to be something else I can help with, though.'

I didn't want to speak up at first; considering Leander's druid background I wasn't sure my suggestion would be what he had in mind. But I figured that after what I did to him, I had to at least give him the option. 'Maybe I can help with that, Leander,' I said. He looked up, his eyes impassive and hard to read. 'I thought that, because the other druids have no way of communicating with each other over long distances, you could stay with me to relay messages from Flego and Krixi.'

The truth was, I had thought about how a battle between Eresa and the Voidshapers would go and figured that the Eresans had no way of getting a birds-eye view of the battle. Flego and Krixi could obviously supply this, but due to the communication barrier, everything had to go through me. With Leander by my side we could get their reports across more efficiently. Unfortunately, this meant that Leander had to consent to a demotion from a capable druid warrior to a messenger boy.

For a moment I was expecting a punch in the face. I could actually feel my own body reacting to my words as though I was the victim of this insult. Nobody spoke; the druids beside me knew what I was asking for even better than I did. A veil of awkwardness blanketed the scene.

As it was, after we got back from our excursion to the Hive's location, I had told Leander about my conversation with Lanike and that she had passed on Leander's apology for what happened at the Phoenix Hall. I was keen to offer it back to him, of course. It was my Shepherd abilities and myself that had been responsible for what happened that day, not he, and I wanted him to find this out from me. But he might have deduced this already when he heard about my Shepherd abilities.

I wasn't sure what had happened that day, I still wasn't, though I was certain it had nothing to do with the fact that I wasn't a druid. Or with the fact that I was from the homeland and that my physiology could therefore be different than his. Part of Ouranis was in me and there could be no doubt, there *should* be no doubt, that this was the reason why I was able to change my shape. Why my abilities decided to kick in at that exact moment I couldn't tell him – it was probably just my fear of the interrogation – and we agreed to leave it at that. Because the fact was that, despite not yet being able to summon a horned owl, Leander felt his energy returning on a daily basis. And even if it was just at a slow pace, he was confident that in time, his owls would conquer the skies once more. I couldn't even express the relief I felt when I heard about this and sincerely hoped his condition continued to improve.

'I'll do it,' said Leander, putting a hand on my shoulder and squeezing it gently. 'The two of us.'

'The two of us,' I returned.

'Then let's move out,' said Lycomedes, his voice flashing with reckless abandon. I too felt empowered. 'Xenokrates, where to first?'

Both elders locked eyes and smiles appeared on both their faces, telling me the answer was obvious. The smiles conjured a mental picture of two teenagers preparing for a practical joke involving a crowded marketplace and a lot of ripe tomatoes.

'To the sea, I think,' said Xenokrates. His face turned serious again. 'Shepherd, you keep me informed of what happens elsewhere. Leander, you do the same with Captains Helios and Cyrene. They should be in the sections to the east and west from where we're going. Aerope, Selena, Briseis, stay close to Lycomedes. From now on, you are under his command.'

Flego, we're on our way to the northern edge of the island. Xenokrates asked Leander and I to keep him informed about what is going on in other parts of the Sanctuary. Do you have anything to report on the Voidshapers?

The seven of us were running up a path that took us through one of the districts I had been before. While most of the Sanctuary was enveloped by tree canopies, the buildings here were more densely concentrated, which meant that nature had a harder time imposing its will on the neighbourhood. I recognised the area from when I observed Eresa from above through owl eyes.

'As a matter of fact, I have, in a manner of speaking.'

What does that mean?

'It means that I am looking at your canine mate. She is with the human girl, it seems.'

Canine mate? For a split second I looked at Aerope, because I still remembered the remark he had made about her. Then the answer hit me like a cake to the face. *Denise! Where is she? I thought she was at the house. She's with Sophia?* The rest of my thoughts became so incoherent, it took Flego a few moments to shut them out and answer me.

'She's on the bigger island. They are running up the path to where we first landed.'

On Delos? That path's going into the forest and... to the temple. What do they want to go there for?

'How should I know? I can't read their thoughts.'

But what are they running from? I cursed as my mind continued to race, trying to picture them in my head.

'It doesn't appear like they are running from anything. There continues to be no sign of any Voidshapers.'

Well, I can't go all the way over there now. They'll be gone long before I arrive, even if you come get me. Can you pick them up and bring them here?

'I think I can manage that. I'm on my way.' Then he yelled, 'Krixi! No, come back!'

What's happening? Flego! Flego! My calls were ignored.

'Don't go in there! Krixi, there's...!' A lion's roar took my head for a spin and drowned the rest of his sentence.

Flego! No! Talk to me, please! But no matter how hard I tried, the connection was lost. Even once we had travelled the path that led us to the northern edge of the island, Flego had still not responded.

'He still hasn't answered yet?' Selena asked as we came to a strip of grass and a stone balustrade, which signalled the island's edge. In my frantic state of mind I had told the others about the conversation with Flego. They suggested to keep trying because there was no sense in making the time-consuming journey to the other island, and I was needed here. And as I stood there watching the druids gaze at me expectantly, the gnawing desire to do something, to know, to help, was slowly devouring me from the inside.

Flego, Krixi, Captain Ione, and all of her fellow Canines were out there. If there was any trouble on Delos, Denise and Sophia could go to them. I knew that. And the druids here needed my help once I re-established my communication with Flego. If I went over to Delos, Leander and I had lost our usefulness to the druid army, and the captains would be in the dark. This meant there was nothing else to it than to trust that Flego and the Canines could handle things on Delos, which was easier said than done when your girlfriend was playing around with an eleven-year-old and you knew what kind of monsters were prowling the waters around us.

The sea before us was calm and unassuming. It didn't make much sense to me to come here of all places, because neither the Voidshapers nor the other druids seemed to have any reason to be here. But I couldn't be bothered by them at the moment. My mind was consumed with thoughts of Denise and Sophia, and again and again I tried to contact Flego or Krixi, hoping to get a glimpse of their thoughts.

'Come on, what's taking so long?' I muttered to myself.

'They could be out of reach,' said Selena. 'Have you any idea of the range of your telepathy?'

I looked at her. I couldn't believe I hadn't thought about this sooner. I had gone over so many possibilities of how this battle could develop and I hadn't once thought to test the limits of the only one of my Shepherd abilities of which I had a reasonable amount of control. It seemed such a logical thing to do and yet… I shook my head.

'Well, you should have,' said Selena primly. 'Now we can't rule out the possibility that they have gone too far for you to probe their minds. Did Flego mention anything about where Krixi was going?'

'No, I told you everything he told me.'

'Maybe you didn't,' said Aerope. *Not you too,* I thought and eyed her questioningly. 'You said he didn't finish his sentence, right?'

'So?'

'So, maybe he did finish it.'

Selena nodded appreciatively. 'You could be right, Aerope.'

'How? I don't understand.'

Selena looked at Aerope as though asking for permission, then said, 'Flego could have finished his sentence inside his head. Perhaps his emotional reaction to whatever happened next simply overshadowed his thoughts.'

'But what if it did? How does it help us?'

'That depends on how good your memory is, of course,' said Aerope. Meanwhile, Leander had lost interest. He was gazing absently at the tranquil surface of the ocean, apparently trying to figure out what the purpose of coming here was. Briseis seemed to be wondering the same thing, but, instead, she was trying to extract this information from the conversation Lycomedes and Xenokrates were having over at low wall. She looked nervous.

'Think, Aaron,' said Aerope. 'Think back and listen to what he said. You have read his mind. You just need to remember it.'

'All right, I'll try.' But with both Selena and Aerope staring at me, I found it difficult to summon the required amount of concentration. I closed my eyes and tried to shut them out. Then with one goal in mind I traversed back down memory lane and found Flego's words.

"Don't go in there! Krixi, there's…!" Again I heard his roar in my head, drowning the rest of the sentence. It was accompanied by a mental image of Krixi diving down the main vent of Ouranis' volcano.

No, they were at Delos, I thought, forcing my thoughts into another direction. *They were near the forest and the temple.* Now I saw Krixi cannonballing into the forest, plunging straight through the canopy of leaves before she disappeared. It was Flego's emotions, or my memory of them, that roared this time. And once more I heard Flego's words. Only this time I focused solely on my vision of Krixi, and Flego exclaiming. 'Don't go in there! Krixi, there's… no way you can beat them,' I finished out loud, my own voice completely in sync with Flego's. 'That's it!'

'That's what he said?' Aerope asked, taken aback. Selena looked shocked and turned to Leander and Briseis, who both peered over their shoulders.

'I think so,' I said. 'He definitely thought about not being able to win against someone.'

'It's the Darkness,' said Briseis, turning. 'It has to be. We have to warn the Canines. Selena?' But Selena had already started talking to Lycomedes and the commander over at the water's edge. She had left the moment she saw the confirmation in Leander's face.

'I knew I should've gone over there,' I said to no one in particular, my hands clenching into fists. 'If Flego and Krixi are recaptured, we'll have no idea of the numbers we're up against.' *Denise, why did you have to take Sophia over there? What are you up to? Or was it the other way around?* The mental picture of several enormous black octopi rising from the ocean's depths invaded my mind. They had their black tentacles wrapped around Denise and Sophia, and the latter was uttering a high-pitched scream of terror.

'That's not necessarily true, Aaron,' said Aerope. 'If you are right about this, Flego only said that Krixi wasn't strong enough to fight them on her own. He's there too, isn't he? And remember, the Canines should be arriving at any moment. Captain Ione won't let anything happen to the girl, I'm sure.'

'I hope you're right.' *Will the Canines even stand a chance?* I added in silence. *And what about Flego? Has he recovered enough since we extracted him from the Vault of Spirits? Maybe I should go over there myself after all. How long would it take me, twenty minutes? Thirty?*

There was a splash of water, followed by Lycomedes' voice. 'Everyone, hop on. Let's go.' While Aerope, Briseis and Leander joined him and Selena, I gave the old man an absent look; my mind was still with those on Delos. He returned it with a knowing one of his own. 'Yes, Bishop, "everyone" does indeed include you.'

'Is that it?' Aerope asked, looking down at a single translucent crocodile lying in the water. 'There are seven of us.'

'It's just for me,' said Lycomedes impatiently. 'The rest of you will follow on Xenokrates' cra...'

Whatever we were supposed to hop onto was swept away by a chorus of gasps and yells; a black, dragon-like head the size of a large sofa had just sprouted from the ocean's depths. The head continued to grow, pushed upwards by a serpentine neck covered with spines and oozing black filth from its skin. I recognised it at once, although the last time I had seen it I was hanging from Ouranis' claws and the great beast was heading for the Phoenix's den.

'Stand back!' said Xenokrates.

The air was infused with energy again. I could feel it on my skin and in my lungs. When I found him, the blue aura around the commander's body had expanded to form a veil of energy that far exceeded the dimensions of his body. Looking through it, the horizon became oddly distorted. It undulated ocean-like, and in places it was barely visible at all.

Something huge began to crawl out of the sheet of energy. At first it was just a giant pincer, then the rest of the crab's body followed. The crab continued to walk sideways out of the sheet of energy as though entering this world from one where giant crabs were commonplace. It was this creature what we probably had been supposed to hop onto. But with the emergence of the Void serpent, I was sure this wasn't the case anymore; the snake's coming had turned the giant crab from a raft into a bodyguard.

Upon seeing the crab sink into the water, the black serpent hissed and drew back its head. I couldn't blame it, for the crab's pincers looked large enough to grab the serpent by the neck and squeeze it to jelly. By the way it snapped its ooze-dripping jaws, the serpent had no intention of backing off, however. It had merely decided to inspect its prey before taking a bite.

'Out of the way, old fart!' said a coarse voice from behind. 'This one's mine.'

The next thing I knew, Kriton, the Bovine clan leader, shouldered his way through the group, and leapt onto the edge of the giant crab's shell. He had barely made it to the top of the crab's shell when nine, ten, eleven serpents joined the first, each as menacing-looking as the next one. I had never seen anything like it. This battle was escalating so fast, I wasn't sure whether even the lot of us combined possessed the weaponry to take these creatures on.

'Yes!' said Kriton in a drawnout, grinding voice, unmistakably savouring the moment. His muscles vibrated with the power of his voice. 'Come at me, you snakehead mongrels!' There was a resounding clap and Kriton had his palms pressed together, ready to fight fire with fire.

The first three serpents were advancing when Selena offered Lycomedes a hand and helped him up. He had been knocked aside by Kriton's charge. 'Are you all right, Master?'

'Do not worry about me, my dear.' Lycomedes got to his feet and began scanning the water. 'My crocodile... there it is. It's so tiny compared to Xenokrates' crab. He's really outdone himself this time.' There was a jealous edge to his voice.

Next to me, Briseis jumped in fright. 'Demonax!' The dwarf-like man I had seen earlier had joined us on her other side, watching the battle unfold. He was grinning appreciatively. 'You almost gave me a heart attack. What are you standing here for? Shouldn't you be helping Captain Kriton?'

'And be trampled by my own captain?' Demonax asked incredulously. 'Our Captain fights alone.'

None of the others had anything to say against this. Even I knew this to be true. But the pack of panthers he had fought two weeks earlier were nothing more than a minor inconvenience compared to the dozen freakish serpents we were up against this time. Meanwhile, at the water's edge, Xenokrates was well underway to summoning a second crab. The first one, now with Kriton on its back, might possess the strength to fight the serpents, but none of its enemies were slow or stupid enough to be caught by the pincers. I figured that perhaps Xenokrates was using them as a decoy, or a living shield.

'Is this all you've got?' Kriton taunted. 'Come on, make yourself worthy of my horns!'

Either through the Captain's building concentration or his raging bloodlust, he too seemed to have generated a large amount of energy around his body. His hands weren't glued together anymore. He was using them to add rude gestures to his taunts, while a thick chain of pulsating energy connected his palms.

The serpents snapped their jaws angrily. Despite his muscular build, Kriton was an elusive opponent and was doing a great job of dodging the attacks.

'Lycomedes,' said Xenokrates as his second giant crab proceeded into the water.

Lycomedes followed his leader's gaze. One of the serpents had coiled its body around the joint of one of the crab's pincers. Selena stepped forwards. 'Selena, no,' said Lycomedes, holding her back. 'Save your energy. I daresay we're going to need your phoenix in the near future.'

'Lycomedes, let me,' said Aerope and she pressed her palms together. She closed her eyes, but was spotted.

'Don't even think about it, woman,' bawled Kriton over his shoulder, his voice minacious and his eyes flashing with anger. His expression was bordering on psychotic. His eyes flicked towards me. I felt them penetrating my body like a scalpel. Without averting his eyes from my face he began to utter a throaty growl and, from his chest, a water buffalo charged across the crab's shell. In a fluid motion the beast pushed off, swung its head at exactly the right moment and raked straight through the serpent's neck. Kriton let out a raspy breath of pleasure.

The snake hissed in anger. Just before it dissipated into thin air, it flexed its serpentine body. The crab's pincer gave a sudden, audible snap and dissolved along with the serpent's body, leaving only a useless stump behind. The stump immediately began to spray blue, glittering droplets everywhere like blood pouring from a wound.

Xenokrates saw it happen, narrowed his eyes, and like Ouranis had done during our fight with the Void crocodile, sealed the wound with an extra layer of energy.

'Incredible,' breathed Selena, watching the bandage form. 'I heard he was able to do it, but I have never actually seen it happen.'

After summoning his first buffalo, Kriton was finally ready to drop his taunts, or most of them, and start fighting. Lycomedes insisted none of us should interfere, for he believed this was only the beginning of what the Voidshapers had in store for us. After the Bovine captain had finished off two more serpents and the crabs had decapitated a third, it seemed like Xenokrates and Kriton had things under control.

During the battle, Demonax, Kriton's vice-captain, informed us that the rest of their clan had remained behind on his captain's orders to defend their assigned part of Eresa. Apparently, the only reason he and his captain were here was because Kriton thought that I was the Voidshapers' intended target. So if there was any good fight to be had, I would be at the thick of it.

There were only seven serpents left when Aerope noticed a foursome of over thirty feet-long, humpback whales with druids on their backs following the coastline towards us. The sight was mightily impressive and I felt my heart lift; even though the fight was going well, there was no such thing as feeling safe enough.

'It's Captain Cheiron and the Piscines,' said Selena, her hand shielding her eyes from the afternoon sun. Apparently, even though whales were mammals, druids who chose them as their avatar were still allowed to join the Piscine clan.

'And the fact that they're here means their patrol hasn't turned up anything,' supplied Lycomedes. 'It is as I expected. The serpents were probably guarding the crossing between Eresa and Delos. Xenokrates must have lured them here when he summoned his crab to get us out to sea.'

'Then they don't know about the presence of the Darkness on Delos yet,' said Selena, rounding on her master. 'We have to tell them so they go can help the Canines.'

'What disturbs me more,' said Lycomedes, 'is why neither Niobe, Helios nor Agelaus have sent people to help us out. They must have heard the sounds of battle. And if all is quiet on their end…'

I watched as the four humpback whales formed a semicircle around the battle scene. There was a level of determination in the Piscines' eyes that seemed to block out all but their serpentine enemies. 'Uhm, guys, what happens if the Piscines interfere?' I asked the group. 'Will Captain Kriton allow it?'

'I'm sure they won't, Aaron,' said Aerope, untroubled. 'The Piscines probably want to make sure that none of the serpents escape.'

There was utter silence except for the continuing battle between the serpents, crabs, and Kriton's water buffaloes. With each of their comrades falling to either horn or pincer, the serpents' rage built to new heights. It was as if the smoke that the destroyed serpents turned into physically added strength to the remaining monsters.

Another serpent uttered its final roar towards the sky and the four that were left watched their companion melt back into the ocean. As the smoke of its dissolved body fused with the surface, my eyes fell on the dozens of the druid bodies behind it, each of them standing in a praying position. With a jolt I realised that Althea was among them as well, even though, at her wishes, she had never officially been recognised as a Piscine.

There was something off in their faces. At first it seemed Aerope was right and the Piscines were just standing guard in case the defeated serpents would reform and attempt to flee underwater. But the longer I looked, the more I had the impression that they were being mind-controlled. Their faces were hard, emotionless, as though something was inhibiting their feelings. Althea looked no different. It gave me the creeps.

As one, the normally invisible auras around the druid bodies coloured blue. Then everywhere I looked, marine animals of every shape and size imaginable poured from the druids' chests, most of them vanishing beneath the surface. This pre-emptive positioning of forces by the Piscines was done with the unassuming air of a crocodile sliding from a riverbank into the water; silently, casually, smoothly.

I could still hear Aerope's reassuring words, but a large part of me no longer believed them. Seemingly on their own accord, my feet took a step backwards. My elbows pushed sideways as though in preparation to sprout feathers. My lips pursed, waiting for the order to turn into a beak. I didn't allow the shapeshifting to continue. But if I wanted to, I was sure I would have been able to take off then and there as easily as running away.

'Captain Cheiron!' said Xenokrates in a majestic voice from on top of the second giant crab. I hadn't even seen him mount it. Kriton was still on the other, cursing the serpents for not continuing the fight now that the area around them was being filled with the oceans' deadliest. This single word was enough for many of the Piscines to turn to Xenokrates. Fear for their leader shone in their eyes.

'There's no way...,' said Selena, breath only and slowly shaking her head. She was a lot quicker on the uptake than Lycomedes and his other apprentices were and still couldn't believe it. 'Captain Cheiron would never betray us.'

Meanwhile, Demonax had leapt onto Kriton's crab and was running across its shell. 'Captain, I'm...!' The sentence ended in a muffled sputtering as Demonax came to a sudden halt, Kriton's hand covering Demonax's face like a squid.

Kriton drew back his hand and growled, 'You better not get in the way.'

'Of course,' said Demonax obediently, wiping his own saliva from his face. Then without showing the slightest hesitation he too rammed his palms into each other and joined his captain by his side.

'I don't understand,' Lycomedes muttered to himself. He was peering into the forest behind us. 'What are the other captains doing over there? The fight is here.'

'I'd better check it out,' said Leander. 'They might not yet know what's happened. With your permission, Master...'

'No, stay,' said Lycomedes. 'There is no sense in going there now. If they indeed haven't heard anything, they must have felt Xenokrates and Kriton raising their energy levels. Something must be happening over there that Demonax didn't know about. Unfortunately, I can't sense the other captains' energy because of Kriton and Xenokrates. I don't know if they are having problems of their own.'

'Maybe they thought the commander was only summoning a crab to take us out to sea,' said Aerope. 'I suppose that was the plan?'

'Who cares what the plan was?' said Briseis, flaring up. 'We have to make a choice, even if Captain Kriton isn't happy with it.'

'Listen,' said Lycomedes, holding up his hand. 'I want to hear this.' Everyone fell silent. The focus was on Xenokrates and the Piscines again.

'What are you up to, Captain Cheiron?' the commander asked, his powerful voice easily carrying across the water. 'Why are you doing this?' It was now clear to everyone that the Piscines had no intention of attacking the Void serpents – and they did nothing in return. By now the sea was teeming with shark fins, killer whales and a variety of fanged fish I couldn't identify, as well as the unmistakable signs of stingrays and a large school of piranhas.

'Do not pretend you don't know, Commander,' said a man with shoulder length hair, twisted into braids. I figured this had to be Captain Cheiron. 'We all know what we are up against. You heard the Linard girl. You heard about her dreams. It's happening, all of it. The beast in flames, the man in feathers, everything.'

'He's talking about Sophia, isn't he?' I asked the group.

'Shh, Aaron,' said Selena. 'I want to hear what they're saying.'

'The girl has a wild imagination, that is all,' said Xenokrates dismissively. 'I order you... No, I *ask* you to reconsider. I know I have been lenient towards our guests, but this is our way. Eresa is first and foremost a sanctuary. Ouranis' teachings...'

'Ouranis has nothing to do with this,' said Cheiron, cutting him off. He gave me the impression the conversation was merely a cursory politeness before whatever he had planned. 'This is about us, about our survival. And yes, you have been lenient.'

Kriton let out a cry of annoyance. 'Stop talkin' nonsense, Cheiron. If you cared about your miserable life you wouldn't be standin' this close to me.'

'I have always had great respect for you, Commander,' said Cheiron, turning away from Kriton, 'but I respect the enemy more.' He paused briefly, then added with finality, 'I regret this has to happen.' He nodded to his left and right. At once, the blue aura around the druids intensified and utter chaos ensued; the battle was in full force once more.

Both crabs began to thrash and fight against the onslaught of marine animals; whatever had made them float earlier was now gone. The serpents joined in and literally had to wade through the pool of wriggling and biting fish bodies in order to get a piece of translucent meat for themselves.

'Selena, Briseis, go!' roared Lycomedes over the sounds of battle. At his command, a phoenix and a bull rhinoceros sprouted from the young women's chests. They had apparently been preparing for this moment while Xenokrates and the Piscine captain exchanged words.

Selena's phoenix went straight for one of the serpents and sore off its head the second it made contact. Briseis' rhinoceros charged towards Kriton and Demonax instead. The translucent beast jumped onto the thrashing crab's shell, continued its way between the two druids and launched itself at a spectral tiger shark dangling from their crab's remaining pincer.

Kriton and his vice-captain jerked back their heads in unison and grinned at Briseis. If either of them had placed one step in the wrong direction they would have been gored by the rhinoceros' horn. But instead of showing anger, they seemed amused by Briseis' disregard for her allies' lives.

'A Bovine,' said Demonax, savouring the word. 'I didn't know Lycomedes was training one.' He exchanged a look with his captain, before they both uttered a warcry and sent an entire stampede of bison and water buffaloes at the beasts that threatened their living raft. Once in the water, the bison and water buffaloes continued to gore at anything within their reach – and that while their masters' energy pushed them inexorably forwards with their minds.

'Aerope, you're with me,' said Lycomedes. Aerope nodded and followed him to the island's edge. There, like an emperor imperiously waving his troops into battle, Lycomedes summoned half a dozen crocodiles. There was a series of splashes before the crocodiles fanned out, snapping at anything that wasn't a bull or crustacean.

From on top of his crab, Xenokrates began pouring out smaller ones. In contrast to their larger kin, the crabs were exceptionally fast and vicious. Seeing them skitter down the giant shell and snap their tiny pincers at their enemies quickly restored the respect I had lost for the commander when I saw the larger crabs fight.

'There must be something we can do,' I told Leander. We were the only two left that hadn't done anything. 'We can't just stand by and watch.'

'There is something you can do,' he said in a curious voice. 'You can close your eyes.'

I turned to look at him, but then something shocked me in a way not even the Void serpents had been able to. Aerope was standing with her back to us. While Lycomedes had been busy summoning his crocodiles, Aerope's aura had turned blue. And now that she had gathered the right amount of energy, a murder of crows, alarmingly familiar, was called into being.

Pelegon..., was the only thing my mind was able to produce over next few seconds, as I watched the crows ascend. In an instant I was back at the ship with Sophia and her father, watching the blue cloud heading our way. *It was her? She executed Pelegon?*

The crows formed a great cloud in the sky and my eyes fell on Xenokrates again. He was amazing. Wave after wave of tiny crabs were sent down the giant crab's shell in rings of clicking pincers. Nothing could even get close to the old man and I could see the frustration building in Cheiron's eyes.

Then the commander and I jumped at the same time; I from shock and Xenokrates from a forceful impact that sent a shockwave through the giant crab on which he stood. A fountain of smaller crabs was launched into the air as a result. As he landed, the old man had only a second to recover when another impact sent him flying again. On the third hit, I saw something huge boring it is way through the slightly softer underbelly of the giant crab. It was as if a maggot the size of a tree was eating its way up through the translucent body.

I couldn't scream. I couldn't yell. Something inside was taking over. This was it. I had to do something. And then I felt my body transform, my muscles change and my senses heighten dramatically. The sight of the black serpent eating its way through the crab's body attained incredible detail, and I could discern one of the serpent's glowing eyes as the light made the crab's wound glisten.

Feathers sprouted all over my body – and it hurt. Inexplicably, my brain was suddenly overcome with agony. I fell down on my spindly owl knees and flapped my wings to prevent my beak from kissing the floor. I had no idea why this was happening, why it was hurting so much. Even worse, I felt utterly exhausted. I could hardly summon the strength to breathe, let alone take off and help the commander.

'Xenokrates, behind you!' said Lycomedes. 'I have a crocodile waiting for you. Use it.'

Lycomedes' voice gave me the strength to lift my head. The pain had made my eyesight bleary. There was indeed a crocodile lying in wait for the commander to jump onto, but there were many creatures waiting for him to try. There was no way he could make it to the bank. Not only that, the serpent that was eating its way through the shell was almost at the top, and I knew by Xenokrates' trembling arms and pained expression that he was using every bit of his power to keep his giant crab from exploding into blue tendrils.

The commander's eyelids drooped. He jerked his head to prevent his body from falling unconscious. He had evidently been trying to keep his giant crab alive by giving it more of his energy, but its tunnel-shaped wound was more demanding than the old man could handle. Age was catching up with him and it was taking every bit of his strength to stall for time. And still he made no move towards the crocodile; he knew the dangers of doing so. There was little more that Lycomedes could do for him, however, for his crocodile couldn't climb the steep shell. And Kriton, Demonax, Selena, Briseis and Aerope were all locked in battles of their own.

A soft voice entered my ear. It was Leander. 'What are you waiting for? You're an owl. Fly.'

As I shot him another look with my bird eyes, the adrenaline kicked in and I pushed myself up. Leander's words and the envious look on his face acted like fuel for my muscles. The pain was pushed into a corner, away from my thoughts. Then I flapped open my wings, hit Leander accidentally in the chest, and took flight.

'Go!' Leander called after me, one hand on his ribs. 'Save him!'

The island was gone within seconds. Then there was nothing but black and blue animals fighting for dominance and, at the centre of my vision, the commander's back. My throat screeched, my wings buffeted the air and my claws seized the old man's robes. I was surprised by his lack of weight – or perhaps the strength of my wings – and together we rocketed skywards.

An explosion of blue energy came from below; the serpent that had been eating its way through the giant crab had finally made it through and the crab had disintegrated as a result. A moment later, Xenokrates let out a cry of pain; something powerful and heavy had grabbed hold.

I felt the old man trying to free one of his legs from the Void serpent's jaws that were gripping his calves. It was too late. Blood had already spilled. And by his frantic muttering I figured Xenokrates was well aware of the consequences. He must have heard all about the Voidshapers and their poisonous bite from Lycomedes and Aristion.

Xenokrates coughed hoarsely. I was still trying to keep us airborne, but there was no getting rid of the serpent. By the time the beast was finally taken care of by Aerope's crows, the commander's legs were already consumed by the Void poison.

Below, people screamed, their voices scrambled into one gut-wrenching noise. 'Xenokrates!'

My claws had completely vanished. They had disappeared into the devouring cloud of black smoke surrounding my cargo. I let go. There was nothing left to be done. The black remains of the old man's body descended onto the blue surface below. His ashes touched then sank beneath the surface, joining the Voidshaper mass. The great druid leader was no more.

Chapter 24

I was hit so hard by the reality of Xenokrates' capture and the feeling of his flesh turning into smoke between my claws, the sounds of battle faded into background noise. Dejectedly I turned and began my way back to the island. I had only traversed a few yards, however, when yet another scream rent my eardrums.

By the sound of her voice, I knew it was Selena. But following the sound, I saw nothing but a giant, black serpent trying to dig its way into the grassy bank like an earthworm attempting to flee into the ground. Its arcing body was wriggling like mad, causing its still-submerged tail to thrash wildly. With a jolt I realised its head was positioned exactly where Selena had been standing last time I saw her.

'Selena, my dear!' Lycomedes exclaimed, as his crocodiles popped out of existence. He seemed too stricken by shock to help her. What the others were doing, I had no idea. All my attention was drawn by the large, grime-sweating serpent head and the pair of phoenix wings that appeared from under it.

Again, Selena screamed, but not for Lycomedes or any of the other druids. She wanted me. 'SHEPHERD!'

All thoughts ceased. I gave a few forceful strokes with my wings, tucked them against my body, and began plummeting towards the ground. Meanwhile, Selena was continuing to keep the maw full of poisonous fangs from puncturing her skin with her summoned phoenix, which was sandwiched between the serpent's gaping jaws and Selena's body.

I had only seconds to think of an attack plan. I shouted that I was on my way, though all that left my throat was an earsplitting shriek. When I reached the arch that was the monster's neck, I readied my claws, opening them for maximum damage. Like a surfer riding a wave, I then planed across the serpent's black skin, whipping up the grime and leaving a trail of black fog behind me.

The serpent snarled in either pain or anger. It did exactly what I hoped and tossed up its head, catapulting me into the air. Several feathers snapped, my flesh felt bruised, though it mattered not. I had only one objective: saving Selena. She, in turn, was watching me tumbling through the air with a worried gaze.

I flapped open my wings, came to a halt, then allowed gravity to take over for a moment. The serpent watched me do it and slowly opened its jaws. But I had seen the attack coming even before the serpent recognised me as a potential meal. It struck, I dodged under it, and before the beast had time to strike again, I had both claws on Selena's belly.

'Shepherd,' Selena whispered admiringly and we locked eyes. During those two seconds it took me to lift my wings, her pupils widened as I blocked out the sun. Then the sand and grass blades blown upwards by my wing strokes disrupted the scene, before we shot away across the bank towards the others. As we did, a herd of transparent animals, consisting of a pair of crocodiles, a rhinoceros, and a murder of crows, passed us from the other direction. When it was safe to do so I let go of Selena, turned, and watched how Lycomedes, Briseis and Aerope took care of my pursuing enemy.

'That's the last of them,' said Lycomedes reassuringly to Aerope and Briseis. They were both panting. I was too, for I had just changed back into my human form and was utterly exhausted, much more so than after my previous attempts. 'Xenokrates…,' Lycomedes added sorrowly, the rest of his sentence inaudible. I watched how a blanket of grief fell over his eyes and felt anger boiling inside.

'You did all you could, Aaron,' said Aerope consolingly, still taking heavy breaths. 'It wasn't your fault.' She paused, then said, 'Selena is alive because of you.'

Selena still hadn't said a word. She was peering down at me with a concoction of emotions I couldn't decipher. I managed a small smile. 'You're welcome,' I told her.

She closed her eyes contentedly. 'I owe you my life… again. Thank you, Aaron.'

Feeling relieved that it was over I turned to the bank, where a loud splashing noise attracted our attention. Kriton hoisted himself onto the low wall that circled the island.

'Spineless worms,' he spat, grinning. At first I thought he meant the Void serpents, but then I realised there was something else missing from the picture; Captain Cheiron and his Piscines weren't here anymore. Apparently, they had left after they saw their commander fall, which I took it to mean they had succeeded in their objective.

'How do you want to proceed, Captain?' asked Demonax, coming up behind him. He evidently shared Kriton's opinion of the Piscines and didn't seem to expect, nor care for, a hand to help him up the bank. Both he and Kriton had clearly expected an act of treachery like this to come to light eventually, and it was evident from the expressions of the others that Xenokrates would still be with us if the Piscines hadn't showed up. His blood was on their hands, not mine.

'Kriton,' said Lycomedes, approaching the Bovine captain, 'this can't have been all they planned. Cheiron wouldn't oppose the clans on his own.'

Kriton shrugged and finished readjusting his druid toga. He straightened up, appeared to make up his mind on the spot, and said, 'If there're more, we'll crush them too.' His hands glowed blue even before he pressed his palms together. Demonax imitated him without a moment's thought. 'You,' Kriton said with a nod to Briseis, 'if you want in on the spoils, I suggest you follow.'

Briseis gulped; despite her love for the charge, she didn't necessarily share her future captain's lust for blood.

'Not so fast,' said Lycomedes. Kriton shot him a nettled look and Lycomedes' lower lip twitched. 'Can you take the lot of us with you?'

'Master,' said Selena, 'don't you think we should warn the other captains first? They also need to know about Commander Xenokrates.'

'We shouldn't split up, Selena,' said Lycomedes. 'There is no way to tell who is still with us. Cheiron's betrayal made that very clear. Our best chance is to team up with Flego and Krixi and move as a group.' The old man looked at me, obviously fishing for support.

'Flego and Krixi would never side with the Darkness,' I told him confidently, 'no matter the odds. But I haven't been able to make contact with them yet.' Then I added loud enough for everyone to hear, Kriton in particular, 'They are probably still engaged in battle with the Darkness. And considering what we just experienced, maybe with druids as well.'

Now Kriton gave me a look that reflected Demonax' earlier words perfectly, that staying with me was his best chance of finding a battle worth living for. This was exactly the result he had hoped for. The captain did a quick headcount, then said, 'All right, you lazy peacocks. Have it your way. Demonax, give me two.'

Not ten seconds later, two bison and three water buffaloes stood gazing puppet-like at their masters. We all took our seats, Kriton and his vice-captain each taking a bovine of their own while the rest of us shared the other three.

'Bishop,' said Lycomedes from on top of his and Selena's water buffalo as our mounts picked up speed, 'no matter what your brain is feeding you, Aerope was right. You truly did all you could.' Selena behind him evidently felt the same way.

'And that's exactly the problem, isn't it?' I told them. 'It *was* my best.' *But not my last*, I went on in silence, steeling my resolve. *I'm coming, Denise, even if I have to sprout wings again and fly.*

We made our way to the crossing on the western side of the island, our bovine transports taking no heed to the fact that sweeping branches and travellers on their backs equated to lot of scrapes and bruises. There continued to be no sign of the Piscines anywhere along the coast. Making sure neither Kriton nor Demonax heard him, Lycomedes suggested they might have gone ashore further east and gone back into Eresa. This only added to the general desire to escape and regroup; our last fight had drained much of our reserve and without backup we couldn't risk the chance of checking in with the other captains. As Lycomedes said, any or all of them would have to be considered enemies at this point.

Lycomedes and his crocodiles helped us the last bit of the way to Delos. During the crossing, I resumed my attempts to contact Flego and Krixi. I didn't understand why I couldn't achieve it. *During our last battle together I had no problem connecting with them*, I reasoned. *So why now? They can't be that far away, can they?*

'Aaron, look,' said Selena softly as we walked up the grassy beach. 'It's Sophia and Denise. They... appear to be fine,' she added in mild surprise.

We halted. The top of the hill up ahead was white with druids. Amidst them stood a young girl with long, black hair that provided a stark contrast with the flapping druid robes on either side of her. And at the tips of her fingers, a black hyena stood gazing down at us, mouth hanging open. I looked at Selena. She gave me a weak smile.

'I told you they would be all right,' said Aerope behind me. 'Captain Ione is with them.'

Neither Sophia nor Denise showed any particular haste to greet me. After they spotted us, they and the Canines came walking casually down the hill. About half way, Sophia moved her lips in an inaudible whisper and the next thing I knew, Denise was sprinting towards me, black ooze gushing from her body with every leaping stride. Everything else simply disappeared. It blurred, then faded, until there was nothing left but my monstrous girlfriend bounding towards me.

My moment of tranquillity was briefly disrupted by Kriton uttering a disgusted noise, followed by Lycomedes blocking him to prevent him from attacking. I did my best to ignore them. 'Denise...,' I said, my voice cracking and my arms widening. I was so glad to see her again that her sudden interest in me didn't register as being weird. *Thank God, you're okay.*

'I'm fine,' replied a voice in my head, which was unmistakably my girlfriend's. The words affected me like a shot of adrenaline, and my mouth fell open. 'It's not your imagination, Aaron. It's really me.' Instead of throwing herself into my arms, Denise came to a gradual halt in front of me. Perhaps she was afraid she would accidentally scratch me and turn me into a Voidshaper. I didn't mind in the slightest. I couldn't care less about anything but her spirit, her voice, our connection. She was here, finally, but...

H–How can this be? I thought. Even my thoughts stuttered. *How can suddenly talk to me?*

'Sophia,' she said simply. Sophia, who was drawing steadily closer behind her, had a satisfied smile on her face. Her health seemed to have steadily improved over the last week, which had done wonders for her appearance. She was actually quite a pretty girl. 'She's been incredible, Aaron,' said Denise telepathically. 'She's prevented me from becoming one of them. And she's helped you with your new abilities.'

You know about my Shepherd abilities?

Her voice dropped. 'It hasn't been easy. This... existence is beyond anything I can describe. At times I didn't know where I was or who the voices that I could hear belonged to. I think I even zoned out occasionally, because sometimes I couldn't remember how I got to where I was. I still do, sometimes. My experience of time has also become rather odd. But for the most part, I like to think I was with you and Sophia. Without her, I would surely have gone over to the other side. Aaron, I've seen the place I was supposed to go, a dark place. Sophia acted as the light that guided me away and brought me back to you every time I lost control.'

It's... so hard to believe. To be honest I didn't know what to think for almost the entire time we've been here. This may sound rude, but you barely seemed to recognise me most of the time. And when it seemed like you did, I thought I imagined it. When did this start? Where were we when Sophia first made contact with you?

'The underground lake. According to Sophia, Ouranis did something to her that pushed her mind into a state of being similar to mine. We were trapped between this world and the one created by the Voidshapers. Eventually she showed me the way back to this world, and then I assisted her from our end when I was back with you at the lake.'

With a jolt the image came back to me of Denise standing inside the cave with her paw on Sophia's chest. Sophia woke up soon after. *That's the first time I thought I saw a connection*, I realised.

'And since then she's been battling the conversion that's going on inside my body to keep me from turning,' Denise added.

So Ouranis brought the two of you together? This must have happened when she touched Sophia inside her den. The Voidshapers discovered our location because of it. But then, who is she really? She is not a normal girl, that's for sure.

'I know what you think, Aaron. She had to do quite a bit of convincing to make me come with her, believe me. I thought she was trying to trick me to stop fighting. But I trust her now, and so should you. She's done a lot to help you as well. She's activated your abilities every time you needed them. She told me all about it. She helped you break me out of that temple by telling Selena about the druid Aristion's arrival in Eresa. Sophia had overheard him talking to the guard, so she hurried back to Eresa and told Selena about it. Then she went with Selena to the temple and helped you transform for the first time to escape those bees. Later she did the same when you were about to be questioned by the druid Council. And then a final time when the Voidshapers had captured Ouranis and we were about to lose you to that Voidshaper crocodile.'

That was all her? But how could she? Who is she?

'She is with us and she is with the Voidshapers. She's been acting as a double agent. Sophia has been branded from birth by the Voidshapers to act as a kind of sleeper agent to find the last Celestial Beast, Ouranis. We've talked a lot about it, particularly since we got back from our journey. But she needed things to play out before I could talk to you. And we needed you to focus on your training.'

She needed things to play out? I felt frustration mounting. *What's that supposed to mean? You mean you could talk to me the entire time and you chose not to?*

'Not because I didn't want to,' Denise snapped back. 'Of course I did. And it is only since a couple of days that your abilities have developed enough for me to talk to you. That's when Sophia told me I shouldn't, at least not yet.'

I can't believe you allowed her to control you like that. You, of all people.

'I owe her my life, Aaron. Please, hear me out. Sophia explained that the reason why she can connect with your abilities is because Ouranis has once been part of the Voidshaper collective. According to her, the Voidshapers have tried to use Ouranis' abilities, but failed to do so. And, after Ouranis escaped, they've been looking for her ever since. Not much of Ouranis' spirit remained behind when she got out, but Sophia told me it was enough to open some kind of connection with you. And it enabled her to accelerate the development of your abilities so we could eventually talk to each other.' There was a pause, then, 'It's been a very confusing time, but an interesting one too. Although you probably don't think that. Knowing you, you've done nothing but worry since you saw me change. I'm so sorry I couldn't talk to you before now, Aaron. Sophia said it was important.'

So you really think we can trust her? How do you know she is not fooling us? And what about everything else that has happened, the death of her father, for example? It barely fazed her, or most of the time. Pelegon was her father, wasn't he?

'Like I said, children like Sophia have only partly been taken over by the Voidshapers, which means that part of their original, human personality survives, as do her emotions. There have been occasions where I too had difficulty connecting with her. Her personality is split in two. And knowing that the alien part belongs to an entire host of voices, I think it's a miracle she even makes sense at all. Well, mostly,' she added more to herself.

During our talk, all around us people had become restless. I had heard something like, "Let them have a moment", followed by an outburst from Kriton, who mentioned Captain Cheiron and the Piscines. At least Lycomedes' laboured breathing was returning to normal. Others, like Selena, were using the time to catch their breath as well. Luckily there was no sign of any Voidshapers yet.

You said, "children like Sophia", I thought. *Does this mean there are more Sophias?*

'Frankly, I don't know,' said Denise. 'I heard Sophia mention, "children like me", once. So yes, it's probably safe to assume she's not the only one.'

I felt a hand on my shoulder. It was Lycomedes. He didn't speak, but didn't need to. His hand was enough to send a soothing wave of comfort across the surface of my brain, taking all tension with it. The look he offered told me he had a fair idea of what was going on. I gave him a nod.

Well, thank God I finally had the chance to talk to you again. I must admit I was losing hope that you were even still in there. I thought you might be floating around in the Vault of Spirits.

'Trust me, I know. I've seen how difficult it has been for you, and again I'm sorry I couldn't talk to you sooner.

Yes, about that. Has Sophia told you why you couldn't talk to me? You said you've been able to a couple of days now.

'She said it would generate too much bias against you if the druids knew you could communicate with… a Voidshaper. You're their Shepherd now, and we felt it would be better if you didn't do anything that could damage their trust in you.'

But you said earlier that Sophia helped me transform a couple of times and that the final time was during our fight against the Hive, the crocodile I mean.

'That's right.'

Then that must be the reason why it hurt so much and drained me of my energy when I transformed to save Xenokrates, I reasoned. *It was the first time I did it myself.*

Denise had evidently heard me. 'You're saying transformed on your own? Today?'

I did. But listen, Denise. There is something else I need to talk to you about, something important.

In the corner of my eye, Kriton and Demonax were walking along the beach, probably in search for any sign of the Piscines. Lycomedes kept a close eye on them. He had released me – he probably thought his message was clear – and was now trying to keep Selena and the others from getting any rash ideas before they had a clear picture of what was going on.

'Yes?' said Denise.

There have been some weird things going on inside Eresa, I thought, turning back to her. *There have been disappearances among the Piscines and the Canines, which have caused quite some unrest among the druids. And now the Piscines have rebelled against their leader, Xenokrates. They killed him, or helped kill him in any case. But more importantly, and this is the weirdest thing of all, there seems to have been another girl like Sophia inside Eresa. Lycomedes and I thought it best not to ask around too much for the time being because of the threat that the Voidshapers posed. He wanted the druids to be focused on the task at hand and not make the situation any more confusing. Luckily for Sophia, she and this other girl haven't been seen together, which helped to make everyone think the girl and Sophia were one and the same. This can't be true, obviously. She was with us. But when we were away, this other Sophia appears to have spread lies about us, and especially Lycomedes, among the druids. Do you know anything about this?*

'You mean do I know if there is another girl with looks identical to Sophia? Not that I know of. But you probably know more about the druids than I do.'

And you didn't notice anything odd about her since we left on the boat? Any change in her personality perhaps?

'Not that I can remember. Like I said, her personality switches sometimes when her masters try to regain control. It makes her very confused when they do, emotional even, and she can react quite… explosively I guess you could say.'

Our conversation was cut short by a roar that could only have come from one source. It vibrated my brain with a ferocity only a lion's throat could produce. 'SHEPHERD!'

My own mind yelled back in shock. *Flego!* The mental connection between us strengthened and Flego's thoughts shouldered their way into my mind, shoving Denise out of the first air lock it could find. *Where are you? What's happened?*

'Do not trust her, human!' he said, throwing the words at me. His voice was frantic, as though he had only moments to get his message across. 'Do not trust the girl! I'm telling you!' In a smaller voice, he added, 'That's good, Krixi. Do it again.'

What's going on? Why shouldn't I trust her? Flego? All was silent again. *Flego!*

An uproar of cracking wood carried across the hills. It was like handful of bulldozer drivers were rampaging through the forest. In the midst of it, Sophia's composed voice popped up. 'He's free,' she announced to the group at large. 'I can't keep him any longer.'

Eerily reminiscent of the fight with the Piscines, the harmonious sound of dozens of hands smacking into each other filled the air; Captain Ione and her fellow Canines were responding to Sophia's statement. The next thing I knew, dogs, jackals, wolves, foxes, coyotes, and even raccoons poured from the druids' chests, forcing everyone back to the waterline. Everyone except Kriton and his vice-captain, that is. They were already there. They turned to face the scene with the interest of a couple of teenage boys reading a review of a new sci-fi blockbuster.

'Don't do anything,' said Lycomedes, commanding his troops. 'Don't give them any unnecessary incentive. We can't win against this many.' For the next few seconds I couldn't see anything but hundreds of bared, translucent fangs. Aerope behind me hissed through clenched teeth.

'Rabid dogs,' growled Kriton, his grin fading. His hands were glowing and a blue chain ignited between them. 'Cowards, all of them. Do you see this, Demonax? Runnin' away with their tails between their legs, same as those fishbreaths.' He raised his voice, which turned even more threatening. 'I'll have your head, Ione! Just you and me, to the death! The rest of those dogfarts can either watch or die like the worms that they are.'

Ione watched her Bovine colleague summon a single water buffalo, her face unreadable. 'That is not how it's going to be, Captain Kriton,' she said, her voice resolute. 'Not this time.'

'Oh, it is,' said Kriton through grinning teeth. 'That fishbreath may have escaped, but not you… Certainly not you.' He jumped onto his buffalo and looking utterly unhinged, he bellowed, 'I'll rip apart your face!'

Kriton charged. The summoned canine beasts crouched down and bared their teeth in anger, but gave no quarter. Then a cheerful screech cut through the sound of thundering hooves and the entire scene was thrown into even greater turmoil by a powerful gush of wind, courtesy of my favourite Gryphon; Flego and Krixi had come.

Most of the canine beasts were blown off their paws, yet the many pounds of muscle of Kriton and his spectral mount made him virtually unbeatable by anything less than a hurricane. He continued his mad charge heedless to anything going on around him.

Kriton stooped low against the wind, his chin hovering between the tips of his buffalo's horns. Then, like a meteor descending from the sky, Flego landed in the strip of no man's land between both parties. Kriton charged right under his wing without the slightest hesitation.

Behind Flego, Ione and her druids had recovered from the gush of wind and I watched the Canine captain powering up. As had been the case with Xenokrates, Ione's blue aura began to expand far beyond her body. I found myself holding my breath out of fear of what kind of otherworldly creature was about to be called forth.

'Bring it, Ione!' roared Kriton, feeding on the mixture of emotions displayed around him. 'If you think size is goin' to matter, you're dead wrong. Now come at me with everythin' you've got!'

The Canine captain was too late. Kriton and his buffalo tore through several of the summoned dogs and jackals. At the last moment of the charge, Kriton jumped and plunged his outstretched elbow into Ione's face. There was a crack, a spout of blood, and she was knocked backwards, hands groping for her nose.

'That's it?' Kriton asked tauntingly, raising himself to his feet. A trickle of blood seeped down his forearm – Ione's blood. 'I won't finish you until you've shown me your full power, *Captain*. Now get up and feed me your worst!'

Flego, what is going on? I asked, my eyes having difficulty leaving the fight. *Why couldn't I contact you before?*

'It's the human girl,' said the Manticore, stepping aside to reveal Sophia. She was standing quite still, collected. Between her and Flego, Denise was having difficulty deciding what to do, a decision only made more difficult by Flego's scrutinising gaze. 'I don't know how she did it, but she trapped my thoughts in some kind of dark place,' he said. 'I can't explain it. I thought I had been taken by the Voidshapers again. You'll have to ask her if she can still talk when I'm finished with that thing. But enough of that,' he added conversationally. He apparently couldn't help but be lured by the battle between Kriton and Ione. 'What's this? Are the druids fighting each other?'

I know, it's crazy. Some of the clans have rebelled, the Piscines, Canines, maybe others too. They already killed Xenokrates.

'Ah,' said Flego disappointedly. 'I liked the old man. He was a strong one.'

You better watch out, Flego, I thought, nodding at the small army of druids and their pets, who had ignored the battle between the captains and turned to us instead. Now that their captain had taken her Bovine colleague for a private lesson, the druids' confidence was visibly building. I already knew the Canines were by far the largest clan in Eresa, but only now that I saw them as actual enemies did I fully appreciate how many of them there were. The druids and the packs of wolves and jackals were already closing the gap that Kriton had punched through their ranks.

'Them?' said Flego, amused. 'Those doggies can't hope to defeat me.'

Krixi landed on my other side. 'They won't, nope, nope. Fleger will stamp on doggies like this.' She seized a bundle of grass with her eagle claws and stamped onto the ground with one of her lion legs. 'And use his skull crusher like that.' With that she stamped onto the ground with her other hind leg.

In the corner of my eye, Denise was inching backwards away from us. 'Denise, where are you going?' I said out loud before repeating the question in my head. Even as I spoke, I became even more frustrated; I was becoming sick of stumbling in the dark. Mysteries were one thing, but enough was enough.

'Sophia!' I called out, forcing her to look at me. Her face was inscrutable, innocent, which only added to my irritation. 'What the hell is going on? What do you want? Whose side are you on? Tell me!'

Denise had stopped halfway between us. Everybody except for Captains Kriton and Ione were watching the scene unfold. Both sides were waiting for either Lycomedes or Sophia to give a command; judging by the way the druids looked at her, it did indeed seem that Sophia was in charge on their end, not Captain Ione. And even if their captain did still have some authority, she was being kept busy by Kriton, who was driving her further up the hill in a battle of horns versus fangs.

Sophia simply stared at me, saying nothing. 'Please tell us why you are doing this,' I said, my voice dropping already; Sophia's look of innocence was disarming. 'Denise has told me what happened. I know all about your efforts to bring us together. So why all this? Why bring the druids into this?'

When Sophia finally opened her mouth to speak, I realised we hadn't actually spoken that much with each other, ever. We were so vastly different that developing a relationship with her was a trying process. And when we did converse, not only was the conversation almost entirely one-sided, Pelegon's horrific death also posed a huge barrier to our interaction. It was a memory that had played and replayed in my mind many times over. And every time I looked at Sophia I heard that same yell in my ears, wintry, demanding, unforgiving.

'We are the same, Aaron Bishop,' said Sophia, her voice soft and kind. 'We belong together. You, me, Denise, Ouranis, Flego, Krixi, Anatin, Lykofos, Iliakos, Kaio, Akhenaten. We are family.'

Flego let out such a roar that, had the foxes and dogs around us spirits of their own, it would surely have sent them yelping away in fear, tails between their legs. Sophia's hair whipped backwards, flapping wildly in the wind, and came to rest on her shoulders once more when Flego's lungs were empty.

Flego, please don't, I thought. *We need answers.*

'That wretched thing!' spat Flego. 'She has no right.'

'It is nothing to be afraid of,' Sophia went on, ignoring Flego. 'It is who we are.'

I didn't know some of the names Sophia mentioned. But judging by Flego's reaction, as well as the fact that together with Ouranis, Flego and Krixi they counted seven, I thought they must belong to the other Celestial Beasts. And then there was Akhenaten, whose name I probably least expected to pass Sophia's lips.

'No, it's not,' I said. 'Do you have any idea who this Akhenaten was? How do you know that name anyway?'

'We are part of him,' said Sophia, touching her belly like I had seen Selena do on many an occasion. 'All of us. We are his legacy.'

'You mean the Voidshapers?' I asked.

Sophia nodded. 'And Ouranis and Flego, Krixi, and all the others. We belong together.'

'No, you're wrong.' In that instant, everything Ouranis had told me about the misguided Egyptian pharaoh came flooding back. 'Akhenaten never wanted to create the Voidshapers. He wanted to create a creature that symbolised the Sun so everyone could worship it. He wanted to create a Sphinx. And he used the goddess Isis' divine powers to do it. Ouranis told me about it. Flego and Krixi and Ouranis are all created with Isis' energy, not Akhenaten's. I don't know where the Voidshapers came from, but they didn't come from Isis, that's for sure. They did,' I said, pointing at Flego and Krixi.

Saying it out loud and explaining it to someone else was even weirder than hearing it from Ouranis. I couldn't believe I was actually talking about an Egyptian goddess as though she was a real person. Then again, I had never believed in Phoenixes and Manticores either, let alone creatures with skin like congealed ink. And this was certainly not the time to deliberate this, especially since Sophia's expression told me she was done chatting. She may be conflicted, but she was also dead serious.

Sophia fell silent. I thought I saw a hint of doubt displayed in her eyes, but it was overshadowed by something I couldn't decipher.

'Sophia,' I said tentatively, hoping that what was holding her back was emotional weakness. I touched Lycomedes with my shoulder to make sure he was paying attention. 'You miss him, don't you? Pelegon.'

Sophia's eyes flicked towards me. Her irises were of the darkest brown, almost black.

'He loved you, Sophia,' I said. 'Do you remember when he stole the ship to get you away from Eresa? Do you remember why he did that, why he took the risk?' Sophia remained silent, her eyes glued to my face. So I pressed on. 'He wanted to create a life for the two of you. He wanted to leave this place and spend his days with you, together. You remember that, don't you? He didn't trust the druids, the same druids that are standing behind you. He knew of their pasts, of what they were capable of. He was afraid of them.'

'Bishop,' Lycomedes said warningly. I shook my head to stop him from interfering.

Now Aerope stepped in, her voice but a whimpering whisper. 'I'm so sorry, Aaron.' She came to stand next to me, her head bowed in shame. 'Pelegon Linard… My mother didn't have a choice. She was ordered by the Council to execute…'

'That's enough,' I whispered a little more harshly than I meant to. She looked up at me and once again I shook my head. 'Please, let me handle this.'

'It was them who killed Pelegon, Sophia,' I said, hooking Sophia's eyes. 'They say they did it because he stole the ship, but the real reason is that they are afraid of the world out there, the same world the Voidshapers are planning to destroy. And they will as soon as the Voidshapers find a way to mine. Those things,' I said with an apologetic glance at Denise, 'don't care about anything but themselves. Pelegon did. Do you remember what happened next?'

'Ouranis,' said Sophia in a voice that was barely audible. She lowered her gaze to the hyena standing between us. 'Denise…'

'Yes. I brought you to Ouranis and she brought the two of you together. You and Denise. You saved her from the Hive. You saved our future together. And you helped me on several occasions. Why did you do that? Why did you accelerate the development of my abilities?'

Sophia's stare found me again. Black droplets had formed in the corners of her eyes and were beginning to fill her eyelids. One of the Canine druids saw it happen. He started, causing one of the foxes sandwiched between a pair of wolves to vanish into thin air, but stayed his ground. By his reaction I knew this wasn't the first time he had seen Sophia display her darker side.

'It was my purpose,' confessed Sophia. 'She needed me to.'

'Who? Who told you to do it?'

'I cannot speak her name,' she whispered, her eyes growing. 'She forbids it.'

I looked at Lycomedes, who raised his shoulders in confusion. 'Have you ever seen her?' I asked. Sophia nodded. 'What does she look like?' Sophia said nothing. With a trembling finger she pointed at Flego. 'She's a Manticore?'

Flego recoiled, his eyes livid. 'It's her!'

I'm sorry?

'The Sphinx,' said Flego. This was the first time I had heard fear in his voice and it was smothered with it. 'She's real. She's alive.'

What? You mean the Sphinx Akhenaten wanted to create? How can it be alive? I thought it split up and gave birth to you and your brothers and sisters.

Once more, as it had several times since I first heard it, my memory of the female, inhuman voice that had spoken to me inside the lagoon replayed. "Weakness spawns folly. Weakness… spawns folly. You know, do you not, *young Shepherd?*" The empty, mechanical chuckle sounded, then, "So entertaining. Come, bring her to me and together we'll play."

But despite Ouranis' wishes, or perhaps because of them, I couldn't ignore it this time. Had this voice actually belonged to a real-life Sphinx? I did know the Greeks imagined the Sphinx as a female creature, but again, Pharaoh Akhenaten was Egyptian, not Greek. And the Egyptian Sphinx was male. What was going on?

'That's what we thought too,' said Flego, overriding my current thoughts of the Sphinx. 'We too thought we had been created from the essence of the Sphinx's body. Until my brother Anatin – you haven't met him yet – noticed another strong mind like ours. The Voidshapers attacked soon after, so we've never been able to discover who this mind belonged to, or if it had been there at all. Anatin was still getting used to his abilities. We all were.'

'Bishop, care to fill us in too?' Lycomedes asked. 'What's going on?'

'Hold on, Lycomedes,' I said. 'Sophia, is this… person… the one who controls the Voidshapers?' Sophia's head bowed, which I took as confirmation. 'Does she control you as well?'

Sophia's head remained bowed. I couldn't see her face. There was only a thick mane of black hair. Droplets of black ink started pelting the grass in front of her. The Canine druids behind her were getting anxious and those closest to Sophia took a step backwards, knocking into others.

Anxiety spread through the ranks of the druid army like a virus. The druids continued to back away as though unsure whether they were about to receive an order to attack or a one-way trip to the Voidshaper collective. Somehow, over the past week, or perhaps more if the stories involving the second Sophia were true, the girl standing between us had generated a frighteningly amount of fear and respect among the druids.

'Sophia, please, talk to me,' I said. 'Explain it to us.'

Denise, who had been watching Sophia wrestle with whatever forces were dividing her, flicked her head towards me. Fangs bared, she uttered a snarl that shattered every positive feeling I had for her. Frantically picking up the pieces in my mind I bumped into Briseis and Leander standing behind me. *Denise, what are you doing? It's me.*

Now another voice came from behind, a female one. People had apparently emerged from the forest of Eresa on the opposite shore. 'Lycomedes, what is going on over there?' one of them asked.

'Mother?' said Aerope, wheeling around. I gave the woman standing on the opposite bank a fleeting look and recognised her as the Avian captain, Cyrene. She was accompanied by several of her druids, all wearing sashes of white. I figured they must have been lured here by the battle between Captains Kriton and Ione.

'Human!' called Flego. He stepped in front of me, his paw acting as a shield. From behind I watched how the air around Sophia, or perhaps her aura, became dark. I still couldn't see her face because of her hair. Nor could I wait for the outcome of the transformation; from beyond the hill behind which Kriton and Ione had disappeared a while back, a horde of Void crabs and scorpions, each the size of one of Briseis' rhinoceroses, came stampeding towards us. Their pincers were large enough to behead even Flego with a single snap.

'Krixi, stay here!' said Flego. 'Protect the humans. These ones are mine.'

'I will,' said Krixi happily, watching Flego push off. 'Fleger will have fun!'

Sophia's hair was whipped from her face by Flego's wings. Her eyes were closed. Her cheeks gleamed black with inky tears. The dark aura around her persisted. Seemingly in slow motion, her eyes opened and she stared straight back at me. When she spoke, her words were like ice. 'Kill them.'

My eyes remained locked with hers. I couldn't look away. Behind the girl, the retreating Canine army began to creep forwards again. It was as they hoped. They were in. They had orders to abide to. Nothing had changed. But for me, everything was going wrong. What had been so wondrous moments earlier was all falling apart. I felt like the responsibility of Lycomedes, Selena, Briseis, Leander, Aerope, and even Demonax was all resting on me. Sophia was my obligation. After I saved her from the druids' execution, I had brought her with me every step of the way. I had taken care of her the best I could. And now she was going to betray me?

As more and more canine beasts were summoned into being, my insides screamed in defiance. My mouth responded and out came a roar of pure fury. 'SOPHIA!'

The adrenaline inside my body was mixed with something else, something alien, I couldn't identify. I didn't care. Everything inside me burned, burning with the desire to keep my friends from suffering from my mistake. This was not going to happen. Not if I had a say in it.

The ground beneath my feet groaned and shivered; Flego had initiated his attack against the advancing Voidshapers. The shockwave acted as a powerful catalyst, shaking my body into motion. Wings, beak, claws, feathers, seemingly in the span of a pin drop my body transformed. It was ready to fly, but this time, it wasn't to save my own skin. I had to get Sophia away from here, for everyone's sake.

The scene around Sophia's face faded. She had observed my shapeshifting with a loving smile that broadened with every feather that sprouted from my body. It was like she was actually willing whatever was going to happen next.

There was no time to think. Out of pure instinct I lunged forwards, digging my claws into the earth. My wings beat the air once, twice, and I found myself inches from my target. I grabbed her waist in both claws and took off, aiming for the open skies. Behind me I heard Lycomedes yell to his students. They were to climb onto his crocodiles, but by no means engage the Canines. The pounding of bison hooves told me Demonax had his own plans for the battle.

Krixi, take Leander and find the other captains, I thought, hoping she was still listening. *There are bound to be some who are still on our side. Leander will know what to tell them.* Leander's cry of surprise made any response from Krixi unnecessary, a cry that dissipated with the speed of a whistling arrow.

Suddenly a dark shadow cast overhead. The sun was gone, blocked out by a ring of Void bats that had come out of nowhere. The ticking noise from the bats' echolocation was loud in my ears, as was the flapping of their many wings. Sophia and I were surrounded. I heard a curse form in my head. It was immediately pushed aside by Sophia's thoughts. They were as clear as Ouranis' had been, yet smoother and more delicate. 'Dive under them,' she said telepathically. 'They won't hurt us.'

What about the others? The Canines... Denise...

'Denise will survive. She is strong. You need this. Now go.'

The fact that she didn't resist did strike me as odd, but I couldn't be bothered with it; depriving the Canine army of their leader was all that mattered. At the very least it brought Lycomedes the time to summon another crocodile fleet and get my friends to safety.

What shall I do with her? I thought when we had cleared the ring of Void bats. I was already imagining myself dropping her off somewhere secluded and continue our conversation in a more private setting; there were still quite some questions I wanted to ask her.

The telepathic link between us was apparently still open, for Sophia answered, albeit in a fading, wispy voice. 'Go... the den... Ouranis... They can't see...'

What are you talking about? Who can't see? The Voidshapers? Sophia's head lolled backwards. She appeared to have fainted. *Fine, have it your way. It's as safe a place as any, I suppose.*

Once at the volcano, my wings brought us up past the bare exterior, sped us down the main vent and finally brought us to a full stop at the centre of the crystal chamber. Carefully I laid down Sophia's body, her head making contact with the crystal first before the rest followed.

Sophia, can you hear...? I began before another female voice entered my mind. The voice was so powerful; it was as if the crystal coating on the inner surface of the chamber had amplified the signal a hundred times. I felt my body collapse a second later.

'Young Shepherd...'

Chapter 25

First there was nothing but darkness. I was standing on something solid, but there was nothing but blackness everywhere. Then a light appeared in the distance, a tiny sparkle. It raced towards me, enveloped me with a white light, expanded, then showed me a live image beyond my wildest dreams.

Before me stood Ouranis, not translucent but colourful, and even more magnificent than the version I had seen with my waking eyes. Her eyes were vibrant, proud, beaming. And even though her beak didn't allow one to form, I could feel the power of her smile.

To her left and sharing her massive size stood a creature composed of a lion, a goat and a snake. It had a lion's body with head attached, an extra goat's head sprouting from its back, and an additional snake head attached to its tail. All three heads bore an expression of the utmost dissatisfaction with their current situation; they didn't seem particularly happy to be put on display like this.

On Ouranis' right, and just as enormous, stood a creature I was quite familiar with, albeit only from pictures. It was a beautiful white horse with great eagle wings. The creature reminded me strongly of the full moon: its mane shone like the orb of the nightly skies.

'This is my brother Kaio, the Chimera, and Lykofos, the Pegasus,' said Ouranis. 'And behind you,' I turned around, 'is Anatin. He is the one who made this meeting possible.'

My mouth fell open. Here stood a creature so odd and amazingly beautiful at the same time, I was rendered utterly speechless. His front part was that of a horse and his back was a fish – or maybe a sea snake. Even more impressive than his shape was the colour of his skin, which was nothing like those of his siblings. He appeared to be made of blue silver, like water turned solid without the coldness or the brittleness of ice.

And he is…? I asked when I regained control over my thoughts.

'A Hippocampus,' said Ouranis. I nodded, but couldn't keep my eyes off him. 'Young Shepherd, we do not have much time.'

Yes, of course. I turned to face her.

'We have been trying to communicate with you for a while now,' said Ouranis. Kaio and Lykofos gave each other a look that told me they didn't necessarily feel included in this group effort. 'Anatin possesses the ability to pass through mental or physical defences or obstacles in ways others might think impossible. We have been waiting for you to use your Shepherd abilities, and by doing so, open a connection with me. We are grateful you didn't wait too long. I was afraid you would be reluctant to do so because of what happened to my body. I can assure you, however, that I am fine and you should concern yourself solely with your own survival. Naturally we've tried to open a connection from our end, several times in fact, but the only thing we managed to do was transfer a portion of Lykofos' energy. How does your shoulder feel?'

The shoulder? It's fine. I turned to the Pegasus. *Did you have something to do with that?*

Lykofos inclined his head, but it was Ouranis who answered in words. 'I was able to pick up the trauma on your body through our energy link,' she said. 'I asked my brother if he could help.'

Thank you, Lykofos, I thought, mirroring the nod he gave me, albeit deeper and slower. *So does this mean you are all together?*

'We are, in a way,' said Ouranis. 'Or we will be until the Hive requires one of our abilities, which are intrinsically linked with our beings. As I mentioned to you before, when the Hive acquires access to them, our spirits relocate, and we have to find each other again. It happened to one of us not too long before I was reabsorbed.'

Do you know what caused it?

'I do not. However, it must have something to do with Iliakos' ability, for it is he who disappeared. I trust it will not take us too long to find him again.'

Then he must be the Cockatrice.

'You have a good memory, young Shepherd.'

I had a good teacher, I corrected her, my voice honest. We both fell silent for a spell. Our emotional moment was interrupted, first by a mental image of Flego and Krixi reacting to me when I would tell them about this unexpected rendezvous, then by another voice entering my head. I saw the Pegasus move her head to Ouranis, though when he spoke, his lips remained sealed.

'Think about the time, Ouranis,' said Lykofos. 'If the Hive needs either Anatin's ability or yours, this meeting is over.'

'Yes,' said Ouranis, a little flustered. 'Very well. We will have to make this quick, young Shepherd. First, I want to correct some misconceptions I had about the Hive, which might aid you in your dealings with the Voidshapers. Do you remember why I needed us to go to the location of the Hive?'

Of course. You said the Hive had moved and you were afraid of losing your connection with Flego. And for me to help you, we needed to be closer. Your brother and sister are doing fine, by the way.

Ouranis bowed her head. 'We know. They have not been reabsorbed during the time that I have been here. Then am I correct to assume you managed to provide them with suitable bodies when you pulled them out?'

Suitable... The question sounded so odd to my ears, it took me a moment to figure out what she meant. Then I remembered Ouranis once telling me that she used her own energy to create the translucent bodies the animal spirits inhabited after she pulled them from the Vault of Spirits. *I did, actually,* I thought to my own amazement. *I haven't even thought about that.*

'It is only to be expected,' said Ouranis. 'When the Voidshapers absorbed us, they took our bodies, but we retained most of our energy. It is for this reason that, when the Hive requires the use of our abilities, it has to actively seek access to them. For our abilities are linked to our spirits, not our bodies. And so is our energy. I am proud of you, young Shepherd. I could not have achieved it on my own. Now, how long has it been since you extracted Flego and Krixi?'

A little over a week. Eight days, I believe. Yes, eight. The rollercoaster of the past few weeks made it difficult to put timeframes on the mountain of memories piled up in my mind.

'I see.'

'Eight days?' said Kaio in a voice not unlike Flego's. Even the way the Chimera's claws reacted to something amusing reminded me of the Manticore. 'The little whelp kept herself out of biting range for that long?' I knew he was talking about Krixi. Hearing him talk like this hinted that the lion heads of both he and Flego, even though quite different in appearance, had to say something about the similarities between their personalities. In contrast, though, where Flego's scorpion tail would have flicked like that of a big cat, Kaio's snake tail coiled and hissed mirthfully.

'Typical,' said Lykofos, looking away disapprovingly.

'As I am sure you have figured out by now,' said Ouranis, ignoring her brothers, 'the Void crocodile we fought was not part of the actual Hive Mind. The Hive Mind should not be able to change its shape. And your memories show that it did. Now, as I mentioned, the Voidshapers themselves do not have spirits of their own. They are merely empty shells like the entities summoned by spiritcraft. This means that the remoulding of the Voidshapers' bodies does not have any effect on the mind that controls them. This is the case for all but one.'

Denise, I filled in.

'That is correct. She has managed to retain her spirit, apparently. To classify her as a Voidshaper is therefore incorrect, which I am sure you are pleased to hear.'

Is this the reason why she can't change her shape?

'It appears so. This is part of why I wished to contact you. Young Shepherd, I implore you, if and when you see Denise change her appearance, albeit an ear, a tail or her entire body, act with extreme caution. If this happens, you must assume she has either lost control or is in the process of doing so.' I couldn't speak, so I nodded. 'Also, it seems that the Vault from which I have been extracting spirits was only one of many. They must be connected, however. For it seems unlikely that the five of us, including Iliakos, are absorbed by the same one. This would be too much of a coincidence.'

'It's no use,' said Kaio, scrutinising me with six eyes between nose and tail. Having no idea who this "Denise" was that Ouranis was talking about – and what she meant to me – he had completely misread both my expression and the silence that had fallen between Ouranis and me. 'The human doesn't comprehend anything you're saying, Ouranis. This was a complete waste of my...'

The Hive's a Sphinx, I dropped at him, alternating my gaze between all six eyeballs. If my dealings with Flego had taught me anything, it was that any being that shared a body part with a lion should be handled with respect and, above all, a heavy bat. And it seemed like I had just hit my first home run.

'A Sphinx...,' breathed Kaio, looking aghast. He was quick to gather himself together and added, 'How do you know that, human? Speak up!'

'Iliakos,' said Ouranis warningly.

My gaze remained fixed on Kiao. I didn't want to give him the satisfaction of thinking he had scared me, or the humiliation of being cut out of the conversation by his feathered sister. *I'll tell you*, I thought with confidence. *My source told me that Akhenaten apparently didn't fail in his attempt to summon his Sphinx. It might not have become the illuminated being he was hoping to create, but there you have it. It's alive, and apparently, it is the one who's controlling the Voidshapers.*

'Your source? What source? Did Flego put you up to this? Ouranis!' Kaio's three heads were now positively rattled.

'Young Shepherd,' said Ouranis calmly, 'are you speaking the truth?'

I am, Ouranis. I would never lie or joke about something like this. The Hive is a Sphinx. It is she who must have contacted me inside the lagoon, remember?

'This is absurd,' said Lykofos. 'Anatin, can you confirm anything about these claims.'

'I'm afraid I can't,' said the Hippocampus behind me, 'or at least not from inside the Vault.'

'Let us, for now, maintain our focus on important matters,' said Ouranis. 'The identity of the Hive is not, for it does not change our situation. Young Shepherd, please heed the advice I gave you before and do not let this information disturb you. It is something we will cope with after we are, once again, free.' There was something in her voice that suggested Ouranis feared mentioning the Sphinx's real identity because she might be listening in.

I won't, I thought. *Or I'm not planning to. But there is something else too that I need to tell you, Ouranis. It's about Sophia, the girl who lived with us for some time.*

'I remember her,' she said distractedly, as though she didn't think it was of particular importance.

She's... not exactly who we thought she was. I'm still not entirely sure what to think of her, but she seems to have some connection with the Voidshapers. I wanted to dance around the words "enslaved" and "mind-controlled", for I didn't want to portray her as some kind of evil demon. Her actions had proven there was a side of her that was still good, and I wasn't prepared to give up on her just yet.

'That much was plain,' said Ouranis.

You knew? You knew about her and you still let her hang around? When did you find out?

'The moment you showed her your mate. Sophia's reaction to her presence told me all I needed to know. I allowed Sophia to stay because I too saw a side of her that did not belong to them.' Ouranis gave me a piercing look, telling me that her reabsorption into the Vault of Spirits had done nothing to her ability to read minds. I looked guiltily back at her. 'This is also the reason why I did not leave her behind after I touched her and we had to leave my den. And why I didn't send her back to the druids when we went to retrieve Flego and Krixi. She asked us, do you remember? She wanted to stay.'

I nodded. *To be honest, I don't really know what I should do with her. There have been disappearances among the druids, and, after what I've seen just now, I suspect she might be behind them. She has also rallied some of the clans behind her. Frankly, I don't even know if there is still an Eresa to get back to when I wake up. It's pretty messed up. They've even killed Commander Xenokrates. And to make matters even more complicated, I also think she knew of your attempts to contact me, because it was her idea to come to your den. And she says she's been helping me develop my abilities.* I sighed. Summing it all up didn't do much to solve the mystery.

'That is curious,' Ouranis said thoughtfully.

But she saved Denise from going to the other side, I thought in her defence. *Your touching Sophia enabled her to find Denise's spirit and pull her back before Denise was fully absorbed. That's why Denise has managed to stay in her own body, or what is left of it. The two of them have been together ever since.* I felt a heavy weight in my stomach.

'Very curious,' said Ouranis. 'I did expect her human side to be a little stronger, however. And I certainly did not expect her to be able to exert this much influence over the druids. I may have misjudged them slightly. And that in only eight days. It seems the timing of your predecessor's departure wasn't in our favour.'

That's the thing, I thought. *According to Selena and others I've spoken to, there has been another Sophia who came to Eresa the moment we left on our journey to the Hive. She somehow disappeared around the time we got back, so everyone thought our Sophia was the one who had been living with them. Our Sophia played her part well, apparently, because as soon as their plan was set in motion, she went over to the defecting clans. With Denise*, I added bitterly.

'Iliakos,' Kaio stated, burning embers igniting behind his eyes. 'He disappeared not long before you arrived here, Ouranis.'

Ouranis bowed her head again. 'At least we now know what his ability was used for. It was he who must have unwillingly enabled the Hive to create an illusion of Sophia. I fail to see another option, because the Voidshapers' secretion could not be responsible.' She looked at Anatin for confirmation; he shook his head in reply.

Because Sophia looks like a human girl, I thought.

'The time, Ouranis,' urged Lykofos.

'Yes, the time,' said Ouranis. 'Now, young Shepherd, the main reason why I needed to speak with you is to keep you from attempting to probe the Hive Mind directly. I know what you must be thinking, but if there was ever a time to heed my advice, it is the present. Listen to me very carefully. If I am right, and I believe I am, something must have happened to you during your transfer to our world that even I could not detect, something unrelated to the Shepherd abilities.' My skin began to prickle uncomfortably. 'I have focused all of my efforts on finding my brothers and sisters, Flego in particular, and therefore did not question some of the events that have happened since your arrival in our world. At long last I found myself close to separating Flego from the Hive Mind and I am ashamed to say it blinded me.' Her giant beak dropped in in embarrassment. 'I even nearly managed to alienate you when you first tried to approach me. Needless to say, I am grateful for your persistence.'

Ouranis pressed on before I had the chance to do more than swallow. 'Young Shepherd, please follow my reasoning and tell me if I am wrong. In order to save the gift, your predecessor, Zeuxis, sacrificed himself during the ritual before the Voidshapers could absorb him. You inherited the gift, and yet the Voidshapers left you alone despite there being only one druid, an apprentice no less, to guard you.'

Selena, I thought, nodding.

'This incident was followed by several others during which the Voidshapers attacked, yet you, no more than an ordinary human, miraculously survived. You were never the target, despite possessing the one thing the Hive Mind desires most.'

The attack by the giant snake when Selena ferried Pelegon, Sophia and I to Delos was pretty close, I thought, purposely dismissing the fact that she called me ordinary. With my mind's eye I beheld the Void anaconda coming for my flesh, mouth wide.

'Was it? Think, young Shepherd.' I could hear in her voice that she wasn't just testing me. She was genuinely interested in the answer.

Well, if Selena hadn't summoned her phoenix in time, I would probably have become one of them.

'Perhaps, perhaps not. But were you the intended target?'

It was either me, or... Pelegon, I thought. Ouranis took a deep breath through her nostrils. *I thought he was trying to save his daughter. I suppose he could also have been dodging the attack at the same time. I'm not quite sure, to be honest.*

'Do you not deem it odd that the Voidshapers did not try to overtake you at times when you were, in their eyes, nigh on defenceless? There were times when they could easily have taken you, made you theirs. Yet they did not. I asked you about this, remember?'

Yes, you did. But... didn't the same thing hold true for Zeuxis? If the Voidshapers wanted our abilities this badly, why have they never tried to attack him? I know they haven't, because the attack on Zeuxis during the ritual was the first time the druids even heard of the Voidshapers, let alone fight them.

'That is correct,' said Ouranis, a hint of pride in her voice. 'However, due to the druids' isolation as well as Zeuxis' duties, your predecessor did not leave Eresa very often. And when he did, I required him to have at least one captain by his side at all times.'

You required him?

'The druids trusted my judgement,' she said simply. By the way she drew herself up she might as well have added, "And rightfully so", yet she didn't. In fact, I had the feeling she was putting on a show to impress upon the other beasts just how much she had achieved while they had been languishing inside the Vault. I guessed this was what it must be like to have a Chimera and a Manticore as brothers.

Okay, so I didn't have the same luxury. But then, why is it that the Voidshapers did not try to take me?

'They did not try to take the Shepherd,' Ouranis corrected me. 'Remember, your predecessor sacrificed himself because he *thought* he was in danger. Considering you have managed to stay out of the Voidshapers' grasp for this long, I am not so sure that he was.'

Then why did the Voidshapers attack the ritualists?

'To infect the Shepherd, meaning you.'

Infect me?

'It is our belief, my brothers' as well, that the Voidshapers have contaminated you in a way that has eluded my detection. Your account of the dark fog in which you entered this world has haunted me ever since you told me about it. But, again, because of my desire to rescue Flego, I never stopped to think what it meant. Now I have, and I believe the attack does not point to one you would expect from the Voidshapers, given what we know about them. Instead, we suspect the Hive has done something to you, or perhaps attached something to the part of me that is in you, during the time you were inside the fog.'

You mean like a parasite? Even now I could still taste the ash on my tongue when I first arrived in this world.

'Something like that, yes. We believe this may have been the purpose of the attack, to dispose of the ritualists and infect Zeuxis. After Zeuxis rid himself of the Shepherd's abilities and passed them to you, it is our belief that the Voidshapers have been trying to isolate, even estrange, you from the druids. They made it so you had only one place to go: my den.'

But why? W–What kind of parasite…? My tongue felt suddenly swollen, as alien as the rest of my body.

'We are not certain. Perhaps the agent only works when you are in close proximity to me. It might also serve as a means to track your movements, and by extension, mine.' Evidently there was more coming, yet she swallowed her words to rephrase them. 'Young Shepherd, heed what I am about to tell you. I urge you to take it as a means to move forward, not to regret your past actions.' She waited for my response.

All right…

'I need you to think back to our fight with the Void crocodile. When you entered the Vault of Spirits that held Flego and Krixi, which you did on *my* orders, my energy fluctuated. I do not wish to make this sound as an excuse for my failure to protect you. It is simple fact, and a crucial piece of evidence. When you went in to find Flego and Krixi, the action caused my energy to spike.' Her voice dropped a little. 'The spike briefly rendered me incapable of moving, allowing the crocodile to take my leg.'

My brain gasped. *No way.* The regret that Ouranis didn't want me to feel washed over me with an unstoppable force. I took a moment to force back the lump in my throat. *But... are you sure this happened because of something the Voidshapers did to me? I mean, couldn't this have happened simply because part of you is in me and I connected with the Hive Mind? Or perhaps because I was brought here by those two strange globes. You too said it was strange. Or maybe... maybe it's because you touched Sophia when you were trying to revive her. It could have affected your abilities in some way.*

'I am confident it shouldn't have. It is true that I am still unsure why you were the one chosen to be the next Shepherd, or why your predecessor's energy behaved the way it did. But neither do I think it has anything to do with the connection between us. And in the case of Sophia, I daresay I should have felt something. If by touching Sophia something of the Hive had transferred to me, I should have been able to recognise the lingering presence inside my body. I did not. Neither did touching Sophia invoke any change in my physical appearance. Considering the way I looked and the way the dark secretion of the Voidshapers behaves, one might expect it to.'

'You, on the other hand,' she went on, 'had next to no experience of sensing your own energy. It is therefore not unthinkable that something might have slipped past your senses. No matter how acute they are,' she added quickly as she saw my eyelids droop in annoyance. 'However, if my fight with the Void crocodile had been a stand-alone incident, I would, perhaps, have doubted my own instincts. But considering what we know, my brothers and I agree the risk is too great not to assume that I am correct.'

'Young Shepherd,' she said imploringly as though I wouldn't otherwise accept it, 'you must not attempt to extract me from the Vault before this problem is solved. We cannot risk the Hive controlling me in any way, or we risk ending up here together, which must be avoided at all costs. In addition, I ask you to be very careful who you entrust with this information. With Flego and Krixi taking my place, it is more important now than ever to keep the image of the Shepherd untainted and unblemished. If word reaches the druid community at large of the Shepherd not being entirely pure, their society and everything I have tried to build will crumble and fall apart. Further apart,' said a tiny voice bearing Ouranis' signature.

I understand.

'In the meantime, I will hold true to my promise to do what I can for your mate. I have not forgotten. However, considering her spirit is with you, not with me, it will probably take a little longer than I expected. It might not even be possible for me to do anything from my current location. We will contact you again when we know more.'

It's okay, really. As long as I know where Denise is, I think I can manage. I can talk to her again, which is a great improvement. And if this Sphinx does get her in the end, you'll be able to find her again, right?

Lykofos gave Ouranis an inscrutable look. 'I believe so.'

Chapter 26

A girly voice, high-pitched and frantic, echoed through the crystal chamber. It was mixed with heavy footfalls. 'Aaron! Aaron!'

I jerked awake and there stood Sophia, calm and composed. She wasn't looking at me, but at something that was charging at us at breakneck speed. My vision was foggy as though I had just awoken from a deep slumber. I wondered how much time had passed since I laid Sophia down on the crystal floor. However long it had been, though, it was apparently enough for my owl body to transform into a human shape again.

I followed Sophia's gaze. Slowly, a black polar bear with a familiar face sitting on top acquired enough detail for me to recognise. 'Sophia?' I asked either one of the girls, or both.

The Sophia who was on a collision course was an exact copy, an identical twin, of the one standing next to me. Or it seemed that way on first glance, for the frantic one on top of the black polar bear sparked something inside me that the one standing next to me did not.

'Don't you dare believe her, Aaron!' said the Sophia on top of the polar bear. In midstride her mount dissolved into black smoke. Sophia kept running until her legs couldn't keep up with her momentum and she fell hard on her hands and knees, hissing in pain. A split second later her head shot up again, black hair whipping her back. Her eyes were livid, her lips crying. 'Don't you believe her,' she said again.

'Sophia…'

I was half way stooping down to help her when it happened. The dissolved polar bear, now a shapeless mass of smoke, moved towards Sophia and rapidly fused with the skin on her ankles. I gave a yelp and staggered backwards, watching the smoke creeping into the little girl's ragged dress. It was like seeing Denise's transformation in reverse, although this time, the black animal had definitely existed outside Sophia's body. The whole event reminded me of the druids' spiritcraft.

'You're smarter than this, Aaron,' said Sophia after the smoke from the polar bear had completely disappeared. She tried to stand up, her knees buckling. Her voice sounded different from what I was used to, and a lot more knowledgeable than I gave her credit for. 'I know you. Don't fall for her tricks. I'm the real one.'

I looked at the other Sophia, who still hadn't said anything, fully expecting her to echo Sophia's words. Not having moved an inch, she stood with her hand shielding her mouth. Freakishly, she flicked her eyes towards me. My stomach did a somersault. Then with a final giggle, as though stepping behind a curtain, she vanished.

Sophia uttered a sigh. Her sigh seemed to physically thin the atmosphere inside the crystal chamber.

'Sophia, are you all right?' I asked.

'I am now.'

'What happened? Where did you come from? Who was that other one?' There were so many questions fighting for dominance, it was hard to pick between the waving hands.

'That bitch!' spat Sophia. 'I wanted to see them too.'

'Who?'

Finally Sophia looked up at me. 'The ones you were just talking to, of course. Ouranis and her brothers and sisters.'

'So you do know about that,' I said, in confirmation of my suspicion that Sophia wanted me here to enable Ouranis to contact me.

'Uh, huh.'

I pointed vaguely at the pocket of air where the second Sophia had just disappeared. 'But then... she must have been the illusion.' Sophia nodded, her lips twisted angrily. 'But I thought she vanished when we got back to Eresa. Or...' A realisation struck me. 'Or didn't you come back with us?'

If she says "yes", it would definitely explain a lot, I thought. *Then the entire coup would've been staged and executed by the illusion, which would mean that our Sophia had nothing to do with it. She would be exonerated from everything that has happened. The only thing I need to do is to convince the other druids, Kriton among them, that they have been talking to a ghost for the past week. That shouldn't be too hard, if Lycomedes backs me up.* I had it all worked out in a matter of seconds. It suddenly all made sense, until...

'No, that was me,' said Sophia.

An image of Denise bearing her teeth at me on Sophia's command bubbled up, shattering the honeyed thoughts of a moment ago. When I spoke, my voice was low and devoid of any feeling of concern for Sophia's well-being. 'Then why aren't you with your Canine friends?' My words gave birth to an emotional distance between us, pushing us apart.

Sophia folded her arms and repeated mockingly, 'Why aren't you with your Canine friends? Denise told me all about you, Shepherd Aaron Bishop. Always thinking you know what's best for everyone. You probably think you have it all figured out, don't you?'

Denise said that? Now she's one to talk...

'Although,' said Sophia, smiling, 'it's nice to know I was convincing enough to fool even you.'

My eyebrows climbed to my hairline. 'What? What's that supposed to mean?'

Sophia's face grew serious again. Then she threw her hands into the air and stated in sudden exasperation, 'I had to do something.' The snappy retort had such force behind it, I literally jumped in shock. Sophia's hair looked as though it was responding to the pent-up rage inside her. 'Like you said, when we got back from our journey the illusion vanished,' she went on. 'I was alone, wasn't I? And here were all these druids, expecting things of me. She,' Sophia gestured at the pocket of air that had been filled with her alter ego a minute ago, 'had done a good job on them. They were scared to death. Of me!' she added forcefully, jamming her thumps into her chest.

For a moment I stood there, flabbergasted. I knew Sophia had problems, which was one of the reasons why I found it so hard to connect with her. But this… I neither had the skills nor the experience to deal with a situation like this.

'And you decided to play along with that illusion?' I asked, my brain barely keeping up with the mystery. 'Why? Why didn't you come to me, or Lycomedes, or anyone for that matter? We would have been there for you. You must know that.'

Probably in response to something going on inside her, Sophia's cheeks wrinkled in anger and her eyes began to roll this way and that. 'NO!' she then screamed to the crystalline walls around us. 'ENOUGH!'

The words continued to bounce around, even through my response. 'Sophia, what's wrong?'

She slapped both hands against her temple. 'I'm so sorry,' she cried. 'So sorry.' Then she clenched her fists and yelled once more, ending in a sob. 'NOOOOO! Stop it! Don't!'

'Sophia, talk to me, please! Is it the Hive? Is it the Sphinx? You need to fight it!'

'I had to do it,' she said, sobbing into her hands. 'I had to. She wanted me to. The druids were going to do it anyway. The Canines, the Felines, the Piscines, they were so afraid. They were afraid they too would disappear. The Sphinx took them one at a time. The other me had told them they would be next. Nothing I could say would change their minds; it would only have confused them more. She said it would. I believed her.'

'You're talking about Peleus and the others. The Sphinx took him away too, didn't she?'

Sophia nodded. 'When we got back from our trip, the clans knew what Lord Arcturus had done, all the sacrifices, and what he was planning for the future. The illusion had told them all about it. The clans were convinced that helping him was their only way out. They said it was the only way they could preserve their "little way of life".' She spoke the last part of the sentence as though the words had done her a great and irremediable wrong.

'Lord Arcturus' plans for the future?' A graveyard at sea rose to the surface of my mind. 'What does he have to do with this?'

'He knows about the door to your world.'

'Yes, I know,' I said more to myself than to Sophia. 'That druid woman with the bears told him.'

'The clans said he wanted to send the Voidshapers here and that he asked me, or the other me, to bring them the message. If they gave up the Shepherd, the clans would be free of the Voidshapers once and for all, because the Voidshapers would go to your world.'

'But that's insane. The clans thought the Voidshapers would just leave?'

'They thought it was the only chance they had to save Eresa. And Ouranis' death proved it.'

'She's not dead. She's alive.'

'So you say,' said Sophia. 'She's gone. That's all the clans know.'

'And because I'm not a real Shepherd, there is no way I can convince them otherwise,' I said to myself. 'That must be why nobody asked me about her. I thought it was because of Xenokrates' orders, but I was sure at least some druids would want to know what happened to Ouranis badly enough. And if not me, they would surely have asked Selena or Lycomedes.' I turned to Sophia again. 'But still, they can't just give up on her. Ouranis is practically their God. And it's their duty to protect her gift.'

Sophia regained a bit of her composure. 'Maybe you don't know the druids as well as you think.'

'Apparently not,' I said. 'But why did you go to Delos just now? And how? I thought the entrance to Eresa was under guard.'

Sophia hesitated, then chose to say, 'I knew where she was sending her Voidshapers. So I decided to go there with Denise and keep them from coming after you.'

'You mean to the temple of Isis?'

Sophia nodded. 'Krixi saw me enter the forest. She went after me. I tried to scare her away, but…' In my head I heard Flego roar and saw him flying after his sister. "Don't go in there! Krixi, there's no way you can beat them!"

'Then the Canines came and I had to play my part,' Sophia went on. 'I needed Captain Ione to trust me. We managed to pin down Flego and Krixi. Flego can't think very well when he gets too excited. I saw that during your last battle with the Voidshapers. But I kept the Voidshapers from reabsorbing him,' she added hastily. 'Then you arrived and I had to continue my act. When I thought it was safe to do so and your friends had time to leave the island, I called in the Voidshapers. The Canines expected me to.'

'I–I can barely believe it. So my whole speech about your father was for nothing?' I didn't know why I even cared about this. The question just sort of happened.

A hint of shame glinted in her eyes. 'I wouldn't have tried to harm you,' she chose to say, taking care for each word.

'And by that you mean...?'

Sophia squinted as though something was pinching her brain. 'I... Aaron... it's not safe. You should leave, quickly.'

'But you just said you wouldn't harm me. Listen, we can work this out. I talked to Ouranis and she reckons...'

'Go, she's getting stronger,' said Sophia, bending over, her knees yielding. Her voice was overlain with agony and her squinted eyes refused to look at me. Desperation was fuelling her next words. 'She switched me for the illusion when you were unconscious. She doesn't want me anywhere near Ouranis anymore. Ouranis knows. She knows...' Sophia gasped and seized handfuls of her own hair. Stretched thin, she breathed, 'Leave... me...'

In literally the blink of an eye Sophia's back straightened, her arms widened and her jaw was thrust open. Then her entire body was turned into a suppurating mass. Black ink began to ooze from every pore in her skin, each of them opening the floodgates for the creature inside her. It seemed to have grabbed her brain in a stranglehold.

Before I even realised what was going on, my legs responded on their own accord; by the time I actively willed it, I was already half way across the crystallised floor. I only looked back when I reached the cave entrance. A seven-strong pride of black predator cats was in pursuit, each of them born from the fountain of black ash that was Sophia.

Now Selena's voice bore down on me from inside the tunnel. 'Aaron, duck!' The next thing I knew a translucent phoenix obscured my vision. I threw myself onto the ground. The phoenix soared overhead and a shower of glittering crystals, taken from the joint craters Ouranis had created during our second encounter, pecked my head and back.

'Get up, quickly!' Selena had halted at a few yards distance. I pushed myself up and went after her, taking no heed of what was happening behind me.

How it happened, I had no idea. But once outside, our hands were embracing each other like old friends. The two of them kissing was the first thing Denise saw when we emerged from the cave, as did Lycomedes, Leander, Briseis, Aerope and, perhaps most surprisingly, Demonax. The latter grinned awkwardly as though not entirely sure what he was doing here.

The space between our palms began to burn. As if struck by a lightning bolt, Selena and I separated. Denise tilted her hyena head and watched my cheeks turn the colour of ripe strawberries.

'You're all here,' I stated unnecessarily.

'Now there's a clever chap,' said Lycomedes.

'So, does this mean it's over?' I asked. But before anyone could answer, another voice, a much more powerful one, entered my brain.

'Don't give me that, Krixi. I thought there were more.' I looked up and saw Flego and his sister flying towards us.

'Fleger always say things like that,' said Krixi, who realised she was closer to her brother than she cared for and increased her speed. 'Krixi can do it herself.'

'Remember what happened last time?' Flego asked her, not bothering to keep up.

'This is not last time. This is this time. Krixi can do it.'

Everything all right? I asked Flego.

He and Krixi landed next to me on the small strip of pebbled beach. 'No worse than you,' he said, taking me in from top to bottom.

Yeah, thanks.

'Shall we give you three a moment, or…?' Lycomedes asked. When I found his gaze I noticed that everyone else was staring at me as well. Everyone except for Selena, that is. She was standing near the entrance of the cave, keeping watch.

'Briseis,' said Selena without sparing a look. She beckoned her over and Briseis complied. Once there, Selena began muttering something inaudible to Briseis.

'Bishop?' said Lycomedes.

'Right, sorry. What happened to you guys? No, wait! There's no time for that. We need to get Sophia out of there. She's inside the chamber, but the Hive, the Darkness, it…' At that moment, a black, winged figure shot out from the main vent of the volcano. It let out a cackling laugh, using a voice that could belong to none other than Sophia.

'Sophia, no!' I yelled, though there was no catching her. Not even Selena's phoenix would be fast enough. I did the only thing I could think of and called after her, infusing my voice with every ounce of reassurance I had in me. 'I will find you, Sophia! I promise! I will find you!'

There was a streak of blue and the black figure exploded into a cloud of smoke. My jaw dropped.

'Krixi,' muttered Flego sternly. I couldn't help but detect a hint of mirth in his voice.

'Krixi told Fleger she can do it,' said Krixi on her way back from the black cloud. 'No problem.' Behind her the ash cloud drizzled down onto the ocean's surface and disappeared. The black figure was gone.

'Was that Sophia?' Selena asked in horror, staring up into the sky. No matter what Selena might have thought about Sophia and her apparent misdeeds, at the sight of the exploding figure the motherly side of her had filled her brain with compassion.

I blinked my confusion away. 'No, it wasn't,' I said in a low voice. 'Or at least not her spirit. The Voidshapers have her now. They were on to her and must not have liked her helping us out.'

'So that was what she was doing,' said Leander, looking doubtful.

'It's a long story, Leander. I'll explain everything later. First, where are the Canines, and the other Voidshapers? And how did you get away?'

'Well, when you took Sophia away, the Voidshapers seemed to suffer a moment of confusion,' said Lycomedes. 'Flego here took care of them. With them gone, the Canines made a run for it. Or a swim, I'd better say. Dogs are a bad match against birds.'

'Oh, right. Captain Cyrene and the Avians. She helped you against the Canines?'

Lycomedes nodded. 'When she turned up, and most of her clan soon after, the Canines thought better of pursuing us. And the Piscines, well, birds are tough to beat for most of us. I'm glad we still have her on our side.'

'I'll pretend I didn't hear that,' said Aerope. 'Or one might think there was any doubt about the Avians' allegiance.'

'What about Captain Niobe and the Felines?' I asked. 'Sophia mentioned them too.'

A grin appeared on Lycomedes' profile and he gave Leander an appreciative glance. 'Krixi took Leander for a swift sweep along the island to bring the word to the Captains.' A gravelly chuckle followed. 'Niobe thought she had it in her to take on both the Vespines and the Viperines. Bad call. She had some help from the Voidshapers, that's true. The Darkness, I mean,' he corrected himself before any of the others could ask questions; they still didn't know about the Voidshapers' real name. 'And Cyrene told us Niobe had Lydus cornered at one point. She threatened to kill him if Helios would take any action against her. That was her second mistake; Helios attacked regardless of Niobe using his vice-captain as a living shield. Lydus still lived in the end, but his condition isn't great.'

Demonax nodded appreciatively, though he seemed to be the only one who sympathised with the way Captain Helios had handled the situation.

'Helios is not one to be commanded,' said Lycomedes, noticing my furrowed eyebrows. 'And now Niobe is ours. Cats hate water.' His grin widened. 'I told her she should have gone with rats.'

'Do you all think Megare will agree to take Xenokrates' place now he's gone?' Briseis asked, throwing the question into the group after a spell. 'She was second in command.' Even though all was quiet inside the tunnel, she and Selena stayed at their posts.

'She's going to have to until the Council, or what is left of it, find a replacement,' said Lycomedes. 'She will do fine, I'm sure.'

'She's a Bovine,' said Demonax, as though that settled the matter.

'No, she *was* a Bovine,' Lycomedes corrected him. He shrugged and said, 'I guess to your captain it doesn't make much of a difference. Things will return much to the way they were when they were living together.' Everyone froze, including Demonax, as if afraid that Kriton would suddenly emerge from the sea and make Lycomedes feel how wrong he was. Then Briseis let out a snort and everyone joined in the laughter.

Before the laughter made us feel too much at ease, however, Lycomedes suggested heading back to the Sanctuary. Nobody seemed particularly keen to come eye to eye with the aftermath of today's events, for the clans' division had cost us dearly, both emotionally and in manpower. But there was no point in delaying it. We had to regroup, assess the damage, and come up with a plan. Because despite today's victory, or "survival" might be a better term, Lycomedes had been wrong in his prediction. The Hive hadn't showed up. In fact, considering what we had witnessed on our journey to save Flego and Krixi, today's attack was but the beginning.

Whether the Hive, or the Sphinx, had counted on the clans' division to destabilise the druid community or today's events were part of a larger scheme, it was too soon to tell. But without doubt, the Sphinx knew about Sophia's presence inside Eresa. The scheming that Sophia's illusionary twin had done when we were away proved it. Perhaps the Sphinx too had sensed the emotional instability of Sophia's young mind, and had thought her a liability. Perhaps that is why she needed the illusion to spread the seeds of fear. But then, had the Sphinx counted on Sophia's defection? Had she known Sophia would betray her master in the end? Or was today's attack simply a means to see if she would, a test?

Like Ouranis had said, the Sphinx was patient, intelligent. She would not rashly siege the Druid Sanctuary. Not if there was a chance, even a slim one, she would not get what it wanted: me. Perhaps she was even afraid that if Sophia would betray her master in the final hour, she could help me find my way back to my own world. Yes, the Sphinx must have known about the shared ability between Ouranis and myself. Otherwise she would not be searching for me. But would she take the chance that I couldn't go back on my own? Wasn't it a safer bet to rely on brains versus brawn? And would it have changed anything if the Voidshapers had charged in with full force? She probably thought a more stealthy approach, one in which a party of Voidshapers would guard the temple of Isis and another party would go and attack Eresa, would be more practical.

If it was a gamble, it had definitely paid off. The Sphinx now knew that either I wasn't capable of going home on my own, or that I chose not to. In addition, by doing it like this and replacing the real Sophia with the illusion during my conversation with Ouranis, she had not only made sure Sophia missed the meeting, she had also discovered Sophia's true allegiance.

Even better, and this was perhaps the most important reason for choosing stealth over force, Lycomedes' predicted division between the clans was now a reality. If the druids had been faced with the utter destruction of Eresa as a whole, they might have come together and stood united against their common foe. This way ensured that the targeted clans at least would defect from their druid family, even if Sophia would choose not to.

Now that I thought about it, I wasn't sure that not going all in had been a gamble at all. Perhaps the Sphinx knew for certain I wouldn't go home if I could. She had penetrated my mind at least once before. And Ouranis had said I had been infected with something that had a direct connection with our abilities. The Sphinx had used this to weaken Ouranis and capture her. So perhaps this parasite, whatever it was, had fed the Sphinx the information she needed. It could be doing that even now, while we stood there waiting on the beach for Lycomedes to summon his crocodiles. If it was, would a druid cleansing have any effect? Would it purge the corruption inside me? But then, would I go against Ouranis' advice and risk the chance of the Eresans finding out about their Shepherd not being pure? And what would happen to Ouranis' gift? Would it transfer to another druid on its own, or would it be lost forever? Would Denise and I still be able to return home?

Lycomedes was standing at the water's edge, his hands pressed together and his back turned to us. Behind him, Selena was allocating the spots on the soon-to-be living canoes. When she was finished, silence stretched. It quickly passed the point of being uncomfortable and was turning awkward. Furtive looks were passed here and there as we all began to chew on different versions of the same idea: was the old man still awake?

'Bishop,' said Lycomedes suddenly, his eyes remaining focused on the open water before him. His voice did wonders to the party's morale. 'How is your training going?'

Selena and I shot each other a surprised glance. 'Fine, why?'

Lycomedes turned, lowered his arms and said with an excessive amount of sternness, 'Good. Then you don't mind proving it. Trionyx should be around here somewhere.'

'You mean you need help?' I asked incredulously. What about your crocodiles?' Lycomedes narrowed one eye and gazed at me with the power of four. 'No problem,' I added quickly. 'I'm on it.'

To my surprise, not ten minutes later the eight of us mounted the mighty turtle in single file. My mind was still with Sophia, though. I felt like I had failed her. Where was she? What had happened to the poor girl? I couldn't shake the image of her yielding body disgorging the fountain of black ash. The image was taunting, infuriating. She didn't deserve this.

When we had all found a place on Trionyx's shell, I looked back at the beach where Flego opened his wings in preparation to take off. The tunnel behind him appeared blue and blurry through his wings. Hoping I would pick up a whisper, a thought, my mind reached out into the tunnel in an attempt to prove that she wasn't gone. She couldn't be.

Denise hit the inside of my knee with her snout. She gazed up at me with a longing in her eyes, but had no words to suit the occasion. I had no intention of searching her mind for any either. I felt bad enough already. *I'm so sorry, Denise. I know what she means to you. I miss her too.*

As I stood there, watching Flego flap open his wings, I braced myself for the impact of the Manticore's liftoff. But then the scene froze. Flego had heard it before I did. Denise had too, and an odd wheezing noise came from her throat. 'Aaron,' she said, her voice hopeful, 'is that…?'

There was a shuffling of feet, a cough, then a plea carried by an exhausted, girly voice. It prickled my ears in a comforting sort of way. My heart was the first to recognise it. The rest of my companions turned around as well, Selena with a gasp. They were just in time to see a small hand with dirty nails groping for the cave's cheeks.

'Wait… for me…'

www.ingramcontent.com/pod-product-compliance
Lightning Source LLC
Chambersburg PA
CBHW021437240626
47153CB00001B/192